ADVANCE PRAISE FOR
PINTIP DUNN'S STAR-CROSSED

"With cleverly written characters, an intriguing world, and heart-wrenching conflicts, Pintip Dunn delights with her exciting science fiction novel. Readers who love tough choices and high stakes will love *Star-Crossed*."
—Jodi Meadows, *New York Times* bestselling author of the Incarnate series

"With a prose as incandescent as a nebula and a romance that blazes like the sun, *Star-Crossed* utterly consumed me from the very first page. Readers will savor this riveting, emotional tale of hope and supreme sacrifice."
—Darcy Woods, award-winning author of *Summer of Supernovas*

"Pintip Dunn's creative world-building brings to life a delicious tale full of depth and complexity. *Star-Crossed* will transport readers to another universe and leave them hungry for more!"
—Brenda Drake, *New York Times* bestselling author of the Library Jumpers series

"A bold and original YA sci-fi novel about love, survival, and sacrifice. Everything about this book is fresh, addictive, and mind-bending. Good luck putting it down!"
—Meg Kassel, award-winning author of *Black Bird of the Gallows*

"Pintip Dunn has crafted one multi-course meal of a story: a fascinating premise to whet the appetite, an entree of utterly compelling world-building seasoned with literary prose, and a forbidden romance that has all the decadence of the richest dessert."
—Jen Malone, author of *Wanderlost* and *Changes in Latitudes*

"The most compelling read all year…This heart-pounding romance of love and sacrifice is impossible to put down."
—Erin Summerill, award-winning author of the Clash of Kingdoms series

Also by Pintip Dunn

Forget Tomorrow series

Before Tomorrow (prequel novella)
Forget Tomorrow
Remember Yesterday
Seize Today

STAR-CROSSED

PINTIP DUNN

Entangled Publishing, LLC
2614 South Timberline Road
Suite 105, PMB 159
Fort Collins, CO 80525
rights@entangledpublishing.com

Entangled Teen is an imprint of Entangled Publishing, LLC.

Visit our website at www.entangledpublishing.com.

Edited by Liz Pelletier
Cover design by Erin Dameron-Hill
Cover images by
Depositphotos, shutterstock, and iStock
Interior design by Toni Kerr

ISBN 978-1-63375-241-2
Ebook ISBN 978-1-63375-242-9

Manufactured in the United States of America

First Edition October 2018

10 9 8 7 6 5 4 3 2 1

entangled teen
an imprint of Entangled Publishing LLC

For my dad, Naronk, who is as wise and loving as a king.

CHAPTER ONE

I break off a piece of raspberry tart, with a crust as light as sunshine, and slide it into the pocket of my caftan. My mouth goes dry in spite of the sweet tang that's about to burst over my tongue.

Because the hidden bite's not for me. It's for my best friend, Astana, and if the royal guards catch me stealing food for a colonist, I could be thrown into the Red Cell Prison. Our laws are clear: actual food, as opposed to nutrition pills, must be reserved for those who can utilize it best.

I shove the rest of the tart into my mouth. It breaks upon contact, littering crumbs across the silver shuttle floor. I'm so nervous, the dessert tastes like congealed space dust and raspberries, but I chew and swallow as if nothing's wrong. As if there isn't a smooshed-up pie staining the inside of my pocket.

Did anyone see me hide the bite?

All around the Banquet Room, the Aegis dig into their mid-afternoon snack. Pecan-encrusted squash, double-mashed garlic potatoes, barbecued tofu drizzled with a blackberry-port reduction. They sit twenty per table, at sheets of metal which would sag if they weren't doubly reinforced. Their silverware clinks together in a high, tinny melody, replacing the conversation that might have occurred back on Earth, where eating was partly social instead of wholly functional.

On our new planet, Dion, no Aegis talks during the first twenty minutes of a meal. It would be a waste, since more food can be consumed before the stomach has a chance to feel full. And an Aegis has only one goal: to consume as many nutrients as possible. We have to, in order to take in enough sustenance for the rest of the colony.

I'm about to finish what's left of the tart when a hand closes over my elbow.

My heart stutters. So it comes to this. After training all my life to eat for my people, I'm caught over a piece of raspberry pie.

Pellets of sweat break out on my neck. I turn to my captor, the excuses ready on my lips. *It's just a single bite. My best friend's been so down lately. I just want to bring her a little excitement, a little joy. Is that so wrong?*

The words melt in my mouth. Because it's not a royal guard who has a hold of me. It's my older sister.

"Sweet before savory?" Blanca asks, moving the hand from my elbow and onto her hip. She's widely considered beautiful, even if she doesn't have the voluptuous figure that is so prized in our colony. It's not easy to have curves when every excess calorie is sucked out of your body six times a day and transferred to the colonists via a pill. "Is that your secret, Vela? You eat a round of dessert before the main course?"

Of course not. I'm only eating this tart because it gives me an excuse to be near the dessert buffet. But Blanca doesn't have to know that.

"You got me," I say. "Sweet and savory foods fill different mental compartments, you know. You can still eat chocolate cake, even though you're full of ramen noodles and pan-fried dumplings—"

"Save it." Blanca arches her back, jutting out her food baby. Fifteen minutes from now, after she pays a visit to the Transfer Room, her stomach will deflate once again, but my sister's always been one to show off her roundness, however temporary. "I don't need your strategies to be named Top Aegis."

I'm a shoo-in for the top prize this year. Blanca knows it, I know it. Half of our Eating class has placed bets on it. If I keep eating the way I have for the next two days, no one will even come close.

Vela Kunchai, Top Aegis. I can taste it. Hot and satisfying, like a tray of lasagna with a bubbling soy cheese crust. It's not the title I want, but the caring that it conveys. The more nutrition pills I produce, after all, the more people I'll feed. My father, the King, has two heirs. Within the year, he'll name either me or Blanca as his Successor. He's been training both of us, from a very young age, to take his place, and a few months ago, the council decided that the transition to a new ruler would proceed most smoothly if the Sucessor stayed within the royal family.

We don't know what criteria the council will use to choose the Successor. After all, our colony has never had to pass the reins before. But winning Top Aegis sure won't hurt my chances. And so, I'd stretch my stomach lining into gauze to make sure it's me. My sister, unfortunately, feels the same way.

"It's not just about how much you're willing to suffer for your people," Blanca says, as if reading my mind. "The King's Successor has to be practical enough to see the big picture. She has to have helped the King from an early age, running scenarios for him in the control room every time he needs data for a decision." Even my sister's raised eyebrow looks smug. "In other words, she can't just flounce around the colony. She can't interrupt her father during important council meetings to show him a Venus flytrap with a broken stalk."

I flush. That was ten years ago, when I was seven and she was eight, but Blanca will never let me forget it. Just like she'll never let me forget that she's useful to the King—has always been useful to the King—and I'm not.

But I refuse to let her get to me. Even if I don't have Blanca's logical mind and analytical abilities, I have my own attributes. "Oh yeah? The King's Successor also has to be compassionate enough to rescue the spider trapped inside that plant."

I lock eyes with her dark brown ones. We weren't always rivals. Once upon a time, my sister and I played rocket ships together. She was the captain, and I was her best mate. We zoomed here to the planet Dion, hundreds of light-years from Earth, and pretended we were one of the original colonists who landed on this world seventy years ago.

Of course, that was before I surpassed my sister's eating ranking. Before my father, the King, announced one of us would be his Successor. Before my mother passed away.

In other words: a long time ago.

"This whole thing is ridiculous," Blanca says. "I can't believe the council's even considering you. How could you possibly be Successor? You can't even stand in front of a crowd without fainting."

"I was a kid, and I hadn't nutritioned all day."

"This isn't something you can learn. You either have what it takes to be Successor..." My sister's eyes hack into me like a cleaver. "Or you don't."

"And you don't think I do?"

She doesn't answer for a moment. The air cleanser switches on. Wind blasts from the vents in the space shuttle's curved walls, picking up the aromas and carrying them outside. Well, not literally outside in the real planet, but outside in our twenty square miles of intersecting bubbles. The two space shuttles, where the Aegis live and eat, are parked right in the middle of our colony, and their solar-paneled exteriors make up part of the energy shields that keep the oxygen-rich air in and the CO_2-dense air out.

"Sorry, sis," Blanca finally says. "Nobody thinks you've got a chance. The council's just indulging Father in one of his whims." She puts a hand on her hip and looks over my shoulder, as if she's bored with the conversation. "You might want to take the pie out of your pocket. Wouldn't want the guards to catch you sneaking food out of the Banquet Hall. Someone might get the wrong idea."

She turns and swishes away, her eating caftan flowing behind her. The material catches the wind from the vents, and for a moment, it billows out, as haunting as a lone kite tapping against our energy shields.

A sharp pain seizes my chest. I can't tell if it's from Blanca's graceful form or from the sudden certainty that I will never be my sister's best mate ever again.

*F*ive bubbles from the center of our colony, in the slags of rock that hold floor after floor of living units, there are no blasts of wind. Instead, the odors sit on the air like the nine layers of my Thai ancestors' most auspicious dessert, *khanom chan.*

Except there's nothing appetizing about these smells. Sweat. Body odor. Insect repellent.

I shudder and ignore the panel next to the front door, which would announce my arrival to my best friend, and walk into a narrow room with furniture set into the walls. All the living units in our colony are equipped this way, so that a single room can serve multiple living functions.

At the moment, a bed is pulled out, and Astana huddles underneath a solar blanket, newly heated from the sun lamps. Her breath comes in uneven pants, and her skin is stretched pale over the bones of her face. She's so thin she could slide between the cracks of the tiled floor.

She props herself on her elbow as soon as she sees me. The blanket slides to the floor, its reflective surface flashing under the lights. "Did you get the pie?"

I shake my head, and she crumples, inches away from joining her blanket.

"Next time, I'll wait until Blanca leaves before I try to take any food."

She wets her lips. "Could I maybe lick your pocket?"

"Oh. Um, sure." My heart shudders to hear her so wistful, but I slip the caftan over my head, leaving a simple tank top. I turn the pocket inside out and hold the raspberry-stained fabric out to my friend. She catches the cotton between her teeth and sinks against the couch, her jaws working the caftan the way a beetle gnaws on bark.

The cloth must've absorbed more juice than I realized. Almost immediately, a bit of color returns to her cheeks.

She sees me watching, and the fabric falls from her lips. "Sorry. I've been craving a taste all week."

"It's okay." This is my fault, really. Back when we were kids, when her mom worked in the royal kitchens, I would sneak Astana bites from my training meals. I wanted to share everything with my best friend, including this weird thing we were learning about in our classes called "eating." By the time I realized I wasn't supposed to share, it was too late. Astana was hooked.

"Besides," she continues. "I don't know if I'll make it to your next visit."

"You're not going anywhere. The nutritionists are going to recalibrate your needs, and in the meantime, I'll give you every excess pill I have. I'll eat until my stomach splits, if that's what it takes."

This is my secret. The strategy that turns my stomach into an infinitely-expanding balloon. The reason I can eat more than anyone else. My best friend in our brand-new world is dying.

We Aegis are assigned a quota every month—a set amount of nutrients we have to consume. Once we meet the quota, any additional nutrients are ours to keep. These little round pills act as currency in our society. We can set them aside to purchase tickets for a virtual vid. Or give them to our friends.

"Your pills can't fix what's wrong with me," she says.

"How can you say that?" I pick up her wrist, my thumb and index finger easily encircling it. "I make the most nutritious pills there are. Everybody knows that."

I smile as I say the words, but I'm only half kidding. Blanca and I have known since we were kids that our genes responded particularly well to the Aegis modification—the one that allows us to extract nutrients from food more efficiently. With this modification, most Aegis can absorb two or three times as many nutrients as the regular person. Blanca and I are five or six times more efficient.

"You have to stop giving me all your pills." Astana's smile, like her body, is a cheap remake of its former self. "Your life's already shortened. You need to enjoy every moment of it."

"Nah. I've got over a decade left on this planet." It's hard for me to be too concerned about my impending death when it's years and years away. Especially when my best friend is in desperate need of nutrition today.

"Can you tell me about the part I missed?" She puts the fabric back in her mouth. "The crust of the pie?"

I bite my lip. How do I explain taste and texture to a girl who's barely known it?

"Oh, come on," she says. "I told you about kissing. Surely you can talk about a measly pie crust."

A few months ago, she painstakingly walked me through every detail of her first kiss with Jacksonville Kim, from his front teeth clicking into hers to the way his tongue cleaned the inside of her mouth like a Hyper Bot.

The memory makes me smile. Even better, Astana's sitting up, and she almost sounds like herself again.

"Just you wait." I aim for light and floaty, like butterfly wings, but relief punches a hole through my voice. "Maybe my mysterious rescuer will swoop back into my life, and then you'll be the one begging me for kissing details."

"That was the only time you ever needed saving." My friend's eyes drift closed. "Not like me. I need rescuing every day."

My stomach falls somewhere near the vicinity of my knees. Because this doesn't sound like my best friend. Gravity has never pulled so strongly on her words. She's never referred to the time I fell into the pond during the King's Birthday Picnic without an exaggerated wink.

I would've drowned that day, ten years ago, had someone not pulled me out and laid me dripping on the shore. But my rescuer left before I could get a look at him. He never even claimed his death debt.

I slide my hand until our wrists are pressed together. Our pulses beat next to each other, our life forces combined into one. The ultimate gesture of friendship and trust. "Do you still want to hear about the crust?"

She nods without opening her eyes. "Please."

"Let's see. The crust of a raspberry pie." I slip my hand into hers and think back to all the times I've eaten the dessert. "Imagine grains of sand as light as dandelion fluff, rolled in the breeze and bursting with sunshine. Threads of brown cut through the flavor, and right when you least expect it, a good strong shot of red…"

I keep talking nonsense until I hear her slow, even breathing. Until her hand goes limp and falls out of mine.

She looks too peaceful, too much like a corpse. Too much like my mother the last time I saw her.

I root in my knapsack and pull out a flat plastic box. Eight round tablets, the color of a juicy peach, rattle inside.

I wrap my friend's hand around the case. That's better. She looks more alive holding the brightly colored pills. As if no harm can come to her, so long as she has this store of nutrients.

If only it were that easy.

"Nice description," a voice says behind me.

I turn. Astana's brother leans against the entry to the living unit, his head a few inches from the doorjamb. Straight hair falls over his forehead, and his caviar-black eyes sink into me.

My cheeks warm. How long has he been standing there? Did he hear me gushing about my mysterious rescuer?

It shouldn't matter what Carr overhears. I've known him since we were kids, and he's not the type to tease. He used to hang around with my cousin, Denver, and sometimes the four of us would play a game of tag. Most of the time, though, Astana and I would stomp around Protector's Pond, catching and releasing dragonflies with fishing nets, while Carr would dig up worms and sell them as bait to the fishermen. He never made much—just one or two of those peach-colored pills—but looking at the dried mud under his fingernails always made me feel like one of his fat-bellied slugs. Spoiled and more than a little lazy.

I'm not that girl anymore, I want to tell Carr. *Any day now, I'll be named Top Aegis of my class, and within a few months, the council might appoint me as the King's Successor.*

But Blanca's words echo in my ears. *Nobody thinks you've got a chance. The council's just indulging Father in one of his whims.* Is she right? Maybe the council members aren't considering me after all. Maybe it's been Blanca all along, and they're just going through the motions.

So I end up not saying anything and simply stare as Carr walks into the room.

"Nice shirt, too." His eyes pause, for a fraction of a second, on my bare arms. "I don't think I've ever seen you in anything like that."

The heat in my cheeks spreads, wrapping around my ribs and stroking its tendrils along my spine. Which is ridiculous. He doesn't mean anything by the compliment. He works way too hard to ever take much notice of me.

And yet, I've always had this reaction to him. He could give me the smallest look, or place the tiniest emphasis on a single word, and my nerves dart around like they're the flame to his flint.

"I, um, took off the caftan because it's hot," I say and then flush. I might as well have told him pills have no taste. But what else could I have said? That I took my caftan off so his sister could suck on it?

Carr yanks on a loop to pull a sink out of the back wall. "What are you doing here?" He passes his hands under a red beam, which zaps the germs off his skin.

"I had some extra pills I wanted to give Astana."

He glances over his shoulder, at his sister's sleeping form, and his eyes fasten on the peach tablets.

My breath gets stuck in my lungs. Colonists don't eat, but that doesn't mean they don't feel hunger. "Carr," I say carefully. "What happens to the pills I leave for Astana?"

He snaps his gaze back to me. "What do you think happens to them?"

"I... I don't know. She never seems to put on any weight. And I've left countless pills."

"I've worked in glasshouses and fish farms all my life," he says, his voice low and controlled. "Day in and day out, I'm surrounded by food. The smell gets into my clothes, the fruit smears onto my skin. Every second of every day, I'm tempted to take a bite. Just one single bite, to see how it tastes. To experience how it feels. And you think I'm stealing from my sister?"

I spring to my feet, heart pounding. This isn't how our meeting was supposed to go. I lay awake for hours last night, imagining what he would say, how he would look. In my head, I made witty comments about the latest news feeds, and he crinkled up his forehead and laughed.

Nowhere in my imagined conversation did I call him a thief.

I grab my knapsack and inch toward the door. "Sorry I asked."

"Wait. Don't go." He scrubs a hand over his face. "I'm not mad. I..." He slumps onto the bed across from Astana, his voice a whisper only used in the deepest night. "She's been throwing up. Every day for the last week. And I've been waking up to her whimpers, because her stomach hurts so much. She's getting worse by the day, and I don't know what's wrong."

"I don't, either." I lift my shoulders, as helpless in my best friend's condition as I am in my response to her brother. I didn't know about the vomiting, about her cramps. Astana's been keeping her symptoms from me. "I didn't mean to accuse you of stealing. I'm just worried. About both of you."

"Me?" He laughs. "Why are you worried about me?"

"You've got circles under your eyes." I sit down next to him, eighteen inches away. He doesn't appear weak, like Astana. Instead, his body is lean and hard, the kind of physique you get from too much labor and not enough pills. "You look like you haven't nutritioned in a week."

"Why do you care?"

His eyes find mine, with an expression so raw and searing I look away. Our hands lie on the mattress, a finger-width apart. All I'd have to do is stretch my pinky, and we'd be touching. Any moment now, he'll move away. Turn so that his hand moves to his knee, a safe foot away. I forget to breathe as I wait for him to shift. But the seconds pass.

I look up to find him watching me. Noticing our hands. And he doesn't move.

"Of course I care. You're my best friend's brother," I say, light-headed from the lack of oxygen.

"I'm certainly not some mysterious prince who will swoop down and save you."

Oh. So he did hear me.

I lift my chin. "That was a joke. I'm as likely to rescue *him* as the other way around."

"I know. That's what I've always liked about you."

Everything freezes. My heart, my lungs. Even the red clock projected on the ceiling seems to stop in mid-blink. Oh. *Oh.* Did he say he likes me? As in his-little-sister's-best-friend-whom-he's-known-forever kind of like? Or something more?

"And you're right," he says. "I haven't taken any pills in the last week. Astana has an appointment at the medic, and I'm saving up to pay for it."

Time wakes up again. My three-dimensional heart squeezes as if it's been stuffed into a flat-surface world. "Oh, Carr. Why didn't you ask me for some?"

"I can pay to take my sister to the medic."

"It's not about whether you can. It's about whether you should skip meals in order to do it."

What about your mother? I want to yell. *Where is she?*

But I don't ask, because I know exactly where she is and what she's doing. Ever since she lost her job as a royal cook, Carr's mother has been strung out on drug pellets—and not the brightly colored ones, either. Many colonists will occasionally indulge in blue pills, which fizz on the tongue and create a temporary, light-headed sensation.

But his mother's pellets are not quite so innocuous. No, the color of these pellets is so dreary they don't have a name, and they do things to your body I've only heard about. Spinning rooms, vivid hallucinations, thinner oxygen. I'm not sure what the draw is, but these pellets can keep her away from the living unit—and her children—for weeks at a time.

"Maybe the medic won't be necessary after all," Carr says, looking at his sister. Her chest moves up and down easily, and her skin has resumed its warm natural tone. "She hasn't looked this good all week."

His lips curve for the first time this visit. "It must be your company that does her good. Nothing else has changed."

I smile back, even as my insides churn. Something's changed, all right, and it's not just my company. It's the raspberry stains lining the inside of my pocket. The tart she was never supposed to taste.

The food she's not allowed to eat.

CHAPTER TWO

I step into Protector's Courtyard, so named because it's located at the apex between the two adjoining space shuttles. The area, however, is used by everyone. It's the only open space in our densely populated bubbles, so all large gatherings take place here, whether it involves a hundred people or ten thousand. The neatly trimmed grass is a healthy, vibrant green, and the space shuttles form both backdrop and border, tall, imposing, and majestic. As always, the view takes my breath away. Not bad for a colony who's only been around for seven decades.

People bustle along the row of shops that borders the bottom of the courtyard, and overhead, the sun lamps inch along a metal arc that spans our entire system of interlocking bubbles. A group of colonists, identifiable by their non-uniform clothes, bunch around a metal platform at the top of the courtyard.

I walk nonchalantly along a path cutting across the open space, my dusty white caftan the same color as the slabs of concrete. Immediately, people begin to call out greetings to me.

One look at my loose-fitting caftan, with plenty of room to accommodate an expanding belly, and the people know exactly what I am. Aegis. Gen mod. Servant of society and revered hero of the colony.

Add the princess insignia pinned to my shoulder, a rose dipped in gold, and they know to press their hands to their hearts. If it were my father, they would tap three times.

As usual, their reverence makes me feel like I've eaten a bad oyster. Sure, I'm sacrificing two-thirds of my own life so they can live the full extent of their ninety years. But it's just one more thing that makes me different from them. One more way that I don't belong. Many of them would love to trade places with me, to be the King's daughter who might one day become Successor. They don't know that being a princess is characterized by one trait: loneliness.

"Princess Vela, I've got a new recipe to show you!" A round woman strolls up to me. She's tied a bright blue sash around her forehead, and a cube containing holograms of her late son hangs around her neck. All around us, people look enviously at her robust body. "Caramel cricket crunch! I think it'll be a big hit among the Aegis, don't you?"

"Sounds delicious to me."

"Come by my room tonight? I want you to be the first to try it." Her voice turns little-girl pleading. It's been almost ten years since her only child died, and as the anniversary approaches, she's been getting more and more melancholy.

"Of course, Miss Sydney." I squeeze her arm, my fingers sinking into her soft flesh. "I wouldn't miss it."

Satisfied, she disappears into the crowd. An instant later, Blanca appears at my elbow. Her hair is a glossy black ribbon under the sun lamp, but the light does nothing to soften her sneer. "How on orb do you know her name?"

I stare. I visit all the Fittest families at least once a week.

Is it possible Blanca's never paid them this same courtesy? "How can you not? Miss Sydney's only lived on the shuttle for the last ten years. Her son gave his life so our father could live."

She shrugs and checks her watch, as though she's sorry she started this conversation with me. "They all look the same to me."

"You just wish you had her figure," I sputter. "They don't look the same. They just have extra curves because they eat real food and their nutrients haven't been sucked out."

But she's no longer listening. I was right. She must've only approached me because she was bored. Conversation over, she drifts away, her eyes trained on a 3-D logo projected by the news feed onto the metal platform.

After a moment, I forget about being hurt. Because my sister's always saying outrageous things in order to get attention, and another outlandish statement she once made, years ago, floats to my mind. *Colonists can't taste*, she had jeered at Astana and me from across the pond, *because then their pills won't work.*

I'd thought she was jealous I had a new friend. But what if she was telling the truth? What if eating actual food is somehow interfering with Astana's ability to absorb the nutrition from her pills?

A hush falls over the courtyard as the news feed begins, and I notice that the crowd around the metal platform has tripled.

I don't know how I could've forgotten. Stress over Astana must be affecting me more than I realized. Thank goodness my feet brought me here of their own volition. Everyone's gathered today to watch the last rites of Kenneth Kendall, the scientist who invented the genetic modification that saved our colony.

"What's so special about them, anyhow?" a woman near me mutters. Her skin is rosy and glowing. I'd take a moment to admire the sheen if it weren't for the venom in her words. "Their excrement might stink less, but they still crap, just like the rest of us!"

My head jerks, even though what she's saying is true. There's food crap—and then there's pill crap. None of it is pleasant, but unfortunately, the nutrient-dense supplements produce even smellier feces.

But the woman's not talking to Blanca or me. She's addressing the news feed at the top of the courtyard.

I study the 3-D image. Master Kendall sits on a bed that spans the entire width of the platform, his long white beard tucked into his button-down shirt, digging into a tray of food on his lap. The holographic image is so crisp I can make out the gold stitching on the pillowcase. The vents around the courtyard blow out aromas, and all around me, people begin sniffing the air.

"What is it?" a girl in an emerald green tunic asks.

"Is he eating cicada? Shrimp paella?"

"I think I smell lemongrass!"

"Maybe they invented a new dish just for him!"

I could've told my fellow spectators they were smelling kimchi-jjigae and scallion pancakes, but what would be the point? They'll never taste either in their lives. The names of food roll off their tongues like the fashion found in old Earth films. Trendy to know, but with no real relevance to their lives.

"We've come to the end of an era," the smooth voice of a female news feeder projects over the loudspeaker. "Brilliant scientist and original colony member, Kenneth Kendall, has reached the last days of his life. His final wish? To eat the food he's devoted his life to amplifying."

As if to illustrate her point, Master Kendall fumbles a spoon to his mouth and audibly slurps the stew.

"Sixty years ago, when the space shuttles first landed on Dion, the people made a catastrophic discovery," the feeder says. "Of the ten thousand pods that were sent to terraform our new planet, only a hundred pods had survived. Instead of a habitable, fully-terraformed planet, the people found only a patch of land on which to live.

"They had two options. Wait for the terraforming to spread to the rest of the planet, which could take a dozen lifetimes. Or hold on until the new pods arrived in the next shuttle, which was hundreds of light-years away—and only if Earth received the emergency message that they sent. Both options meant the original colony would be decimated, as there was simply not enough land to grow the food necessary to sustain the population. The people were cut off from all communications with Earth, so they were on their own. To live…or to die."

A guy with full facial hair gasps, although we all learned this in our first history lesson at school. His affected drama is the result, I suppose, of taking a group of people and flinging them into the deep reaches of space. Without any other colony to distract us, we're singularly obsessed with our own past.

"And then Master Kendall proposed a third option. Turn the human body into an incubator, so it becomes more efficient at extracting nutrition from food. Suction the nutrition from these incubators and distribute it to the rest of the colony. With this genetic modification, a person can eat a single portion of food and extract several times as many nutrients. It's not a perfect solution. We know this. But it was the best option we had at the time. And so, Master Kendall moved forward in recreating a miracle that's been talked about since the early days of Earth: he took five barley loaves and two small fish and fed the masses."

The crowd bursts into whoops and cheers. I clap along with everyone else, even though the feeder failed to mention the side effects. But why should she? This is about commemorating Master Kendall, not me. Not the other Aegis. So what if the transfer itself is exceedingly uncomfortable? What if the genetic modification damages our cells, so we perish six decades sooner than the normal lifespan?

Everyone knows about these side effects, of course. That's why the colonists showed me so much deference. We are a society built on sacrifice. Layer upon layer of sacrifice. It is not only the honorable thing to do. It is normal and *expected*. This colony wouldn't exist if it weren't for the sacrifices of our original colonists. That is why we are called the Aegis. The protectors. The personification of the shield that Zeus carried in Greek mythology.

And so, everyone who tests positive for the Aegis gene, the one that shows if a person will respond to the genetic modification, is expected to forego their selfish interest for the overall good of the people.

"Waste not," the feeder says. "The First Maxim of our colony. Many have petitioned the King, Adam Kunchai, to make exceptions to this Maxim, for holidays, for anniversaries, for the milestones in every person's life. He has always declined. And for good reason. What little food we have cannot be squandered. It must be reserved to those who can utilize it best."

"Please!" The rosy-skinned woman next to me shifts, bumping into my shoulder. "Like a single bite would make a difference. The King wants to hoard the food for himself."

Blanca and I look at each other, in a rare moment of camaraderie, ready to defend our father. But we don't need to. Even as my heart leaps at our shared connection, the other spectators shuffle together until a ring of space forms around the woman. The Circle of Shunning. The easiest—and most effective—way to tell a person: *we do not condone your behavior. You are not one of us.*

It works as well here as it does on the playground. The woman looks at the absence of bodies around her, and her skin ripens to the color of tomato. "I was joking," she says. But it's too late. She's spoken against their beloved King, and this crowd does not forgive easily.

Above our heads, the news feeder continues: "…only under the most extenuating of circumstances will the King and his council make an exception to the First Maxim. In order to award the family of the Fittest candidate, for example. Or to honor the man who saved us all."

Master Kendall finishes his meal and wipes his mouth with a silk napkin. He leans against his pillows. Even as his body relaxes into the mattress, however, he darts his eyes from one unseen spot to another, so quickly a lesser technology might be accused of broadcasting a blurry image.

The news feeder's voice lowers as if she's telling us a secret. "As Kenneth Kendall lies on his deathbed, he has given the King his final request. Give him a taste of heaven, and then, before his body can reject the food it's not used to eating, end his life the way he tried to live it. Heroically."

Master Kendall's eyes focus as a thick gray gas begins to cloud the holographic air onstage. For a moment, he freezes. Then he straightens, lifts his arms in the air, and takes a deep breath.

Each rise of his chest fills his lungs with the gas. Dark. Odorless. And deadly. I can hardly make out his features through the vapor anymore. But there's no mistaking the instant his body slumps to the side.

"Rest in peace, Master Kendall. You were the very first hero in a colony founded and sustained by heroes."

The news feed is cut, and we all drop to our knees, our hands pressed to our hearts. But even in this moment of silence, my mind doesn't stop churning. I'm as grateful to Master Kendall as anyone else, but this ceremony has made me realize more than the heroism of my fellow people.

It's reminded me the council rarely makes exceptions to the First Maxim. In fact, other than the Fittest families, Master Kendall is the first colonist who has been granted permission to taste food. And so, it doesn't matter if the medics figure out what's wrong with Astana. If I'm right about what's ailing her, they may not be allowed to give her the one thing she needs to get better: food.

Only I can do that. And judging by the severity of Astana's symptoms? If I don't get her real food soon, she could very well die.

Half an hour later, I'm standing inside the Banquet Room, watching the food preparation team set up the early evening meal.

Fondue tonight. Pots of melted soy cheese, flavored with white wine and roasted shallots, sit on every table, along with mountains of crusty bread and brightly colored bell peppers, sliced into perfect cubes. Fat bee larvae wait next to the smoking hot oil, ready to be dipped for mere seconds.

I can smell the crisp scent of fried insects. Feel the rich, fatty bite melt on my tongue. According to the archives, bee larvae is supposed to taste like the bacon they had back on Earth. I wouldn't know. Although we have frozen embryos of every Earth species stored in our space shuttle, we don't have any livestock in our colony. Not yet. We simply don't have the land.

Right now, though, the last thing I feel is hunger. All I crave is a successful getaway.

I should probably wait a while before making another attempt. Lie low until Blanca turns her microscopic scrutiny somewhere else. At least ride out the next two days until I'm crowned Top Aegis.

But Astana doesn't have a while. Carr says she's getting worse. I need to alleviate her symptoms now, before it's too late.

I pull back my shoulders, trying to trick myself into feeling confident. A hurricane roars in my ears, and the thin cotton of my trousers sticks to my legs.

My best friend needs me.

The thought propels me to the dessert table, where Barbados, one of the food preppers, is arranging the chocolate fondue. Streams of dark liquid chocolate wind around islands of strawberries, while graham cracker towers spiral into the air.

Sweet and bitter, moist and crunchy. In spite of my mission, my stomach growls its approval.

Barbados squints at his creation, turning one of the graham crackers a few degrees.

"This looks beautiful, Barbados," I say.

He straightens and beams at me. "I'm glad you noticed. It takes me hours to build these scenes, but the Aegis seem to decimate them in a matter of seconds…" His voice falters with the last word, as if he's realized he's speaking to an Aegis. "What I meant to say, Princess Vela is, uh, I hope you enjoy the presentation."

I pick up a strawberry from his stash and pop it into my

mouth. The juices squirt over my tongue. "Delicious. I'm sure I'll eat more than my stomach wants, thanks to your hard work."

Which is Barbados's entire purpose in creating this edible landscape. The purpose, in fact, of the entire food preparation team. Manipulating flavors, texture, aroma, and colors to entice us into taking one more bite.

When my fellow Aegis and I first started our training classes, food was this miraculous adventure, this whole new world of unexplored tastes and sensations. But now that it's our job? Now that we must stuff ourselves at six different meals, day in and day out? I'm still able to take pleasure from food most of the time. But some days, eating is nothing but a chore. Those times, I even wish that I'd never tested positive for the Aegis gene.

But there's no point wishing for a different life. Being an Aegis is who I am. Providing for my people is what I've been called to do. I leave Barbados to his work and walk around the room, saying "hi" to the other preppers and sampling a cube of bread from this pile and a scoop of cheese from that pot.

No one blinks at the few bites that find their way into my mouth. They might look twice if they notice the food that's disappearing into my clothes.

Five cubes of bread nestle at my elbow. Two plump strawberries lodge in my left pocket, three bee larvae in my right.

My heart pounds. I've never taken this much food before. Every other time, it's been a bite of tart or a quarter-cookie or half a spring roll. Items I could feasibly pass off as absentminded mistakes. But now, I've got a whole meal hidden in my caftan. If I'm caught, there will be no excuses.

I bend my elbow and casually wrap my arm around my

torso, surveying the room. A royal guard stands in the corner, but she's grinning at a female prepper as she constructs a heart out of veggie strips. The other preppers are scattered across the banquet tables, busy with their work.

So far, so good. I start moving toward the door. Twenty more steps, and I'm out of here.

I try to control my breathing, aiming for the even in-and-out we used to practice during our training classes. Not only did we learn the most efficient ways of eating, but we also built up our physical stamina and practiced fortifying our wills. I wasn't half bad at meditation—but now, my nose sucks in air before my mouth can expel it, and I end up with jerky, overlapping pants.

Fifteen steps.

The strawberries squish against each other, and juice drips down my leg. A few drops blossom like blood in the white cotton.

Ten steps.

The cubes of bread slip. I bend my elbow harder, but the cubes fall from their cradle, forming noticeable lumps at the bottom of my sleeve.

Oh Dionysus, don't let the guard look now. Please keep her focused on her prepper girlfriend.

Five steps.

I'll do anything if I get out of here safely. Give up the title of Top Aegis. Concede the Successorship to Blanca. Just let me get this food to Astana.

Four, three, two...

I take one step across the threshold, and then a hand claps onto my shoulder.

My blood freezes, falling apart like shaved ice as an authoritative voice floats over me. "Princess Vela, you are under arrest for the smuggling of edibles on your person."

CHAPTER THREE

*U*nder arrest.

Me. Vela Kunchai. Princess of Dion.

I turn slowly, as if my limbs push against a medium denser than air.

The guard cuffs my wrists and recites the rest of the custody warnings. "Do not speak now. You will be given the opportunity to testify before the King and his council. At that time, you may deny or excuse, justify or explain. But choose your words carefully because the council will reach a verdict upon your Testimony, and like all council decrees, the verdict will be final."

Her eyes meet mine for a fraction of a second, and something I can't read flits through them.

Probably just as well. My legs seem to be holding up, but my mind is numb and cold, like someone doused it with a dewar of liquid nitrogen. A million emotions swirl, trying to surface, but the ice cage locks them up tight. If I look into the guard's eyes and see disappointment—or even worse, shame—in the actions of her Princess, my emotions might split the cage wide open.

She leads me out of the shuttle and to the Red Cell Prison, at the back of the center bubble. In the processing room, a warden empties my pockets and strips me of my caftan. She tells me her name is Palmetto and lays the contraband on the table. Bread. Strawberries. Bee larvae.

A few thoughts break through. It's just food. Not a weapon. Not illegal drug pellets. Not flammable, toxic, or poisonous.

Just. Food.

But I don't protest as she hands me a slimmer version of my eating caftan and urges me into a Transfer Room. I strip and lay on the table, slipping my arms and legs into clear plastic tubes. A local anesthetic is misted all over my body, and then Palmetto adjusts the plastic shield around my torso and flips on the machine.

A powerful vacuum suctions my entire body off the table. My skin is a glove I've put on backward, and my organs feel like they're being squeezed out of my body: my lungs out my chest, my heart dragged up my throat, my stomach through my belly button.

The procedure is highly uncomfortable—but at least the anesthetic guarantees that there's minimal pain.

Six times a day, every day for the last two years, and I've gotten used to the strange sensation by now. Maybe, one day, I'll even forget the discomfort.

After the machine extracts every excess nutrient, I get dressed, and Palmetto takes me into a room the size of the Banquet Hall. The smells hit me first. Urine. Underwear. Unwashed bodies. I pull my shirt over my nose, but the stench is like a gruesome crime scene—one contact, and no amount of time or scrubbing will ever get it out.

Palmetto continues walking, and I have no choice but

to follow. The room is divided into cells by intersecting red beams, and inside each cell, men and women with greasy hair and identical uniforms sleep or stand or pace. As soon as they see us, they stop whatever they're doing and stare.

Their eyes sink into my skin like poisoned barbs, and a single step feels like a thousand. My stomach twists with fear and pity. Some of these people might have been incarcerated for a nonviolent offense, like mine. But others might be assaulters, kidnappers—even murderers. Still, I wouldn't wish these living conditions on anyone. A lifetime passes, and then Palmetto stops in front of an empty cell. She pushes a button on the square device hanging from her belt, and a section of the beams blinks off.

"In you go, Princess. Don't touch the rays. They'll cook you like a wonton."

"I want to talk to my father." The words are flat and unfeeling, the product of a frozen mind, but the very act of talking is melting, melting, melting the bonds. I notice, for the first time, the way my toes slide against each other, slick with my body's sweat.

"After your Testimony. Red-cell policy," she says and then leaves.

Through the red beams, I have a clear view of the detainees on either side of me—and glimpses of the detainees on the other side of them.

One woman is topless, nasty red streaks across her breasts, as if she would slice herself into ribbons to scratch an itch she can't reach. Another guy does push-ups as if the demon that drove him here still rides his back, whipping him into submission.

I take a shaky breath. It's going to be okay. I know all about the red cells. I learned about them in school a decade ago. Once, I even came here on a field trip. I'll be fine.

Funny how no one ever told me the guy in the next cell might be sitting on a toilet. They forgot to say his face would scrunch together, as red as vine-ripened tomatoes, as he defecates.

The foul smell of pill crap washes over me.

Although it makes my stomach turn, I sniff the air again. Yep. Urine, underwear, unwashed bodies—and pill crap. My neighbor has been taking nutrition supplements instead of eating.

My heart strikes against my chest. I suck in mouthful after mouthful of air, my lungs punctured tires. But it's not enough.

Because I only had a few meals left before my title was official. Before I would be named Top Aegis.

"Hey!" I stand as close to the red beams as I dare and shout, "Hey!"

After four or five iterations, Palmetto returns. She's only a few years older than me, and her eyes are kind, although she has the hardened features of all the colonists who work in close proximity to food. It's as if steeling the soul against daily temptation sands the softness right off your face.

"Yes? Is there something you need?"

I stuff the panic down my throat. As if on cue, my stomach growls. Of course it does. It's been three hours since I last ate. The colonists' stomachs make plenty of noise, but only the digestive juices of an Aegis are so routinely exercised you could set a clock by the tell-tale gurgle. "My next meal's coming up. When do I go to the Banquet Hall?"

She frowns. "I'm sorry, Princess. You don't get to resume eating duties until after you're sentenced." She pulls a peach pill out of her pocket. "You can nutrition with this until the council has a chance to hear your Testimony."

I take the pill from her. It's not like I've never taken one before. In fact, they supplied the majority of my nutrition before I became an official Aegis when I turned fifteen. Even now, I might take one in a pinch. But this pill means more than a skipped meal.

I won't be eating tonight. I won't make my quota. Blanca will swoop right past me in the standings.

This innocuous peach pill means I've just lost the title of Top Aegis.

I lie on my back in the middle of the cell, as far as possible from my neighbors. My stomach grouses and grumbles like a mad baby, but I ignore the noises. The guy to my left battles with his toilet, and the girl to my right claws at her legs. I ignore them, too.

The concrete is cool and smooth against my skin. If I close my eyes, I can pretend I'm not here. I can go to that moment, ten years ago, when I coughed and gagged on the muddy shore, spitting up sludge and pond water and possibly a lung. My throat burned like bubbling magma; my chest ached like I was popped into the wrong dimension. I was sure I was going to die.

But then a hand pressed into my back. A boy said, "This pain, too, will pass. Just hold on, and life will get better. It always does."

I was so confused and water-logged that I didn't register much else about the voice, other than the fact that it was masculine. But I held on for a moment, and another moment after that, and then the pressure unlocked around my chest and I could breathe again.

The hand disappeared from my back, and by the time

my eyes started working again, he was gone.

I wish I had seen his face. I wish he would come back now. Not just because he's played a starring role in my daydreams, but also so I could thank him. For that moment, and for a thousand other moments since. Any time I was lost or unsure, any time I felt like there was no way I could survive, I think of his words.

This pain, too, will pass. Just hold on, and life will get better. It always does.

Somebody clears her throat. The sound is too close to be coming from the next cell. I open my eyes, and Palmetto is bending over me, her fine hair dangling around her face.

"Your Testimony is in half an hour. You get one holo-call before that." She shakes the phone in her hand. "Who would you like to reach?"

I sit up, still smelling the damp scent of pond moss. "My father."

"Not possible. He's not allowed to speak to you until after your Testimony. How about another family member? Your sister, Blanca?" Her tone is even, without a hint of sarcasm. Is it possible she doesn't know about the rivalry between the princesses?

"Blanca will want to know I've been red-celled, all right. But her joy's not what I want to hear right now."

"Oh." Palmetto flushes. "No family then. Anyone else?"

I give her Astana's code. She sets up the call and leaves, presumably to give me privacy. Which is nice but unnecessary. Itchy Girl and Defecating Guy have abandoned their obsessions and stand nose-to-red-beam, peering into my space.

I give them a wave and turn my attention to the holo-phone. An instant later, an image of Carr is projected in front of me.

Talk about not being able to breathe. The cell is suddenly sauna-hot, and I feel like I have too many arms and legs. The hologram is so precise I can see the stubble on his jaw and the way his too-long hair brushes over his ears.

Maybe that's why I obsess over my mysterious savior. He's never comng back, and that makes him a whole lot safer than a flesh-and-blood boy—or even the holographic image of one.

"Vela." Carr's eyes flicker from my face to the slimmer-fitting caftan to the red beams behind me. "What happened to you?"

Ah. The question worth a life's supply of pills. How I answer here and more importantly, during the Testimony, will make all the difference in the world.

My world, at least. Free or red-celled. Princess or convict. Successor or loser. These things are grains compared to the sandstorm that is my best friend's life, but even the smallest particle can sting when it's wedged in the silent space of the soul.

Ever since I was a little girl, my father taught me a few basic lessons. Tell the truth. Value all life. Accept responsibility for my actions.

And yet, my decision's not clear. I could say that the food was for me. That I was saving it for a midnight snack, even though the pantries are open to us at all times. I could say that I was being lazy, that I didn't want to budge from my bed in order to shore up my calories. Or…I could tell them the truth.

If I thought being honest with the council would save Astana, I'd do it. But can I trust them to do the right thing? Or will Astana just get in trouble for eating?

"Never mind what happened to me. How's Astana? How are you?" I take an involuntary step toward his image. I just left him this morning, but he looks like he's aged five years. The bruises under his eyes almost match the blacks of his cornea, and his lips are a bindle stick carrying too much weight.

"She's worse." He glances behind him. I can't see what he's looking at, but his view must be bad. I can tell from the jerk of his elbows, from the tremor in his eyelashes. "The improvements didn't last long after you left." He faces me again. "I sent a message to the gorge, asking my mom to come home."

I go still. Carr's never asked his mom to come home before. Not when he lost his job at the apple orchard, not when their holo-feed got turned off. Not even when the unit-lord threatened to evict them.

Lucky for him, things always seemed to work out. A new job would pop up out of nowhere, or an unexpected deposit would show up at the pill bank. As if someone was looking out for him. His mother, maybe. Or more likely, a guardian angel.

"Did you ask her because you think she might be able to help?" I try to wet my lips, but my mouth is suddenly, desperately dry. "Or because you want her to say...goodbye?"

The word feels foreign in my mouth, maybe because I haven't uttered it for years. I never got to say goodbye to my mother, and so now, I make a point never to say it at all.

"My sister's lost consciousness." His voice trembles like the ground during an orbquake. "I took her to the medic, but he didn't know what was wrong, either."

My saliva is a rock I can't swallow. His despair matches the one inside me, the one that's been growing ever since I wrapped my arms around my best friend and felt like I was hugging a skeleton.

Here's my answer. It doesn't matter if I'm red-celled for

the rest of my life. It doesn't matter if I lose the position of Successor. My best friend is unconscious. She won't be able to tell the medics what they need to know in order to help her. So I have to. Right here, right now, no matter who might be eavesdropping.

"Carr?" I edge closer to his image. "You know how Astana's symptoms improved earlier? And you thought it was because of my company?"

He nods, leaning forward, too. At least I'm not the only one deluded by a field of light.

"Well, that wasn't the reason at all." I fill my lungs to capacity. I'll need the air. Once I say the words, there's no going back. "I think she got better because I gave her food to eat."

Someone gasps. It's not me or Carr, so it's got to be Palmetto or one of my cell neighbors. I'm now committed to the truth—and its consequences. With these witnesses, I'll have to tell the council the same story.

"I've given her bites in the past. And I think that's why she can't absorb the nutrition from her pills. That's why she's been starving. I tried to sneak more food out of the banquet hall this afternoon. Not crumbs this time. An entire meal. But I got caught."

"You're in the red cells now? Because you stole food to help my sister?"

"Yes. I give my Testimony before the council in a few minutes."

He looks over my shoulder, toward the itchy girl with the red streaks, although I know he doesn't see her. My heart constricts into a tight ball, as if it's been strapped behind a plastic shield and all the blood has been sucked dry.

"My sister's dying," he says roughly. "And now, you're imprisoned."

"I should've said no." The words shoot out as though from a speargun. "All those times she asked me for one more bite, I should've refused."

"My sister can be very persistent." If his mouth wasn't anchored down, it might've smiled.

"You're not mad?"

"Under these circumstances? No. I'm sorry she's so sick. I'm sorry you're in the red cells. I'm sorry any of us are in this pill-suck of a situation. And you know what else I'm sorry about?"

"What?"

Instead of responding, he holds his hand in the air, his fingertips reaching for me. My mind knows this is just a recording that's reconstructed a split second later. There's nothing in front of me but a structure of light with varying density, intensity, and profile.

But when I lift my hand and touch his, I swear there's a spark. My fingers burn. My skin turns to static, and my heart swells to twice its normal size. I thought only the stomach had the capacity to stretch and expand. I never knew my heart had the same elasticity.

"I'm sorry I didn't touch you when I actually had the chance." His voice is a low, dark rasp. "A million chances over the years, and I've wasted them all."

Everything I've ever wanted to say to him comes brimming to my lips.

I used to watch you for hours, digging in the dirt. Do you remember finding a dish of worms one morning, waiting for you on the shore? That was me. I woke up before the sunlamps, and I kneeled in that mud for hours, so I could make your work a little easier. So that you would have time to play with Astana and me. But that pile of worms only made you work harder.

I want to say all of this, and more, but I don't get the chance. Palmetto rattles back into my cell, and I snatch my hand out of the air.

"I'm sorry to interrupt, Princess Vela," she says. "But it's time for your Testimony."

CHAPTER FOUR

I tell the council everything.

Looking into a holo-cam, in a small room with a one-way mirror, I tell them how I gave Astana a taste from my training meal before I even became an official Aegis, how I've been sneaking crumbs to her over the years, how she's been slowly but steadily getting sicker.

I tell them about how food seems to improve Astana's symptoms, about watching Master Kendall's execution on the news feeds, about my decision to sneak an entire meal out of the Banquet Hall.

On the other side of the mirror, the members of the King's council listen as I give my Testimony.

What do they see? A screwed-up Princess who threw away her future before it began? Or a girl who's made a series of mistakes?

More importantly, what does my father think? Is he disappointed in me, or does he understand?

I'm not a bad person. I was trying to help my friend. I don't belong here in the red cells.

I scream this out with every confession, every detail, every word. But I don't know if and what they hear.

I tell them everything and then I beg them to help Astana. I am willing and ready to accept the consequences for my mistakes, but please. Don't hold my actions against my friend. Help her get better.

When my Testimony's finished, I go back to my cell and wait.

And wait.

And wait.

One day, six pills, and zero words on Astana later, the council summons me to the Royal Towers, a tall building at the junction of the two space shuttles. I stop in front of the double doors of the King's chambers, my heart racing like I've been running through the wheat fields. My palms won't dry, no matter how many times I wipe them on my caftan.

This pain, too, will pass. Just hold on, and life will get better. It always does.

My savior's not here, but I can follow his advice. I think about his words and study the mural etched in the doors. A man and a woman, naked except for a few leaves and the flowing tresses of the woman's hair. They stand underneath a lush, bountiful tree, and a serpent slithers its body around an apple, as if offering it to the woman.

Their names are Adam and Eve, and the scene is from one of the religions back on Earth. As the story goes, the world's troubles came when Eve first took a bite of the apple. The picture's carved here not only because the man is the King's namesake but also to remind us never to take eating for granted.

As if we would. I don't think I've ever forgotten the countdown to my death began the moment I received the genetic modification.

But the serpent scares me. It always has. When I was a kid, I used to have recurring dreams about its coiling, twisting body. About a shiny red apple on the ground, with a bite taken out of it. If I'm being honest, the nightmare still shows up now. Maybe it's all the more scary because we don't have any real snakes in our colony.

I'd rather face a snake, real or imagined, than what's inside that office.

I square my shoulders and look into the camera positioned above the serpent's head. The lens scans my face, and the door slides open.

The King stands in front of his desk with a group of council members. His face is square and placid, his formerly black hair shot through with silver. I used to say the color reminded me of the mane of a unicorn. He would respond that if the mystical creatures actually existed, their manes would be gray and dusty, on account of the dirt.

Today, my father is neither gray nor dusty. He wears a gold brocade jacket that hangs straight to his knees, over white pants and a white shirt, along with his royal insignia, a pine cone dipped in gold. The royal uniform alone should remind me I'm appearing before him not as his daughter but as a subject.

I pay no attention.

"Dad!" I shout as I run to him. He spreads his arms wide. I leap into them, and he pulls me to his chest, crushing my cheek against the pine cone. He smells like the woods behind the shuttle after the rain spigots have been running.

I feel six meals lighter. He still loves me. I'm still his

daughter, no matter what I've done. "I've missed you," I say.

"You're shaking." He kneads my shoulders, as if he can stop the vibrations. As if searching for the missing nutrients. I feel in his squeeze the words he cannot say. *What have they been doing to you in the red cells? Have you suffered?*

"I'm fine. I've been taking pills instead of eating," I say. "I missed winning the title of Top Aegis by a few meals."

The council member closest to me, a woman with skin a few shades lighter than my medium brown, nudges her companion and tilts her head toward me. I flush. I was doing what I always do: giving my father a rundown of my day. But that's not how they see it. They think I'm complaining. They think I'm a spoiled princess, used to getting everything I want. Maybe they're right. But the King's never given me special treatment because I'm his daughter.

I've been in the red cells for two days! I want to shout. *Why would the King let me stay there if what you believe is true?*

But shouting is not the way to impress the council, so I take a few steps back. Hands clasped, head inclined. Subject once again.

The leader of the council, Master Somjing, shuffles forward on his mechanical braces. He wears a hologram pendant around his neck, and he's almost ninety, the same age as my father. Without the benefit of the King's transplants, however, he looks considerably older. The skin sags from his bones, so you can't tell where his cheeks end and jaw begins, and his bushy, white eyebrows point in every direction. The braces wrap around his legs and help him get through his daily routine. Walking, standing, even jumping.

"Shall we begin the formal sentencing?" His tone implies the father-daughter moment was a courtesy to the King.

My father sits on his throne, and the council members

shuffle themselves into a semi-circle. The council is made up of colonists, old and middle-aged, male and female. Each member also doubles as head of the various departments in our government. Master Somjing is one of our few remaining original colonists.

"Princess Vela, you've made a full confession," Master Somjing says, his voice low and gravelly, the way a serpent might sound if it could talk. "We are not here today to issue a verdict on your guilt but rather to sentence you for your crime."

My heart ricochets into my mouth. I try to summon my rescuer's voice, but here, in front of this semi-circle of eyes and expectations, it won't come.

"I'm ready," I say, my voice two decibels above a whisper.

"The council has carefully considered your Testimony. While the reasons you stole food as a child were frivolous—in order to share a taste with your friend—there are some of us on the council..." His eyes slide to my father. "...who believe the motivation behind your more recent violation was based on loyalty and friendship. Surprisingly, CORA agrees." *Even if I don't*, his tone implies. "We on the council have taken that into consideration, even as we deem your actions a clear transgression of the law."

CORA, short for control room analytics, is a computation engine that runs scenarios, using every piece of available data and extrapolating from all known human behavior, to calculate a percentage of success or failure. Every decision the council makes is backed by CORA's findings. In fact, every aspect of our life on Dion has its roots in this computer.

The best of both worlds. Machine-like objectivity, powered by human subjectivity. The highest level of statistical success, tempered by moral judgment. Whatever my sentence is, it'll be the best possible decision, based on the history of human experiences from both Earth and Dion.

I don't know if that's supposed to reassure me, but I nod, not daring to speak. Hardly daring to breathe.

"Therefore, you will not remain in the red cells."

The air *whooshes* out of my lungs. If it weren't for my father's gaze reining me in, I would've swished around the room like a leaking balloon.

"You may return to your residence in the shuttle and resume your eating duties," Master Somjing continues. "However, you will be sentenced two years' worth of excess pills for violating the law."

"Two years?" I blurt. "That's not fair."

The woman closest to me knocks into her friend so hard he stumbles.

Okay, I get it, lady. You don't approve. I take a deep breath. I'm guilty of the action. Therefore, I must accept the responsibility. "I mean, it is fair. I apologize."

If I were the girl they trained me to be, I would shut my mouth now. But if I were that girl, I wouldn't be here now. "What about Astana?" I ask. "Is she in trouble?"

"Your friend will have to give Testimony but not while her health is compromised." Master Somjing glances at Mistress Barnett, the council member with the long silver hair and wine-red lips who heads our medical facility. "You are right that we do not easily make exceptions to the First Maxim. We cannot waste our limited supply of food. But we shall see."

What, exactly, will we be "seeing"? Does he mean the council might make an exception, after all? Or simply that Astana may get better through other means?

I learned long ago Master Somjing only says what he intends, and if he's being vague, it's deliberate. Even if I ask, I won't get any more answers.

"The council understands her addiction to taste began when she was a child, too young to understand the ramification of her actions," he continues. "She will be shown the same leniency given you."

My shoulders relax. I guess that's it, then. I couldn't have hoped for a better outcome. Sympathy from the council, my friend under expert care. Master Somjing didn't say anything about my candidacy for Successor, but perhaps that consequence is understood. I'm a criminal now, confirmed and sentenced. It goes without saying I'm no longer under consideration.

The disappointment is a fishbone stuck in my throat. Now I'll never help my people the way that I want. Now I'll never live up to my father's high expectations of me. "Thank you. I appreciate your understanding."

I bow to Master Somjing and prepare to leave, but then, my father stands and breaks through the line of people. "Wait, Vela. There's more."

He nods at the council members. As if by prior agreement, they begin to file out of the room.

He turns back to me. "A whole lot more, I'm afraid."

CHAPTER FIVE

My pulse leaps. Something more? What can he mean?

I watch the council members walk out of the Royal Office, each disappearing body turning the crank on my pulse. By the time Master Somjing lurches out the serpent door, his mechanical braces scraping over the door jamb, my heart feels like it's busted the dial.

"Is it good news or bad?" I ask.

The words are from a game I used to play as a little girl, when my father would sit Blanca and me down in the evenings for a "talk." I could never stand the anticipation back then. I always had to know, as soon as possible, if I should steel myself or bounce in my seat.

And then came the day my father turned into a stone carving and said, "It's bad news, girls. Your mother passed away."

I never asked the question again. Until now.

Three creases appear in my father's forehead, and for a moment, he looks as old as Master Somjing. "A little of both, I think. Let's go for a walk."

So I'm going to have to wait, after all.

We exit the back of the building into a thick throng of trees. Like everything else inside the bubble, the trees are crowded together, roots overlapping roots, as they perform their job of sucking in carbon dioxide and spitting out oxygen.

The trunks stand tall and pristine. Back on Earth, forests were cut down for lumber and paper products. But wood is a scarce resource on Dion. We only have what we can grow inside our bubbles, so the trees remain.

We squeeze behind a trunk as thick as my arm span and duck underneath a low hanging branch to take a path I know well. The dirt is moist, as if the rain spigots have just rotated through this sector, and the trees are plump with colorful leaves.

Three turns and a few scratches later, we enter into a copse of C-trunks. The trunks of these genetically engineered trees curve in a C-shape, perfect for the human body to sit. We plant them all over the colony, in lieu of actual chairs, to maximize oxygen. But what makes these trees unique is that they're planted ten feet apart, rather than crowded together.

That's because this copse isn't part of the air-producing machine, but rather, a tribute to all the boys and girls who have sacrificed their lives to save the King. The copse was my idea, and this memorial was built five years ago. I fertilize the C-trunks and trim the grass. And once a week, I bring a fresh bouquet of flowers to place at the base of each tree.

My father places his hand fondly, almost reverently, on a C-trunk, where a boy's name has been carved. I know, without seeing the letters, whose name it is.

Cairo Mead. He died for my father thirty years ago, before I was born. His brother tells me Cairo had bright green eyes and was always playing practical jokes. One time, he taped a faucet handle down, so whoever turned on the tap would get sprayed in the face. Another time, he took his baby sister out of the cradle and bundled up a butternut squash in her place.

They say he died with a smile in his eyes and a punchline on his lips.

"Do you know why we're here?" my father asks, his fingers dipping into the grooves of Cairo's name.

I nod. "The Fittest Trials are coming up."

Every five years for the last five decades, we hold trials to select the candidate who is most physically strong. Most morally worthy. Most deserving to be memorialized in our colony's history, forever.

In short, the person most fit to die for the King.

My father received the genetic modification when he was twenty, and thus he should have reached the end of his shortened lifespan fifty years ago. But our colony was young and unstable, and CORA predicted that without a consistent leader, universally beloved by his people, it would dissolve into chaos. The Fittest tradition began, and every five years, my father receives a transplant of all the major organs from a colonist to replace his own damaged ones.

As this cycle's Fittest Trials approach, I sense a shift in the families of the previous Fittest candidates. First and foremost, there's pride. Out of all the eligible people, their sons and daughters, their brothers and sisters were selected to be honored. To be placed on a pedestal above everyone else. To be awarded the privilege of performing the greatest sacrifice of all—a sacrifice that will save an entire colony.

But at the same time, the parents and siblings seem to draw closer together, as they prepare to welcome a new family into their fold. A family who will share in their grief and loss.

"Master Somjing typically administers the trials, and CORA selects the Fittest. But this year, we're doing things a little differently." My father's hand closes in a fist on the bark. "This will be my last transplant."

The words sucker punch me in the throat. "What are you saying? Are you...dying?"

"We all die, my eye-apple. My body's getting old, and there's a limit to how long we can extend my life through artificial means. Five years from now, I will retire from the throne. That's precisely why we need to choose the Successor now. We need adequate time to prepare her to take my place."

The pressure around my heart eases. Five years. Half a decade before he leaves me. And only a few years that I'll have to live on this world without him. I can handle this.

He gestures for me to sit. I choose a tree carved with the name "Branson Steel." Miss Sydney's son. And one of three Fittest boys who have been sacrificed in my lifetime.

I settle my spine against the curve of the trunk. The rough bark bites through my caftan. Unlike the C-trunks in Protector's Courtyard, which have been worn smooth by thousands of bodies, these trees have hardly been used.

The King sinks into the C-trunk next to mine. "Your Testimony shocked us, me most of all. We were stunned you had been violating the law this entire time, especially since we were in the midst of debating your merits as the Successor."

I rub my fingers along the rough bark. I can't look at my father. Don't want to see how much I've let him down.

"CORA predicted you and your sister were equally likely to succeed as a ruler, and the council was undecided which of you we preferred. Obviously, your Testimony changes things."

"Obviously." If the word had a shape, I would've choked on it.

"The council spent the entire night discussing exactly how much. I'll be frank with you, Vela. The vote was unanimous. Every council member voted to disqualify you and elect Blanca as the next Successor."

I squeeze my eyes shut, every cell in my body deflated. I was always a long shot. I know this. So why does the news feel like a cake knife to my gut?

"There was only one holdout," my father says, his voice fierce with something I can't identify. "Me."

I shiver, even though there's no breeze in the copse. Even though the wind fans are probably on the opposite end of the bubbles by now. Other than Astana, my father has always been my biggest champion. He believes in me, even—and especially—when I don't.

"When we plugged your transgression into CORA, surprisingly enough, it didn't change the analysis. Not by a single percentage. So, the council had no choice but to listen to me."

"Listen to you about what?" My voice is as small and timid as one of the moles we use for agriculture, reluctant to poke its head out of the ground for fear of what it might see. "Are you saying I'm not out of the running for Successor?"

"Not yet, my eye-apple." He gives my chin a tweak, the way he used to do when I was a little girl. "The council and I have decided on a test. You and Blanca will each be given a task, and your performance on the tasks will determine who will be the Successor."

I collapse against the trunk, my mind spinning.

"Each task is designed to test your respective weaknesses," my father says. "You see, the reason we had so much trouble deciding between the two of you is because you're opposites.

Blanca is a thinker. She's logical, quantitative, practical. When it comes to balancing the competing interests and determining what is best for the greatest number of people, she has no equal."

I nod. Everything he's saying is true, but now I have even more evidence that I'm not a very good sister, since I can't bring myself to feel happy for her.

"We fear, however, that your sister lacks the ability to empathize with people. And a ruler must understand when a moral imperative trumps everything else."

He taps his fingers against the bark, and I realize, for the first time, a serpent has been carved underneath the boy's name. It seems I can never get away from the snake, no matter where I go.

"You, Vela, have no such problem. You feel so passionately for the individual that sometimes you fail to see the bigger picture. I had almost convinced the council that with time and experience, you could overcome this characteristic. But your action this past week raises grave concern. It makes them wonder if your personal feelings will always interfere with your ability to make the right decision. You have to show them otherwise. Do you understand what I'm saying, my eye-apple?"

"Yes, Dad." As always, he is my teacher, and I am his student. He wants me to echo his lessons back to him, to make sure that I understand. "I have to show the council that I can make the correct decisions, in spite of my personal feelings."

"That's my girl."

I'm almost afraid to ask. "So, what's my task?"

He doesn't speak for a moment, and every hair at the base of my neck prickles. Somewhere, between the thud of my heart and the roar in my ears, I know, with absolute certainty, that my life is about to change. And no matter what I do, it will never be the same again.

A broad, palm-shaped leaf flutters from a tree. The King grabs it from the air and offers it to me. We're forbidden by law to pick leaves off the branches, so to catch a falling leaf is considered good luck.

"You will administer the Fittest Trials this year. You will narrow the candidates on the criteria of your choice, and you will select the challenges in which they compete. More importantly, you and you alone will have the power to veto CORA's verdict. There are some things a machine cannot calculate. This decision is one of them."

He looks me straight in the eye. "In essence, Vela, your task is to choose the person fit to die for the King."

CHAPTER SIX

*C*hoose the Fittest? Be responsible for a person's death? I shake my head and keep right on shaking it, as if the action can take away this decision. Propel me into the past, where my biggest concern was being named Top Aegis of the year.

"I can't." I mouth the words rather than say them, but my father understands me. He's never needed anything as pedestrian as audible speech to hear what I have to say.

"You can. I have complete faith in you." He cups my chin, and because it is him, because I've done nothing lately but disappoint, I stop shaking.

Instead, I stand and walk to the center of the copse. Ten C-trunks surround me, one for each Fittest candidate. Their palm leaves turn inward, as if the trees are embracing me. As if they're protecting me from this task.

I was only twelve when Branson Steel died, and I'll never forget the moment he was crowned. His jaw hardened to cement, and he lifted Miss Sydney right off her feet, as if he was trying to cram a lifetime of love into a few short seconds.

I couldn't help it. The tears poured out of me the way lava rushes from a volcano—fierce and unstoppable.

Blanca gripped my wrist. "Quit it. You're disgracing the ceremony."

"What do you mean?" I wrenched my hand away and pressed my sleeve against my eyes. "He's going to die. Shouldn't we be sad?"

"No, Vela. Branson has been distinguished with the most honorable position in our colony. This is a happy occasion."

That's when I first learned the fiction we have to tell ourselves to allow the Fittest Trials to occur. As I grew older, I understood it was a necessary fiction, since the rule of my father was vital to our colony's very survival.

But that doesn't mean I have to be a co-conspirator.

"When this copse was planted, I swore a tree would never be planted here because of me." My voice is as low as our underground caverns, as forceful as the waters that rush through them. "I swore I would never allow anyone to die, just so I could live."

"If and when you become ruler, that decision will be yours to make," my father says, his lips straight, his cheeks relaxed. I call it his "King face," the one he wears when he wants to conceal his thoughts. "But that day will never come if you don't participate in this task."

"Can't you give this task to Blanca? She doesn't even know the names of the Fittest candidates. This test would be a cinch for her."

"That's precisely why it's your task and not hers. The council knows how many hours you spend visiting the Fittest families. We know how much this copse means to you. Prove to us you can rise above your emotional attachments and make the right decision, and you'll show us you're ready to rule."

My father unfolds his body from the C-trunk and crosses the clearing to join me. Two, three, four leaves flutter around us. Neither of us makes a move to catch them. The greatest luck on the orb isn't going to get me out of this dilemma.

"I never said this would be easy. But the life of a ruler isn't easy." The corners of his lips twitch in a quarter smile, less serious than sad, more tired than anything else. "Are you fit to rule, my daughter? A ruler must be willing and able to make the tough decisions. The decisions no one else is willing to make, for the good of the colony." His voice is heavy, as if it's filled with all the choices he's had to make during his reign. The tragedies he's authorized. The casualties he's deemed acceptable. "Can you do that?"

Can I? Miss Sydney's face drifts across my mind. The last time I visited, we watched the holograms of her son from the cube. When we finished, her blue sash was askew. And she'd taken no less than five swipes across her eyes.

Can I be responsible for that? Can I look into a mother's face, a brother's eyes, knowing I approved the death of someone they loved? My father believes in me. He stood up for me when every other council member voted against me. For his sake, I'd like to try.

But I can't. Out of all the tasks they could've picked, this is the hardest possible one. I cannot be responsible for another person's death. Something shriveled inside me the day I caused my mother to die, never to be revived, and I cannot—will not—go through that pain again.

"I guess I'm not fit to rule, then." Each word is a pin jabbing into my heart. "Go ahead. Give the Successorship to Blanca. That's what the council wants, anyhow. She'll make a far better ruler than me."

"If I believed that, we wouldn't be here." His hand claps onto my shoulder, large, warm, and reassuring. Always reassuring. "I told the council this would be your response. And since it is imperative we choose the proper Successor, we've declared this an exigent circumstance. The council is willing to make an exception to the First Maxim."

My mouth goes dry. "What do you mean?"

The King smiles, but it's the same sad one he wore for days after my mother passed. The one that suggests his insides are so ravaged they're beyond tears.

"It's simple, really. For every day you participate in this task, we will give your friend Astana one day's ration of food."

My knees buckle. My father knows me so well. He can predict what I'll say and how I'll react. And he knows, with this one sentence, he's taken away every choice I have.

CHAPTER SEVEN

*I*f I crane my neck, I can see the candidates in Protector's Courtyard out of my small shuttle window. Lined up in rows, put through a series of grueling exercises by the royal trainers. As they were yesterday. And the day before. Their backs form a sea of gray, uniform but for the different splotches of sweat that have soaked through their T-shirts.

In half an hour, I'll be standing before them. Addressing them for the first time. And making my first cut.

I move from the window and wipe my palms down my trousers. All the furniture has been packed into my walls, and the tiled floor gleams. I can't quite make out my face in the reflection, but the outline of my form is clear in each tile.

That's how I feel sometimes—an anonymous girl stuffed into a royal position. It hardly matters which girl, so long as she makes the right decisions. Wears the right clothes.

Today, I'm wearing my official Princess gear, a brocade jacket similar to my father's, over a white top and pants. Instead of gold, however, the jacket is purple.

Purple like the eggplant in last night's early evening

meal. Sliced into quarter-inch coins and dipped into a mixture of flour and water. Fried to a crisp golden brown and layered with cheese, tangy tomato, and basil leaves. Ordinarily, eggplant parmigiana is my favorite dish, and after a couple days in the red cells, I should've savored every tingle of my taste buds.

I didn't.

My mind was too full of the meetings I'd had with the council. Too jam-packed with the considerations of my task.

A person will have to die. And I'll be responsible.

A slim figure bursts into my sleeping unit, flinging the waterfall of her black hair off her shoulders. I've only seen her practice that motion in front of the mirror a hundred times. Blanca.

"Dad said I should check on you," she says flatly, so I don't think that she's here of her own volition. So I don't think that she actually cares. Heaving a large sigh, she stalks around me, scrutinizing me from head to toe. "You're not appearing in front of the candidates like that, are you? Your skin's the color of almond gelatin."

Pale, in other words. Pale and jiggly, which is quite a feat considering the natural brown hue of my skin. She reaches for my cheek, and I push her hand away.

"Maybe I'm just shocked to see you," I say, fighting the tremor in my voice. "I mean, you couldn't even visit me in the red cells. I guess Dad didn't order you to come see me, then?"

She pauses, her heel striking extra-loud against the tile as if it hung in the air an instant too long. "Nope. And I had no reason to think you wanted me to visit."

I clench the back of my teeth. Same old story. Same old Blanca. That isn't moisture nipping at the back of my eyes. That isn't pressure pushing against my chest. It didn't bother me when she failed to show at my birthday party last year, and her indifference doesn't get to me now.

"Go away, Blanca. You've fulfilled your obligation, and I'm busy, if you can't tell."

"I'm not finished. Are you really going through with this task?"

Every inch of my clothes is steamed. My hair is freshly washed. And yet, all I can see, under my sister's scrutiny, is the faint smudge on the cuff of my pants. "Why wouldn't I?"

She abandons her orbit around me and drifts to the door, where she tugs a holo-cube from its home in the wall. The cube fits comfortably in her palm and is made of shiny, black glass. Identical to every other holo-cube in the colony, and yet, Blanca handles it a little too assuredly, as if she knows exactly what's inside.

"Are you still having nightmares, Vela?" Her voice is sweet, innocent. A frozen fruit treat on a day when the sun lamps are cranked. "You know. The ones where you wake up sobbing for our mother's forgiveness?"

Silver flashes as the cube spins in Blanca's hands. I lace my fingers together to stop from snatching it out of the air. "I haven't had one of those dreams in ages."

"That's not what the royal cleaner said. She said she had to change your bed linens mid-rotation, they were so soaked with tears."

"I spilled water on my pillow."

"Salt water, you mean?" She wiggles the cube in front of me.

It's a test. If I take the cube now, I'll be admitting how dependent I am on the hologram inside. How I still project my late mother's image several times a month. When I can't sleep, when nervous embers pop and sizzle inside me. Sometimes just because I want to hear her voice again.

"There's no reason to feel guilty." Her voice softens. "You

were a kid. How were you supposed to know the shuttle would be put on purple alert when you fell asleep in the apple orchard? You didn't make Mom go out without her allergen tabs. You didn't make her step on a hive of bees."

"I…" My throat closes up, the way Mom's must've when the bees swarmed out and attacked her. Three hundred and twenty-seven stings, the coroner said. Swollen red bites ballooning her face, closing her eyelids and puffing out her cheeks. Seems like overkill when it would've only taken one.

"It *was* my fault," I say slowly, relenting and taking the cube from her hands. I'm not sure why I'm telling her this now, other than the fact that she seems gentler than she normally does. More approachable. More like the Blanca I used to know. "Because I wasn't asleep. I was hiding, calculating how long it would take Mom to find me. Except I forgot to tell her we were playing a game."

Her mouth falls open. I'm not surprised. My confession is far beyond the terse, combative exchanges of our normal conversation.

"You…you should've told me." The last word tilts up as if Blanca herself isn't sure if it's a statement or question.

"Why? So you can have one more reason to hate me?"

"I've never hated you," she says. I almost can't hear the words above the drills outside my window. "And I don't blame you, either."

In all these years, it's the closest she's come to comforting me. It's like my mother was a buffer between us. The former Queen was the most important woman to the King, to her daughters. To the entire colony. When she died, everything became a competition. From my father's affections to the people's respect. And my relationship with Blanca was never the same.

"You really don't blame me, Blankie?" The childhood

endearment slips out. As the story goes, on the first day of my Aegis training, the teacher instructed the children to stow their favorite toy or blankie in their cubbies. "No!" I shouted, horrified. "I can't put Blankie in the cubby! She's my sister!"

At the sound of her old nickname, Blanca's features shutter down, and she turns from me to look out the window. The candidates are doing push-ups now, the row of their backs moving up and down like the segments of a centipede.

"Do you actually think you can perform this task?" she asks. "Be responsible for a boy's death?"

Her words slice through my chest, straight to the freshly baked walnut bread and hazelnut spread I scarfed down this morning. I sway on my feet, and my father's words echo in my head. *It's not meant to be easy. A ruler must make the decisions no one else wants to make.*

"I don't have a choice." I don't tell her about Astana, about how the council made me an offer I couldn't refuse. Knowing Blanca, she'll find a way to use the information against me. "Besides, I see it as maintaining Dad's life, not taking one of theirs. And maybe…" I lick my lips. "Maybe, if I can save him, it will be a way to atone for Mom's death." Or will it? Sometimes, I'm not sure there's anything I can do to make up for my childish prank. But doing my part to keep the King alive would at least be a start.

She puts her hand on my arm, but it means nothing. The motion is too practiced. The sincerity doesn't reach her eyes. "For your sake, I hope that's true."

I doubt it. If I quit now, before my task even begins, her path to becoming Successor will be that much easier.

"What's your task, Blanca?" I ask, realizing the council never told me. "Are you considering dropping out?"

"No way." She sneers at the holo-cube I'm still clutching.

I don't have any similar baggage, her look seems to say. *I don't need to rely on an inanimate object, no matter whose image it projects.* "If you're determined to play, then I wish you luck. May the best princess win."

She spins on her heel and leaves my unit, not answering my initial question about her task. I think about going after her, but the digital clock on my ceiling begins to beep and flash.

Time to find the boy who will die for the King.

*T*wo hundred candidates stand before me in Protector's Courtyard, in ten rows of twenty. That means four hundred eyes are trained on my purple brocade jacket, dissecting my posture, my figure, my face. Four hundred ears wait to hear the words scrambling around my brain. Two hundred hearts beat inside two hundred bodies, but I'm willing to bet mine is louder than all of them.

Sweat breaks out on my forehead, and black spots zoom like angry bees across my vision. I grip the podium, and the platform tilts beneath my feet.

Dear Dionysus, don't let me pass out now.

Help comes not from Dionysus, god of wine, but from deep in my memory. My mysterious savior presses a phantom hand against my back. *This pain, too, will pass. Just hold on, and life will get better. It always does.*

I hear those kind and gentle words, and my heart rate slows. The black spots stop dancing, and I can see again.

Above me, red and gold flags wave from the top of the space shuttle, dangerously close to the energy shields. Behind the candidates at the bottom of the courtyard, triangles of blue dot the ground of the athletic field. Tents. Of course. Some of these boys have come from the edges of our colony's bubble, two miles away. Making the trip every day would be burdensome. They have to sleep somewhere, and the shuttles aren't so big they can absorb two hundred extra bodies at a moment's notice.

Master Somjing creaks up to me, his braces sounding like the rusty wheel of a bicycle.

"Remember. The more physically fit the candidate, the more successful the transplant. That should be your first criteria in narrowing them down." His gruff tone turns the words into a threat. "It was always mine."

I nod, even though I have no intention of complying. This is my task. The council manipulated me into participating, so Master Somjing will have to live with my decisions.

I climb the three steps onto the raised podium, trying to keep my knees from shaking, and survey the crowd. My eyes stumble on individual features. A green spiked mohawk. Dimples as deep as ice cream cones. A smattering of freckles.

But these features don't coalesce to form any distinct personalities. There are too many boys, and I don't know them. At least not yet.

"My name is Vela Kunchai." My voice wavers like a five-year-old's. No. I can't sound like this. I need to be authoritative, in control, especially since the boys are more or less my age.

All teenagers, every last one of them. Our ideal candidate is a person whose body has stopped growing and whose organs have matured but are still healthy. CORA predicted that the people would more readily accept the sacrifice if we alternated between a male and female Fittest. During the last trial, Romania Cayan emerged as the best candidate, and so this time, we must select a male. Thus, every boy between the ages of sixteen and eighteen has been rounded up to participate in this year's Trials.

I conjure up an image of my father's square jaw and alert eyes. He believes in me. I can do this. "I'm the King's daughter, and I've been tasked with administering the Fittest Trials."

Better. At least my voice holds the same note, instead of jumping from one end of the scale to the other.

"You have been called upon to serve your colony. To prolong the reign of our beloved King. But in the process, you will forfeit your life."

I wet my lips. The rows of boys waver like the current of a river, but the ten-by-twenty formation holds.

"There will be rewards, of course. You will hold a place of honor in our history, and your family will be invited to move into the shuttle. They will reap the benefits of being an Aegis without the cost." I pause to make sure my words sink in. "Without the cost. This means they will receive a monthly stipend for the rest of their lives. They will eat a daily ration of food. And they will *not* receive the genetic modification. The nutrition will *not* be extracted from their bodies. Your family will thus be among the few in our colony who have the best of both the Aegis and colonist worlds. They will enjoy the taste of food, without sacrificing a single day of their lives."

A whistle pierces the air, and two boys in the front row whoop and give each other a high five.

"The Fittest will sacrifice himself for the colony, and so the colony, in turn, will sacrifice for him." As I continue talking, I forget my nerves. My entire focus is on these boys and what they're about to give up for my father. "In the entire history of Dion, this is our only regular exception to the First Maxim. This is how much we honor the Fittest candidate."

More whistles and a few scattered cheers. This is what humanity understands, after all. A fair trade. More than loyalty to a colony, more than duty to a king. If the Fittest is to give up his life, he must receive something in return. Even if he's not around to enjoy it.

"I will now make the first cut."

The murmurs die. I feel Master Somjing's eyes blistering my back. "In spite of the rewards, if there are any of you who do not wish to be here, you may leave. It is a noble thing to sacrifice yourself for your country. You will be remembered as a hero forever. But it is also strictly voluntary."

I stop talking. And wait. Nothing happens for a few seconds. A boy with tattoos covering half his face looks at me as if he can't believe his ordeal is over this easily.

Well, it is. This is my first criteria. And the most important one. "Did you hear me? This is voluntary. So please, if you want to go back to your family, if you want to continue to live, do so now. You not only have my permission; you have my blessing. Go."

The boys move then. The formation breaks like a puff of dandelion, and the majority of them scramble for their tents.

Master Somjing steps onto the podium next to me. His normally oaken face has turned birch white. "What if they all leave?"

For a moment, panic clogs my airways. Breathe. Just breathe. "Then, they'll leave," I say, my voice smooth, even as my intestines tie themselves into macramé.

"You might've let our most physically fit candidate go!"

"I don't care." I clench my jaw so hard my teeth ache. "You wanted me to do this task, so I'm doing it. My way."

He peers at me, the lenses in his eyes, which correct for near- and far-sighted vision with the flutter of an eyelid, making them abnormally large. "Your stubbornness doesn't endear you to the council."

"Sorry to disappoint," I say, not sorry at all. "But I'm not trying to impress you."

I turn back to the candidates. To my relief, approximately fifty boys remain, and they bunch together in a confused mass, formation forgotten. I adjust the microphone at my collar. "There's going to be a second cut."

"What? But we always have only one cut on the first day!" a scrawny boy with a pill-necklace exclaims. "We're supposed to go straight to the challenges."

"Not this time." Taking a deep breath, I address the rest of the crowd. "I don't want your reasons for competing in the Fittest Trials to be financial. I will not allow a boy to give up his life because he needs to pay his family's rent. Therefore, by being here now, all of you will receive one year's supply of pills. So, if finances were your primary reason for volunteering, you may leave."

The scrawny boy hoots, jumping into the air with his legs kicked to the side. He lands and takes off for the athletic field. Approximately half of the other boys follow him.

Beside me, Master Somjing groans. "A year's supply of pills for all these boys? The council's coffers will suffer for it."

Good. That wasn't the reason I offered the incentive, but a small, petty part of me wants to make the council pay—literally—for forcing me into this situation.

"This isn't what the council intended when we gave you control." His hand taps, taps, taps the side of his brace, as though he's counting the candidates and calculating the costs.

"Should've thought about that before you put me in charge." I make my voice as cold as his must've been when he voted to manipulate me.

The twenty or so remaining boys gather in front of the podium, forming a semi-circle. I can make out individual faces now. Turning away from Master Somjing, I scan the lineup. And then, all the blood drains out of my body and seeps through the metal slats onto the ground.

I recognize one of the faces. It's a face that's taken permanent residence in my mind, but one I'd never, ever expected to see here.

Carr Silver.

CHAPTER EIGHT

What is Carr doing here?

The world spirals into a kaleidoscope of purple skies and red and yellow flags. I grip the podium to stay on my feet, and even then, my knees have the consistency of a chocolate soufflé.

Make that a soufflé that falls flat.

He's nineteen years old. One year older than the conscription age. So how is he here?

Oh, I can guess why he would want to be. Astana needs to eat real food, and Carr can give her that right if he's selected as the Fittest. But surely he knows she would never allow it. Surely he knows I could never, ever let him die.

I stumble over the next lines of my speech. I have no idea what I say, but I must be somewhat coherent because the boys begin to disperse.

Frantically, I search for Carr among the retreating bodies. Maybe I didn't see him, after all. Maybe it was a trick of the eyes, the energy shields bending the light in weird ways. Before I can confirm or deny, Master Somjing appears at my elbow. Again.

"Vela." His bushy white eyebrows climb toward his scalp. "I really don't think you should interview the candidates. I don't see what good can come out of it."

I struggle to focus on his words. Interview? Right. At least I managed to tell them about the next phase of my selection process. "Of course I have to interview them. How else will I figure out who's Fittest?"

"The physical trials!" He pulls a fistful of black and blue wires from his satchel and waves them in the air. A round adhesive sensor is attached to each wire. "Stick one of these on each boy and run them through my trials. Then, feed the data into CORA, and it will spit out your answer."

"What about the moral character of each candidate?" I ask. "How do your physical trials determine that?"

He presses his lips into a thin line. "Look, the moral character of the candidate is a bonus. CORA predicted the Fittest Trials would be more palatable to the people if the winner was held in the highest moral regard. The very fact that these boys are willing to die for the King makes them worthy enough."

I press one of the sensors against my wrist. It feels cool and sticky, like a frozen ice that's been forgotten in the Banquet Hall.

His suggestion is tempting. I could hide in my living unit for the rest of the selection process. Leave the work to the physical trials and then come out for the final veto. Astana would get her daily ration of food, and I wouldn't be intimately involved in the selection. Wouldn't have to face Carr in the event he remains in the competition.

Of course, if he were to win, your problems would be solved, a voice inside me whispers. *Astana would be saved. She would get food for the rest of her life.*

No. I could never choose Carr to die. Never.

I yank the sensor off my skin, and my wrist screams. Good. "The council didn't assign me this task so I could let CORA do my thinking, Master Somjing."

"Fine." His nod is a sharp slice in the air, but something flashes in his eyes. He didn't expect me to stand up to him. He thought I would cave at the first opportunity and take the easy way out.

That's when the knowledge sinks to my stomach like a pound of pasta. My overall task might be to administer the Fittest Trials. But the council is testing me every step of the way.

*I*t takes me half an interview to figure out Master Somjing has a point. Getting to know the boys is a bad idea. Before the interviews, the candidates were a set of statistics, an abstract idea that might be able to extend my father's life. Now, I'm putting names to faces, and my heart breaks to think about any of them dying.

There's Fargo who longs to be an Aegis. He dreams about food, day and night, because he once snagged half a cookie from a transport cart. Ever since, he's spent every moment chasing another taste. He wants to give his family the life of his dreams, but as his final request, he'll ask for the most sumptuous feast imaginable. A meal to die for.

Baton is so poor he sleeps in corridors, curled up against the doors of living units to absorb the escaping heat. When people find him, they shoo him away like a stray mole. He could take the year's supply of pills and run. And he will, eventually. But in the meantime, he'd like to spend a few nights in the insulated tents.

And then there's Jupiter. He's scaled Protector's Slag, jumped out of moving transports, tried every pill that's ever existed. He's on the search for the next big adventure, and he thinks the Trials will top each of his previous experiences. "It will be," he says, "an orgasm in parts of my body that have never felt orgasms before."

I like them all. I'm charmed by the earnest ones, I feel sorry for the less fortunate ones. I'm even touched by Jupiter's passion. These are my boys. Every last one of them. They've entrusted their futures to me, even though I'm not at all sure I can figure out my own fate, much less anyone else's.

And then Carr walks in.

Everything falls away. Every artifice, every coat of polish, every facade to make me appear more confident, more authoritative, more legitimate.

All that's left is the girl from the red cells, with no title and no status. The one who held up a finger to touch a ray of light and wondered if she would ever feel the real thing.

And now, the real boy is here. Right in front of me.

"What's going on, Carr?" My voice is shivering, and I'm grasping, grasping for the cloak of authority. "Last I checked, you were nineteen, and the conscription age is from sixteen to eighteen."

He sits in the C-trunk across from me. If I've shed layers, he's piled them on. His face is tight, unreadable. A mask that hides his true feelings as effectively as a pie crust conceals the filling. "You're allowed to volunteer, so long as you pass the physical requirements."

Oh. I didn't know that. Master Somjing never mentioned it.

"So, you're administering the Trials." He tugs at the silver disc around his neck. The disc is the counterpart to Master Somjing's sensors. It can be scanned at any holo-desk to reveal his address, his genealogy. Every bit of physical data picked up by the black and blue wires. "Wouldn't have thought you had it in you."

"Why?" My neck stiffens. "Because I'm a kid who knows nothing about making decisions?"

"No. Because I've seen you in Protector's Courtyard with the Fittest families. Because you bring bouquets of flowers to the memorial copse every week."

Some of my tension leaks away. "How do you know that?"

"The flower glasshouses are right next to the airlock, where we exit the bubble to terraform the outside planet. I noticed you."

Our eyes meet and hold. For a moment, we're back in the red cells, with nothing to lose. Where we can do what we want and say what we feel. Only this time, he's not halfway across the bubbles.

My fingers creep onto the table, as helpless as steel shavings in the presence of a magnet. His hand inches forward to meet mine—and then, he pulls away and lurches to his feet, severing our connection.

"The medics confirmed it," he spits out. "Astana's body can no longer absorb nutrition through a pill. The medical team put in a request to the council, for permission to give her food, but they aren't optimistic."

My stomach falls down a well with no bottom. I suspected, of course, but now I know for sure. Unless we find a way to give her food on a permanent basis, my best friend is going to die.

"The council is forcing my hand," I say dully. "For every day I administer the Trials, they'll give Astana a daily ration of food. But the food will only last as long as the Trials."

His eyes laser into mine. "That's why you agreed to be in charge of the Trials."

"Yes. I'll do anything to help Astana."

"Then you'll select me as the Fittest. It's the only way."

I shake my head automatically. "Your sister would never let you give up your life for her."

He plants both palms on the table. "It's not her call."

"You're right. It's not." I get to my feet, and even though my hands are cold and trembling, I slap them on the table right next to his. "It's mine."

"And you want your best friend to die?"

"That's not fair, and you know it. I don't want either of you to die." The trembling spreads up my arms. "I might be able to negotiate a solution with the council. Maybe the medics will find a different cure. We don't know."

His face softens. "It's my life to sacrifice. You're willing to kill a boy to save your father. All I'm asking for is a fair chance. Let me compete in the Trials along with the others. Let CORA evaluate me on the basis of my merits. That's all I'm asking."

I squeeze my eyes shut. It sounds so reasonable. I weighed the evils and decided to give in to the council's bribe. Why shouldn't Carr have the same choice?

Because it would crush Astana to lose her brother, my heart whispers. *Just as it would crush me.*

"Even if I tried, Carr, I couldn't be objective with you."

"Because I'm your best friend's brother," he says.

"No." I look at the shiny plates of his fingernails, no longer lined with dirt. Part of me wants to dive behind the shelter of our noncommunication. The passing glances that might or might not have been intentional. But the time for pretending is over. Too much has happened. Too much is at stake. "Because of who you are."

I cross my arms over my chest, as if that can shield me from what I'm about to do. "I'm sorry, Carr. But you're not staying. As administrator of the Trials, I can narrow the candidate pool however I wish. I don't even have to give a reason. And I'm tossing you out."

"No, you're not." His voice is calm. Too calm. "Because I'm calling in my death debt."

I freeze. "What are you talking about?"

"Even back then, you were the brightest thing I ever saw." His voice is so low I feel like I'm eavesdropping on my own conversation. "Your dress was as white as clouds, your hair as black as the underbelly of a bee. Your laugh called to me, pulling me from behind one tree to another, as you skipped around Protector's Pond.

"I couldn't take my eyes off you. That's what saved your life, you know. You stepped into the pond and disappeared in an instant. By the time someone else would've thought to look, you would've been gone."

"I don't understand." My heart throbs, each beat propelling me back in time, until I feel the water closing over my head, the lace ribbons of my dress tangling like seaweed between my legs. The air pounded against my chest, struggling to be let out. I couldn't breathe; strong arms yanked me out of the water; and then I could. "You're my rescuer?"

He nods, once.

My lungs fill with cotton. My brain turns to flax. You could sew buttons over my eyes and stick me on a shelf.

This whole time. The rescuer over whom I fantasized. The voice in the back of my head, the one who never let me down, the person who was always, always here for me. This whole time, it was him.

"How come you never said anything?" I swallow my shock, but it snags on the corners of my voice. I've finally found my mysterious savior, and I couldn't have chosen better.

He turns away, and a rush of cool air replaces the heat emanating from his body. "You dreamed of a prince, as shiny and clean as yourself. While my hands left smudges on your skin, even as I pulled you from the water."

"That's not true!" I step closer, desperate to feel the warmth again. "All my talk about a mysterious rescuer—I was fooling around. I never wanted a stranger. All I ever wanted was—"

I snap my mouth close before I say too much. But it doesn't matter. He fills in the blank for me.

"Me? Yeah, right." He laughs, in a short, harsh way that leaves splinters all over my skin. "Sorry to disappoint you."

"I'm not disappointed." I lick my lips. "There's no other rescuer I'd rather have. Honest."

He closes the gap between us, seizing my arms with his calloused hands. My skin sizzles as though it's wrapped by a live wire. "You owe me. If you have any honor within you, then you'll grant my request. A life for a life, Vela. I saved yours. Now, name me as the Fittest. The worthiest candidate to die for your father."

I squeeze my eyes shut. "You know I can't do that. Master Somjing, not to mention CORA, are watching my every move. I can't fake the results. If you want to be the Fittest, then you're going to have to earn it."

"Fine," he says. "I'll earn it. But you have to give me a legitimate chance. A real chance. You can't manufacture a reason to toss me out. Do you agree?"

Astana will never forgive me. I may never forgive myself. But even though hairline fractures spider across my heart, even though every cell in my body rebels against the thought, I do not—I cannot—argue.

The death debt is one of Dion's oldest tenets. Honor the ones who save our lives. This tenet arose with the system of Aegis and expanded to include the individual. Nothing is more sacred than the bond between savior and saved. There is no greater debt I could possibly owe.

So I say the only thing possible: "Yes. I agree."

CHAPTER NINE

*T*he mother-daughter moons shine high in the midnight sky, one big and one small. They're obscured only by wispy clouds that move across their faces like fingers of smoke. For a moment, I worry they will go up in flames and disappear, like the fabled phoenix. Like so much of my life lately.

But they don't. The sky deepens, the clouds shift, but the moons remain, as constant as ever.

Oh dear Artemis. What should I do?

I move into the memorial copse. They look different with the sun lamps darkened. Lonelier, with the extra spaces between them. Even sad.

I sit down, not in the trees but on the ground. It makes me feel closer to the candidates whose lives are remembered here. This task was hard enough when I had to sacrifice a stranger. How can I possibly consider choosing someone I've admired all my life?

When I was younger, I hungrily witnessed all the gifts Carr brought home for Astana. Bottles of scents and necklaces made of polished rocks. She would squeal and laugh, throw her arms around him and declare him the best brother in the world.

But I'm not sure she ever noticed the smudges under his eyes, the sand that lined his voice and spoke of the many hours he labored in order to give her such gifts.

I saw. The smudges and the sand, the lean, handsome face and the long, artisan fingers. And I fantasized. How would it feel to be so loved? What would it take to put a smile on those serious lips?

On two occasions, he included me. An extra length of ribbon, a particularly shiny rock. Presented to me as if I were an afterthought. With the offhand remark that I probably already had drawers full of such trinkets.

Little did he know that the only trifles I ever saved were the two presents from him.

Sighing, I take the holo-cube from my pocket. Is Blanca right? Am I too dependent on the cube?

No. I need it—I need her—now. With the tip of my fingernail, I push the button on the side, wondering which one of the ten holograms will show up this time.

An instant later, my mother appears in the copse above me, her fingers busily weaving together the long black strands of a little girl's hair. My hair.

I shift on the ground, adjusting my head so it aligns with the hair in the hologram. I can't see my mother's face this way, but I don't need to. I've memorized the softness around her mouth, the low light in her eyes as she hums.

Just a field of light. A memory recorded long ago and brought to life today.

And yet…and yet…I can almost pretend she's here with me, her fingers untangling, braiding, smoothing my hair. I can almost smell the eucalyptus that used to cling to her skin, the scent that stops me in my tracks whenever and wherever I am.

"Now what?" I whisper to my mother. "What do I do now?"

My mother, of course, has no response other than to continue humming her song.

The melody is haunting yet uplifting. I wish I knew the words. The song has lyrics, of that much I'm certain. I can remember my mother singing them to me. But the words weren't captured in the hologram, and when I downloaded the tune into CORA, there was no match.

One more thing lost by my mother's death.

I have to let Carr stay in the candidate pool. There's no question about that. I can't dishonor a debt signed by my life.

But I also knew, when I watched my mother's lifeless body enter the incinerator, when I pressed my lips against her too-cold skin and came away with a dusting of foundation powder, I would do everything in my power to prevent anyone I cared about from dying, ever again.

This means I have to find a way to save Astana. But it also means Carr can't be my answer.

The last bit of my mother's song drifts over me. The words are at the edge of my memory. If I concentrate hard enough, I can almost bring them back into focus. Something lost and lonely, like the C-trunks in this copse.

But the lyrics don't matter. Because I suddenly know what I have to do.

Carr will do well in the challenges. He spends his days engaged in hard, physical labor. Plus, he's so honorable. He has all the qualities of someone CORA would select to represent our colony.

I have to allow Carr Silver to compete in the Fittest Trials. But that doesn't mean I have to let him win.

I step onto the athletic field. The sun in the outside planet is actually out, for once, and it peeks over the space shuttle, streaking the sky with violet flames. Most of the two hundred tents have been taken down. The few that remain hunker on the ground like stubborn stink bugs.

My insides slosh around. Maybe it's my dream of the serpent last night, its fangs glistening and poised for attack. Or maybe it's because I still haven't gotten in touch with Astana. Master Somjing assured me she's safe and her daily ration of food is being delivered. But she's not registered at the medical facility, and she's not at her living unit. Could she be under a different name? Or is the council lying to me?

At the thought, rage rushes through my veins. I want to punch somebody, hard. But Master Somjing promised leniency, and the council's never lied to me before. So I settle for ramming my fists against my thighs.

A guy pops out of his tent twenty yards away, and my hand flies to my throat. Oh Dionysus. His brown hair sticks out like the spines of a sea urchin, and he's wearing nothing but a pair of shorts.

I drop my eyes. You could sauté an onion on my cheeks. It seemed like a good idea when I woke up, to conduct the second half of my interviews here. I need to get to know these boys. Find out who they really are. What better way than to go on their turf? What could possibly go wrong?

Half-naked boys, that's what.

I keep walking, my eyes measuring the dirt. Not a problem. Surely, they'll scramble for their clothing once they realize the Princess is here. It'll be fine.

Except it's not. I skirt around a tent, and a tinkling laugh shoots straight through my gut. I'm too late. A princess is already here.

Blanca perches on a rock at the edge of the courtyard, next to the blackened remains of a fire. She's cut holes in her eating caftan so that her bare shoulders gleam in the dawning light, and a blinking amber necklace circles her collar. Surrounding her, latching onto every word, is a group of boys. My boys.

At least they're fully dressed.

My feet stop as if they've hit an invisible wall. I haven't spoken to my sister since she came by my living unit.

She glances up and rises to her feet in one boneless motion. The boys' eyes follow her. I don't blame them. Blanca was beautiful when she sucked on nutrition pacifiers in her crib.

She sweeps over to me. "I was getting to know some of your candidates. Do you have any early favorites? I know I do."

She wiggles her fingers at Jupiter. Trust Blanca to zero in on the thrill-seeker of the group. Jupiter grins and waves back. The two boys behind him, however, dart guilty looks at me and take off for the wash basins behind the tents.

"You're so lucky." She plants a hand on her hip, striking a pose. "All these guys. So many muscles."

I stare. "Blanca, one of them is going to die. This is hardly the time or place for you to be breaking hearts."

She smirks. "At least he'll have fun in the process."

"You're disgusting. What are you doing here, anyway? Shouldn't you be working on your own task?"

I realize I still don't know what her task is. When she ignored my earlier question, I thought it was just an oversight. But what if there's another reason? What if she's hiding something?

Before I can ask again, the light around her neck blinks. Oh. The amber circle isn't a necklace, after all. I should've known the thin wire was much too utilitarian for Blanca's taste.

"That reminds me." She pulls an identical loop from the deep pockets of her caftan and hands it to me. "Special delivery from the council. That's the *only* reason I'm here." Disdain drips from her words. Hardly a conversation goes by without her reminding me, in some way, that she's only talking to me because she has to. "It's a recorder. You're supposed to wear it every time you're in the presence of one of your candidates."

I slip the recorder over my head, but I don't turn it on. The metal is both cool and biting against my collarbone. "Why are they making us wear these?"

"It was your brilliant idea to interview the candidates. I don't think the council expected you to have so much interaction with the boys. They must've realized they have one more way to evaluate us." She pulls up the loop so that the mic is at her lips, although I'm pretty sure, technology being what it is, that the device could pick up sound within a fifty-foot radius. "So thank you, dear sister. I've always wanted a team of psychologists dissecting my every word."

She looks up and catches my eye. We exchange conspiratorial grins, like we used to back in our space explorer days.

And then, the moment disappears like aromas sucked out of the air. "Who's that?" she asks.

I turn. Carr approaches the tents, a towel slung over his shoulder, his black hair slicked off his face. He's not wearing a shirt.

Quickly, I drop my eyes. I've seen him without his shirt before. In fact, I used to hide with Astana behind heavy machinery and spy on Carr and his crew in the apple orchard.

She had a crush on the foreman. I only had eyes for Carr. When the sun lamps climbed to the highest point of the metal arc, the crew would shed their shirts. That's how I can picture, without looking, his leanly muscled pectorals and the hard, distinct ridges along his stomach.

"That's Carr Silver," I say, looking up at my sister but keeping my eyes carefully averted. "You know, Astana's brother. Don't you recognize him?"

"Oh." She bites the inside of her cheek. For the first time in years, she looks unsure of herself. I thought she was seconds away from propositioning him. Instead, she looks left and then right, as if searching for an exit in the wide, open space. "I have to go."

Before I can respond, she practically runs off the field.

I frown. Is it Carr? What did he ever do to her? They couldn't have had a previous…relationship. Could they have? No. Now I'm just being paranoid. But oh Dion, what if they did?

When I look up, he's watching me. Not Blanca, her stride graceful even in her escape. But me. There's a first for everything.

"Good morning, Vela." Will I ever get used to that voice? Deep and smooth, like a stone that's been polished round by the current of a river.

"I don't know how to act around you anymore," I blurt out. "I don't know what to say."

"Something wrong with 'hello'?"

I shake my head. "We spent the last ten years being casual friends—and then yesterday…" I swallow hard, not sure how to put into words how yesterday felt. "I'm not sure if I should treat you like a candidate or my best friend's brother. Like my mysterious rescuer…or…"

"How about just Carr?" he says. "I've always had to be

someone for everyone. The responsible brother. The hard-working son. It would be nice to just be me."

"I can do that," I say, and the pressure retreats from my chest.

We exchange a smile, and I'm very aware—and very glad—that I haven't turned on the recorder.

He looks in the direction of Blanca's departure. "Was that your sister?"

Pop goes the bubble rising in my chest. The worst part? I hadn't even known it was forming.

"Yep." I struggle to keep my voice even. "You remember her from when we were kids?"

"She's hard to forget. She certainly made an impression on the guys."

"Blanca always makes an impression." I'm so ridiculous. Of course Carr noticed her. Everyone notices Blanca.

"See, I never got that." He takes a step closer to me. "Back when my mom worked in the royal kitchen, everyone always talked about how beautiful she was, despite her slenderness. But you know what I think when I look at her?"

"What?" I ask, not sure I want to know.

"That I never heard anyone scream so loudly after accidentally touching a worm."

I giggle. "She was the champion screamer, wasn't she? Still is."

This would be the time to tell him about the dish of worms. I open my mouth, hoping the courage will magically appear, and then, the loop around my neck vibrates.

I jump. Blanca didn't tell me it could do that.

"Princess Vela." Master Somjing's voice emits from the wire. Blanca didn't say it was a two-way transmitter, either. "Your first interviewee is waiting."

I look toward the arches separating the courtyard from

the athletic field, where a tent's been erected for me to conduct the rest of my interviews. Master Somjing stands next to the blue canvas, his mechanical braces glinting under the sun lamps.

"Please remember to turn on the recorder in the presence of a candidate," Master Somjing continues.

Hastily, I reach behind my neck and flip on the switch. "I'll talk to you later?" I say to Carr.

He places his hand on my arm. The touch isn't urgent, the way it was yesterday, but the spark is just as burning, fire-poker hot. One shift forward. That's all it would take to close the gap between us. To turn my fantasies into reality.

"I'm counting on it." His voice—and his words—make me shiver, even if the sun lamps are directly overhead.

I swallow hard and hurry to the tent. My goal is still the same—to make sure Carr doesn't win. But for whom am I really saving him? For Astana?

Or for myself?

CHAPTER TEN

"**Y**our parents own a perfumery?" I ask the candidate across from me. We don't have too many "luxury" industries in our colony. But if the business doesn't take too much space, the council may approve a proposal to open a new shop in the interest of balancing survival with societal advancement.

"Oh, yes." Freckles spill over York's cheeks like cinnamon dashed over a pie, and his big voice fills the dome-like interior of the tent. "I've been apprenticing in the lab for the past couple years. My dad insists that people will always prefer the florals, but I've been experimenting with some food scents. You know — Baked Bread, Apple Strudel, Spaghetti Marinara." He leans forward, placing his palms on his thighs. "Go ahead. Test me. I guarantee I'll identify more scents than any guy here."

I shift on the ground, where we're both sitting with our legs crossed. "Uh, I don't have any food with me."

"Oh." Everything about York droops. His shoulders, his mouth, his voice. Even his hands slide off his knees. It's like he's been waiting for this moment to shine, and I've shut him down before he can even begin.

"Maybe we can go to the Banquet Hall later," I offer. "I'll blindfold you, and you can tell me what you smell."

He smiles so broadly his freckles smash together. "You are a class act, Princess." He picks up my hand and gives it a chaste lick, and I start. The gesture is one of the ways the people express gratitude and respect, but it's reserved for a particularly close mentor or counselor. I've always been the people's Princess. But I've never been their friend.

"What's more, you would smell absolutely delicious in my new Mashed Potatoes & Gravy scent," he continues. "If you wear it, maybe my dad will be convinced to give my experiments a try."

I smile and nod, even though my throat vibrates with the need to laugh. "Anytime."

He leaves the tent. Yesterday, I would've taken notes, so that I could input the data into CORA later. Today, the recorder eliminates the need for this step.

York seems like a nice guy. I know I'm supposed to be evaluating his worthiness as a candidate. Is this the boy we want to represent our colony? Are these the qualities we want to put on a pedestal? But I can't focus on these questions. All I can think is: *I don't want him to die, either.* In fact, I don't want any of them to die.

All of a sudden, I understand the motivation behind Master Somjing's physical trials. It wasn't just to discover the most athletically fit candidate. It was also a way for *him* to survive. Since the Fittest Trials began, Master Somjing has been the one in charge. Ten times CORA's chosen a candidate, and ten times the final veto has come down to him.

A pang slices through my chest for the gruff, old

councilman. It's all the more piercing because I know exactly how he feels.

I'll need a miracle to get out of this one with my heart intact.

*A*s soon as my last interviewee ducks under the tent, I sense he's different from the other candidates. Zelo Hale is not as muscular as Jupiter or Carr, but he walks with a physical grace, as though he knows exactly where his body is, and what it's doing, at any single moment. His lips are relaxed, his eyes so calm I might think he was sleeping if he wasn't lowering himself onto the ground across from me.

An eerie sense of familiarity washes over me. "Have we met?"

"I don't believe so," he says. "Unless you've prayed at the Temple."

Ah. That's why he seems familiar. He's part of the order that worships the gods from the old religions. They talk and move in the same way, each word and footstep a measured beat, and they dress in plain, simple robes. If he weren't wearing the candidates' uniform of gray shirt and navy pants, I might've recognized him by his attire.

"If you aren't part of the Order, maybe you subscribe to the new trend of calling on our mythological gods," he says. "Zeus and Hades and the like."

"Neither, really," I say. "I may use those words, but it's cultural. They don't reflect what I truly believe."

"And what's that?"

I blink. Not once, in any of the interviews, has a candidate turned the spotlight onto me so efficiently.

"I believe in my mother," I say quietly. "I believe she didn't cease to exist when her physical body expired. I've felt her presence as I walk in the woods. Her touch whispers over me when I tilt my face to the stars, looking for answers. I know she's here with me, even if she's in a different realm."

He nods, as if satisfied with my answer. I, in turn, feel as though I've passed some kind of test. As though I've been deemed worthy to hear his answers.

"You'll understand, then, why I'm competing to be the Fittest." He folds his hands together, as though in prayer. "I believe it is God's will."

My eyes widen. He actually thinks it is God's will that he *die* for my father?

"Let me explain." He leans forward and gestures to my handheld. "Does that tell you why they call me 'Zelo'?"

I shake my head.

"I was dumped in front of the Baby Unit a few weeks after I was born. I had zero family and zero prospects in life. I was nothing but a big, fat zero, with a birth certificate to prove it. Some nice worker at the orphanage took pity on me and changed a single letter on the certificate, so the rest of the world wouldn't know how much my parents loathed me."

My mouth falls open. "You're telling me your parents named you 'Zero'?"

"You can clearly see the smudge over the *L* where the certificate's been fixed."

I curl my hands into fists, trying to imagine a world where my family didn't want me. Where I had no father, no mother. No Blanca. "I'm sorry," I say. Completely inadequate. But how else can I respond?

"Don't be. Even today, zero people would miss me if I were gone. I have a few fond memories of those Baby Unit workers, but I've made no lasting connections in my eighteen years. No friends, no relationship. The others in the Order respect me, but they don't know me. They don't know my thoughts or feelings, my likes or dislikes." He stops, as if the words are a squirming squid that's difficult to swallow. "I've moved through life looking for meaning. That's why I started praying at the Temple. Because I was trying to understand my purpose here. And for a long time, I came up with nothing.

"Then, you spoke to us yesterday. And it all came together. I felt God speaking directly to me. *This* is why I was set on this planet. *This* is why I've been alone and unloved. I was born to die for the King, and my death is meant to leave as few scars as possible."

My skin begins to tingle. His words are passionate and powerful. But more than that, they reach deep inside me because they feel like the truth. What if he's right? What if he is fated for this role?

A boy who will leave no loved ones behind. One who will fulfill his life's mission through his death. One who sincerely and rapturously wants to follow God's will, even if it means dying.

I think I've found him. A boy fit to die for the King. A boy who will save Carr.

For the first time since the Trials began, my stomach isn't tied up in knots.

For the first time since I learned about my task, I see a way out of my conundrum.

For the first time since I agreed to choose a boy to die, I feel one unconflicting emotion: relief.

CHAPTER ELEVEN

*Z*elo may be fit to die for the King, but is it too much to ask that he also be physically fit?

I pop a tortilla chip into my mouth and wish I were eating Miss Sydney's caramel cricket crunch instead. Wish I had time for more than a quick visit with her this morning. I could barely look in her eyes when I told her I was administering this year's Fittest Trials. But she just wrapped her arms around me and said she was sure I would make the right decision, one that would honor her son.

The air in the glassed-in spectator box is cool and crisp, with a scent of pine needles blowing from the vents.

Below me, on the quarter-mile track that winds through the wheat fields, all twenty of the remaining candidates trudge, carrying sacks of rocks on their shoulders. Sweat streams down their backs, and their feet kick up storm clouds of dirt.

It's the first event, and I opted to use a challenge from my own Aegis Trials.

The current leader, Carr, is going strong with twenty-three laps. And Zelo, the candidate on which I've pinned all my hopes, the boy who's been sent on a mission by God himself? In last place with a measly ten laps.

I shove another chip in my mouth and then cram in another six. I have a lot of nutrition to make up if I'm going to meet my quota this month.

"This is awful, just awful," I mumble. "How can he be last? CORA's never going to pick a physical cream puff."

"Cheer for him," a voice behind me says.

I whip around, the nachos flying in the air. I thought I was the only person in the spectator box, but grinning at me, and now covered in crickets and salsa, is my cousin.

"Denver! You scared me!" I crunch past the chips littering the floor and press my wrist against his.

He leans in and takes a whiff. "You smell nice. Like jalapeños and onions. Trying out one of that boy York's experimental perfumes?" He plucks a chip from my hair. "Wearing the food as accessories, too, I see."

I roll my eyes and lead him back to the window overlooking the track, where three platters of nachos await. "What are you doing here? And how do you know anything about York?"

"Master Somjing told me. I came by to see you. And Carr."

My foot catches on the metal floor, and I stumble. Of course. His friendship with Carr goes back almost as far as his relationship with me. But while they were drawn together by common interests like tree-climbing and fishing, Denver and I are bonded by blood. His late father was the King's brother, and we were playmates, and then classmates, for most of our lives. When his father passed, however, his mother petitioned the King for a living unit separate from the rest of the colony.

Not easy to find isolation in twelve square miles of bubbles. The best the King could do was set them up in a small cottage in the Agriculture Bubble, behind the dense mass of fish farms.

I get my aunt's need for isolation. But I miss my old friend. Once upon a time, I could've ordered his daily snacks. Now, I can't predict his tastes or thoughts about anything.

"Are you mad that I'm letting Carr participate in the Trials?" My voice is so small it could hide between the tongue and grooves of the floor.

"Carr's always done what he believes necessary. It's why we're friends. Once we've settled on a goal, you couldn't stop either of us if you tried." He places a plastic box tied with a blue ribbon on the table.

Which means he's staying. And not mad.

My chest lighter, I perch on a chair next to him. "Astana doesn't know. I have no idea how I'm going to tell her."

"Don't. It will only upset her."

True. But I've never lied to my best friend before. Never omitted anything, either. But I don't intend to let Carr win, so maybe Denver's right. Maybe there's no need to say a word.

"Are you going to cheer for him?" my cousin asks.

"Who?"

He gestures out the window. "The pill popper about to lose it. The one you obviously want to win."

"You mean Zelo?" Of course he means Zelo. No one else has that lurching gait and flambè-apple-face. "And don't call him pill popper."

"You know I don't mean anything by it."

And he doesn't. Denver is the son of a colonist mother and an Aegis father. Such unions are always heartbreaking, as one spouse is guaranteed to die decades before the other.

"Why do you want him to die?" my cousin asks in his direct way.

I grab another tortilla chip. It's cold and chewy, and there's no way it can get past the lump in my throat. "I don't. But if I have to pick someone, Zelo is the best choice. He thinks he's fulfilling the will of God."

Denver whistles. "There's no better reason than that."

My throat relaxes, and I can swallow the chip, after all. He doesn't argue with my explanation. Doesn't judge me for allowing his old buddy to take part. He's just Denver. The guy on whom I've always been able to count, from helping me catch glass-jar grasshoppers to now.

"I wish I could cheer for Zelo. But that would be favoritism."

"Speak straight into his earpiece," he advises, in the confident tone of someone who was born knowing how to get what he wants. "The others won't hear you, and the voice of the Princess will spur him on."

No way. I want Zelo to win, but that would be cheating. Right?

Carr's in the lead, a voice inside me says. *And Zelo's last. Not second to last. Not bottom quartile last. Dead. Last.*

What can a few phrases of encouragement hurt? They're just words. Intangible things that disappear as soon as they're said. Like particles of dust that blow away when the wind fans pass overhead. Like dew drops that disappear as the day progresses. How can a few measly syllables qualify as cheating?

Quickly, before I change my mind, I turn off my loop, detach the transmitter from the wall, and key in the code for Zelo's earpiece.

"Come on, Zelo. You can do it." My voice is as flat and impersonal as CORA's.

Denver pulls me to my feet and dances me around. "You're trying to motivate him, not put him to sleep."

"Looking good!" Now I sound like one of the Peppy Bots. "Keep up the great work! You've got this!"

"Better. Now say it like you mean it."

I keep going, babbling countless permutations of "Go, go, go!"

The cheering works. Zelo looks up at the spectator box, and his strides become longer, more forceful and deliberate. Pretty soon, he's no longer gasping for breath, and he appears to be getting a second wind.

I return the transmitter to the panel, my mouth as dry and gritty as desert sand. I did it. I threw my support behind Zelo. I influenced the outcome of the challenge.

I targeted a boy to die.

Oh, Dionysus. What have I done? I collapse into the chair, but my heart keeps going, through the floor of the spectator box, past the grass, into Dion's bubbling core. I try to breathe, but my lungs have locked up. I try to sit up, but my shoulders have turned to stone.

"I'm sorry I wasn't here sooner, but I was talking to the King." My cousin's tone is light and jocular, as though he's unaware of the turmoil inside me. But this is Denver. He's not oblivious. He's just distracting me.

A horn sounds, signaling that a candidate has dropped out of the race. I check the scoreboard to make sure it's not Zelo—it isn't, thank Dionysus—and look back at Denver. "Oh? What about?"

"I've asked the council for a laboratory to experiment with my flowers, and I was hoping the King could put in a good word for me." He grabs a handful of chips and piles them into his mouth. "I want to breed some new varieties. Introduce the people to pure, unadulterated beauty like they've never known. Of course, your sister walked in on the conversation, and she gave me the evilest look, as though I'm trying to usurp her affections with the King or something."

Bits of food spray out with his words. I wipe the spittle crumbs from my face, but instead of grossing me out, they make me smile. Denver would never act so uncouth with anyone else. In front of the public, he's as smooth as Blanca's fall of silky hair.

But I'm not the public. I've been his ally since we used to build dirt forts and lie inside, quizzing each other on nutrition charts as the drying mud crumbled in our faces.

"Don't worry about Blanca," I say as the horn blares again. I find Zelo on the track. Still going strong. "The King is your uncle, and he loves you. My sister's so paranoid she even thinks I'm competition."

"You *are* competition. And don't you forget it." The smile flatlines. The dimple disappears. For a moment, my charming cousin looks deadly serious. "It's easy to get lost underneath Blanca's glow, but I've never doubted you're every inch her equal. And probably more."

I blink. "That might be the nicest thing you've ever said to me."

His eyebrows do their wiggle-dance. "Just trying to get in good with the Princess before she becomes Queen. Lookie, I even brought you a present." He hands me the box from the table. "My newest breed of azaleas. This is my first contender for the royal flower. What do you think?"

He lifts the lid. A flower lies at the bottom, its petals round and delicate. Tiny black buds sit on top of wispy stamens, and the deep, deep pink reaches inside me and pulls. I didn't even know this color existed in nature. I thought it began and ended with the sticky rice and tapioca layer cake we sometimes have for dessert.

"It's beautiful." I stroke a finger across a powdery petal.

"Could you send a hologram to my mother and let her know?" His lips twist. It creates unattractive lines in his cheeks, but this is how I like him. Showering me with spit and a little bit ugly.

"Is she still giving you a hard time about being a horticulturalist?"

"She wants so much for me," he says, his voice soft like the flower and just as vulnerable. All it would take is one hard blow to smash them both into spacedust. "I'm such a techie genius, she says, I could conquer the planet. I told her I'd developed a new variety of flower that neither Earth nor Dion had ever seen. She told me to grow up."

My heart squeezes. The King may not rely on me the way he does on Blanca, but he's never asked me to be someone I'm not. Denver's been on a lifelong quest to earn his mother's approval. My father only wants me to be true to myself. "I'm sorry, Denver."

"Yeah. Me, too."

The horn sounds once more. I look at the scoreboard, and the air coming out my lungs stutters at my throat. Because this time, it's Zelo who's dropped out of the race.

And in the lead, going strong with a cool thirty laps, is Carr Silver.

*C*arr wins, of course. It's not even close. The second-place finisher, Jupiter, takes one last gasping breath and falls to his knees on lap forty-nine. Carr continues for one more lap, back straight and head high, his chest pumping up and down like a metronome.

Not good. If we continue with these physical challenges, Carr will be named the Fittest by the end of the week.

I need to step up my schemes. Chanting encouragements in Zelo's ear brought him up a few places from last, but it's not enough. I need a trial that will test not just physical strength but also moral character. One that will give Zelo a chance to display his strengths.

You're doing more than targeting now, a voice inside me whispers. *You're manipulating the Trials so that you can help a particular boy die.*

It's what he wants. I'm helping him fulfill God's will.

Do you believe it's God's will? the voice says. *Or are his religious beliefs merely convenient for your purposes?*

My stomach heaves, threatening to empty the chewed-up mass of tortilla chips onto the steps leading down the spectator box. Dizzy with self-revulsion, I leave Denver and descend onto the track.

The boys sprawl in the field, limbs draped over stalks of wheat and each other. They look like a painting from Earth, the one with the pocket watches melting onto the landscape.

I wind through the candidates, congratulating each boy on his effort, lingering with Zelo to press his hand and tell him I believe in him. Then, I make my way to the edge of the track, where Carr and Master Somjing stand next to a pile of burlap sacks.

"An impressive showing, Mr. Silver," Master Somjing says. As usual, his legs are propped up by mechanical braces, and the hologram pendant dangles from a chain around his neck. "Although you didn't beat the record for most laps in an endurance trial."

"Is that right, sir?"

"In fact, here comes our record-holder now." Master Somjing looks up as I approach. "Princess Vela lasted fifty-two laps at her own Aegis trials."

Carr's eyes widen, as if the council member told him we only had one moon. "Really?"

I stiffen. I'm smaller than him. Definitely not as muscular. But I'm in great shape, and the number of rocks we carried were in direct proportion to our weight. "I never would've passed the Aegis Trials without physical strength."

"I thought those Trials measured your aptitude to enter a life of sacrifice?"

"We also need to be physically fit because eating can be an athletic activity."

"I see." He runs his eyes over my caftan, as if he's trying to see through the thick material. I try not to fidget, even though I know he's imagining the shape of my limbs. Maybe he's even remembering the way my arms looked when I took off my caftan and gave it to Astana.

Master Somjing's earpiece buzzes, and he moves away to answer the call. I take a step closer to Carr, and everything else fades. The council member yammering across the track, the water bottles strewn across the thick stalks of wheat. Even this competition in which we're embroiled.

"Carr," I say softly. "How do you celebrate?"

"The usual way. Parties and the like."

"Yes, but…" My mind races to the few parties I've attended. My own birthdays, my sister's. Being a princess means that I don't have many friends, even among my own classmates. Pathetically, all I remember is the food. Escargot hushpuppies, battered and perfectly fried. Platters of crispy green kale dressed with walnuts and beets. Freshly shucked oysters, so sumptuous you would think each one contained a pearl. All food. Just food.

I try to push my mind's eye deeper. There must've been decorations, but I can't see them. There may have been music, but I can't hear it. I return, again and again, to the vivid colors, the enticing smells, the brilliant tastes of the food. What's wrong with me that I can't remember anything else?

"Can you describe it to me?" I ask. "Exactly what do you do at these parties?"

Something I can't read flickers over his face. "We have music. And dancing under the purple sky. If the sun lamps are turned up, our clothes stick to our skin, but the wind fans cool us enough so we don't feel sweaty in each other's arms. We string tiny lanterns between the trees so it feels like we've brought the stars down to our level. We talk and laugh and sing until half the night is gone, drunk in each other's words. Each other's company."

"And there's no food?"

"Of course there's some, for the Aegis in attendance. They can't go more than a few hours without upping their calorie intake. There's also blue pills for the colonists, but neither food nor pills are a focal point."

I shiver. I can almost see the lanterns reflecting off his dark eyes. I can also feel the warmth of his hand as it clasps my neck, our bodies moving to a music that pulses all the way through my bones. How much have I missed by being a princess? Have I ever danced under the stars? Have I even stayed awake past midnight?

Hardly ever. And why not? It's not like I have a curfew. But I almost always conk out two hours after the late evening meal, which is especially large due to the upcoming nighttime fast. Food coma at its finest.

All of a sudden, I want more than anything to experience the dancing and the laughter.

I turn to the candidates still lounging on the field. "We're having a party tonight," I announce, my voice getting stronger and more certain with each word. "A proper one, with music and lanterns and song and dance. You've worked hard today, and you deserve to celebrate the beginning of the Fittest Trials."

The boys cheer. The sound is not quite loud enough to drown the voice inside me. *You mean, to celebrate the beginning of the process that will lead to a boy's death?*

But I push the voice away. The Fittest Trials have been going on for decades before I was born. Its necessity was mandated by CORA. What's a voice inside me compared to the weight of human experience?

Master Somjing walks back to Carr and me, his eyes blinking rapidly. "You're both to report to the medical facility immediately. Go to the Protector's wing."

Both of us? Why?

My chest contracts so hard I feel my joints pop. "The King? He's dying."

"What? No, no." Master Somjing shakes his head. "You've misunderstood. Your father's fine."

Relief slams into me like a wall of water, but before it can sweep me away, Master Somjing reaches out his hand. I think he's going to pinch my cheek, or some other weird Earth custom. Instead, he picks up the loop around my neck and switches it on.

"It's Astana. She's been admitted, and you're both to report to Room 108 immediately."

CHAPTER TWELVE

"Astana's in the Protector's wing?" I ask. "But she's not an Aegis."

"She's the one who's dying, isn't she? Oh Dion, tell me. Is she dying?" Carr slumps, his entire body a question mark.

"No one is dying." Master Somjing blinks again. "Astana is in stable condition."

There's logic here. I know there is. I just can't seem to grasp it. "So why is she in the Protector's wing? They only treat eating-related issues there. Is it because she's receiving the daily ration of food?"

"No. She could receive food anywhere in the facility. But that's all I may divulge at the moment, so please, no more questions."

"But why? What's the big secret?"

He blinks again. The motion is less precise this time, although no less deliberate.

And then I get it. This is another one of the council's tests. That's why Master Somjing turned on my loop. I am being fed information little by little, so they can gauge my reaction. It's one more data point to evaluate my suitability as the Successor.

I glance at Carr. His arms are wrapped tightly around his torso, as if to subdue tremors that run far beneath the surface. It must kill him to know and not know about his sister. Just as it kills me to watch him.

"Astana's life isn't a game, you know." My voice is low, but it's on simmer. Provoke me long enough, and it will boil over. "There are real people involved. Real lives at stake. The way I react isn't to please you. It isn't to prove to the council or anyone else how suitable I am."

"What do you think the role of Successor is, Princess Vela? Do you think the future ruler of our kingdom will make decisions that affect real people?" Master Somjing angles forward, a muscle in his jaw twitching. "You're right. This isn't a game. But the very fact that you question me makes me wonder if you really understand the big picture."

His words slice through my small, fast pants. Even now. Everything I say, everything I do contributes to their analysis of me.

"Keep your recorder on," Master Somjing says and lurches away, dismissing us.

I think about disobeying, just to be contrary, but childish reactions aren't going to do anything but annoy the council. They make me want to scream—but I need them. They alone control Astana's food supply. As much as I hate to admit it, I'm better off with them on my side.

"Does this mean what I think it does?" Carr asks, his voice a closed door and optimism a stranger he doesn't dare admit.

"I think so." I can barely say the words since the hope bubbles inside me so strongly. "As the name implies, the Protector's wing is reserved for the Aegis. The medics there have a specialty in digestive diseases. So if Astana is there, that must mean—"

"She's been cleared to eat food," Carr finishes for me. "Permanently."

For a moment, we grin foolishly at one another. This could be it. Our deepest wish fulfilled. Astana saved.

Without another word, we take off. Who cares if the council wants to be sly and secretive? Astana's in the Protector's wing, and I'll be talking to her in a few short minutes.

We run full-out, faster and faster, spurring each other on. Even after fifty laps, Carr's able to keep up with me. Off the wheat fields, through the arches, across the courtyard. We collapse on the grass in front of the double doors of the medical facility.

"Have to…catch our breath…before we see Astana," Carr says, in between pants. "She'll wonder…why we're together. Why we're both breathless."

"Yes," I gasp. Similarly winded. Maybe even more so. "We need to figure out what we're going to tell her."

The purple sky wavers overhead. If I focus on this small patch, away from the generator towers spearing the air, I can almost pretend there isn't an energy shield separating me from the rest of the planet. Pretend we're free to roam wherever we want. Pretend there's no such thing as a food shortage and no reason for the Fittest Trials.

I prop myself on my elbow and think of Denver's words. Astana will only be upset if she knows her brother is a participant in the Fittest Trials. "If she's safe, I don't want her to know that I allowed you in the candidate pool."

"You didn't have a choice." He imitates my position, so that we're lying face-to-face. Elbow to elbow. Lip to lip. "I called in the death debt."

"Doesn't matter. She'll never forgive me. Please." I lean closer. His eyes are so black, so urgent. I might even be willing to drown again, so long as it's in their inky depths. "We'll say you were making a delivery to the shuttle, that's how you were able to get to the medical facility quickly after being summoned."

He looks at me for a long moment. "I won't lie. But I won't go out of my way to tell her the truth, either."

"Thank you."

The conversation is done, but he doesn't move away, and I don't either. I can feel blades of grass tickling the bare skin at my waist, where my caftan's bunched up. Worse, I can imagine his fingers replacing the grass.

All of a sudden, my heart pounds harder than it did when we ran across the courtyard. My nerves feel like grasshoppers about to jump from my skin, and I can't look away from his lips.

He trails his fingertips along my cheek. "Vela?"

My name is both a question and an answer, an invitation and a response. He lowers his head, and I stretch up. We align our mouths and move in another inch. Any moment now, our breaths will mingle. Any moment now, our lips will touch. Any moment now—

"Princess Vela, is that you?" A bot whirrs out the double doors and onto the grass. "I haven't got all day. Do you want to see your friend or not? Let's go!"

"*L*ike I have nothing better to do than lead the Princess around," the bot says in its robotic monotone. It speeds down a corridor to the Protector's wing. "Fast, fast, fast. Not my problem if you can't keep up."

Carr and I trot after the bot, our rubber-soled shoes squeaking on the tile. We pass carts filled with gauze, syringes, and electronic equipment. Patients lean heavily on metal walkers, the strings of their open-backed gowns trailing behind them. A loudspeaker blares overhead, and the smell of bleach perfumes the air.

"Are the bots always this unhappy?" Carr asks.

"Just the grumpy ones." The bots can't think for themselves, of course. All they do is access data stored in CORA, but that didn't stop the programmers from giving each one a personality. The Grumpy Bots are my favorite. Their surliness never fails to put a smile on my face.

The bot rounds a corner and zooms down a second corridor. We increase our speed and follow. Without warning, it lurches to a stop in front of an open door.

"Consider yourselves delivered. Thanks for nothing," the bot says, rolling away. "Now I'm off to do something actually worth my time."

I turn to Carr. He swallows, and if he weren't a colonist, I'd swear he had food in his mouth.

"Is it silly to be nervous to see my own sister?" he asks.

"Is it silly to be nervous to see my best friend?"

We exchange wobbly smiles and walk into the room. The far wall is made of glass, and since the medical facility sits at the edge of the bubble, we can see the dry desert of the outside planet. Slabs of rock jut out of the craggy landscape, large and imposing.

But no view can ever compare to the real, live people in the room. My cousin Denver stands beside the bed, and my best friend rests on it.

"Astana!" I fly to her side, knocking into a bed tray, tripping over a nest of wires. Don't care. What matters is

I'm with my best friend again. "You look so healthy."

Her skin no longer looks stretched like a straining cloth over a pot. Her face actually has hues and depth, instead of that eerie, one-dimensional hue. She's even sitting up, with the help of some pillows and Denver's hand on her shoulder.

Every doubt I had about my participation in the Fittest Trials melts away. It's worth every bit of anguish to see Astana looking so well.

"I've had better compliments in my life." She laughs, and her hand creeps up to touch Denver's, as though to make sure he's still there. She's known him almost as long as I have, but I've never seen them look quite so…comfortable.

I glance at Carr to gauge his reaction, but he's got the frozen smile and dilated pupils of the shell-shocked. I'm not sure he even sees Denver, much less notices that his old friend's hand is entangled with his sister's.

"Why didn't you tell me Astana was here?" I demand.

"Sorry, cuz." His wide grin matches the one growing on my face. "The council didn't want me to say anything. It about killed me to keep the secret inside, but I knew you would be seeing her beautiful face soon. Do you forgive me?"

"I forgive you," I murmur, taking Astana's other hand.

"I'm sure you have a lot to talk about," he says. "I'll leave."

I should protest, but I don't. I love my cousin, but at this moment, I kind of want my best friend—and her brother—all to myself.

Denver leans over and murmurs something in Astana's ear. His lips brush her earlobe, and she giggles like he's the stand-up comedian of Dion.

He straightens and slaps Carr on the back. "Good to see you, old friend. We'll catch up another time."

Carr doesn't respond. In fact, he hasn't said a word since we entered the room. We watch Denver leave, and then

Astana grabs her brother's hand with her now free one and draws him to us. "I'm so happy to see you."

Still, he doesn't say anything.

My throat closes up. I can't see Carr's face, but his expression is reflected in the softening of Astana's lips, in the tender creases at the side of her eyes. So similar, the Silver siblings. They look like they could even be twins, despite the two years separating them. In some ways, they may even be closer than twins, as they're each the only family the other's got.

"My brother doesn't talk when there's something important to say." Her smooth delivery hitches on a few syllables, the way a flowing river hiccups around a surprise boulder. "I guess that's when you know he really loves you. If he's at a loss for words."

My heart twinges, and the pressure builds behind my eyes. It doesn't even matter that Carr's emotions don't include me. I'm connected to him through Astana, through the circle of our hands, and at the moment, that's enough.

"Did they make you an Aegis?" I ask.

"Not quite," a familiar voice says behind me.

Too familiar.

I turn, and Blanca walks into the room, followed by a girl about our age with a riot of curls tied into a ponytail. They're both wearing the long gray jacket of the medics.

I gape. She doesn't even like Astana. Why is she visiting her?

Not for the first time, either. Blanca leans against the glass wall, relaxed, casual, as if she's been here many times before. The girl mimics her pose, as though she is Blanca's clone…or an assistant. But why would Blanca need an assistant? What on orb is going on?

"You knew, didn't you?" The words twist on the way out

of my throat, coming out garbled and betrayed. "You knew the entire time that Astana was here."

Blanca pushes herself off the glass with so much force I'm surprised the window pane doesn't pop out. "Well, of course I knew. Astana is my task, after all."

CHAPTER THIRTEEN

"**A**stana is your task?" My voice echoes too loudly in the small room. "How can she be your task? She's a person."

"Yes, and there are others like her. Others who have developed an intolerance to the nutrition pills. Others whose futures I must determine." Blanca glances at her curly-haired shadow, and she looks less sure, less in control. Less like the Blanca who's a shoo-in for Successor. "The medics couldn't figure out why their pills didn't work. Until your Testimony."

"You mean, all the others like Astana have also eaten food?" Carr asks, his first words in this room.

"In every single case."

I frown. "But none of us ate food regularly until we took the Aegis Oath at fifteen. Why didn't we end up like Astana?"

She nods toward her companion. "This is Hanoi. She's one of the patients like Astana, and I've hired her as my assistant for this task. Hanoi? Do you want to take this question?"

Clearing her throat, Hanoi fishes a handheld out of her

pocket while Blanca drifts to the wall, where a solar blanket lies on a recharging rack. "The intolerance doesn't affect everyone," Hanoi says in a voice as clear as bells as she consults her handheld. "Just the people with a predisposition for it. The medics believe that the intolerance slowly builds over time, with each subsequent exposure to food, until the patient can no longer absorb nutrition from their pills. That's why Astana and I are only showing symptoms now, in our teens, while we've got a two-year-old girl in our pool already sick. Her parents must've been sneaking her food every day."

Blanca nods, like a teacher proud of her student. I'm still puzzled about their relationship, but I can't focus on that right now.

A sick toddler. Other patients like Astana, weakening because they're unable to absorb nutrition the regular way. There's one main difference, however. She's getting food. And Hanoi and the others are not.

The room spins, and I grab the object closest to me, a metal pole on a stand, like a coat rack but slimmer. Two cylindrical bags hang from the top of the pole, and a clear liquid drips into a tube that attaches to Astana's wrist. Another denser formula flows through a tube attached to her belly.

Carr looks at the bags. "Tube feeding."

"A stop-gap measure," Blanca says softly. "Astana's body can only partially absorb the formula, but at least it's better than the pills. Back on Earth, our ancestors were able to keep people alive through tube feeding for years. But those patients couldn't absorb food. Astana has the opposite problem, since she has difficulty absorbing nutrition through *supplements*. She needs the real thing, so I'm not sure how long we'll be able to keep her alive with tube feeding alone. The others—" She cuts off, glancing at her assistant like she doesn't want to say too much. "The others don't look nearly as good, since they haven't been supplementing with real food. Hanoi here is the healthiest of the bunch."

Glancing at Blanca's assistant, I notice for the first time what her curls distracted me from earlier. The sallowness of her skin. The way she sways slightly on her feet.

"I had no idea there were others. Others even worse off than you." I grab my head, trying to stop the images that flit through my mind. A little girl, unable to get out of bed. Her tiny eyelids veined with blue. A rack of ribs as flimsy as matches. "Hanoi, I'm sorry. I didn't know. Otherwise, I would've asked the council to give you food, too."

Hanoi presses her lips together, as though she would like to agree, but Blanca strides to the center of the room.

"That's not your responsibility." My sister might as well drill the warning across my forehead. Her tone says it all: don't interfere. "In fact, that's my Successor task. Proposing a blanket policy that will determine what to do with the colonists who can no longer sustain themselves via a pill."

My knees turn to IV liquid. I'm not sure I can rely on Blanca to braid my hair. How can I trust her with my best friend's life?

"How are you going to decide?" Carr asks, his voice raw and trembling.

Again, Blanca looks at her assistant. Again, she shrinks into herself. She's been running scenarios for the King for years, and she likes her numbers stark and precise. And confined to the data screen. The only uncertainty she's willing to tolerate is in the wild thought experiments she indulges in with Master Somjing, such as time travel or extraterrestrial life. She doesn't like unknowns sitting in front of her, with pesky questions and even peskier emotions.

"I... I..." She clamps her mouth shut. A look of horror

crosses her face, and she runs from the room.

My mouth drops open. I've seen Blanca's departing back many times. Flouncing off, with her caftan sailing behind her. Stalking away, when she knows she's won an argument. But never, ever because she doesn't have the words.

"Be right back," I mutter to Hanoi and the Silver siblings and dash after her.

My sister stumbles down the corridor and latches onto an empty stretcher. She's not sobbing—Blanca doesn't cry, it makes the eyes red and the lids puffy—but buries her face into the mattress on the stretcher.

Hesitantly, I reach out my hand, and it hovers in the air above her shoulder. As if sensing my presence, she jerks up, her nose drawing in air with quick, halting snorts.

"This isn't easy, you know," she says. "It wouldn't be much of a task if I came up with the answer on the first day, would it? There are a ton of considerations. If we carve out a regular exception to the First Maxim, it will prompt even more colonists to try to fit into that exception. People with other diseases will argue that they, too, should be allowed to eat. It could be a slippery slope to utter chaos."

"Then make Astana and the others into Aegis," I say. "The genetic modification might cut short their lives, but ten more years is better than one."

She shakes her head. "I've already thought of that. They're too weak. The medics don't know if the modification will take. And the council doesn't want to create a class of inefficient Aegis. It's not entirely my decision, anyway."

I want to be sympathetic. I do. But it takes all my strength not to wrap my hands around her neck and tell her to forget the council. "Why not?"

"My task is the same as yours." She swipes a finger under each eye. "Collect the data and propose policies for evaluation. But CORA makes the ultimate decision."

"You have veto power."

She pauses a beat and then nods. "Yes. But I'll only use it as a last resort."

"Does Hanoi know that?"

Blanca clamps her lips together and turns away. My sister's thrown up so many walls between us, I can recognize one that she's erecting with the very first brick. She doesn't want to talk about her assistant. That much is clear. But I'm just as unwilling to let the subject go.

"Why on orb did you hire her?" I ask. "Her presence clearly makes you uncomfortable. You're hesitant to talk about your task in front of her, and you've never needed—or wanted—help from anyone." *Least of all me*, I continue silently. "It doesn't make any sense."

"I don't *need* her." Blanca whips her head back around. "But she required the pills, okay!"

I blink, as much from my sister's outburst as from what she's telling me.

She takes a step back, breathing hard. Her eyes shutter down, and another row of bricks settle on the wall between us. She continues backing away—the bricks continue piling up—but I reach across the space and touch her elbow. "Blanca, please. There's so much I don't know, about your task, about mine. The confusion's about to split my head apart. Help me understand *something*."

I'm barely touching her, just two fingers on the bone of her elbow, but she stares at the contact as if it's a physical message from Earth. "Hanoi lost her job as a shrimp farmer when she was too sick to go to work," she mumbles. "She's just a kid, like us, but her mom took off when she was young, and her dad was injured on an expedition to the outside planet. She's got four siblings who rely on her to bring home pills...and I had to do something."

I stare into her symmetrical eyes. Her cheekbones slash across her face, and her lips are full and lush. She's so beautiful, lack of curves notwithstanding. I wonder, sometimes, if she would be as lovely if she *weren't* my sister — or even more so.

Blanca offered Hanoi a job, when she didn't need the help. I have to believe there's goodness in her. I have to believe all that beauty is more than just a mask.

"Blanca. You will do the right thing for Astana and the others, won't you?"

"You're such a child." Shrugging off my touch, she shoves the stretcher, and it rolls a few feet down the hall. "One of these days you're going to learn 'right' and 'wrong' are dynamic concepts, changing with every day. Every minute."

She stalks away, caftan whipping the air. Showing me her shoulder blades.

Clearly, Blanca's recovered from whatever it was that shook her. Too bad. I never thought I'd miss *any* version of Blanca. But the more vulnerable one, the one who gave Hanoi a job? With time, I might've actually grown to like her.

*W*hen I return to the room, Hanoi is gone — probably trailing after her boss's vibrating caftan — and Astana is showing Carr her gifts from Denver. Her eyes shine brighter than the moons of Dion. The moons can only reflect light from an external source, after all, while her glow radiates from within.

"And then yesterday, it was honey-scented perfume, made from his bees—" She stops when she sees me. "Well?

What did Blanca say?"

I pick up the glass bottle from the table and smell the stopper. Yum. Honey toast and ice cream, my dad's favorite snack. I wonder if Denver's been talking to York. "She wouldn't tell me anything. I have no idea if she's going to make you an Aegis or not."

"I should've been nicer to her when we were kids." Astana sighs. Taking the bottle from me, she dabs the scent on my wrist. "At least Hanoi seems nice. Maybe she can convince Blanca to go easy on us."

"My sister was the one who was too good to play with us. The one above mud puddles and dragonflies." My stomach growls. Great. Is it time to eat again?

I press a hand over my caftan to muffle the noise. An Aegis would've ignored the rumbling. But Astana and Carr stare at my torso like it's an artifact from Earth.

"You've got to hear this, Carr," she says. "It's the wildest thing."

I move my hand. "He doesn't want to listen to my stomach."

"Of course he does. Our tummies grumble, too, but not like yours." She pushes Carr toward me. "Go on. She doesn't mind, I promise."

He takes a few steps toward me, his eyes soft around the edges. "May I?" he asks.

"Um, sure. Go ahead. I mean, if you want to." The heat hikes up my cheeks, and I glare at Astana. Her smile back is moonlight innocent.

But then Carr kneels in front of me, fitting his ear to my stomach like a jigsaw puzzle, and my embarrassment is crowded out by other sensations. His breath pushing against my caftan. The brush of his thick hair. A live, humming spark where our bodies touch.

The air is suddenly more liquid than oxygen, and my heart sprints like it's running a race. Just an ear. Just a stomach. Just a boy.

And yet, I know, from the soles of my feet to the top of my heart, Carr Silver has never been just anything.

A few seconds later, a few hours too soon, he stands and walks around the bed. "Thank you. That was…an experience."

An experience. Good or bad? Weird or nice? But I can't possibly ask without revealing to Astana how her brother's touch affected me. My moment with Carr on the lawn, and now this, have caused all sorts of emotions to swirl inside me. I don't quite understand them yet—and I'm certainly not ready to share them.

Instead, I turn to my best friend and try to remember how to breathe. "Don't worry. Between the two of us, Blanca and me, we'll figure out a way to make you better."

"The three of us," Carr says, his eyes drilling holes through me. "You know I'll do anything to save you, sis. If I have to, I'll even kill."

I laugh, but it comes out as brittle as cracked glass. "That's hardly necessary."

"We'll see."

We stare at each other over the rumpled bed sheets. Those warm, swirly emotions that I associated with Carr? The coldness of his tone, the distance of his words have doused my feelings with liquid nitrogen, so that they freeze right where they had been dancing. I don't know how he can listen to my stomach one moment and be my adversary the next. But then Astana grabs our hands, tugging us close and breaking the tension.

"I'm so lucky to have you both in my life." She beams like she might power an entire grid.

Beams? That's a little extreme. We haven't found an

answer yet. We're not even close. I've only seen her this happy once, and that was when she was bot-mindedly in love with Jacksonville Kim.

She couldn't be…? Oh my goodness.

Pulling my hand away, I flick my fingers against the intravenous bag. The medication drips, drips, drips into her veins. "You must have happy potion in here. Is this because of Denver?"

I expect her to laugh or roll her eyes. Instead, she blushes. Honest-to-Zeus red flushes her cheeks. From the girl who can stand naked in front of me without flinching. "Oh, V. You know me so well."

"Denver." I just saw them together, and I'm still having trouble processing the relationship. "The same boy who smeared mud in your hair. The one you swore you would never kiss if he was the last boy in the colony."

"He didn't even care that I looked a nightmare today," she says, her mind light-years away. "My hair wasn't brushed, my face hasn't been primed. But he called me beautiful. That's never happened unless I was fully accessorized."

"Because you never leave the living unit otherwise," Carr says.

"No. This is different. He makes me feel special. Me. Not my face or my body. But who I am when everything else is taken away." She looks at her arm, which is still more bone than anything else. "As it has been these last few months."

My hands clench on the intravenous tube, and the hollowness inside my stomach spreads, up my core and down my legs, until it fills every nook and cranny of my body.

My best friend is dying. Her fate is up to my power-hungry sister. Her brother is competing to die in her place.

And now, she's crushing on my cousin. As much as I love Denver, I'm not sure if this is the right time for romance.

"Astana, you know what a flirt Denver is," I say carefully, making myself let go of the tube. "His attention might not mean anything. You know that, right?"

But if she hears me, she doesn't respond. Instead, she plucks a flower from the vase on her nightstand. Not just any flower, either. One with pink petals and black-tipped stamens. A new breed of azaleas, grown in a certain glasshouse on the edge of the Agriculture Bubble.

She strokes her finger across the petal, like I did. Except not. Because my touch was an appreciation for the beautiful. Hers is a tender caress for the boy behind the gift.

CHAPTER FOURTEEN

*O*ver my head, tiny lights are strung across the courtyard.
Instead of stars, they look like fluorescent butterflies
commissioned to hover above the dance floor. Fluffy pom-
poms and rainbow confetti are scattered across long, white
tables. Not as popular as a platter of spring rolls—but not
as distracting, either. And the black night sky covers us all,
the mother-daughter moons full and round, peeping at us
like the eyes of curious children.

A worthy backdrop for the first party I've ever hosted.
My birthdays are always organized by the royal staff. But
this get-together is mine. My idea. My execution. Too bad
all I can do is worry about Denver and Astana. How can I
be sure he's not toying with my best friend? Ever since he
brought three shiny apples to three trainees on the same
day, I've made it clear to him that the girls in my Eating
class were off-limits.

Silly me. I never thought to include Astana in the
proscription. But why should I have? He's known her since
she had to clutch a stuffed grasshopper to go to sleep, and

there's never been any kind of spark.

Until now.

I catch a flash of Denver's face at the other side of the courtyard, and I start making my way through the crowd. Not easy when everyone's mingling, laughing, and—judging from the number of pom-poms sailing through the air—having a great time.

Despite myself, a smile tugs at my lips. Maybe there's not such a big divide between the Princess and the rest of the colony, after all. Maybe I just need to learn to relax.

As I get closer, Denver's entire body comes into view. He's not flirting with any of the girls. Not talking or dancing, either. In fact, his shoulders are hunched, and he looks… lost? Can that be? My center-of-attention cousin, lost at a party? Apparently. His feet drum the ground, and he keeps checking his red-beam watch, as if he'd rather be somewhere else. Somewhere like sitting on a hospital bed next to my best friend.

I trip over a rock. Could I be wrong? Could this thing between him and Astana actually be real? He's a good guy, my cousin. His only fault is his inability to commit. But maybe he's changed. Maybe he's beginning to see what I see, that Astana is one of the most wonderful people on Dion.

I open my mouth, about to call to him, and then strong arms lift me into the air.

"Dance with me," Jupiter says, his face crinkled with joy and adrenaline.

Fun. Handsome. Coordinated. I couldn't ask for a better dancer partner. And yet, my heart plunges below my feet. Because he's not Carr.

Of course, Carr never said he would come. He's probably sleeping, so he can be at his best for tomorrow's trial. Still, after our near-kiss on the lawn, after he pressed his ear to my stomach, I was hoping he would show.

Jupiter twirls me and twirls me, and my feet step-step-step in response. It's not the arms I imagined around me, but still, I'm dancing. The laughter bubbles inside me like carbonated soda, as if it was always there, waiting for the tab to be pulled. The conversation with Denver can wait.

It can wait until after I introduce York to the royal cook's assistant—and giggle when he leans in and sniffs her neck. It can wait while Zelo points out the space shuttle constellation in the night sky. And it can really wait when I see Blanca hesitate at the edge of the crowd, twisting her torso as if to go, before Hanoi whispers a few urgent words to her and tugs her onto the dance floor.

By the time I think to look for Denver again, I no longer care that I can't find him. Because I've thrown a party. A real, actual celebration. And I've never had so much fun in my life.

And then I see him. The person who will make my evening even better.

He stands under the archway, melting into the stone, as though he doesn't want to disrupt the festivities. I walk toward him, smiling. Doesn't he know he's always welcome at any social gathering?

I take his hands and lead him into the yellowed glow of the twinkling lights. "Dad. I didn't know if you would make it."

"And miss my little girl's first hosted party? Not a chance." He holds me at arm's length so he can examine my dress. It has a simple shape—fitted through the waist with a flouncy skirt. But the color is the fresh, vibrant green of pea shoots poking out of the soil.

"Your mother had a dress this color," he says.

"I know. She's wearing it in one of my holograms. I took the cube to the clothier to see if he could match the color."

"You remind me more and more of her every day."

I startle. "She's tall like Blanca. Not me."

"Not in the way you look." His words are strong, his voice misty. He yearns for her. Every minute of every day, he yearns for her with a ferocity that reaches into the heavens and tries its damnedest to force her back again. I know because I feel the same way. "You remind me of her because of the strength I see in your eyes. Because of your ability to discern the moral core of a situation and your courage to act upon it."

I try to swallow, but the saliva won't go down. It pools at the top of my throat and threatens to choke me. "How do you know I'm strong enough, brave enough to do the right thing?"

"I don't. I can only hope."

The soft strums of a guitar emit from the speakers. A slow song, to cool the frenzied dancers in the courtyard. My father holds his hands out to me, and I step into his arms. We rarely dance in the shuttle, but I remember being a little girl and placing my slippered toes on his feet as he demonstrated how to step in an invisible square.

"I spoke to the council about your request to give the patients in Blanca's pool a daily ration of food," my father says. "And they're amenable. But it'll come at a price. Remember, for every meal we give, we take many times that amount away from the rest of the colony. So, the council suggests we eliminate a meal a day from the family members of the Fittest candidates."

He spins me in a circle. "If you agree, we'll change the deal. For every day you continue in the Trials, every patient—not just Astana—will receive food."

Hanoi's face floats across my mind, the wan smile, the brilliant burst of hope in her eyes. But immediately, other faces crowd into my vision, chasing her away. Miss Sydney and her blue sash. Cairo Mead's brother. Lenox Gray, with a gray beard to match, the father of the very first Fittest girl. I'm not sure what he thinks about the children dubbing him "Santa Claus," on account of his round belly.

But I know exactly how all of them will feel about a portion of their reward being taken away. Not. Happy.

"Is there any other way?" I ask.

"The food has to come from somewhere." He places his fingers under my chin. "We're not placing conditions to be mean, my eye-apple. The council has always had one purpose—to do the best we can for the overall colony. Sometimes, in order to do that, we have to make unpopular decisions."

Unpopular. Ha. I'll be the serpent from the carving come to life. But how can I let these patients, how can I let Hanoi, starve? Sure, they have Blanca's feeding tubes, but she said so herself: the bags of formula aren't a pill replacement.

I nod slowly, like a bot in need of oil. And hope this is what my mother would've done. "Okay. Let the council know I agree. But can it be a permanent solution? If the families give up their meals forever, Astana, Hanoi, and the others will be saved."

His hand drifts to my elbow. "We made the families a promise, and we can't go back on that promise. Just like we can't undo the deaths of their sons and daughters. In exigent circumstances, such as the selection of the Successor, we may take extreme measures. But only then."

"What if they voluntarily gave up their meals?"

"If anyone can convince them, it will be you, my eye-apple." His voice tells me how impossible this task is. "But please remember, this is Blanca's task. We need to let her act as she sees fit. Besides, you can't save everyone."

"Why not?" I ask fiercely. "What's the point of being a ruler if I can't save my people?"

"On the contrary, a ruler must pick and choose whom to save. That's what makes the position so difficult."

We continue dancing. In the middle of the dance floor, a crowd forms a ring around a boy. But it's not the Circle of Shunning. It's just Jupiter refusing to be cooled. Spinning on his head, his back, his hands. If the music won't aid him in working up a sweat, he'll do it himself.

The tempo's gotten too lethargic for me, too. I don't want to be moving gracefully anymore. I want to be Jupiter, my sweat swinging out in an arc and spraying everyone in a five-foot radius.

"I wish I remembered Mom better." I spin out of my father's arms.

"Why? You think she'd be able to give you the answers?"

"Maybe." I stare at the pine cone insignia on his shoulder. "If I knew her better, maybe I could guess what she would do. You've always been so generous with your stories, and I have the holograms on my cube. But when I think about what I actually remember—something that's not filtered through your memory or a mechanical lens—there's very little."

"You don't need to remember her," my father says. "Because she lives in your heart."

I lay my head on his shoulder and get a whiff of eucalyptus perfume. Am I losing my mind? I take another sniff and realize it's not my mother's ghostly presence, after all. My father's just mixed the eucalyptus water with his aftershave.

Tears sting my eyes. Our ancestors on Earth thought that by hurtling hundreds of light-years from the original planet, we'd somehow get closer to heaven. But they were wrong. Heaven is in the same place it always was. Infinitely far.

"Do you ever think about entering another union?" I ask. "I mean, you've had other wives before Mom. Other families before us."

At ninety years old, my father is the oldest Aegis on this planet. He suffers the same tragedy as the colonists who choose Aegis spouses—he's had to survive his wives and children by decades.

"I don't think so, my eye-apple. I loved all my families. You know that." He puts his chin on my head. "But you, your sister, and your mom were the family I was waiting for. You are who I want to think of in the last moments before I die."

My chest constricts. "You're not going to die anytime soon, Dad. You've got five whole years left."

"I know it." His voice is thin and distant, as though it were flung into space with my mom's ashes. "But what I'm trying to say is: I'm perfectly fulfilled. After all these years, there's nothing more I need to feel. Nothing more I want to accomplish. I've been with this colony from the moment we discovered the pods were destroyed and were convinced our mission was an utter failure. To now. When our society is alive and blooming. When we can look forward to both stability and progress for centuries to come. I have one duty remaining, and then my life will be complete."

"What's that?"

He moves back, so I have to lift my head off his shoulder and look at him.

"To find the proper Successor to rule in my place."

CHAPTER FIFTEEN

*C*ome on, *Zelo, you can do this.* The words run through my head like a bot stuck in the same programming loop. *You can do this. You can do this.*

You. Can. Do. This.

I look through a one-way window, into a room where Zelo stands on a flat stone, one foot wide by one foot long. There's no table, no desk, no holo-feeds. No food. Nothing but concrete floors and white plaster walls.

All the other candidates stand on their own stones in their own empty rooms. It's the second event, and I've chosen another challenge from my own Aegis Trials.

The boys may step off their stones at any time, and the last boy standing wins. The twist? The candidates will be offered incentives to quit. Incentives specifically designed to entice them, based on information collected during the personal interviews. Incentives meant to show exactly what is important to them—and by how much.

The most important thing to Zelo is serving his god. So he has to do well today. He'd better. I picked this challenge just for him.

My face feels hot, like I've stuck it over a pot of boiling water. I look up and down the corridor, certain any passerby can see the guilt etched in my features. My actions are more suspect than what I did in the first challenge. A step more manipulative.

But I'm not targeting a boy to die, I tell myself. *I'm helping the worthiest boy win. The one who won't be missed by anyone in the colony.*

Except, perhaps, by me.

My ribs squeeze together, as if the serpent from the mural has wrapped its body around my torso. Master Somjing plods down the hallway, peering into each window, and I struggle to break the snake's hold.

"One hour in, and half the candidates are gone," he says, coming up to me. "Once the incentives came out, they folded like laundry from the smoothing press. A warm bed. Dissolvable strips flavored like chocolate-chip cookies. Pills. Even more pills."

Pulling out my handheld, I scan the next round of incentives. "Next, we'll offer the opportunity to go on an expedition in the outside planet. A position as aid to a council member. A featured spot on the news feeds."

Master Somjing clicks his tongue, which is all the approval I ever get from him. "Getting to the core of their true characters. Not bad, Vela."

"I remember the stone challenge well from my own Aegis Trials."

"How long did you last?"

I bite my lip. Why is he asking? Master Somjing doesn't make conversation with me. But ever since I made the decision to take away food from the Fittest families, he's been friendlier. As if he can better relate to the cutthroat side of me. The side that's more like Blanca.

"I lasted an entire day," I say. "They offered the usual. Longer life, more pills, political power. That kind of thing."

"I heard it came down to you and your sister." He scrutinizes my face, as if searching for a tell. Blanca should've had her Trials the year before me, but she missed them due to some analysis she had to do for the King. My sister insisted that the work was so important she was willing to delay her entrance into eating for a year—but I always suspected that she just wanted to compete directly against me.

"You were both offered the same incentive in the final round," Master Somjing continues. "That's when you caved, while Blanca remained strong. Yet, you were recorded as the winner of the challenge. How can that be?"

I glance through the window. Zelo's eyes are closed, head tilted toward the ceiling. He hasn't moved an inch.

Master Somjing wouldn't know what happened in my final challenge, of course. The records of a person's Aegis Trials are highly classified. Even council members don't have access to them.

"It was a trick," I say finally.

"How so?"

I turn and look at him. The light at his collar is off, which means this conversation isn't recorded. There isn't a team of psychologists somewhere dissecting my every word. Could this mean Master Somjing is actually interested in me? As a person and not a data point?

"They gave me an ultimatum. Get off the stone, or my sister gets tortured. It wasn't a choice for me. I got off the stone."

His mouth opens. "And Blanca stayed on?"

My eyes feel wet. This is ridiculous. The challenge happened over two years ago. I didn't cry then, and I'm not going to cry now. "I guess it wasn't a choice for her, either." My voice cracks, and I hate the tone, hate the pitch, hate my vulnerability. "She stayed on."

Long moments pass. Inside the room, Zelo stretches his arms overhead. Shakes one leg out and then the other.

"I have a confession to make," Master Somjing says, his tone changing. Without the stiffness shoring up each syllable, he sounds like a completely different person.

"What is it?" I keep my eyes on Zelo and his standing-in-place calisthenics. Zelo is safe. If I watch him, I won't have to see the pity on anyone's face. The mocking ridicule of the poor little Princess, who continues to idolize her older sister, even though the feeling isn't mutual. Has never been mutual.

The air whistles in and out of Master Somjing's mouth. "After you got caught stealing food for your friend, I was one of your...well, I was your most vocal opponent. In fact, I didn't even want to give you another chance. I always knew you were a sweet girl, Vela, but I thought you were soft. Malleable. I thought there was no way you were qualified to be our next ruler." He stops. "And now..."

"Yes?" I sneak a glance at his face. He's watching me, as usual. But instead of searching for a mistake, he's looking at me like I might have something to teach him.

"Now, I think I was wrong. I hope you make the right decision. I hope you prove to the council, and everyone else, that you're worthy of your father's confidence. Because I'm starting to root for you."

"I'm trying." The words get stuck in my throat and come out as half air.

He shakes his head. "Not good enough. Try harder."

*T*he day is a slow-burning candle, melting time in small, imperceptible moments, leaving behind an ever-growing pile of cooled wax and minutes. One by one the candidates drop out, until there are only two left. Zelo, that lovely boy. And Carr.

"The examiners have been interrogating both boys." Master Somjing skims his finger over his handheld. "Running through a list of human desires and noting when their vital signs change."

"And what have they found?" I ask.

"From Zelo? Nothing much. The boy's blood is ice. We couldn't get a rise out of him, no matter what we said."

Good for him. Must've been all the time he spent meditating in the temple, tuning out the everyday noise.

"He seems too good to be true." Master Somjing squints at the data on his screen. "I can't get a good read on him. Neither can CORA."

"Maybe he *is* that good. Maybe some people really are that noble."

"Maybe," he says doubtfully. "What's next? Should we threaten to torture someone they love?"

"What? Oh Zeus, no. *No.*" He's kidding, right? He's got to be kidding.

But I can tell from his unsmiling mouth that he's not. Especially because I know this strategy would work. Carr would step off the stone before we even finished the ultimatum. Zelo has no one he loves. He would stay on. Since this isn't a reciprocal relationship like mine and Blanca's, it wouldn't be considered a trick. Zelo would be deemed worthier, as he has no other allegiances that can sully his obedience to the colony.

I wanted Zelo to win today. But not like this. "No torture."

"We wouldn't actually—"

"Not even the threat of it. We can't condone torture in any shape or form. Not even in a game. Not even to find the Fittest."

He tilts his head, considering me. "I guess I understand why you would feel that way. What do you suggest, then?"

I stare at the transmitter in his ear. It's the size of a cherry pit and nearly undetectable. "Let's talk to them."

He snorts. "We're not going to be able to talk them down. What do you think the examiners have been doing for the last eighteen hours? If you're unwilling to go the torture route, I think we're at a standstill."

"The examiners are strangers. We aren't. Carr and Zelo will respond to us. They may slip and tell us more than they intend." Acid spurts into my mouth with each word. The boys don't know they're being recorded. They don't have any idea that their vitals are being transferred instantaneously to their interrogator's ear. What I'm suggesting is disingenuous…but no more manipulative than my previous actions. "The point of this challenge is to learn more about their true characters. So, if we can dig deeper into their motivations, then I'm satisfied with declaring this challenge a tie."

A tie. That's the best I can hope for. Dion knows, I don't want this challenge to turn into a contest of physical stamina. We all know who has the advantage there.

"What do you say, Master Somjing? I'll take Zelo, and you can talk to Carr."

He nods, signaling for a bot to roll over with a tray of ear buds. "Fine, but let's switch it around. You take Carr."

"But—"

He holds up a hand, stopping me. "Zelo's vitals never changed during the interrogation, but Carr's did." He selects a bud from the tray and offers it to me. "His heartbeat spiked every time we mentioned you."

CHAPTER SIXTEEN

Carr's head snaps up the moment I open the door, his eyes watchful and wild. Prey. Hunter. Or a combination of both.

I ease into the room. The air is drenched with sweat, the temperature ten degrees warmer than the corridor. Cracks in the plaster snake through the ceiling, and the one-way window reflects Carr's image, making him look like he's drowning in shiny, black glass.

The ear bud vibrates. "Good. His heartbeat is racing already."

The high, nasal voice belongs to a psychologist I've never met. I clamp my mouth to keep the words inside. *Not your business. Get OUT!*

"If you're here to convince me to quit, you can leave right now." Carr's voice is low and raspy. His lips are cracked and bleeding. He needs water. He also needs lip balm and sleep and a shower, but a drink is the only thing I can offer at the moment.

I find a pitcher on the floor and pour some water into

a cup. "I just want to talk. I didn't see you at the party." I approach him, not sure how much to reveal. "I was hoping you'd come."

"Didn't feel like partying after I found out my sister was in Blanca's care. Sorry."

He might've been sorry, once upon a time, but he's not now. This challenge seems to have wrung every dispensable emotion out of him.

I move closer. His hair is plastered to his forehead, and his face looks ravaged. Slashed by an invisible claw from forehead to chin. Of course, the only demons who might rip him apart are the ones inside him.

Two years ago, in a room like this one, I faced my own monsters. Sometimes, I wonder how long I would have lasted if they were able to give me the one thing I really want: absolution for my mother's death.

I offer him the water. "You and Zelo are the only two left. If we can learn enough about your motivations, we'll declare a tie and this whole thing will be over. Would you like that?"

"No. I'd rather win." He waves away the cup, rejecting the water. Rejecting me.

The voice chirps in my ear. "A spike in his pulse. Something's getting him worked up."

I ignore her. "Why are you standing here, Carr?"

"You know why. So I'll be named the Fittest. So my sister can eat."

"Is there anything—anything at all—that would make you step off?"

"No."

A crackle of static from the earbud. "He's telling the truth. Or at least, that's what his body thinks. But don't you believe it. We all have a price."

I grit my teeth. My price, right now, is getting rid of this yammering in my ear. *Try harder*, I remind myself. *Try. Harder.*

"Can we talk about your parents, Carr?" I drink the water myself and set the cup on the floor. "Your father left when you were nine, is that right?"

According to Master Somjing, two topics agitated Carr. One was me. The other was his family.

The already hard lines of Carr's face turn to granite. "I've already been over this with the examiners. I'm not going to rehash it again."

"I remember him a little." A memory comes to mind. A handsome man with a mustache, patting Carr's mother on the behind as she fussed with the pots in the royal kitchen. Astana, Carr, and I sat like roaches in the corner, the most well-behaved insects you ever saw. Not once did the man glance in our direction.

"He called you 'boy,'" I say. "I always wondered about that. Didn't he know your name?"

Carr shuffles his feet a couple inches to the right, as if to get away from me, but the stone is only so big, and he can only go so far. "He remembered Astana's name. She was so pretty he always fetched extra pills at the market if he brought her along. My mother was 'Lima,' but she did everything for him.

"Me?" His eyes close. "I wasn't any use to him. So I guess I didn't deserve a name."

A few dots connect in my head. "The year he left was the year you started selling worms for peach-colored pills."

He opens his eyes, and his steady, black glare squeezes the breath out of me.

The earbud comes alive. "Deadly Dion, you've done it. His vitals are going through the stratosphere."

I yank out the bud and shove it in my pocket. I don't need this useless analysis. Like I can't guess how Carr's feeling by looking at him. "Why were you trying to earn extra pills? Did you think you could bring him back?"

He winces. "Silly, wasn't I? To think my father's love could be bought with a few peachies. I should've aimed for the blue pills, at least."

"You shouldn't need to buy his love at all. Parents are supposed to love their children, no matter what."

He snorts. "Who told you that? The bedtime stories from Earth? They're called fiction for a reason, Vela. Because they're not true."

"Nobody had to tell me. The King showed me every day of my life. If I fail at this task, he'll be disappointed. But I know he'll still love me."

"That's the King. Regular people can't afford to be so free with their love. We have to reserve it for the people who will benefit us."

"You've got it all wrong," I whisper. "You do things for people because you love them. Not the other way around."

"Yeah?" He pushes his hair off his forehead and teeters to the edge of the stone. "My mother never paid attention to me. My clothes could be in threads, I'd come home from work with bleeding palms, and she never said a word. It was up to Astana to clean those wounds. Never her.

"But one day a month, my mother saw me. Because that was payday and that was the day I brought home pills. No one in this colony was treated better. She'd hug me and dance with me around the living unit. 'How did I ever get so lucky?' she would say. 'You're the best son a woman could ask for.' The next day, I would be invisible again. I didn't exist until the next payday."

"She was strung out on pellets." My words are harsh, my

voice harsher. But I have to get through to him. He has to understand that her behavior wasn't right. "She can't be your model for how to love."

He moves his shoulders, not looking at me. And I get why he's not hearing me. I do. We look to our parents first to learn how the world works. To determine our self-worth. And Carr's parents taught him that he is only loved for what he can do for them.

My heart is a caged thing, beating against too narrow walls. Is this why he's always worked so hard? I've never seen Carr do anything for himself. Now I understand why. In his mind, every pill was an opportunity to secure his family's love.

"What about Astana? She loves you. I've never seen a sister so devoted to her brother."

"Of course she loves me." He jerks his chin, and my words flick away like specks of dust. "I've been buying her gifts all my life."

"That's not why she loves you." I want to shake him. Hard. But then he might fall off the stone, and we'd have to disqualify the results due to my physical interference. "Sure, you gave her presents. All those bows and scents and things. She was probably the most spoiled girl in our colony. But don't you think she'd trade all of that for your happiness?"

He lifts his face, uncertainty reflected in his features. He really doesn't know. He has no clue how much his sister loves him.

The box around my heart tightens. "What about me?"

"What *about* you?"

His eyes land, not on me, but on the blinking amber light around my collar. I remember that there's more than the two of us in this room. There's a team of psychologists, and the nameless examiners, and every member of the council.

Not anymore.

My hands close around the loop. I switch it off and toss the metal necklace into the corner. And then I walk to the door, lock it, and flip a switch on the wall. A solid panel rolls from the window frame and slides over the one-way glass.

No one's watching now. No one's evaluating. I stand before him not as the Princess, but as Vela. The girl who's always crushed on him. My actions now aren't about the Trials. They're not about the council finding their answers. And they're certainly not about treating Carr like a data point.

"I care about you." I step closer, so he can't ignore me. "How do you explain that?"

"If you like me, it's only because I saved your life."

"Really, Carr?" I'm not a violent person, but I wish there was something in this room I could throw. A table, a chair. Something for me to wrap my hands around and hurl at the wall. "Is that why I like you? Because last I checked, I didn't even find out you rescued me until last week. What about in the red cells? What about when we almost touched? When we should've touched, just like this?" I grab his hand and jam our fingers together. Electricity snaps between us. "Did I like you then?"

He stares at our fingers. "I don't know."

I take his other hand, and the electricity cycles in a closed circuit between us. "What about the worms?"

He shakes his head, as if my words are from an Earth language he doesn't understand. "What worms?"

"When we were kids." I weave my fingers through his, so he can't pull away. "Do you remember coming to the pond one morning and finding a plate of worms waiting for you? That was me, Carr. I dug for hours before the sun lamps turned on, so you could have the day off."

His eyes widen. "That was you? Vela, I…" He swallows hard. "That was the nicest thing anyone's ever done for me."

"Now do you believe me? Now do you believe you don't need to buy someone's love?"

He gnaws on his cheek, and I see the doubt in each quick bite of his teeth. He still doesn't believe he's worthy of love. And how can I blame him? The barter system is all he's ever known.

I have one more argument up my sleeve. One last move. The final way I have of convincing him.

My entire body thrums, and my heart beats so fast it might break out of this cage yet. Quickly, before I change my mind, I close the gap between us. Stepping up onto the stone, I reach up and wind my arm around his neck.

"What about this?" I whisper.

And then I press my lips against his.

CHAPTER SEVENTEEN

My entire body tingles, every last nerve. My fingers twine in Carr's hair, and his stubbled jaw rubs against my skin. And his lips. Oh, those warm lips contain the secrets of our world. They may be cracked, but they burn all the way through me, welcoming me back to a place I've never been.

If this is home, I never want to leave.

Blanca once dared me to dive to the bottom of one of Dion's many ponds. This body of water isn't manmade, she'd said, but a chasm in the ground caused by a striking meteor. If I dove deeply enough, I wouldn't touch the rich, black dirt of our terraformed ground, but the hard, jagged rock of the original planet.

I believed her, of course. I always believed my sister, no matter what she said. But I dove anyway, and I knew I would never forget the bubbles fizzing all over my body, the breath that got pent up in my lungs. That deep, deep satisfaction when my hands finally touched rock.

Well, that's how I feel now. As if I've discovered something that has always existed. I only had to dive deeply enough to find it.

His arms wind around me, and I press my body against his. Too much clothing between us. Too many layers. I want my skin sinking into his, I want to feel the hard angles of his torso. I want our hearts beating as one. I want, I want, I want.

But we're in the middle of a challenge. And standing on a single square tile.

I pull back and lay my head on his chest, listening to his ragged breaths.

"Now do you believe me?" I ask.

His lips curve, and I can feel the shape of his smile against my scalp. "I don't know. I think I may need a little more convincing."

He moves his mouth back onto mine. His teeth scrape gently against my lips, and then his tongue tangles with mine. I'm drowning, drowning, drowning in this heat. Nothing in my life has prepared me for this feeling, and I'm about to be swept away, forever.

And then, I see the door flashing out of the corner of my eye.

"Princess Vela! Are you okay? There's a malfunction in our monitoring equipment. Do you need us to break down the door?"

It's Master Somjing. His words are concerned, but his tone is wry, as if he knows exactly how the malfunction occurred. And exactly who caused it.

"I'm fine." I fight to keep my voice steady as Carr presses floating-lily-kisses along my collarbone. "I'll be right out."

"Is the candidate still on the stone?" Master Somjing asks.

Carr and I look down. An inch of tile surrounds our feet. It's a wonder we haven't lost our balance.

He plants his feet more squarely on the tile. "I'm not getting off this stone, not even for a few steamy kisses."

I jerk like I've been slapped and stumble off the tile. The words don't slash a new wound. They rip open an old one. It hurts all the more because this isn't my pain—it's his.

"Is that what you think? That I kissed you to get you to drop out of the challenge?"

He doesn't respond, but his eyes say it all. Big, black pools of purpose and resolve. The characteristics our colony admires most. These qualities elevate Carr to the most noble of our candidates—but they also erase every trace of the boy whom I just kissed.

"How can you think that?" Oh, the rational part of me knows the answer. A single kiss—no matter how perfect—doesn't change a lifetime of hurt. But the other part, the part that poured myself into our embrace, the part that I thought he saw, above anyone else—that part can't understand. "My feelings for you have nothing to do with the Fittest Trials."

"Don't they? You told me you would make sure I didn't win. Has that changed?"

"No. But I didn't kiss you because of this challenge, either. If you don't believe me, I don't know what else to say."

We stare at each other, the weight of the planet between us. Barren, craggy rock with too much carbon dioxide and not enough life.

"Vela?" Master Somjing calls again. "Has Carr stepped off the tile?"

I turn toward the door, as much to avoid Carr's gaze as to pitch my voice in the right direction. "No. I don't think he'll ever step off."

The door handle rattles. "Put on your ear piece."

I fish the ear bud out of my pocket and fit it into place.

"Did you get the necessary information?" Master Somjing asks. "Can we declare a tie?"

I look back at Carr. At the firm set of his jaw, at the lips that will always seem gentle to me, no matter how hard he presses them together. In some ways, I've learned so much. I've learned that something can warm me from the inside out. I've learned why Carr works so hard. I've learned that he may never let himself have the only thing he really wants—love.

And yet, he's as inaccessible to me now as he was all those years ago. I can't reach him any more with a kiss than I could with a plate of worms.

"Declare a tie." I don't give up, as a rule. But I've failed with gifts and words and touch. I'm not sure what else is left. "I'm not getting anything more from this candidate."

An hour later, I walk along the edge of the bubble, on my way to visit Astana at the medical facility. It's raining outside, in the real planet, and colored ribbons of water sluice down the side of the energy shield.

I watch the red rain fall from the sky. When the drops hit the bubble, they burst into other colors—the smaller, lighter dribbles into blues and greens, and the larger, heavier plops into yellows and oranges. The colors streak downward, growing fainter and bluer as the energy dissipates.

It doesn't rain like that in here. Inside the bubble, the color's been filtered along with the bacteria, so it rains clear and boring and only at night. There's no energy field for the water to hit, so no pretty sunbursts of color, either. If I close my eyes, I can pretend there isn't a shield between the water and me. Squeeze them even tighter, and I can almost feel the splatters against my skin, leaving rainbow splotches like a paintbrush flicked against a canvas.

Silly. If I were really in the rain, the bacteria would make me sick. Even sicker than I feel now.

I catch sight of the medical building and cut toward the center of the bubble. I still see the rain, high overhead, but it's not the same as the brilliant streaks coming down beside me. The drops that fall on top of the shield are like the single pinprick of a distant star compared to the sunflower explosion of a nebula.

What could have possessed me to kiss Carr like that? And how exactly am I supposed to explain this to Astana? *Um, I kissed your brother, and it might've been the best experience of my life, but don't worry. It will probably never happen again.*

Right. That will go over well.

As I reach the entrance of the building, Miss Sydney walks out, carrying a basket of her caramel cricket crunch. After she tests her recipes on me, she generally tries them out with the patients at the medical facility.

"Miss Sydney, hi!" I perk up, as I always do, at the sight of her blue sash. "Do the patients love the cricket crunch as much as I do?"

But she doesn't smile at me the way she usually does. She doesn't offer me a sample of the crickets, either. "They didn't give me any dinner last night. Instead, I had a nutrition pill and that was all." She slits her eyes like the serpent's. "They told me you were responsible."

I wince. I meant to go to each of the Fittest families and tell them personally, but I've had so much on my mind. I guess I forgot.

I reach for her wrist, but she twists away, so I end up with her sleeve. "I'm sorry I didn't explain. You see, there are some colonists who are unable to absorb nutrition—"

"Yes, they told me." She's shorter than me, but her stiff

anger elongates her, so she seems to tower over me. "And of course, these patients need to eat. But what we don't understand is why you're taking *our* food away. Surely there are extra stores somewhere else."

"There really aren't," I say helplessly. "Other than the gen-mods, the Fittest families are the only people who eat. You know I wouldn't have decreased any part of your reward if I had another choice."

"Do I?" Her eyebrows disappear under the blue sash. "Because some of the Fittest families are questioning your motives, Princess. Clearly you would do anything to save your best friend—even at our expense. We're beginning to wonder if you still value what we gave your father. If you've ever valued us at all."

"Of course I value you! I'd give up my own meals, but I need to eat to produce pills." I grab her sleeve, too hard, too much, but if all I get is a square inch of fabric, I'll take it. "I'll make it up to you. I promise I'll find a way to make this right."

She tugs her shirt, and even that small inch falls away. "If I held my breath every time I heard someone say that, Princess, I'd have joined my son years ago."

"I don't suppose you would consider giving up your evening meal permanently?" My voice is weak and faded, like a ghost who's overstayed its time in the physical realm. Try harder. Try. Harder. I force some life into my words. "You want my friend Astana to live, don't you? She'll die without food."

"Maybe you should've thought of that before you broke the law." She adjusts her basket and stalks away.

My insides feel like someone's whipped the very life out of them. But instead of fluffing like coconut cream, they're wilted and flat.

The King was right. It won't be easy to convince the Fittest families to relinquish their rights. But I'm not giving up. Not now, not ever. Not when the stakes are so high. Not when those stakes include my best friend's life.

CHAPTER EIGHTEEN

When I enter Astana's wing, a mother and daughter are in the corridor. The little girl is about two years old, with flaxen pigtails and dimples as deep as chasms. She scampers across a stretcher as though it is playground equipment, and her mother, who is hardly more than a girl herself, follows close behind, holding onto a metal stand.

"Brooklyn! How many times do I have to tell you? Stay still or the tube's going to fall out," the woman says.

The girl grins at me with her whole face—with her too-thin cheeks and her long eyelashes. "Catch you!" she says and leaps off the stretcher, directly at me.

Oomph. She lands in my arms. My knees buckle, but I manage to remain standing.

"Oh Dion, I'm sorry." The woman hurries to us, holding the now-detached and dripping intravenous tube. "She's just so excited to be out of bed. To be detached from the feeding tube for a few minutes. You wouldn't believe it, but two days ago she couldn't even sit up. It's amazing what a difference food can make." Her voice is equal parts relief, wonder—and hope. As though she resigned herself to the worst and can't believe her baby's being given a second chance.

I swallow hard. This must be the little girl Hanoi mentioned. The one who's as sick as her and Astana.

I lower the girl to the ground, and she scurries onto the stretcher once again.

"Catch you?" I ask.

"Brooklyn is still learning her pronouns, and she thinks 'you' is her name." The woman makes an exasperated sound, but I can tell from her soft smile that she thinks it's the most adorable thing on Dion. "So all day long, it's 'catch you,' 'hold you,' 'give you.'" She snags the back of her daughter's gown as the girl runs past and reattaches the IV.

Brooklyn beams at me. "See you."

"Hey, that was right!" I smile back. I can't help it. "See you later."

I continue walking down the hallway, the confrontation with Miss Sydney leaking from my heart. I helped this little girl out of bed. I gave this young mother hope. If I had to do it over again? I'd decide the same way, every time.

As I approach Astana's room, I hear raised voices. Shouts. Maybe even an object being thrown.

The hair on my neck stands up, and I rush inside.

"He's doing *what*?" Astana paces in the small space in front of her bed, the metal stand dragging behind her.

Denver reaches out to pat her arm, but she swishes away before he can reach it.

"Vela." She pounces on me, her voice cracking like too-dry cake. "How could you do this to me? How could you let Carr compete in the Fittest Trials?"

Oh. That *he*. And that *what*. I guess my cousin has been whispering more than sweet nothings in her ear.

"The Fittest is the, um, the most revered person in our

colony." I stumble over the words. I wasn't going to be able to keep this a secret forever. I don't even know why I tried. "He'll be remembered forever as a hero."

"Yeah, but he'll also be dead. I don't want a C-trunk in your silly memorial copse, okay? I want my brother alive and next to me."

This is why I tried. My best friend's anger fills the room, suffocating me. It makes Miss Sydney's annoyance look like a single, colored drop in a torrential downpour.

I shrink back. "I don't want him to die, either, Astana."

"Then kick him out. Denver tells me you're in charge of the Trials, just as Blanca is in charge of me. Disqualify him. Right now."

"It's not that simple." I blink rapidly at Denver. The fluttering of eyelashes is our old distress signal. The one we'd shoot each other when we were cornered by an obnoxious classmate. Even now, when he was the one who got me into this mess, I still expect him to rescue me. The trust must come from building all those forts together. Mud forges a bond that's thicker than blood.

Denver snags Astana's hand. When she stops pacing, he pulls her to him and brushes a kiss across her lips. The gesture is so tender, so intimate, I move to the side window and look out.

The view here is not nearly as majestic. Instead of brilliant streams of color, I see one of the generator towers that spear up like tent poles all over our colony. The towers are black, metal structures connected at the top by a series of scaffolding. They may be necessary—without the generators perched at the apex, we'd have no shield—but they're certainly not pretty.

Ugly or not, the tower keeps me from intruding on someone else's kiss.

"I'm sorry, Astana," Denver says. "It was wrong of me to spring the news on you. Let me give you and Vela time to talk."

"I don't want to talk—"

I stare as hard as I can at the bolts in the tower. I really don't want to think about what they're doing. Really don't want to know what those little smacks mean.

"Please," my cousin says, sixty long seconds later. "I feel awful for telling you in such a crude way. Talk to Vela. We'll all feel better. Besides, I need to speak to the King. He's approved my new azalea as the royal flower."

"That's wonderful." Astana's voice is as pure and open as a bud unfurling in the new season. As pure and open as she is.

My heart thumps. This is just like Astana, to fall in love so quickly and so hard. She doesn't know how to crack open a seam and let a person in bit by bit. When she loves, she does so irrevocably, without holding anything in reserve.

Her capacity to love is one of the reasons she's my best friend. But it's also the reason she could get hurt. Badly.

Denver comes to my side. "Let's give her a few minutes," he whispers. "Come with me."

I nod, and we walk out of the room.

"Sorry, V. I didn't realize she didn't know," he says when we're in the corridor. Brooklyn and her mother are gone, and a puddle of fluid sits on the floor in front of the stretcher.

"Really?" My voice takes on an unfamiliar edge. One I don't often use and certainly not with my cousin. "I could've sworn I told you I was keeping Carr's participation a secret. In the spectator box, during the first challenge. You even advised me not to tell her. Remember?"

He winces. "I guess I forgot." He holds up his wrist. "You'll forgive me, won't you?"

I sigh. I can never stay mad at my cousin for long. But

even as I press my wrist against his, I know the conversation isn't finished.

"What are you doing with my friend, Denver?"

He scuffs his foot against the stone floor, where the treads of bots have worn slight grooves. "I really like her, V. This thing with Astana... I've never felt this way before."

I want to believe him. Because if there's anything my cousin deserves, it's love. The last couple years haven't been easy for him, with his father dead and his mother depressed. If the romance between him and Astana is real, I'll be their biggest supporter. But if it isn't...we'll see just how strong those mud bonds are.

"Forgive me for not taking you at your word. But Essex wouldn't eat for three days after you lost interest in her. My stomach still hurts thinking about the extra food the rest of us had to eat to make up for her quota."

"You'll see. With time, you'll see how sincere I'm being."

"I hope so. I really do." Because if we all come out of this alive, with our hearts unscathed, it would be a fairy tale from Earth.

Even if we have to eat poisoned apples and be baked alive before we reach our happy ending.

*O*nce the details start spilling out of me, they won't stop. I start from the beginning and tell Astana the whole story. Not just for her sake, but also for mine.

With each word, a water balloon pops in my chest. I tell her how Carr confessed he rescued me and called in his death debt. Pop. How I found the perfect candidate in Zelo, even though he's lacking in physical skills. Pop. How neither boy would get off his stone, no matter what incentives we offered. Pop, pop, pop.

And yes, the kiss. I even told her about that.

Her eyes get big and bulging. She looks like the test mole that burrowed under our energy shields and emerged in an air too rich with carbon dioxide. "You kissed him? You made the first move?"

I sit at the foot of the bed. If I'm going to come clean, I might as well confess the whole truth. "I like him, Astana."

"Well, of course you do," she says, as if I told her the sky was purple. "All the girls love Carr. Even Hanoi confessed that she thought he was cute. He's never had time for any of them, that's all."

She cocks her head. "Did he kiss you back? How was—" She snaps her mouth shut and flops against the stack of pillows. "Never mind. I don't want to know. If you're going to get involved with my brother, don't tell me any of the specifics. Okay?"

"I don't know if we're involved." I look at my hands. The same ones that intertwined with his. The same fingers that touched a ray of light. "He seemed to think I was only kissing him to get him off the stone."

"Were you?"

"No! I've liked him ever since we were…we were…" My voice falters, as I realize this is one more secret I never told her.

"You can't possibly want him to win."

Fine tremors run up her arms. I grab the solar blanket off the recharging rack and hand it to her. "I'm doing everything in my power to make sure he doesn't."

I tell her about cheering for Zelo, about choosing a trial suited for his particular strengths. Either my words reassure her, or the newly heated blanket warms her up.

The trembling stops. But her anger doesn't.

"You're not trying hard enough. We're halfway through the trials, and Carr's won both challenges."

"Don't you think I know that?" The dread seeps through my veins, watery and cold. Like Astana's intravenous fluids but worse. Because no blanket, no matter how warm, can take the edge off. "I knew Zelo would excel at the incentive trial. How was I supposed to know Carr would be as good?"

"You can't just tailor a trial to suit another candidate and hope for the best. You have to go out of your way to stack the odds against Carr."

"What do you mean?"

"I'm not sure," she admits. "What's the next challenge?"

"The Orange Temptation." I drop my head, and my hair swings forward to cover my face. I can't bear to look at my friend. This challenge is further proof of how spectacularly I've failed at protecting her brother. "The candidates will be placed in a room filled with oranges. The fruit will be sprayed with a fragrance that will make them virtually impossible to resist. We expect every candidate to succumb to a bite eventually. It's only a question of when."

Taking a quick breath, I hurry on before Astana can protest. "This is a challenge that's traditionally been part of the Fittest Trials, before we knew that a bite of food could trigger the intolerance to the pills. But you don't have to worry. We've tested all of the candidates, and none of them have the predisposition, so they aren't at risk. I never would've allowed the challenge otherwise."

"That's not what I'm worried about," Astana says. "I mean, yes. I'm glad your challenge won't produce more patients like me. But what's more pressing is that Carr's been in and out of glasshouses, resisting food, half his life."

"I know." My voice is a pebble in an infinitely expanding

universe. I attacked the challenge from every angle, but Master Somjing insisted it had to be included. In the end, I couldn't dispute his logic. The Fittest will live in the shuttle for months before the transplant. He'll be surrounded by food, day and night, and yet, he can never succumb to a bite or he'll risk damaging his organs. We have to know he'll be able to resist the temptation.

Astana drums her fingers against her cheek. "What if you changed the temptation from oranges to apples? Is there still time to make the switch?"

"I guess. What difference would it make?"

"Carr would be able to abstain from oranges all day. But apples…not so much."

I shake my head. "Not following."

My friend pushes herself off the bed. The attached tubing limits her movements, so she grabs the stand and takes it with her. "I overheard Blanca talking to the medics. She said once you've had a bite of a particular food, it becomes harder to resist. And you can't tell anybody this, but, well… Carr's tried an apple before."

My mouth drops. Carr, the disciplined one, the one with the iron-nickel will, has tasted food? I don't believe it.

"It wasn't his fault." The words rush from her mouth. "You know how he always has nightmares?"

I didn't. I would've thought he was too sensible for nightmares.

"This one night, the dream was especially bad." She opens and closes her hand, as if to increase the flow of fluids. As if she knows she'll need the extra medication for this story. "He was shaking and moaning. I couldn't get him to stop. I couldn't wake him up. And then he started to cry. I've never heard my brother cry before."

She lifts her eyes to me. I might as well be looking into a

mirror. Her eyes are black instead of brown, heavily fringed instead of sparsely lashed. But the same emotion clouds her irises: guilt.

"You'd given me a slice of apple that day, and I saved it, in order to savor it." Her face crumples. "I thought he was crying because he was hungry. You know he never keeps enough nutrition for himself. I didn't have any pills left, but I did have the apple."

My throat closes up. "You fed him the apple? In his sleep?"

She nods, once. But once is all it takes.

I rock forward, my mind racing. "What happened?"

"He choked a little, but once I talked him through it, he was able to get the apple down. I was so pleased I was able to do something for him. But when he fully woke up, he was livid.

"Work was hard for him after that. He'd never had any trouble resisting food. You can't be tempted by what you've never had, after all. But when he came home from work the next day, his clothes were drenched with sweat. Every minute was pure torture for him. All he could think about was taking that next bite. He lasted a week. When he felt like he couldn't bear the temptation any longer, he quit his job rather than break the law. Rather than follow in the footsteps of our mother."

I take a shaky breath. "He never took another bite?"

"Not a single one."

My heart feels heavy, as if the tears of my body have been collected to rain inside its chambers. Anyone else would've given in. But not Carr. He'd give up his livelihood before compromising his morals.

I remember now the time he left the apple orchards. He was offered another job the very next day, as a terraforming specialist to cultivate the barren areas of the planet. The weird part was: he never submitted an application. The circumstances of the new job were so bizarre, I never thought to ask why he quit his original job in the first place.

"Are we settled, then?" Astana asks. "If you swap the oranges for apples, then Carr is done. I doubt he'll last five minutes."

The room is suddenly too small. I jump to my feet and pace from one wall to the other. "I can't. He already thinks I'm trying to manipulate him. This switch will only prove I care more about the Trials than him."

"Not to put a damper on your romantic pursuits," she says, her voice as cool as the IV dripping into her body, "but we're talking about my brother's life."

"This isn't about me!" I spin on my heel and walk even faster. "Did you know Carr believes he's not worthy of love unless he's done something in exchange for it?"

"That's ridiculous—"

"He told me himself. He said you and your mother only love him because of what he can do for you." My voice drops. "I was trying to convince him otherwise. If I betray him, he'll never believe me."

She reaches for my hands. "Look at me, V."

My eyes slide into hers. So black. So piercing. Just like her brother's.

"Our first priority is saving Carr's life. If he's dead, then all your other concerns are irrelevant. Got it?"

I don't want to agree. There's a line inside me between right and wrong, and I know her suggestion crosses it. But when I think about losing Carr, everything inside me sags, and the line disappears like matter sucked into a black hole.

So, against my better judgment, against my sense of

morality, against a lifetime of lessons from my father, I nod.

"Promise me you won't let my brother die. Promise, V."

Carr may hate me for it, but at least he'll be alive. That's what's important. Right?

"I promise."

CHAPTER NINETEEN

*P*iles of apples line four sides of the room, stacked floor to ceiling, stretching wall to wall. A large square in the middle has been left empty, as well as a path running from the door to the space. But the sheer amount of fruit is deceiving. It tricks my mind into believing all I see is apple. Red, shiny apple. Crunch-in-your-mouth sweet. Exploding-on-your-tongue tart.

"Apple pie, apple turnover, apple fritter, apple ice cream, baked apples, stewed apples…" Denver says.

"The possibilities are endless." I blink, and the fruits seem to multiply. Blink again, and my senses swim in a churning river of red. "Apple curry, apple salad, apple soup, apple chutney, applesauce."

"And we'll be eating them all in the next few days."

My taste buds rejoice. Waste not. The First Maxim of our colony. The fruit has been sprayed with an irresistible fragrance, but it's perfectly safe to eat. As soon as the challenge is over, every bit of apple that's salvageable, from the juices to the bruised flesh, will be collected, sanitized, and recycled.

Denver and I stand in front of the one-way window, along with several Aegis who have gathered to watch the show. Even Blanca and Hanoi are present, halfway down the corridor. Blanca's whispering to her assistant, a mile a minute, while Hanoi taps furiously on her handheld. Hanoi's warm complexion glows, and she seems steadier on her feet. The meals must be doing their job.

Still, I frown. Why are they here? I'm glad to see Hanoi looking so much better, but shouldn't Blanca be working on a solution for her patients? How is she going to save my best friend's life if she's wasting time attending my challenges?

"I heard there was a last-minute switch," Denver says, interrupting my thoughts. "The bots in the orange orchards were about to pick the fruit when they were told the royal order no longer needed to be fulfilled."

"Who told you that?"

"Oh, you know. I hear things here and there." He smiles glibly. No bit of gossip is safe from Denver. I don't know if he has a secret underground network or if he just has a lot of friends.

"We decided apples were more symbolic, since they're carved in the wall of the Royal Office." I hate lying. I don't think Denver would judge me, but now that I've decided to cheat, the less people who know, the better. "Since these trials are historic—the King's last organ transfer—we thought apples would be the better choice. Even if they're less enticing."

"I don't know." He looks back into the room. "They look pretty tempting to me."

I agree. My mouth waters, and I clasp my hands together to keep from reaching through the glass.

At that moment, the door opens and the bots stacking

the apples exit the room. A sweet, crisp scent drifts into the air, assaulting my nose, stirring an age-old hunger. For one wild moment, I want to leap on those apples. I yearn for the flesh on my tongue. I can feel the juice slide down my throat.

I wrestle a muzzle onto my hunger, but not everyone is as successful.

A nearby Aegis lets out a tortured howl and lunges through the entrance, grabbing an apple and shoving it into his mouth. He manages to snatch a second and a third before the bots converge on him, locking their metal arms around his torso and dragging him out.

"Please. Just one more." His hands claw the air, his eyes feral, as if he's lost all thought and reason. "Let me have one more."

The bots roll down the corridor, taking him with them. His screams continue to ring in my ears, leaving behind a physical mark of his hunger.

"That was weird," Denver says.

I shiver. "Did you feel it, too? That uncontrollable urge to gorge on the apples?"

"Yeah. I thought it was just me."

We look at each other, as if we can find the answer in the other's eyes, and then Master Somjing lurches toward us, his fingers hopscotching over his handheld. Denver excuses himself to join a group of our former classmates, who are buzzing over the scene they just witnessed. I can't help noticing that Blanca and Hanoi have drifted to the end of the corridor, as if to get as far as possible from the smell.

"That was a brand-new Aegis," Master Somjing says as soon as Denver is out of hearing. "His test scores show the least amount of control in his class, and the apples have been sprayed with an irresistible formula."

"Still, he shouldn't have reacted like *that*." I frown. "Is something wrong with the formula?"

"I don't think so. The fragrance reacts most violently with someone who's tasted the food recently. Enough to recall the flavor, but not so frequently as to sate the appetite. He's a new Aegis who's not acclimated to the taste of apple. That would explain his reaction." Master Somjing looks into the room and quickly averts his eyes, as if afraid of being infected. "Do you think the temptation will be too much for the candidates?"

My stomach churns. If all the boys fall the moment they enter the room, we won't have any scores to differentiate them. We won't gain any new information. And this challenge will be a failure.

"We have to test the fragrance," I say. "That's the only way to find out if the candidates have a fighting chance. A colonist has to go inside that room and remain for ten minutes."

Master Somjing's eyes open so wide I'm afraid his lenses will pop out. "Who, me?"

"You're the only colonist here," I say gently.

He slips the handheld into his pocket, even as his ears flush red. "I beg your pardon, Princess, but I've never had resistance training. I don't have any experience steeling my will against temptation."

"Your job requires you to fortify yourself on a daily basis." I put my hand on his arm. "Besides, I'll go with you. I'll talk you through the test."

The council member glances at my hand. I don't know when our roles changed. I'm not sure when he started talking to me, instead of lecturing. But over the days, we've somehow stepped into a relationship between equals. With honesty, respect. And mutual trust.

He nods, and then we walk into the room.

*T*he fragrance surrounds me as soon as I enter, and my taste buds spring alive. I'm bombarded by a hundred memories of eating apples, each one more sharp and poignant than the last. The flavor of nectar and honey explodes on my tongue, and the beast roars to life. I want that taste in my mouth. I need it now.

But then, the desire recedes. My body isn't hungry. I've had a full early-morning meal, and the many memories of the flavor take the edge off my craving. I don't need to eat because I know how an apple tastes. I know I'll be eating it soon enough in the Banquet Hall.

Not the case for Master Somjing. Sweat beads on his forehead, and he skips his eyes around the room, as if trying to land on each and every apple. He hasn't tasted the fruit since Earth, before he boarded the space shuttle that would bring him to Dion. With the ensuing decades, he's probably forgotten the taste. And yet, his body yearns for the flavor.

"Master Somjing, look at me."

He doesn't hear. His eyes continue their erratic jumps; his throat bobs convulsively. I dig my fingers into his shoulders. Underneath the coarse fabric of the council member's uniform, I feel his muscles spasm. "Master Somjing, listen to my voice," I say. "Look straight into my eyes. We are not here to eat. We are testing this challenge. Do you understand?"

He doesn't answer, but with great effort, he drags his eyes to my face. He's gulping air like a nearly drowned victim, but there, in the deepest part of his irises, I see a glimmer of his old steadiness.

"Talk to me," I say. "Tell me about the hologram pendant hanging from your neck." I touch the reflective black cube, so similar to the one in my living unit. "Who do you wear so closely to your heart? Who matters so much that you must keep their presence with you at all times?"

"My wife?" The words are a question, not a statement. As though he's not sure of the answer. As though he's not sure of his own name.

I've always known Master Somjing as a childless bachelor, without any family. But I've heard rumors of a woman long ago, someone he loved with his entire soul. I can't imagine the old councilman rapturous about anything, but maybe he loved so thoroughly and so deeply, his passion expired along with his lover's death.

"My wife," he says again, but this time, the words are a sigh, a settling into the one trance that can distract him from the apples. "She was the very first gen mod, you know."

"I didn't know." I align my eyes with his so he can't look anywhere else. Won't see the red temptation surrounding us. "Can you tell me how it happened?"

He nods, and the many lines in his face soften. "We'd woken up from the cryogenic chambers and discovered the pods had malfunctioned. The air was largely unbreathable, due to volcanic eruptions that threw massive amounts of carbon dioxide into the sky. The engineers were building the energy shield as quickly as they could, scavenging parts from the broken pods to build the generators, but in the meantime, people were starving. There just wasn't enough food to feed everyone.

"And then, Master Kendall approached us with a solution. The genetic modification was in the newest phase of development, and no one knew what the side effects would be. But there was no time to test, no time to perfect. Dozens of people were dying every day, and nobody wanted to step up. So my wife volunteered."

I hardly remember to breathe. Somehow, in the countless lessons about our colony's history, I never heard about his wife. Never knew about this first gen mod. Master Somjing's face has that distant look again, but he's lost in the past now, not the present.

"She was such a hero, Vela. So stoic, so gracious. After they saw her example, a few more people became Aegis. This small group single-handedly saved the entire colony. A few months later, the shield was finished, and more food could be produced. The scientists developed a new version of the gen mod to minimize the side effects. But it was too late for my wife and the others. The damage to their genes as a result of the modification was hefty—and permanent. She, and the rest of this first group of Aegis, passed within the year."

When he finishes, tears coat the inside of my throat. I, too, made the same choice. To sacrifice years of my life so that others may live. But I was given fifteen more years to live. Master Somjing's wife only had one.

"What was her name?" For some reason, I need to know. I, too, want to hold her memory close to my heart.

His eyes refocus, and he glances around the room. Apples, still there. Fragrance, still present. But his desire is now held in check. "Viola," he says.

At first, I think he's saying my name, and then it sinks in. Viola is his late wife's name.

"Your father named you after her. He was a great friend to us both. And indispensable to me since she's been gone."

My heart thuds, a percussive beat to accompany the rushing in my ears. The trend on Dion has been to name children after geographic locations back on Earth, a way to memorialize the place from which we came. I remember crowding around the maps of our mother planet when we were kids. My classmates would yell and point excitedly whenever they found their name. But I never found mine.

The King explained that Vela wasn't a place back on Earth. It's not a traditional Thai name, derived from my ancestors, either. I never understood why he chose it.

"How come he never told me?" I ask. "How come I've never heard about Viola and the other original Aegis until today?"

"That was my fault. In those early years, any reminder of her was a stab in my heart. As a favor, your father kept her name out of the history lessons. But enough time has passed..." He pinches the bridge of his nose. "She should be remembered."

"Yes. She should be remembered." That one sentence says it all.

Something in my pocket beeps, and we both jump.

"What was that?" he asks.

I pull the handheld out of my pocket and switch off the alarm. "Congratulations, Master Somjing. You've lasted ten minutes in this room."

CHAPTER TWENTY

*T*he candidates file down the corridor and line up in front of the glass wall. Their eyes widen at the stacks of apples, and a few of them turn their backs to the glass. Smart. No reason to look at the apples longer than necessary, especially when the challenge hasn't even begun. I tap their names into my handheld.

My stomach hasn't settled. Something seems off about the formula. I can't shake the image of the Aegis with the wild eyes, being carted off by the bots. But Master Somjing was able to last ten minutes in the room, so all I can do is hope that the candidates emerge similarly unscathed.

"Good luck, Fargo," I say.

"You can do it, Baton."

"I'm rooting for you, Stowe."

My words are an echo of the Endurance Challenge, when I dreamed up countless ways to wish Zelo well. This time, however, I spread out my encouragement among all the candidates.

Jupiter grabs my hand and licks it, the grin practically

splitting his face. To Zelo, I simply nod. I slipped him a note earlier with my instructions for this challenge. He spreads his palm across his chest, tapping three times.

The gesture makes me stumble. Maybe he only means to acknowledge my message, but it's also the royal salute. The one reserved for the ruler of our colony. I'm not ready for that show of respect yet. I don't know when—or if—I'll ever be ready for it.

And then, I reach the last candidate in line. Carr. My smile sticks, as petrified as the C-trunks in the memorial copse. I haven't seen him since we faced each other during the Incentive Challenge. Since we kissed. Since I decided to sabotage him.

I turn, but he reaches out and touches my elbow. He's not as suave as Jupiter. He could never be as reverent as Zelo or as charming as Denver. But one look into his deep black eyes, and I'm lost.

"May I speak to you, Vela?" he asks, his voice low and grave.

I tuck my chin into my chest. "The challenge is starting at any moment."

"Fifteen minutes, Master Somjing said. We have time."

I should say "no." The other candidates are watching. Master Somjing is down the hall. If I turn off the recorder one more time, I don't know what the council will think.

But these are my last moments with Carr before the Betrayal, as I've come to think of it. He'll know. If not now, then as soon as he enters the room and feels the overwhelming temptation. The only food he's ever tasted is an apple. This challenge revolves around apples. The coincidence is too big.

We step into the alcove at the end of the corridor, the one with floor-to-ceiling windows. The light from the sunlamps falls across Carr's cheekbones, and his eyes appear even darker against the lit-up skin.

"You didn't wish me good luck." He glances at the cameras mounted on the ceiling and then at the blinking light at my collar. "You wished all the other candidates luck."

There's nothing I can do about the visual, but council be damned, I reach up and turn off the loop. He eases closer, even though there's no one around to hear us.

"I can't wish you luck because I don't want you to win," I whisper.

"I know." He touches me with a single finger. My nose, my cheek, my lower lip. "I've always appreciated your honesty. You don't play games. You say what you feel, and you do what you say. I like that."

I shiver, my body vibrating with uncertainty and his touch, but I don't grab his hand. Don't tell him to stop. "Does this mean you're not mad?"

"You've never lied to me, so I shouldn't have doubted you. I'm sorry." He takes my hand. "But my feelings for you are so big, so unexpected, I don't know how to trust them. That's why I jumped to the worst conclusion."

My palms break out in sweat, and I pull my hand away. If he only knew. He shouldn't trust me. I'm much worse than a manipulator now. I'm a traitor.

His finger drifts under my chin. "You might not be able to say the words. But would you kiss me for luck?"

Would I?! My pulse skitters away, and I'm not sure I'll ever catch it again. But a line of candidates stands, not twenty feet from us, and I can't forget my official capacity, no matter how much my body yearns.

"You know I can't. Not in front of the others." Have I ever regretted any other decision so much? Have I ever been so tempted to grab his hand and run far, far from the colony? Away from the Fittest Trials. Away from this task looming before me.

"After the challenge, then?" he asks, his eyes as dark as night. "A congratulation or a consolation prize. Or maybe just because you want to."

"If you still want me," I whisper.

"I will."

I'm not so sure. I wouldn't place any bets on him talking to me, much less kissing me. But maybe I'm wrong. Maybe he won't discover what I've done. The switch is small, from one innocent fruit to another. Even with my concerns about the formula, what could possibly go wrong?

A lot, apparently.

Half the candidates drop to their knees as soon as they enter the room. They cram apples into their mouths, much like the Aegis that had to be dragged away. Except they aren't used to eating. So instead of chewing and swallowing, they choke and spray stuff and gag.

The neat stacks collapse, and apples roll everywhere, smashing into the floor and slicking the plastic-covered tile with their juice. The bots part through the chaos, wrap their metal arms around the disqualified boys, and carry them out.

Only two minutes have passed.

I dig my nails into my palms. Groups of Aegis clump in front of the window, straining to see even as they cover their mouths. I feel like I'm watching my mother burn in the incinerator. There's nothing worse than seeing someone you love turn into charred, crinkly ash, but I would not—could not—look away.

I scan the room, trying to make sense of the confusion. Zelo is in the center, exactly where I told him to go. A few apples bounce around his feet, but he's not moving so he doesn't trample them. Doesn't splatter himself with their flesh.

He closes his eyes, like I instructed, and cups his hands over his ears, blocking his senses. His lips move. If he's following my orders, then he's chanting a series of prayers to himself.

A few of the other candidates follow suit. They must've figured out the only way to resist is to find a way out of the room—if not physically then mentally. One of them is Jupiter. Before I can take note of the others, I find Carr.

No wonder I didn't see him earlier. He's curled into a fetal position on the floor, his head tucked into his knees. He's blocking his senses, too, but not in the best way. He's too close to the apples, his skin has too much contact with the floor—and the juices flung on it.

His hands wrap around his knees, and the white of his knuckles contrasts starkly against the red apples. The pulse at his temple throbs, and his jaw is clenched so tightly that the skin stretches taut over his bones. He is the picture of suffering.

My knees turn to liquid, and I clutch the window frame.

"What is Carr doing?" a voice says at my shoulder. I've only heard her speak once, but I'd recognize the bell-like tone anywhere. Hanoi. "Why doesn't he take a bite?"

I turn and practically fall into the arms of my sister's assistant. "Why didn't we think of this?" I moan. "He's not a quitter. Why didn't we think he might refuse to give in?"

"He doesn't even have to take a bite," Blanca muses, a foot away from us. "He can just walk out of the room and disqualify himself."

Obviously, she doesn't know Carr very well. Obviously, neither do I. Obviously, neither does Astana.

"I need to talk to him." The words pour out of me. "Let him know that it's okay to give in. Okay to lose this challenge. Oh Zeus, why doesn't he just give in?"

"No microphones," Blanca says as Hanoi pats my back soothingly. I realize, then, that my sister was mistaken. She does need her assistant. Hanoi is literally the hand that Blanca doesn't know how to extend. "You and Master Somjing set the rules, remember? No communication during the challenge. The candidates have to find the strength within themselves."

Carr's face turns bright red, and the pulse at his temple looks like it might explode. More candidates fall. Six minutes pass. Still, Carr remains.

"Has he passed out?" I hide my eyes in Hanoi's shoulder.

"No," she murmurs in my ear. "See his ankle? It's moving."

I have to look. If I've put him in there, the least I can do is look.

Hanoi's right. His ankle moves. Not a twitch or a tremor, but in slow, deliberate circles. This small action somehow pushes me over the edge. He's inside that shell, conscious and suffering. Because of me.

"I'm sorry," I moan, even though he can't hear me. "I'm so sorry."

Hanoi is talking to me. She's saying how no one looks good now, their faces are lined with fatigue, their muscles twitch from being held so still, but I can't really listen because I'm so miserable.

"I'm sorry," I continue mumbling. "I don't know what got into me. I would change my decision if I could—"

"Vela, *look!*"

The words slam into me like a rock. Carr's limbs unfurl,

and then he's shaking. Teeth clacking, arms jerking, knees knocking. Uncontrolled muscle spasms rack his entire body.

"He's having a seizure." I stumble out of Hanoi's embrace and scream into my collar. "Bots! Get Carr Silver out of there now! Take him straight to medical. This is an emergency! I repeat, this is an emergency!"

Four bots zoom inside, whirring so loudly that Zelo and the other candidates' eyes pop open. The bots pick up Carr by each shaking limb. Within seconds of my command, they have him out of the room and rolling toward the medical center.

I sprint after the convoy of bots, begging the stars it's not a moment too late.

CHAPTER TWENTY-ONE

*T*he next few hours pass like a swarm of bees—chaotic and fast, with one minute blending into the next. But once in a while, a moment lifts out of the fray and descends like an individual sting.

I bury my face in my hands, nearly hyperventilating. A hand presses on my shoulder. I jerk up. Blanca. My sister and her assistant have followed me to the medical wait lounge, and Hanoi urges her forward, encouraging her to speak to me.

Vaguely, I remember thinking that Hanoi was the hand that my sister wanted to—but couldn't—extend. What? My sister, as a sympathetic supporter? What would possess me to believe that? I rest my head on my knees again.

"I'm sorry," Blanca whispers finally, "but I don't know how to do this." And then she is gone, her assistant giving me a squeeze and following her.

*T*he next time I raise my head, Zelo is sitting on the edge of a C-trunk. "I was passing by," he says. "And I saw you in here."

"Oh, Zelo." My voice is as dull as a jelly knife. "Did you win?"

"Yeah." He slouches into the curve of the branch, not meeting my eyes. As if he feels guilty that he's healthy and well, while Carr's in a medical bed somewhere. "You really like him, don't you?"

"Yes. I really do." The admission rips and tears on its way out of my throat. Because what good does it do to confess now?

I was trying to save him from death, but that's not a good enough excuse. He might suffer permanent physical damage. Or maybe, he'll never speak to me again. Either way, I'm slayed.

"*S*omeone tampered with the formula, Princess." Master Somjing maneuvers first one mechanical brace and then the other so he can sit next to me. "I just received word from the lab. The concentration of the fragrance was double what it was supposed to be."

I massage my temples. Tampered? I knew the formula was off, but I never suspected foul play. "But why?"

"Why do you think?" He shoves a stick down the side of his brace and scratches. "Half the candidates disqualified the instant the challenge began. Your front-runner injured and in the medical facility. If someone wanted to disrupt the Trials and make you look bad, I'd say they succeeded. Wouldn't you?"

I sleep, but I don't. Tree-chairs forgotten, stretched on the concrete floor, my body mimicking the position of Carr's body right before the seizure. Torso curled, fists clenched, even my ankle slowly, but deliberately rotates.

Hands pull a blanket around me. I creak my eyes open. The sky has turned black, and the mother-daughter moons shine through the window at my father's back.

He used to tuck me in like this every night. For years after my mother passed, the King was the last person I saw before I went to sleep. In his way, I think he was trying to reassure me. *You may have lost your mother, but I'm not going anywhere.*

"Rest, my eye-apple," his shadowy figure says. "You'll need it in the days to come. This is only the beginning."

The beginning? What does he mean? We have only one challenge remaining. Shouldn't he be telling me the task is almost over?

His words are so strange, and I want to ask him to explain. But sleep is too strong, and it tugs me under. Or maybe I'm not awake at all. Maybe I never opened my eyes, never saw my father standing there, and this is only a dream.

Or a nightmare. Like the serpent who visits me in the night, its body wrapped around the tree trunk, choking the life out of me and everyone I love.

*M*y eyes feel gritty in the morning, and my body aches in those places you feel only after a night on the floor. A blanket is wrapped around my mid-section, and a pillow is squashed between my knees.

Not a dream, then. My father was here last night, bringing me the blanket and pillow. What's more, a meal cart sits in the corner of the room, with a pitcher of freshly squeezed orange juice and plates of thickly sliced honey toast topped with whipped cream.

The scent of fried dough and powdered sugar tickles my nose. The King's favorite snack. The royal cooks prepare honey toast for him once a week, and it is just like him to order a cart for me, so I won't have to leave the medical facility to go to the Banquet Hall.

I pick up a fork and begin to eat. Normally, the cubes of bread, at once chewy and crisp, combined with the sweet taste of honey, set off an explosion in my mouth. Today, I barely taste the flavor.

If my father's appearance wasn't a dream, then the rest of the visits weren't, either. The conversations with Blanca and Zelo. Master Somjing telling me someone tampered with the formula.

An entire cube of bread slides down my throat. Who would want to discredit the Fittest Trials? Or does someone have a personal vendetta against me? Could the culprit be my sister? Or one of the Fittest family members?

No. I refuse to believe it. Blanca and I haven't been close for years, and the families are annoyed at me. All true. But my bonds with each of them go far deeper than these recent disagreements.

I finish eating and step into the Transfer Room next door to convert my calories into pills. When I emerge, a familiar figure strides down the corridor, the gold tassels on his shoulders gleaming under the fluorescent lights.

"Dad! I'm here!" I rush after him and then stop short. A bot is leading him toward the patients' rooms, instead of toward the wait lounge. Toward *me*. "Are you coming or going?"

My father ruffles my hair. "I wouldn't leave without finding you, my eye-apple. I was merely checking on Blanca's patients and, of course, young Carr."

"You know Carr?" We continue walking down the corridor. Bots wheel meal carts identical to mine to each of the recovery rooms. Blanca's patients must be eating the same thing as me for their daily ration.

"I've been keeping tabs on all your candidates. But you could say I have a special interest in Carr."

I frown. Not good. I want Carr mediocre and nondescript. Indistinguishable from the other boys, so when he loses, no one will think to question why. "Why?"

"He was the top candidate before the last challenge, and he's my daughter's best friend's brother. But if those reasons aren't good enough... I suppose I care because he once sold me a worm."

I raise my eyebrows. "Huh?"

The King pauses in front of an open door. Inside, a little girl squeals as she digs into her honey toast. "Feed you! Feed you!"

She's the same pig-tailed girl who leaped off a stretcher into my arms. The one who was doing so much better after the daily rations began. Brooklyn.

In spite of the anxiety bandaging my heart into place, the organ manages a single leap. At least one person is happy today. My father and I exchange a smile and continue walking.

"I met Carr ten years ago, when his mother worked in the royal kitchen," he says. "I was strolling around Protector's Pond, wearing my old straw hat. I guess Carr mistook me for a fisherman. I bought his worms because I thought he was enterprising. We became friends and strolled together nearly every night.

"He never knew he was friends with the King. A month later, his mom left the kitchen, and we lost touch. But I never forgot him."

His voice is too complex, too layered with emotion for a simple reminiscence. All of a sudden, I know.

Things always seemed to work out for Carr in his times of need. Almost as if there was someone in the background smoothing his path. Not his mother, after all. Someone like a guardian angel. Or maybe the King.

"That was you?" The breath rushes out of my mouth. "The time Carr lost his job at the apple orchards and got a new one the next day? When a cache of pills arrived to settle their debts right as the unit lord was about to evict them?"

My father nods.

The words jam in my chest. The people are right. He is a good King. Over the years, I've witnessed his generosity dozens, maybe hundreds of times. But I've never felt his kindness more keenly than I do at this moment, standing in a corridor, the patients savoring their breakfast all around us.

"It saddens me, as much as it does you, to learn that Carr is in the candidate pool." He shouldn't even be admitting this much. As the King, he must remain completely impartial to the selection process.

I'm glad he chose to bend the rules this once. "Thanks for telling me, Dad."

"King Adam?" A medic appears beside us, his jacket the same murky gray as the stone walls. He drops into a low bow, touching his forehead to the ground, and taps his chest three times. "I'm told you've given up your own meals so these patients can eat. I'd like to express my humble and unworthy gratitude, Your Highness."

I stare at my father. One more thing he hasn't told me. "You have?"

"As you know, I stopped transferring my nutrition a few years ago, because of my health, even though I still eat real food. A concession for which the council voted, despite my misgivings. But Mistress Barnett worried that the sudden switch to nutrition pills would be a shock to my system, so I assented. Thus, I am the only person in the colony besides the Fittest families who eats without having to make a nutrition transfer." He helps the medic to his feet. "If they must sacrifice, then so will I. Under Mistress Barnett's care, I've been easing off real food. She made me promise to revert to eating at the first signs of distress, but there's been no shock yet." He smiles. "I guess this old body is sturdier than any of us expected."

"Dad, that's amazing." My mind races. Surely, if the Fittest families knew about the King's sacrifice, they would follow his example. Surely, this will convince them to give up their own meals permanently. "You're an inspiration. A model for others to follow." I can hope, anyway.

The King waves off my words and addresses the medic. "You have news on Carr Silver?"

"Yes, sir. He is in stable condition and will make a full recovery." The medic shoots a glance at me. "However, he will need to be on bed rest for the next two days."

"Two days?" I blurt. "But the final challenge is tomorrow."

"I'm aware of the timing." The medic holds up his hands

as though to brace himself for attack. "Unfortunately, his recovery doesn't revolve around the Fittest Trials."

My neck sags, my stomach clenches, my heart leaps. I don't know what to feel. Emotions shoot inside me like a comet trapped inside a box. Joy that Carr will recover. Heartsick that my sabotage was even more successful than I planned. Pure, liquid relief that I did it. I saved him. He cannot possibly win the Fittest Trials now.

"He's cleared for visitors," the medic says. "Would you like to see him?"

I turn to my father, questioning him with my eyebrows.

"Go ahead, my eye-apple. I haven't spoken to Carr since our days by the pond." He moves his shoulders. On the King, even a shrug looks royal. "I probably shouldn't interact with him until the Fittest Trials are officially complete."

I nod. All the disparate emotions coalesce into my next words. "Okay," I say to the medic. "Take me to see Carr Silver."

CHAPTER TWENTY-TWO

My heart thumps so loudly as I walk down the corridor it could be a signal from Earth, the one for which our computers are constantly searching—and have yet to find. Does Carr know I'm coming? Is he mad? Will he even look at me?

There's no one to ask. The medic left me in the care of a bot and disappeared to his duties. The bot zips down the hall, lights blinking on its head, oblivious to my distress. It doesn't even pause as it passes the turn-off to Astana's room.

"Wait!" I dash down the hall toward my best friend. I stumbled to her room twice last night, but both times she was sleeping.

I didn't wake her to tell her about Carr. There was nothing she could've done, and, well…I'm a coward. One more item to add to my ever-growing list of faults.

When I screech into the room, the meal cart's waiting, steam rising from the honey toast. But no one is here to eat the food. "I don't get it," I say out loud. "Where is she?"

The bot whirrs up next to me. "Princess Blanca is conducting some tests on the patient named Astana Silver," it says in a sultry robotic tone, its eyes fluttering. Great. I've got a Flirtatious Bot.

"Tests? What kind of tests?"

"I'm not sure," the bot coos. "But when I find out, you'll be the first to know."

I roll my eyes. It will do no such thing. The programmers just added that line of dialogue for fun.

"Princess Blanca files a report with the council every two days, detailing her experiments and theories." The bot flips its nonexistent hair over its shoulder. "She's been varying the composition of the formula, to see if it'll lead to a better absorption rate. Getting desperate, if you ask me."

I blink at the last sentence. That's not a line the engineers would've programmed, and the bots can only regurgitate something they've heard or read. Does that mean there's a report somewhere with that characterization of Blanca? And if so, who wrote it?

I return to the corridor. The bot zooms in front of me, swaying its nonexistent hips before resuming its forward progress. Blanca must be approaching her deadline for making a recommendation. And from the bot's information, she doesn't seem to be any closer to a solution.

No matter what her findings, she has to advise the council to make all the patients Aegis. She has to. She might be cold, but even she wouldn't let all those people die. She wouldn't let her assistant die. Right?

With my sister, you can never tell.

The bot slows in front of a doorway, points, and then sashays away. Anxiety slams back into me, and my heart rate doubles. I take a large breath, which is a total waste, because when I round the corner, it gets knocked out, anyway.

Carr's on a medical bed, wearing a flimsy tunic. A few wires trail from his body to machines monitoring his vitals. His olive skin is a couple shades off, but his eyes are as black and focused as ever.

More importantly, he's smiling. At me.

"I was hoping you'd come visit." Even his eyes smile, as flirtatious as the bot but a whole lot sexier.

Relief flows through me. He's doesn't know. He's doesn't know. He's doesn't know. His smile loosens my neck, my shoulders. And, unfortunately, my tongue. "You look good."

He grins even wider, and I flush.

"I was talking about your health, not your attractiveness." Oh crap, crap, crap. "I mean, the way you look is good, too. If you like the lean, muscly type. Which I do. I mean, who doesn't?"

Dear Dion. Can the airlock open and suck me out now?

"Is that all?" he asks.

I nod mutely, since clearly, I can't be trusted to use any more words.

"Why don't you come here, then?" He scoots to the side of the mattress, rearranging the wires, and pats the space next to him.

I climb onto the mattress, and my shoulders brush against his chest. His very warm, very strong chest. Heat emanates from his skin and wraps around me.

"Vela?" His lips graze the shoulder of my caftan and then slide up the cotton seam until they touch the bare skin at my neck. I shiver, ridiculously glad I'm not wearing the loop.

"You still owe me a kiss." The lips travel up my neck.

"Are you sure you want to? I mean, are you well enough?"

"Why don't we find out?"

He closes the gap between us. Or maybe I do. Only an inch separated us—either of us could have swayed forward.

But then our lips touch, and that inch is the difference between night and day, Earth and Dion, inside the bubble and out.

I feel alive in a way I've never felt. There's a life force that starts deep inside me and spirals outward, so I don't need a bed in order to rest. Don't need the shield in order to breathe. Don't need food in order to live. Don't need anything except Carr.

We pull back, our grins as big as the ones painted on the Jolly Bots' faces.

"I'm sorry you can't compete in the challenge tomorrow," I say without thinking.

He stiffens. "Who says I'm not competing?"

Oh Dion. Not jolly. Make that intoxicated. So drunk off Carr I don't know what I'm saying. But it's too late to take the words back now. "The medic says you need two days of bed rest—"

"Forget the medic!"

He sits up, and I move to the bottom of the mattress, cheeks flaming.

Despite our embrace, his skin is waxen, and his breath comes in quick, shallow pants. The seizure might not have affected his ability to kiss, but he's definitely not in top form.

"You're in no shape to compete," I say. "Look at you. You can't even sit up without getting tired. How can you possibly hope to win?"

"I have to try. My sister's counting on me. Don't you see that?"

"No, she's not. She burst a bubble when she found out you were competing. And I don't blame her." I sweep my hand out, encompassing his bed, the wires, this whole awful situation. "Why didn't you take that bite? Why did you have to go and give yourself a seizure?" My voice shivers and breaks. I wrap my arms around myself, afraid the rest of me will follow.

"I'm not a quitter. And I didn't come this far to give up over a piece of bad luck." He picks up one of the wires and rolls it between his fingers. "I've had misfortune all my life, and it's never stopped me before. If it had been any other fruit, this wouldn't have happened. Grapes, oranges, peaches…"

He trails off, and my face turns into the freeze frame of a hologram. I try to unstick it, mold it into something more natural, but the more I try, the gummier it feels.

"What is it?"

"Nothing." Not good enough. I ransack my brain, searching for something, anything to say. But I come up with nothing. *Nothing*.

He studies my face, pixel by untruthful pixel. "You know how I said I've never heard you lie?" He drops the wire. "Well, something tells me you're lying now."

I swallow hard. I can't deny it. And yet, how can I tell him the truth? I knew switching the fruit was wrong the moment Astana suggested it, but I went along with her idea anyway.

Just like I shouted encouragement in Zelo's ear. Just like I picked a challenge at which Zelo would excel. My conduct since this task began has been one wrong after another.

If anything is sacred to us, it's the Fittest Trials. Dying to save the King—and thus our entire colony—is the most honorable sacrifice that a person can make.

None of us wanted the terraforming pods to malfunction. None of us asked to live inside a set of intersecting bubbles without enough land to feed us all. The Aegis system we've developed is a last resort, just like the tradition of selecting a Fittest. In order for our colony to thrive, we have to make hard choices. And we justify those choices by putting the

Fittest on a pedestal. By remembering, above all, what the Fittest is giving their life for.

And here I am, being dishonorable at every turn. By manipulating the outcome of the Trials, I've sullied the meaning of the Fittest. I've made a mockery of the sacrifices that the previous Fittest boys and girls have made for my father. For my colony.

I thought my actions were justified. I thought Carr's life was worth me turning into a liar and a cheat.

But now, looking at the boy across from me, the one who's so honorable he won't even succumb to a bite, I'm not so sure. Maybe some things aren't worth any price. Maybe there's a fate worse than death.

All I know is, I'm not proud of the girl I've become. And I know my father wouldn't be proud of me, either.

"There was a last-minute change." My words are slow and hesitant, like water that has to be coaxed from a pump. "The challenge was supposed to use oranges. They were swapped out for apples."

"Who made the switch?"

I take a deep breath. This is it. After I confess, he'll either hate me or forgive me. But at least he'll know the truth. "I did."

"Why?" He wrinkles his forehead. I know the instant the answer dawns on him, because the creases disappear. "Astana told you about that night, didn't she? When she fed me the apple while I was asleep."

"I didn't know you would get hurt," I whisper.

"Do you think that makes any difference? You cheated!" He shakes his head, back and forth and back and forth. Each motion slices through me. Because his words aren't a rejection. They're total and complete repudiation. "You're sullying what it means to be the Fittest. Taking what should be good and noble and turning it into something selfish and base."

"Carr…" I reach out, hoping to remind him of what we had a few minutes ago. Of the person I used to be before the Trials.

He jerks away, so hard one of the sensors pops out of his wrist. *Beep! Beep! Beep!* the machines yell at me. *Beep! Beep! Beep! Beep!*

"I was wrong about you." His eyes are cold, so cold they burn right through me. "You're not the girl I thought you were. Not the ruler I thought you could be."

His statements slam into me, leaving me gasping for breath. He's right. He's confirmed what the council's known all along.

I'm not fit to rule.

I have no words. Even if I did, they wouldn't matter. A team of medics rushes into the room to deal with the incessant beeping, and Carr pronounces his final verdict.

"Please leave."

CHAPTER TWENTY-THREE

"Some of the stones are lighter or heavier than the weight that's been assigned to that particular candidate," a bot reports to me above the roar of the waterfall. "Just as you suspected."

Aha! Gotcha, Mr. Saboteur.

I jam my hands on my hips and scan the spectators who have gathered to watch the final challenge. A group of boys play catch next to a trough of stones, and a little girl and her mother splash in the stream near the waterfall. Bubble Falls, the water's been dubbed, since the hillside is part of our colony's energy shield. A few Aegis lay out spreads to rival all picnics. Mountains of sandwiches, craters of chips, oceans of lemonade.

No one notices my perusal.

No one disturbs the stones in the trough.

No one acts like a potential saboteur.

"How's the quality of the stream?" I ask the bot.

Its digital eyeballs bounce, and the bot spins first to the left and then to the right. Must be a Hyper Bot. "Fine. No foreign substance has been detected in the water."

"And the chasm floor? Any disturbances there?"

"No." The bot pokes its mechanical arms into the ground and hops forward. "Other than the stones, everything looks to be in proper order."

"Good. Please make sure all the blocks conform to the assigned weight for each candidate before the challenge begins."

The bot hops backward and whirrs away. I continue patrolling the area, making sure nothing looks out of place. I may not be fit to rule a colony, but I still have a challenge to run. And if my saboteur is out there, trying to cause trouble, I'll be ready for him.

Or her, my mind whispers. But I don't like thinking that way. Because if it is a "her," there's one person who emerges as the primary suspect. And I'm not ready to entertain that possibility.

At least not yet.

An hour later, I focus on a single spot in the water, looking for the smallest ripple. Willing Carr to appear. *Come on, Carr. You can do it. Break through that surface.*

An instant later he does, limbs flailing and eyes bulging. The pressure in my lungs relaxes. I've been holding my breath as long as he has. He made it. He's safe. At least for the moment.

Water splashes throughout the stream, in big surges and small, as candidates claw their way out of the depths. They bring up stone blocks — rectangular, heavy, and proportional to the candidates' weight, no thanks to the saboteur — and deposit them on the shore before diving down for another. Again and again and again. Until one of them does so forty times.

"He's not looking good, is he?" Astana asks. This is the first challenge she's been well enough to attend, and she sits in a wheelchair next to my C-trunk.

"No, he doesn't." Worry ricochets around my insides. Carr's hanging onto the shore now, his forehead pressed against the mud as his chest heaves. "But he won't have to last much longer."

I skip my eyes from one pile to another, counting the number of rocks. Jupiter, 18. Zelo, 13. Carr, 4. The first boy to retrieve forty stones wins the challenge — and stops it. The remaining candidates will be ranked according to the number of blocks they retrieved.

Any other time, Carr would have led the pack. Today, two days after his seizure, every stroke is a victory. Every rock recovered, a miracle.

"He's so mad at me." My friend adjusts the portable stand on her wheelchair. "You should've heard him last night. I thought my skin was going to blister. On and on about my lack of character. If I didn't have my integrity, I didn't have anything. And if I couldn't see that, then he'd failed in teaching me." She blows out a breath. "I don't know which is worse. His disappointment…or the fact that he blames himself. As always."

"He's only two years older than us. Why does everything have to be his fault?" I can't decide whether to be confused or exasperated. Carr's hands dig into the mud, holding onto the stalks of plants as if they alone can keep him afloat. Yep. Exasperated it is.

"You have no idea what integrity means to him. His, as well as mine."

She's wrong. After all these years, I'm finally getting a clue.

We fall silent as Carr dives back down. I jump to my feet. I can't sit here any longer. I didn't tell Astana about the weight of the rocks being off, but I can't shake the feeling my saboteur's here, watching the challenge to see how it will play out.

"I'm going to walk," I say to Astana. "See who's here to cheer on our candidates." And see who's watching the stones a little too closely.

As I weave through the crowd, a few colonists press their hands to their chests. Essex and Genoa, two Aegis from my class, rush up to share their predictions with me. Jupiter, with his finely chiseled muscles, is their guess for the top contender. Meanwhile, Miss Sydney pulls the blue sash over her eyes and pretends to sleep when she notices me.

I want to tuck my limbs into a precisely shaped fish ball, sufficiently packed so that it doesn't fall apart. Between the Fittest families and the saboteur, I'm beginning to feel downright unpopular.

I'm beginning to feel like a ruler.

I walk the length of the bank and am about to turn back when Cairo Mead's brother, Cyprus, approaches me.

"Thanks for the concession, Princess." He must be around fifty years old, with serpent tattoos decorating both forearms. "The others might complain, but I much prefer choosing the menu than having an evening meal."

"Glad to hear it." I ignore the tattoos and give him my best smile, carefree and light, the kind that belongs to girls who never have to deal with serpents, real or imagined. "You know, those meals you're giving up are keeping my best friend alive. She's over there if you'd like to meet her." I point to where Astana sits, looking as pretty as the purple skies.

"There are a dozen others like her." I smile again, but the curve of my lips feels more like a stretch across my cheekbones. Here it comes: the pitch I've practiced ten times in front of the mirror. "The meals are your right and your reward. I recognize and value that. But it would mean so much if you relinquished them on a permanent basis. You could save Astana's life—and all the others', too."

He traces his shoe on the ground, turning up clumps of dirt and pebbles.

"The King's already given up his meals." The words tumble out. Too fast. Not the way I practiced. "He enjoys eating, but not at the expense of someone's life."

"I want to help your friend." His voice is as gritty as the rocks beneath his feet. "But it won't do any good unless the rest of the families agree. One or even two people's meals can't save them all."

"Will you talk to them? Try to get them to see our perspective?"

"I'll do my best."

"Thanks, Cyprus." I press his forearm and don't even mind that I'm touching the serpents. "One more thing. I know the Fittest families have been unhappy. Have any of the grumbles risen to the level of violence? Or, I don't know, sabotage?"

His eyes narrow, and I get the reason for the tattoos. The resemblance is uncanny. "Why? Are you having some trouble?"

"No, no trouble," I say quickly. "I want to be prepared, that's all."

"I haven't heard anything." He glances at the far side of the bank, where some of the Fittest families have gathered. I can't tell if he's imagining their culpability or protecting them. "But I'll keep an ear out."

I thank him once more and head back to my seat. Cyprus didn't agree to my proposal, and I didn't learn anything new, but I feel less jumpy. More like I might have an ally.

Carr surfaces when I reach Astana. He hoists his eighth rock onto the shore and falls back onto the long grasses that extend over the water, completely spent.

I check Jupiter's pile. He's stacked his rocks in groups of ten, so they're easy to count. Thirty-six. Just a little while longer, Carr. Hold on, and you'll be done soon.

"I can't believe he'll work himself to physical collapse when all I've ever done is disappoint him," Astana says, tears ringing her voice as her brother dives back down.

"He loves you. No matter what, he'll always love you. That's not how he feels about me." I force myself to laugh. "I don't think he'll ever speak to me again."

I want her to contradict me, to tell me her brother only needs time to come around. But she doesn't.

Her silence, more than anything else, makes me wilt. Astana knows him better than anyone. If there was any hope, she would tell me.

At that moment, Jupiter deposits his fortieth rock to the pile. And then, Carr's hand breaks through the surface—only to sink down again.

I leap off the tree trunk. "Did you see that?" I rush to the edge of the stream and squint. There, under the water's splashes, is a thrashing form.

Without another thought, I dive into the water. I can't see past the bubbles, but I propel myself forward as fast as I can, and when I hit a solid mass, I wrap my arms around him and yank up.

Nothing happens. He's too heavy, and I can't get any traction in the water. *No.* I've got Carr in my arms now, and I won't let him drown just because I don't have the strength.

Gritting my teeth, I wrap my arms more securely around his chest and scissor my feet as hard as I can. We move forward a few inches, but then begin to sink down in the water again.

My lungs burn. The air inside is becoming short; panic makes it even shorter. But I won't give up. Not yet. Not ever. I lock together my fingers, trying to get a better grip, when his body is jostled against me. Suddenly, York has a hold of his legs, and Jupiter latches onto Carr's upper body, easing my strain. Reinforcements. Thank you, Dionysus.

Together, we kick upward and break the surface. A few of the other candidates have reached us, and they help us drag him onto the shore. Carr sputters and chokes. A long, torturous moment later, he rolls onto his hands and knees and continues to cough, expelling a lungful of stream water.

After an entire minute, he sinks to the ground, and his cheek squishes in the mud. The medics on standby descend on him with a stretcher.

"Carr. Are you okay? Please say you're okay. Please."

He opens his eyes as the medics move his body onto the stretcher. "I always knew you would save me back."

My heart breaks. Splits cleanly in two like it's been whacked by a cleaver. This outcome was exactly what I wanted. There's no way Carr can win now.

So why do I feel like I've lost everything?

CHAPTER TWENTY-FOUR

"**J**upiter!" half the crowd screams the next day.

"Zelo!" the other half thunders back.

"JUPITER!" The first group shouts even louder.

"ZELO!" The second group will not be beaten.

Master Somjing and I stand on the metal platform at the top of Proctector's Courtyard. The entire colony has turned up to watch the Fittest announcement ceremony. People stand shoulder-to-shoulder on the lawn, and I can't see a single patch of green grass.

Horns blare incessantly, and colorful streamers shoot across the courtyard like volleyballs. Banners featuring Jupiter's and Zelo's faces wave in the air.

Everyone has their favorites, but no one knows who will win. One thing is clear: either Jupiter or Zelo will emerge as the Fittest after the ceremony. There's no other choice. Both boys had strong showings in all four challenges. Jupiter won the last task, but Zelo won the third. Jupiter finished second in the endurance challenge, but Zelo tied for first in the incentive one. CORA itself will have to compare the relative strengths of each boy and determine the winner.

I thought I'd feel differently right about now. Knees liquid with relief, heart pulsing with victory. I achieved all my goals—Carr's not the Fittest. And Zelo, the candidate I'd pushed from the beginning, is one of the two final contenders.

Instead, my stomach feels like it's plummeting off the side of Bubble Falls. One of these two boys is going to die, and I helped put him here. Out of all the people in this colony, I am the single most instrumental person in this boy's death.

This scenario is exactly what the council intended. They wanted to see how I would hold up under the weight of such responsibility. The answer? Not well.

"What do you think, Princess Vela? Are you ready for this announcement?" Master Somjing watches a guy climb onto his friend's shoulders, beat his naked chest, and let loose a primal yell. "Are they?"

I skim my eyes over the candidates in the front row. I can't bear to look at Zelo or Jupiter—much less Carr. Blanca stands with Hanoi and some of the Aegis around the refreshment table. The Aegis munch on thin wafers topped with avocado and fish roe. They're certainly not hungry— we finished the mid-afternoon meal an hour ago—but this ceremony is one more opportunity to boost their caloric intake. Even Hanoi nibbles delicately on a wafer. This snack must be part of her food allotment for the day.

At the side of the stage, hands flash as a pair of guards exchange pills, no doubt placing a bet, and Denver stands by himself on the edge of the row of candidates, Astana conspicuously missing.

"Master Somjing, would you mind reading the name CORA chooses?" My voice wavers. I don't bother to hide the tremor, the way I would've at the beginning of the Trials. "I don't trust my reaction."

"Certainly," he says, with a sympathy which makes me wonder if he understands more than I assumed.

It's raining outside, in the real planet, and the red drops hit the shield in colorful splatters high over our heads. Inside the bubble, the sun lamps cast everything in a warm glow. You might not even know the light wasn't natural if you didn't look up.

Does anyone else see the irony of this setting? The celebration of an entire courtyard, while somebody, somewhere, mourns the impending loss of their loved one. The cheers on the outside, and the tears on the inside. We are the exact opposite of the drops outside the bubble, but both the rain and the tears are dangerous. The former, because it is acidic. The latter, because it can just as surely burn a hole through your soul.

A bot enters the courtyard and rolls down an unfurled carpet, and the chanting dies. It is a Regal Bot, its procession slow and stately, one of its mechanical arms held at a right angle and waving from the wrist. It carries, in the opposite hand, a folded cloth.

CORA could've zapped the name of the Fittest directly to one of our handhelds, but Master Somjing wanted drama and ritual. He wanted to honor the Fittest boy from the first moment.

Back on Earth, the winner of any major contest was revealed in a white envelope made of a substance called paper. On Dion, we don't have paper products of any kind, so a scrap of fabric will have to do.

The bot reaches the platform. Master Somjing bends down to take the cloth, and a girl clutching Jupiter's arm moans. My heart pounds, so loud and hard that my entire body becomes one pulsing point.

Master Somjing unfolds the cloth and hesitates. I brace myself, not sure whether I want to hear Jupiter's or Zelo's name.

"Ladies and gentlemen, Aegis and colonists." His amplified voice booms over the courtyard. "I am honored to announce that CORA's choice for the Fittest is…Carr Silver!"

CHAPTER TWENTY-FIVE

*T*he Fittest is Carr Silver…Carr Silver…Carr Silver…

For one long, unending moment, there is silence. In my mind, the moment loops around to infinity and back, in between the space of each tightly pressured heartbeat.

Impossible. How could CORA have spit out Carr's name? How? He lost the last challenge by thirty-two blocks. There's no way his previous performances could've made up for that. No way. There has to be a mistake.

One of the candidates begins to clap. Another joins in, and then another. Denver adds his hands to the noise. And then Blanca and Hanoi and Master Somjing and two or three other council members and the royal guards ringing the crowd. Pretty soon, everyone is clapping and cheering.

Everyone, that is, except for me—and maybe Carr.

I find him in the front row, five people to the right of the flagpole. As much as I tried not to see him, I always knew where he stood. I expected triumph or maybe shock, his mouth smiling or his features frozen.

But I see neither. Instead, he stares at me, his eyes wide

and imploring. Begging me…for what? CORA already made its decision. What else does he want from me?

And then I remember. Of course. I have one more decision left. The veto.

Even now, Master Somjing's moving toward me, his fingers outstretched as the clapping dies. He clasps my upper arm and turns me to face the crowd.

"Before we crown Carr as the Fittest, is there anything you would like to say, Princess Vela?"

"I…" The words get stuck in my throat.

Just say it. *I choose to exercise my veto. Carr is not a worthy candidate. He is not fit to represent our colony.*

The ground tilts, and I stumble, trying to find my balance. Sweat beads on my forehead, and a drop slips past my brow and into my eye. I blink rapidly, but it still burns, as though I've been splashed with hot oil from a frying pan.

It would be so easy. This nightmare could be over in a matter of seconds. My one chance to turn things around. It's what I'd planned all along, should we come to this.

Well, that unthinkable moment is here. I can make the horror go away. All I have to do is say the words. Don't look at Carr.

Just. Say. It.

"I…"

Of their own volition, my eyes seek him out. The boy of my dreams glares at me, and even though everything about him is hard—hard lines, hard muscles, hard ridges—my eyes automatically find the soft parts of him. A square of cheek, underneath the slash of his cheekbones. The hollow below his Adam's apple. His lower lip, full and pink below the thin upper line. It's these soft parts that clog the sentence inside me. They are the underwater vegetation that stops my words from draining out.

"Do you know of any reason why Carr should not be selected as the Fittest?" Master Somjing prompts.

I look at Carr across fifty feet. *I am trying to save your life. Who will care about honor and integrity when your body is nothing but ashes released into space?*

His spine straightens, his jaw clenches. And I can hear his words as clearly as if he's spoken them. *I am trying to save my sister. This result is what we've both been working toward since the beginning.*

My knees slosh around like gelatin. Any moment now, they'll spill onto the platform and bring my whole body down. *No. You don't have to do this. Cyprus Mead will bring the Fittest families around. Blanca will come up with a solution. We can save you both.*

If he understands, he chooses not to listen. His eyes continue to glare. *This is your chance to redeem yourself. To show me and the world you can make the right decisions. To prove to the council you have what it takes to be the Successor.*

"Vela?" Master Somjing's voice is gentle, as if he understands the debate raging in my head, the one taking place in sharp, silent glances across the courtyard. "We need an answer. Do you choose to exercise your veto? Is Carr Silver worthy to represent this colony?"

Worthy? The word washes over me, chopping my joints, puréeing my muscles. I'm back in Protector's Pond and my breath comes in gasps, as if I only have a moment to fill my lungs before the water drags me under again.

Memories assault me. Carr in the royal kitchens, handing peach-colored pills to his mother for a pat on the head. Astana dozing under two heavy blankets, while her brother sleeps by her side in threadbare pajamas. Carr telling me he is loved only because of the things he does.

Can I really announce before the colony that this boy is

unfit? Integrity is everything to him. Without his character intact, he'll never be proud of who he is, ever again. He'll never believe he's worthy of love. Can I destroy, in a single moment, everything he's worked for in his nineteen years?

I open my mouth. The cool air hits the back of my throat, and my tonsils shiver. Every last inch of me cowers at the decision before me.

Because there's only one possible answer. Only one response I can give and still live with myself.

"Is Carr worthy?" My voice is raw and hoarse, as if it's been years instead of a few minutes since I last spoke. The crowd before me spins in slow, undulating waves. "Yes, Master Somjing. Carr Silver is worthy. In fact, he is the worthiest, most honorable boy I know."

Someone gasps. It might be one of the council members. Perhaps the sound comes from Blanca. I don't turn to find out who. I lock my gaze with Carr's. Instead of cold and hard, his eyes are now pools of caviar, dissolving in my mouth, melting my insides.

"Let me be perfectly clear, Princess Vela," Master Somjing says. "You are choosing not to exercise your power of veto?"

There's got to be some other way. To prove this is all a mistake. To save him still.

"That is correct."

"Then, Carr Silver..." Master Somjing pauses. His words ring out across the courtyard, powerful, authoritative. Legally binding. "I pronounce you the boy fit to die for the King!"

A piece of my heart detaches from the whole, burning itself out of existence the way the incinerator obliterated my mother's dead body. But I don't regret my decision. I can't.

It is the right thing to do.

*T*he next few minutes pass in a blur. Carr disappears from my vision as the crowd swarms him. Rainbow confetti blasts out of the air nozzles hidden in the four corners of the courtyard, and the King's anthem pipes through the loudspeakers. An instant later, Carr pops up again, hoisted onto the shoulders of his fellow candidates, so high he is framed against the red raindrops falling on our energy shield.

I suppose they mean to put him on a hero's pedestal. But all I can think, when I see him up there, is of a lonely strip of plantain jerky, left out to dry.

My shoulders tense into thick, hard knots. *This isn't a celebration*, I want to shout. *The only thing Carr's "won" is a death sentence.*

But the people are well past speeches. They drop Carr to the ground and surge toward the libations that have magically appeared on long white tables. Champagne in glass flutes for the Aegis, hydrangea-blue pills for the others.

I sweep my eyes across the crowd, looking for Carr. In the space of a second, he's disappeared again.

Zelo lopes up the steps to the platform. As he approaches, he spreads his long-fingered hand across his chest, both a salute and a resignation.

"I'm sorry," I say and then cringe. Sorry for what? Sorry CORA didn't pick him? Sorry he's not going to die? "I thought you would win. Either you or Jupiter. But if there's been a mistake, I'll find it. I can promise you that."

"That's the way life goes. I suppose I'll have to find some other way to fulfill God's will." His voice is a mixture of sorrow, loneliness—and relief? Can that be?

He turns to leave.

"Zelo, wait. Are you happy you didn't win?"

"Of course I'm not *happy*. This was my choice, my destiny." His eyes flash, and something I can't read, something I don't understand passes through them. "But in the end, nobody wants to die, Princess. Not even me."

He takes the steps two at a time and almost runs across the courtyard, tracing the Regal Bot's path on the red carpet.

The acid begins at the bottom of my chest and burns its way up, like it does after a particularly excessive meal. Zelo was the perfect candidate in so many ways. Except one: CORA didn't choose him.

I resume my search for Carr. Before I can find him, Master Somjing shuffles to my side.

"I'm intrigued. You may have made a noble decision. Quite possibly, you may have sacrificed someone about whom you care deeply. But I'm not sure."

He's still holding the cloth from the Regal bot, the one with Carr's name on it. He tries to hand the cloth to me—for what? as a souvenir?—but I shake my head.

"You see, there are too many gaps in your recorded conversations with Candidate Carr," he continues. "Too many places where the data stream stops for the council to understand the exact nature of your relationship with him."

So, I'm still being evaluated. There's probably a team of kinesiologists watching my feed this very instant, taking note of my every movement. Forming a hypothesis of my feelings, complete with margins of error.

My hands close around the thin wire around my neck. Flipping my collar up, I slide the loop over my neck and hand it to the council member. "Here. I won't be needing this anymore."

But he doesn't take the loop, just as I refused the cloth. "You're not finished."

"The task is done. The Fittest has been selected. What else is there for me to do?"

"Acclimate Carr to life in the shuttle. There are two more months until the transplant takes place. As the day approaches, the Fittest sometimes has a change of heart. It's your job to make sure that doesn't happen."

Relief rushes through me. Two more months that I can continue to earn daily rations for Blanca's patients. Two more months to uncover CORA's mistake. Two more months to save Carr.

"A word of advice." The lines in his face are deep and unfixable, like a chocolate cake that's been baked in a too-hot oven. He may be my friend now, but he is still head of the council. "Keep the recorder on when you interact with the Fittest. We can't evaluate your actions unless we know what they are. We've been lenient with you up to this point. But if you don't keep your end of the bargain, then neither will we."

My heart lodges in my throat. "Are you saying…?"

"Yes, Princess. If you don't leave the loop on, then we will no longer give food to Blanca's patients."

Straight to the point. As clear as the planet air on a cloudless day. This is how Master Somjing and I communicate best. No fancy words, no blustery threats. Just plain and simple cause and effect.

I slip the loop back on. "When will the council be done with its assessment?"

"When we're sure we have the right Successor."

The right Successor. Would the right Successor let her best friend's brother die for the King? Or would she lie, cheat, and steal to save the ones she loves?

Maybe neither. Maybe there's a way for me to save Carr—and maintain my integrity. Because somehow, some way, something went wrong in CORA's calculation. Carr couldn't have won that competition, not with those scores. I know this to the very core of my being.

And I won't rest until everyone else knows the truth, too.

CHAPTER TWENTY-SIX

"What do you mean, the files are wiped?" My voice is so loud the analysts closest to me stop what they're doing. At a look from their boss, they return to tapping on their holo-desks, launching see-through images and diagrams into the air.

"Exactly what I said, Princess," Captain Perth says. He's not really a captain, of course. The space shuttles are permanently fixed on land; they're not going anywhere. But he's in charge of CORA, which is located on board the ship, so the name stuck. "When an analysis is complete, we copy the inputs and outputs in triplicate. And then, once a week, we transfer everything to a secure off-line storage. Unfortunately, the Fittest files disappeared before we could run our weekly backup."

"And there's nothing you can do to get them back?"

He shakes his head. Wall-to-wall panels of electronics blink behind him, and so many holograms crowd the air, they overlap. I feel like I'm standing inside the heart of a computer. "We can't run the algorithms again because the inputs are gone, as if they never existed."

Gone. Disappeared like the steam that rises from the craggy rock of the outside planet. It sure puts a damper on my plan to double-check CORA's analysis. But what if that was the point? What if somebody deleted the data so no one could examine it?

The hair at the back of my neck stands up. Because the result might not be a simple mistake anymore. It might not be a wrong variable or a mistyped data point. It might be something—or someone—a lot more malicious.

My saboteur.

"Can we recreate the inputs?" I force my voice sun-lamp-bright, as if that alone can combat my creeping sense of unease. "Replay all the recordings. Collect the silver discs with the metrics from the candidates. The raw data is there. We only have to reassemble it."

"We could." He taps a disc, similar to the ones Carr and the other candidates wore, on a glass desk. "But that's a lot of extra work. Why is this data so important? The Trial is over. The Fittest has been named." His tone is stiff and condescending, as if I'm a little girl who wants to play when the adults are working.

He looks nothing like Master Somjing. He's about thirty years younger, for one, and while Master Somjing is slender and bent, Captain Perth has one of those oversize frames with shoulders wider than a doorway.

But at that moment, he reminds me exactly of the head of our council at the beginning of this task.

I want to shrink into myself. Captain Perth would never belittle Blanca this way. But she's in the control room on a daily basis, running the King's scenarios and researching her own wild thought experiments. They know and respect her here.

Me? I'm just the Princess who prances around the colony, picking Venus flytraps and shoving them in her father's face.

"A lot of people were surprised by the result, and now the data's missing." I look him straight in the eye, my voice stronger than I feel. "Someone's been sabotaging the Trials. We need to make sure he hasn't been manipulating the data, too."

Captain Perth taps the silver disc on the desk some more. *Tap, tap, tap.* And then he nods.

The pressure crawls off my chest. "How did the files get wiped?"

"Either our firewalls were breached"—his tone makes clear how unlikely this scenario is—"or someone with access tampered with the data."

"Who has access?"

He exhales, and his breath stirs the stifling, recycled air. "The control room employees, which we can rule out. They've all been vetted through extensive investigations. That leaves the council members. And the royal family."

My eyes widen. "Why would any of us mess with the data?"

"Why would somebody want Carr Silver to be the Fittest?"

Good question. Who would want Carr dead? His parents? As his legal family, they would receive the same benefits as Astana. And they may not care enough to mourn his death.

Blanca, a voice inside me whispers. *To hurt me so much I drop out of the race for Successor.*

The hairs on my arm match the ones on my neck. "I don't know who wants Carr dead," I say. "But I'm going to find out. No matter who he—or she—is."

*I*round a path and come face-to-face with a bee. Sweat breaks out all over my body. My throat feels sticky, like it might be gummed up with honey from the combs. After trying to save everyone else, my life is going to end like my mother's—by the sting of a bee.

Except this one's behind the mesh screen of a cage. And I'm not actually allergic to the insect the way my mom was.

Still, I take a deliberate step back.

The Bee Park, located behind the medical facility, is one of the few places in our colony where there's space for space's sake. Part honey farm, part garden, and part escape, it boasts twisting pathways, shady trees, and flower beds. And, of course, bee hives. Hundreds and hundreds of bee hives.

Closing my eyes, I breathe in the rioting scents of azaleas, roses, and hydrangeas. The low, incessant buzzing hums in my ears. I'm acting ridiculous. It's just a bee. It can't hurt me.

I force myself to turn down a path in search of Astana, passing honeycombs in stackable boxes and cross-pollinators flying freely in cages. The colony founders probably thought the bees would make good pets. The medical patients seem to enjoy watching them buzz back and forth, anyway.

But I wish we had real pets, like the soft, furry animals I've seen in the data feeds. However, the scarcity of food means we can't waste any of our nutrition on non-humans. The only exceptions are creatures that can aid us with farming or terraforming: insects and moles, fish and plankton.

Five turns and three cages later, I finally spot Astana, like the bot said I would.

Her wheelchair's been pulled onto a grassy knoll, and Denver holds a cage in front of her. Carr stands behind the chair, his hands wrapped around the handles.

"Get that thing away from me." My friend's shrill voice pierces through the insect drone. She's not crying, but old tears track down her cheeks like the veins on a pregnant woman's legs.

Denver strokes his finger along the cage, as though caressing the insects. "The bees are supposed to be therapeutic."

"I told you she wasn't going to be comforted," Carr says. A few seconds later, he looks up and sees me. "Vela." His teeth clamp down, as though my name is an admission ripped from his mouth.

"You!" Astana lunges from her chair, the intravenous tube ripping from her wrist. "You promised! You promised you wouldn't let Carr be the Fittest. How could you do this to me? To us?" Her voice pitches, so hysterical it knocks us both over. Or maybe that's just her body. We fall to the ground, and my breath flattens out of my lungs. The purple sky wavers above me, and pain roars against my cheeks.

"This is your fault. My brother's dead because of you. Dead."

I feel my cheeks and come away with blood. She scratched me. My best friend, who wouldn't swat a fly, just raked her nails across my face.

The talons rear up, ready to take another swipe, when they're caught in midair. A moment later, the weight disappears off my chest.

"I'm not dead." Carr scoops up his sister and carries her to the wheelchair, a safe ten feet away. "I'm right here next to you."

"You will be. She could've saved you. And she didn't."

"I didn't want her to." He unfolds first one footrest and then the other, tucking her feet onto them. "I want to be the

Fittest. I want to die to save the King. To save you."

I sit up. The scratches sting, but they're nothing compared to the welts swelling up my heart. "I haven't given up." I taste blood along with my oath. "The transplant's not for another two months. A lot can happen in that time."

She buries her face in her hands. "Like what?"

"Like, maybe Carr isn't supposed to be the Fittest. Maybe there was a mistake in CORA's calculation. Maybe somebody messed with the data." I tell them about the tampered challenges, the wiped files. "If there's sabotage, I'll find it. You'll see."

Astana peeks over her nails, interest taking the edge off her despair, but Denver's hands tighten on the bee cage. "I don't think you should give her false hope." My cousin's voice shakes, as if worry over Astana has used up all his warmth. "It'll only make things worse."

"The Trials are finished," Carr adds. "You have to let me go."

"I can't." I crawl to Astana's wheelchair, even though it puts me within range of her nails. She might be mad, but she's my only ally in this whole mess. "This hurts me, too." My voice breaks along with my heart. "Don't you see? Making that decision destroyed me, but I couldn't dishonor Carr by announcing to the entire colony that he was unfit."

"At least he'd still be alive."

"Not on his terms."

Her head snaps up. "Yeah? You want to hear my terms?"

She jumps out of the chair and shuffles over to a free-standing bee cage. The three of us freeze, like candidates an instant before the starting horn.

"I never asked you to give up so much for me," she says to her brother, the bees buzzing like royal guards at her back. She shifts her eyes to me. "And I never expected you to make a promise you couldn't keep. If you won't save my brother, I'll do it myself."

She turns, and time slows as if we're approaching a black hole. An eternity passes as her hand reaches...up...up...up toward the door of the cage. I have another year to think: Bees. My mother. She's taking away his reason to be the Fittest.

She's taking away his reason to be the Fittest.

Time speeds up again, and she's moving fast. Too fast. Hand grasping the handle, latch twisting, door opening.

"Denver!" I scream. "The bees! She's trying to kill herself with the bees!"

He leaps and knocks her hand away, slamming the door closed before a single bee can escape.

I drop to my knees, and sobbing overtakes me. The kind of sobbing you hear from the universe when a star is cleaved out of existence. But when I lift my eyes and meet Carr's, I realize I'm not the one crying, after all.

The keening comes from Astana. Her knees are pulled to her chest, and she rocks on the ground as though she will never stop.

Denver presses his forehead against hers and whispers. Yet, I hear the words so clearly they might as well be branded in my heart.

"Don't you ever leave me," he says. "I will never get over missing you. Do you understand? The most important part of me dies with you."

CHAPTER TWENTY-SEVEN

"This is the residential floor." I lead Carr down the narrow, steel-plated hallway. The ceiling starts twelve inches above his head, and every twenty feet, an oval hatch is cut into the wall, with a wheel in the center of each door. "My father, Blanca, and I each have a unit near the center capsule, and the rest of the Aegis sleep in one of the side corridors. During the space journey, these cells were used to store raw materials from Earth. One cell for each material…"

I keep up the constant monologue. Ever since we left Denver and Astana in the Bee Park, we haven't exchanged a single personal word. In fact, we haven't really spoken, not about anything that matters, since he asked me to leave his recovery room.

Me, because my emotions are all used up. Carr's been selected as the Fittest. My best friend's no longer speaking to me. She's finally guaranteed to receive food—although not in a way I'm willing to accept.

I don't have any real words left. Even for Carr. Especially for Carr.

Him? I'd guess it has something to do with the recorder around my neck. When I glance over my shoulder, he's not looking at me but at the blinking amber light at my collar.

I wish I could turn off the loop, give us a chance for private conversation. But I can't. The daily food rations of a dozen patients are at stake.

Clearly, Carr no longer hates me. Ever since I chose not to exercise the veto, his face has been softer when he looks at me. His body less rigid. But I don't know what that means. I don't know if he's forgiven me or is merely tolerating me. Are we headed back to where we were? Or is polite civility the best for which I can hope?

If it's the second, I think I'd rather not know.

"Stop here." I spin the wheel on a door, and it swings open. "This will be your living unit. This cell was used to store frozen embryos, so there shouldn't be any lingering smell."

Carr steps into the cell, and I follow him. The room inside is more spacious than you'd expect, with the same built-in furniture as the colonists' living units.

He fiddles with a latch and out pops a sink. Another latch, and out comes the bed. It's like the hologram cubes: you never know what you're going to get.

I tap the black cube embedded in the wall, and immediately we're surrounded by holographic water. Not the plain, clear water you find inside the bubble, but rings of iridescent color as brilliant as jewels—sapphire, emerald, topaz, garnet. The kind of waters you only find in the real planet. The kind Carr used to encounter in his job as a terraforming specialist.

"You can upload the cube with any holo-vid you want." I look at the fake water swirling around my feet. Instead of the stunning blue, somehow all I see are the deep black coals of Carr's eyes. "I chose the hot springs because of your job."

"You knew I would miss the view." It is a statement, not a question. "Even if these colors come from bacteria and algae, you knew they would calm me if I ever woke from a nightmare."

I flush. I *wish* I knew him so well. My mother used to be able to look at a dinner menu and know exactly what my father would order. Knowing a vid preference is similarly intimate, especially since Carr doesn't eat. But the truth is, I was only guessing.

"I've never seen these waters in real life." I shuffle my feet through the image. "I've never even been outside the bubble. My father thinks it's too dangerous."

"I'd like to show you sometime." His voice is gruff with an emotion I don't understand. But whatever he's feeling, it's not polite civility.

He sits on the bed. Although there's room for me to join him, he doesn't ask. The last time he cleared a space for me, I snuggled against his chest—and he kissed me. I can still feel the tingles in my toes.

All of a sudden, I can't bear if I'm misreading his signals. What if he's waiting for me to leave so he can take a nap?

"I have to go," I blurt, stumbling across the holographic water to the door. The illusion looks so real, I'm surprised my feet don't get soaked.

"Vela, wait," he says. But when I turn, his eyes fasten on the loop. "There's so much I want to say to you."

I know exactly what he's asking. I've done it so many times, the motion's starting to feel automatic. See Carr; turn off loop. Only this time, I can't.

"I can't turn off the recorder," I say. "The council will take away the patients' daily food rations if I do."

We stare at each other. The urgency of what we might

have said disappears, and the minutes pass as the colored water laps at our feet, again and again.

"Will you sit down?" he says finally.

It is—and isn't—the invitation for which I've been waiting. I sit at one end of the mattress, my arms stiff at my sides. Leaving at least a foot between us.

He looks once again at the blinking amber light around my neck. And then he grasps the loop and turns it around, his fingertips brushing against my collarbone and igniting a trail of fire. "There. At least we won't have to look at the light."

I touch the skin where he touched. I almost feel like I'm back in the red cells, holding up my finger against a ray of light.

"Do you think my sister will try to commit suicide again?" he asks.

Her sobs fill my ears like a recording. "I think—I hope—she was as scared as we were. Denver seemed to get through to her. And if not, I've got a bot on her every moment of the day."

"When can we get her off the feeding tube?"

"Not for a while." My skin still burns from his fingers, but our conversation is stiff. What did I expect? With the council listening, all we can do is talk logistics. "The crowning ceremony is tomorrow, and the King will welcome your sister and parents into the shuttle. Even though Astana's been consuming a daily ration, her stomach's not used to eating much food. She'll have to be on a regimen of expander pills for at least a week before she transitions completely." I stop, a thought occurring to me. "Your parents are coming, aren't they?"

He fixes his eyes on the floor, as if he's never seen this particular hue of yellow before. "I don't know. I sent word to my mother after Astana got sick, but she never responded. I haven't spoken to her in months. With my dad, it's been more like years."

"But the royal guards contacted them about your selection as the Fittest?"

"As far as I know."

The silence settles between us like a sponge, getting heavier with every moment. And there's so much water in this room.

I don't know how long we sit there, but then he shifts, and the rough fabric of his pants brushes the cotton of mine. I look up, and the expression in his eyes makes me forget the loop, forget the council, forget the team of analysts listening to our conversation.

He sees me. Finally, at long last, he sees the girl I am when no one else is watching.

"I know it wasn't easy, what you did for me," he says. "Given how you feel, I don't think one person in a hundred would've passed over the veto. You'll have my respect forever."

I swallow. "Carr—"

"The most unforgivable thing," he rushes on, "is when I said you wouldn't make a good ruler. That's the kind of decision *only* a good ruler could make. Our colony should be so lucky to have someone like you leading us."

He seizes my hand. "I'm sorry, Vela. I was so fixated with saving Astana, I couldn't see your side. If the situation were reversed, maybe I would've cheated, too."

"You wouldn't," I say automatically.

"I don't know. That's the thing with ideals. They're easy to impose on other people. Not so easy to practice yourself." He skims his thumb over my knuckles. "I don't have much longer, but if you'll let me, I'll make it up to you every day for the rest of my life."

My throat closes, and I blink, blink, blink to keep the tears from falling. "I don't want you to die, Carr."

"I don't, either." It's the first time he's said that. The first time he's admitted he has any selfish interest in this whole process. A heart to give, years and years to live. "I have two more months. And I don't want to waste a moment of it."

I don't respond with words, but with my whole entire soul poured into my kiss.

The water sloshes on the floor, colors swirl all around us, and we pull our feet onto the bed, creating an island of our very own.

CHAPTER TWENTY-EIGHT

"**P**roblems, Princess." Captain Perth strides over the moment I enter the control room. His hair stands up, like he's been shoving his hands through it, and he doesn't even bother to frown. Either he's preoccupied with his news, or he's finally getting used to me. "We've collected the silver discs from all the candidates except one—Zelo Hale. We can't find him anywhere."

Behind him, everything looks the same. Same analysts tapping on their desks. Same holograms floating in the air. Same lights blinking on the circuit boards. I get the feeling I'd find this same scene, no matter what hour or day I entered.

"Can't you look him up in the system?" I ask.

"We tried. He's not listed. According to our records, there's never been a Zelo Hale living in our colony."

"How can that be?" I make my voice calm and mild, even though each syllable wants to dart in a new direction. "All the candidates were vetted when they signed up for the Trials. Fingerprints, retinal scans, DNA samples. How can somebody fake an identity?"

"Don't get me wrong. I believe his record *did* exist. I think it got erased along with the files."

My mind whirls. Out of all the records, only Zelo's is missing. One of the two candidates who should've beaten Carr for the title. It can't be a coincidence. "If his record was erased, this means—"

"You were right." The frown finally comes to Captain Perth's face. But instead of disapproval, I think the downturn of his lips means I've found an ally. I want to save Carr. He wants to protect his data. We can work together. "Someone tampered with the Fittest results. Someone doesn't want us to find Zelo Hale."

*T*he space shuttles stand majestically at the top of Protector's Courtyard. From my angle at the base of the platform, all I see are steel plates and curved lines, sleek and striking under the sun lamps. In less than two hours, no one will even notice the shuttles. All eyes will be on the King placing a crown of ivy on his newest savior, the Fittest.

A hint of eucalyptus floats from the trees, and the gnawing inside me intensifies. Memories of my mother mix with the dread of the ceremony to come.

Sure, the crowning ceremony may be a formality, but it's also one step closer to the conclusion I don't want. A bit more momentum to push Carr toward one fate over another. The longer this course goes on, the harder it will be for me to stop.

I will stop it. That much is certain. The only question is how.

An Orderly bot swerves around me, picking up trash

from the emerald green grass, and technicians roam the courtyard, installing speakers and holo-screens at regular intervals. I retreat a few steps, trying to get out of their way, and almost plow over a woman so bent with age she looks like a folding chair.

"Sorry!"

"I was searching for you, anyhow," the woman says.

I take a closer look at her. Her skin is pocked by countless scars, but in her dark eyes, I see a glimmer of someone familiar. Someone whose hands never used to stop—kneading dough, slicing an apple, peeling the blistered skin off a roasted red pepper—as Astana and I perched on stools in the royal kitchen and regaled her with our latest adventures.

Carr and Astana's mother, Lima.

"You're here." I want to throw my arms around her. Thank Dionysus. Carr won't have to be crowned without his parents watching. "We weren't sure if you would come."

She scowls, the scars on her face rearranging like an interactive map. "You're not as pretty as I remember. Shorter than I expected, too."

I smile as I've been taught. I've heard much worse from the Surly Bots. "We have time before the ceremony. I can take you to your children. Astana's resting in the medical facility, and Carr's probably with her."

"I'm not staying." Her face betrays no indication that she recognizes her children's names. "I'm only here because the guard said something about a monthly allowance. You can pay me, and I'll be on my way."

"But the ceremony." Maybe she doesn't understand. Maybe the message got garbled. Maybe she doesn't know what a huge deal this crowning is. "The whole colony is coming out to honor Carr. He's giving his life to save the

King, and in return, you get all the benefits of being an Aegis without the shortened life span. Don't you want to witness that?"

"Listen. My man and I could care less about food. I've lived in that tin can before, when I worked in your kitchens. Not shredding my skin to go back. If you ask me, this whole ceremony's rubbish. What makes it okay to kill someone just because you're rewarding his family?" She leans so close drops of spittle land on my face. "But nobody asked me, and my man and I could use the extra pills. So fork 'em over."

I open my mouth to tell her about the tradition of sacrifice, one as long-standing as Earth itself. About soldiers who gave themselves for their country. About heroes who risked their lives to protect the innocent. But I doubt she'll listen. Just as I doubt she would know how to breach a firewall.

"I could have one of the royal guards locate Carr. He could be out here in a few minutes."

Her laugh is as harsh as splinters. "You don't get it, do you?"

My blood heats up. Oh, I get it, all right. His entire life, Carr's been working to please his mother. To earn her love. He's taken care of his sister, paid the rent. Took over each and every one of Lima's responsibilities so she can spend her days strung out on drug pellets. And now, she won't take a few minutes to see him?

I wipe the spit off my face. "A mother should want to see her children."

"You've never been a mother, so how would you know? You've obviously never been in love, either."

My mouth opens and closes. "Of course I have. That's what my life is about. The people I love."

She clucks her tongue. "I'm not talking about family

ties. Societal constructs that tell you who and when to love. I'm talking about real love. Soul-mate love." She straightens her spine, and I hear a loud "pop" as her bones shift in their sockets. "My man gives me first choice of pellets. He even shares his favorites, so I can feel what he feels."

"Are you talking about Carr and Astana's father?" I ask incredulously.

"He's always been the only one for me."

"He also neglects your children and encourages you to do the same. He's never taken responsibility for anything in his life."

"I love him," she says. "When you find love, you'll understand. There's not a thing I wouldn't do for him."

"What about your children?" My voice cracks, not for this pitiful person in front of me. But for Astana, for Carr. For myself. Not a single one of us has a mother anymore. "Don't you love them, too?"

"Sometimes there's only room in your heart for one person."

She doesn't elaborate. Doesn't explain or excuse. It's as if she's been telling herself this lie for so long she believes it as truth.

"My children will take care of themselves. They always have. They don't need me like my man does."

I can't listen to this garbage anymore. The stuffing's coming right out of my heart. The same white fluff has been leaking out of Astana and Carr for years now, but she doesn't see their pain. She doesn't care. Her love is like a fire held to their toes, straddling the line between heat and danger, and maybe it's time to send her away before we all burst into flames.

"Go. Before one of your children sees you." My voice is high and thin, as if it did come from a doll. "I'll have someone get in touch about the monthly allowance."

"That's all you had to say in the first place." She turns and clomps away.

I don't watch her go. She's taken too much of my time already. Stolen even more from her children. I'm not about to give her another second.

I hope to Dionysus that Carr feels the same way.

CHAPTER TWENTY-NINE

*T*en minutes and counting.

We're in the antechamber of the shuttle, waiting for a Regal Bot to lead us onto the stage at the appropriate time. Carr, as the Fittest. Astana, as his recipient family. Blanca and me, as the Royal Princesses.

The only one missing is the King. And the only one extra is Denver.

I squeeze my cousin's shoulder. He's not going onto the platform with us, but I'm grateful he's present. While the rest of us are mute with tension, he points out the hooks in the wall to Astana, explaining that astronauts used to suit up here before exiting into space. He also brought Blanca and me our favorite snacks—candied crickets and roasted almonds.

I crunch a few bugs, even though I'm not hungry. Even though I may never be hungry again. The sweetness coats my tongue, and the red digits displayed on the ceiling tick down. I can't delay anymore.

"I saw your mother." My voice comes out excessively

bright, like a spotlight on top of the sun lamps.

Carr's foot stops tapping, and Blanca squints from her seat on the white storage lockers, where she's been waiting, separate from the rest of us. For once, she is without her trusty shadow, Hanoi, and she seems lost without her. Maybe she's beginning to rely on her assistant more than she realized.

I wait another beat, until Astana turns from her post against Denver's chest. She hasn't spoken to me since the Bee Park.

"She, um, she couldn't stay."

"You mean, she didn't want to," Astana says. Her words are a response to mine, but they don't count in breaking our wall of silence. Not when she can't even look at me. "Let me guess. She took the pills and ran. Nothing new there."

Carr swallows again and again, as if trying to get down an uncooperative pill. Each bob of his Adam's apple tightens my own throat.

"Did she say anything about my dad?" he asks, his voice rough despite the multiple gulps. "I thought this win might be enough. I've gotten them an allowance every month for life. That's pretty good, isn't it?"

My heart lurches. Even now, he hopes. Even now, he's trying to earn their love.

Astana hobbles to her brother and seizes his hand. "You are done trying to please that man. Do you hear me? You are worth a thousand—no, a million—of him. He's not fit to trim your toenails."

"He's my father," Carr says quietly.

Brother and sister look at each other with so much aching emotion it turns the rest of us into outsiders. Blanca, Denver, and I have many shared experiences. We're even related by blood. But at that moment, the thing that unites us most is that we can't share their pain.

Astana and Carr's hands drop to their sides, still connected, and we wait like that, not speaking, until the bot rolls up to the door.

"Today is a bittersweet day for me," the King says. His words, amplified by the microphone in his collar, carry over the crowd, and a sheen of sweat covers his forehead. Instead of his usual pine cone insignia, he wears one of Denver's new breed of azaleas. The unique pink color has been covered by a layer of gold, but the shape of the flower is unmistakable. My cousin will be pleased his royal flower is debuting at such a large gathering.

Not everyone in the colony showed up. I know of two people who are conspicuously, offensively missing. But judging from the sea of people pushing up against the metal railings, I'd guess we're close to full attendance.

"I get to honor one of the worthiest young men I've ever met." My father's voice is heavy, as though saturated with the drops of our manufactured rain. "At the same time, I have to accept his gift: the sacrifice of his life for mine."

He steps from behind the podium. Despite the royal insignia at his shoulder, despite the fact that he's orating in front of a crowd of ten thousand, he turns into just another colonist. Someone to whom we can all relate—a father, a brother, a son. This is his strength as the King. He rules not by his authority but because he is loved.

"I've crowned many worthy young men." He lowers his voice, so that it seems like he is talking to each of us individually. "And always, I am humbled by the extraordinary heroism of the boys and girls who have laid down their lives for me. But today is different. Because today, I am accepting the sacrifice from a friend."

A murmur ripples through the crowd. Carr's eyes widen, and he takes a couple steps off the X that was added right before the ceremony. He doesn't understand what the King means. I never told him about my father's role in his life. The subject never came up, and besides, it wasn't my story to tell.

The King turns to Carr. "I've taken you by surprise. For that, I apologize." He looks at the audience once more. "You see, this is the first opportunity I've had to speak to young Carr since he's been named. I would've saved our conversation for later, but then I thought: What better way to honor this boy than to show the entire colony what he means to me? So I hope you'll indulge me for the next few minutes."

The men and women in the front row press even closer to the railing. Of course they'll indulge him. He is their king. They can't learn enough about his personal life.

This is why my father wasn't present in the antechamber. This is why their spots were marked right before the ceremony, to make sure the crowd can see the King's and the Fittest's profiles when they faced one another. The King's speech was changed at the last minute, and this conversation was added. But why?

"I suppose nearly a decade has passed. And I'm not wearing my straw hat." A bot rolls up to my father and gives him a tattered hat, which he places on his head. "Is it possible you've forgotten your old buddy? I have more than a few pleasant memories of us walking around Protector's Pond. Do you?"

Carr's mouth falls open. He closes it, and then it opens again. "That was you? You walked around the pond with me?"

"My dear friend," my father says. "How could you not recognize my face on the news feeds?"

"I remember your eyes." Carr's words are a mumble, but the microphone in his collar broadcasts his voice, loud and clear. "They were kind. And your face on the feeds did look familiar, but that's to be expected. The King and his daughters always look familiar to us, on account of our love for them."

"Well said!" a woman shouts, and another colonist whistles his agreement.

Several people in the front row spread their palms against their hearts and tap three times. My chest tight, I catch Blanca's eyes. She stares into my gaze briefly and then looks away. This is the first time we've been included in the royal salute. The first time the people have signaled they would be willing to accept one of us as the King's Successor.

"We drifted apart a month into our friendship," my father tells the crowd. "Young Carr moved away, and we weren't able to continue our walks around the pond. But I never forgot him. I kept tabs on him and helped him out whenever I could."

Carr's jaw twitches, as though he is sifting through the past and putting his life back together like a jigsaw puzzle. The month's rent that showed up out of nowhere. The employer who called him the day he left his job at the apple orchard. *That was the King,* I want to shout. *That was my father helping you because he values you.*

"Some would say I was his guardian angel." My father touches the brim of his straw hat. "But to me, it was more than that. To me, I was looking out for my son, if not by blood, then at least by feeling."

My breath hitches, and Carr stumbles. My father catches his hand and draws him up, so that they stand together, straight and proud.

And I understand. I understand everything. The last-minute change, the decision to have this private conversation in front of the rest of the colony.

The King has followed Carr's life too closely not to be aware of his family situation. When he learned Mr. and Mrs. Silver wouldn't be attending the ceremony, he must've decided to give Carr the next best thing. A father figure who loved him, even when he received nothing in return. Someone who was willing to help him in the past, with no credit at all.

The King wanted to honor Carr, and this was the best way he knew how.

The bot rolls back to center stage, bearing a crown of ivy and holly. Back on Earth, crowns were made out of metals and jewels. On Dion, a crown is constructed out of the most valuable, the most precious of our resources. The living plant.

My father picks up the crown, panting a little with the effort, and places it on Carr's head.

"With this crown, Carr Silver, I name you as the Fittest, the candidate who is *more than* fit to die for the King."

Never, in previous ceremonies, has the King put that spin on the description. More than fit. What does that phrase mean? Is he implying Carr shouldn't be dying at all? Or are the words merely a slip of the tongue?

"I welcome you and your sister Astana into the shuttle." He stops and takes a shaky breath, his stomach ballooning out with the effort. "Not as guests, but, if you'll accept it, as members of your true family."

Carr nods, his eyes glinting under the sun lamps. Thunderous applause erupts. I leap out of my tree-chair and smash my hands together. Never have I clapped so hard for anything in my life.

The King embraces Carr and then turns to salute the crowd. My skin prickles, recognizing before my eyes that something's wrong. Is my father swaying? What's going on? Some kind of orbquake?

Like a data feed, images of the last few minutes flash through my mind. The sheen of sweat on my father's forehead. The small pant from picking out the crown. His body working overtime in order to breathe.

With a shout, I break out in a sprint. Before I can reach him, however, my father flings his hands out as if he can grab hold of the air.

And then he pitches face-first off the stage.

CHAPTER THIRTY

I rush forward to break my father's fall, but of course it is too late. I see, rather than hear, the sickening crunch of his bones as his body smashes into the ground.

Someone, probably Master Somjing, issues a command, and as I stand, looking at what could not possibly be real, the bots load the crumpled heap of my father onto a stretcher and take him away.

The railing splits, and people spill onto the stage, shouting, screaming, jabbing fingers at Blanca and me.

"What happened to the King?" A man with a tattoo stretching across his cheek shouts in my face. "Where are they taking him?"

"Has he been ill?" A flagpole of a woman yanks my sleeve.

"He's going to die. I know it." A girl with twin braids bursts into tears.

Normally, Blanca takes charge of this kind of situation. I remember stuffing my knuckles inside my mouth when I was nine, as hands grasped my cheeks and pinched at my clothes.

Even though she'd been bawling a few minutes before, my sister shoved me behind her back and said, with an authority she had yet to earn, "We are grieving our mother. Please respect our privacy."

I wait for her to speak now. But she just wraps her icy fingers around my wrist. "Noooo," she whimpers. "We can't lose him, too."

My intestines tie themselves into a knot. She saw him as invincible, and so did I. The King has a million resources at his disposal. People lined up to give him their healthy organs. Nothing has ever happened to him that can't be fixed.

At least up until now.

Fear claws its way through my torso, slashing through my kidneys and lungs. But I don't have time to be scared. Carr does his best to hold the people back, but they continue to push, to demand, to cry.

"Stop!" I pull Carr's collar toward me, since I'm not mic'd. But I've never spoken to a crowd this size, and the platform tilts wildly. But Carr looks into my eyes and nods. The nearness of his skin centers me, and the dizziness melts away.

"That was shocking for all of us to see," I say into Carr's microphone, amazed at how strong and certain my voice is. I sound like I know what I'm talking about. I sound like I don't have worms wiggling in my stomach. I sound like Blanca.

"Rest assured, we have an excellent medical staff. The King will be under the best possible care. We will update you as soon as we have any information. But for now, my sister and I need to be with our father."

I drape my arm around Blanca and push my way through the mob. Carr steps in front of us and clears a path with his body.

"Take your time," Master Somjing says as we pass. His

hand is pressed against his earbud. "The King is with the medics now. He's alive, but it'll be a while before they know anything."

We make our way across the courtyard. The crowd disperses, but we're still hounded. The difference is, I've known these people all my life. I can't brush them off. I have to stop and smile and accept their condolences.

"Your father saved my job," one of the royal guards tells me. "I would've been fired as a trainee because I missed too many shifts. But your father listened when I said I had to visit my sick mother, and he got my boss to give me another chance."

"The King is as kind as they come," a food prepper says a few steps later. "I'll never forget the time he gave the entire cooking staff the day off to celebrate the New Year with our families. 'You've fed us so well the rest of the year,' he said. 'We can fend for ourselves for one day.'"

Another few steps, and an Aegis presses my hand. "Your father once saw me in tears, after my boyfriend dumped me. Even though he had better things to do, he listened for ten whole minutes to my tale of heartbreak.

Over and over again, people give me examples of the King's kindness. I usually love hearing stories like these. But not today. Because these people are acting like the King's already gone, and that's not the case. I have to believe he's going to be okay. I have to believe he'll be our king for many years to come.

We finally arrive in the wait lounge, the same one where I passed a dreamless night on the concrete floor.

"Oh good, you're here." A medic enters the room, moments after I deposit Blanca on a tree-chair. "Mistress Barnett would like to speak with you. She has news about your father."

My kneecaps evaporate, and my body shakes, a marionette without a master, and then I feel a hand on my back.

Carr. He's still with me. Through all the people and all the words, he's still here.

"You can do this," he says, and I hear the echo of his words from so many years ago. *This pain, too, will pass. Just hold on, and life will get better. It always does.*

As much as that advice has meant to me over the years, it means so much more today, now that I know it belongs to Carr.

"You're strong. Strong enough to steal my sister a meal. Strong enough to forego the veto. You're the strongest person I know. You can do this. You can do anything."

I don't feel strong. But this is Carr's gift. He gives other people power by the force of his vision alone.

I glance at my sister, who's curled into the curve of the C-trunk. "Watch after Blanca?"

"As if she were my very own sister." His eyes find mine. I don't know to which family he's referring. My father's offer of a true family? Or something more permanent between us? How do I even begin to hope when his life might end in two months?

"Go. I'll be here when you get back."

I nod, grasping his hand for one last shot of courage. And then I follow the medic out of the room.

The head medic's office is a simpler version of the Royal Office. The mural displays a single panel of the serpent's story, the one where it whispers in the woman's ear, its tongue forked and pointy. A glass desktop covers one bank of computers, and the chairs are half the size of the King's throne.

I sit on the living wood, bracing myself to hear the bad news. My dad's heart is giving out. His lungs punctured, his appendix burst. Any and all of his internal organs failing in a body too worn out for a transplant to save.

"Your father's been poisoned," Mistress Barnett says instead.

My clasped hands break apart, and the air leaks from my mouth. Nothing seems real. I feel like I'm in an abstract painting from Earth, about to melt off the canvas. "Poisoned?"

"Yes. Most likely, it was ingested. It could've been an insect bite, but the point of entry is usually obvious—swelling, discoloration—and there are no marks on his body."

"But he is so loved." I think of the waver in the food prepper's voice as she told her story. The gratitude on the royal guard's face. "Who would poison him?"

"I don't know." The head medic fidgets in the tree-chair. Her long silver hair gleams underneath the sun lamp, and she's chewed off her lip paint, so only the red outline of her mouth remains.

I try to swallow, but my mouth is a child's sandbox. "Will he get better?"

She straightens, as if relieved to get a question she can answer. "I don't think the poison was meant to kill your father. The dose was too small. There's the risk of cardiac complications, but at the moment, his main symptoms are vomiting, dizziness, loss of coordination, and muscular weakness. Those will subside in a few days. More worrisome are the two ribs he cracked in the fall. He'll heal, but it may take months."

I can't breathe. The serpent laughs at me from the mural, each jab of its forked tongue a strike against my wounds.

My dad has an enemy. Someone who wishes to hurt him. Maybe even kill him.

But for now, he's going to be okay. That's what's important.

A few breaths later, I no longer feel like someone's stuffed crickets under my skin. "When can I see him?"

"As soon as he wakes up. We've given him a sedative so he can rest."

She walks me to the door, squeezing my shoulder in what seems like true sympathy. And yet, she voted against me in the Successor ballot. Every council member did. Can I trust her show of support?

Some people would say her previous vote no longer matters. My father overruled, and I was given the chance to prove myself.

But now that the King's in the medical facility, with broken ribs and an unseen enemy, I think the past does matter. It matters more than ever to know who's on my side.

*lanca's sitting up when I get back to the lounge, her knees tucked into her chest in a vertical fetal position. The C-trunks bend their leafy boughs over her head, providing shade even though there are no sun lamps inside. "Well? How is he?"

"Not good." I tell them everything I know, which isn't much.

Carr puts his hand on my shoulder. "Why would someone poison the King?"

I shrug, and his knuckles brush against my neck. I want to shrug, again and again, so that I can feel his skin on mine.

I want all of this to be a nightmare. I want to go back in time, a year or two or ten, to a past where no one I loved was sick or poisoned or dying.

But there's no past like that, at least in my lifetime. As long as I've been alive, people have been sick and dying. Their deaths might be slow, like the Aegis', or fast, like the Fittest candidates'. But until we get outside these bubbles and eradicate the need for the genetic modification, I'll never know how it feels to live in a healthy world.

"Why would someone poison the King?" Blanca echoes. "Lots of reasons. Because they want his throne. Because they think the new Successor will have more favorable policies." As she talks, her voice grows stronger, until she sounds like her old self again. "Or maybe because they don't want Carr to die, and if there's no ailing King, then there's no need for a Fittest."

She stares pointedly at Carr.

I gape. "Are you accusing him of poisoning our father?"

"No, not Carr. But maybe somebody close to him."

My mouth opens even wider. "Astana, then?"

I want to tell my sister she's wrong. The Astana I knew wouldn't hurt an insect. But I can still feel the scratches on my face. I remember her hand reaching up for the latch to the bee cage. And I can't dismiss anything.

Blanca tilts her head, looking at the leaves as if searching for answers. "Anyone could be responsible. The motivation could be anything—greed, jealousy, lust, hunger."

"Maybe not." A broad palm leaf flutters out of the tree, and I catch it in the air. With my other hand, I take Carr's fingers. Luck and love, and those two things might not be enough to fight what I'm up against. "Today isn't the first instance of treachery. If the same person has been sabotaging the trials, we can narrow down the motivation to something political. Something directly related to the Fittest task."

The three of us look at each other, a round robin of stares that keeps our eyes bouncing from one person to the other. This is the first time I've brought up the sabotage in front of Blanca. The first opportunity I've had to gauge her reaction.

"Master Somjing mentioned some weird things were happening." She flips her hair over her shoulder. "It wasn't me, if that's what you're thinking."

I have no idea what to think. Blanca is the consummate actress. Her denial doesn't reassure me in the slightest.

Carr clears his throat. "Maybe we should figure out *how* the King got poisoned. I could talk to the royal cook, get a list of everything the King's eaten in the last day."

I turn to him. "Good idea. The list won't be very long, since he's given up his meals for Blanca's patients, but he may still be eating snacks. You don't have to involve yourself, though. This crime is more our problem" — I gesture between Blanca and me — "than yours."

"I'm part of the royal family now, remember?" He extracts his fingers gently from my grip. "The two of you need to wait here in case your father wakes up. I might as well make myself useful."

"He's right." Blanca's voice is soft again, as though she's remembered why we're here. "You should let him go."

"Okay." My fingers thick, I unpin the personal insignia from my chest and hand him the gold-dipped rose, along with my unlocked handheld. "Take these. That way, they'll know you're acting under the authority of the Princess."

Carr's eyes flash. He swoops down and presses his lips against mine for one hot second.

"I'll see you soon," he says against my mouth. And then he is gone.

Blanca gives me a sideways glance. "Did you know that when an Aegis gives someone her personal insignia, she's declaring her undying devotion to him?"

I did know, actually. I know that very well. I rub my fingers across my lips and wonder if Carr knows it, too.

CHAPTER THIRTY-ONE

Blanca and I wait in silence, as if we've exhausted our allotment of words for the day. But the silence is companionable rather than strained. Restorative rather than exhausting. Hanoi stops by briefly, to bring us our lunch and to give each of us a sympathetic hug. I'm not surprised by her embrace. The little I know of her suggests that she is a warm, loving person who communicates through her touches. But my jaw hangs open a little when she moves from me to my sister.

"Hey," she says, squeezing Blanca's shoulders. "Your reserves are waiting, underneath that steel. All you have to do is gather them."

"I'm not very good at gathering," my sister mutters with a vulnerability I've never before witnessed.

"You are," Hanoi says. "I've seen you. When you thought nobody else was looking. I've seen who you are then."

She leaves soon after that, but I continue to stare at my sister. Who did Hanoi see that I haven't? Is this person a stranger—or is she the old Blanca that used to play space explorers with me?

We still haven't spoken when Miss Sydney shows up in the lounge an hour later. She wears her signature blue sash, but the arms that usually carry a basket of food are empty. In addition to the last meal of the day, her access to the food supplies have also been cut as part of my deal with the council.

A surge of guilt moves through me. Miss Sydney loves nothing more than experimenting with her recipes. But I had no choice.

"How's the King?" Her words are hesitant, as though she's not sure where we stand.

I'm not sure, either. I thought she was my friend, but an unknown enemy lurks in our colony. Until we find him—or her—everyone is a suspect.

"The King's recovering." I shoot a glance at Blanca. She nods, as if approving my vague word choice. "We haven't seen him yet."

"I won't keep you." She shifts from one foot to the other. "Cyprus Mead told me the King fainted because he was giving up his own meals. Not one meal every evening like the Fittest families, but breakfast, lunch, and dinner. Is that true?"

I nod. "That's not the reason he collapsed, but yes, he's been nutritioning with pills instead of eating real food."

"I need to apologize, then," she says. "I didn't believe you when you said the food couldn't come from anywhere else. But if the King himself is sacrificing…" She straightens, and her sash swings like one of the flags on the space shuttles. "I'll help Cyprus talk to the other families. Some of them are so furious they're forgetting themselves."

So furious they would sabotage the Trials? Forget themselves so much they would poison the King?

Before I can ask, Miss Sydney and her sash back out

of the room. I unfold my legs, which have gone numb from their criss-cross position. Blanca leans her head against the trunk and closes her eyes once more. Did she understand the importance of Miss Sydney's offer?

"You know, the Fittest families could be the solution to your task." I make my tone casual, as if I'm remarking on the trajectory of the rain spigots. "If they give up their meals permanently, then the other patients can be saved."

"That's a big *if*," she says, her eyes still closed. "I'm not about to base my entire strategy on an *if*."

We fall silent once again and go back to waiting some more.

*T*wo hours pass. Finally, the medic comes back into the lounge. By now, I've figured out that he's Mistress Barnett's apprentice. Once the head medic passes, he'll take her place.

My mind flashes forward ten years, and I see an older version of the medic, his black hair shot through with silver, working alongside the reigning Queen. But try as I might, I can't see her face.

"Your father's awake." The medic takes off his stethoscope and rubs his neck. "He'd like to see both of you, one at a time. I'm sorry I won't be able to give you more than a few minutes each. The King needs his rest."

I look at Blanca. Any color she's regained in the last hour has bled out again. "Do you want to go first?" I ask.

"No, you go," she says. "You've been so good since this whole thing happened, and I'm a total mess. You should see him first."

"I don't think I've ever seen you give up a first turn at anything." I try for light and teasing, but the words come out forced and childish. Little wonder. I haven't teased my sister in years, and I'm not sure how to do it now.

"People change." Her faint smile is a relic from our childhood. "Or sometimes, they've been a certain way all along, and they only just remember."

What has she remembered? Are we friends, rivals, or something in between?

I don't ask. So long as she doesn't contradict me, I can answer the question however I want.

A hologram is playing on the wall when I enter my father's recovery room. Nebulae from our home galaxy. A crystal-blue light cracks open the deep black space, surrounded by an algae-gold cloud and twinkling pink spots. If I didn't know better, I could believe I was looking into the gates of heaven. The image changes. This time, electric-blue lightning snakes through a dragon's flaming breath. This would be hell.

The pictures flash across the wall, each nebula more breathtaking than the last. But I ignore them all and hug my father. "Dad. I'm so glad you're okay."

He kisses the top of my head. "Me too, baby. Me, too."

I pull back. His skin sags with as many wrinkles as there are stars, and deep circles bruise the underside of his eyes. His eyes themselves seem lost. A million light-years away with the nebulae.

"No, don't you worry about me, too." The lines around his mouth crease, as though he's trying to smile. "Mistress Barnett will tell you herself, the poison has left my system.

With the exception of my ribs, I'm back to normal."

"But you're sad." Simple words, but they stick and tumble on the way out of my mouth. I don't normally associate sadness with the King. In fact, I've only seen him truly melancholy one other time—the day we sent my mother's ashes into space.

He fixes his eyes on the nebulae. After all these years, could this be where my mother's ashes have traveled? Is this my father's way of being with her?

"When your mother died, a gash was ripped in my heart," he says, as if I'd spoken out loud. But I don't need to. My mother's presence is in this room, as real and tangible as any physical body. "People told me, over time, the gash would mend itself. It would get smaller until I wouldn't notice the pain with every breath, I wouldn't feel the gaping hole with every beat of my heart. It might even disappear, they said.

"They were right. But they were also wrong. I got used to the gash, but it never closed. Time was nothing but a series of bandages I slapped over the wound. Not for a moment have I ever forgotten how much I love your mother."

He catches my chin with his hand. Tilts my face so it catches the light, not from the nebulae but from the sun lamps outside the window. "As you grow up, Vela, I see her in you more and more. Your mother lives for me again, in the ghost of such moments. I can almost believe she waits for me in a different realm." He smiles, as wistful as a child. "I miss her."

I don't know what to say. I don't know how to feel about his confession. Even as I watch, he puts on his kingly role the way one might button himself into a coat. He buries the tragedies of his personal life behind his responsibility. The emotions melt from his face, so when I look at him, I no longer see a man grieving over his dead wife.

All I see is the King.

This camouflage is perhaps his greatest lesson to me. It's not that he doesn't feel. Indeed, he feels as much as the next person. But what supersedes his emotions is the duty to his colony.

My father taps the holographic cube to turn off the nebulae. "So tell me. What have you discovered about my poisoner?"

I tell him about our plan to check his food and my theory that the poisoning is related to the Fittest Trials.

"You might be right. I'll increase the number of bots watching all of us." He sighs and then winces as the breath moves along his ribs. "I don't think even the council predicted how hard this task was going to be."

"What do you mean?"

My father untwists the wires on his torso. "You're so young, my eye-apple. Too young, some of the council members think, to be considered for such an important role. I disagree. I think your youth is a strength. You're not entrenched in the status quo. You don't accept something just because that's the way it's been. There are some… lessons…that have taken the council and me a lifetime to see. And you're on the verge of understanding them now."

I get the feeling he's alluding to something big, something vitally important to the future of our colony. And it's all related, somehow, to my decisions in the Fittest Trials.

"Are you trying to tell me something about Carr?" I watch his face for every nuance of expression.

"You know I can't talk about the Fittest." He drapes a hand on his forehead, as if to shield himself from my scrutiny. "I can't help you with this decision. You must make it alone. That's how we'll know if you're ready to be the Successor."

What decision? I thought the veto was my last move, and

I already made it. Master Somjing said the council was still evaluating me, but on what? Helping Carr get settled into the shuttle? Investigating the firewall breach?

A thought occurs to me, so terrible it makes me stumble backward. "Dad, is the council behind the wiped files? Are they responsible for your poisoning?"

"What? No. *No*." He tries to sit up, his face contorting with pain. "I give you my sovereign word the council has nothing to do with either. Our focus is finding the next Successor, and whoever is causing this trouble is making our job more difficult."

I exhale. I don't know how to feel. Relief the council isn't involved. Or frustration that I'm back to my original questions.

Before I can probe any further, a bot rolls in and tells us my time is up. I give my father a kiss and turn to leave the room.

"One more thing, Vela." My father's eyes are beginning to close, and his face looks shadowed even in the light of the sun lamps.

Guilt slithers through my digestive tract. I've worn him out, and he'll have nothing left for Blanca. Crossing back to his side, I pick up his hand, careful not to disturb the wires. "Yes, Dad?"

"As the King, I would choose again and again to have you participate in this task. I firmly believe you have the most potential to be the kind of leader I would be proud to follow. But I want you to know…" His eyes close all the way, and I'm no longer sure to whom he's speaking. To me or himself. Or perhaps to the ashes of my mother, floating along a distant nebula. "As a father, I will never, ever forgive myself for asking you to make this decision."

CHAPTER THIRTY-TWO

When I return to the lounge, Carr's waiting and Blanca's gone. I walk straight to him and wrap my arms around his torso, trying to soak up his warmth, his goodness. My head's like the planetary water before they filter it. Full of too much bacteria, too many colors. But this. This doesn't confuse me. If I could live in a world of his arms, maybe everything would be okay.

I stay there, trying to memorize the rhythm of his heartbeat. After a minute or an hour, he whispers into my hair, "We have company."

Two bots stand ten feet away. I didn't hear them approach. The engineers specifically designed the bots to roll with a mechanical whirring sound, but I guess they didn't take Carr's mesmerizing heartbeat into account.

"May I help you?" I ask.

One of the bots whirrs closer and pokes a mechanical limb in the air, a few inches from my kneecap, doing a remarkable imitation of a jabbing finger. "I'm watching your every move, Princess. Master Somjing says you don't need to wear the loop any longer."

"Who are you with? What are you doing? What are you thinking?" the other bot asks.

I roll my eyes. Great. Nosy Bots. One for each of us. That was fast. My father must've put in the order for increased surveillance as soon as I left his room.

Unlike the messenger bots, every surveillance bot has a set of human eyes watching from a control room. And I thought the recorder was bad.

I turn off the loop, unwinding it from my neck and stashing it in my pocket. "Did you get the list?" I ask Carr.

He nods and gives me the handheld. I open the appropriate document. "I was right. The only food he ate yesterday was his favorite snack, right before the crowning ceremony. Honey-apple toast with vanilla ice cream, drizzled with honey."

"I gave the ingredient list to CORA, but I'm not sure it'll get us anywhere," he says. "More likely, the poisoner added a toxic substance to your father's food."

I feel as though we're searching for the one red pebble in a riverbed of brown stones. You know it's got to be there — the composition of the planet dictates as much — but you have no idea where to start.

At that moment, Master Somjing lurches into the room, followed by his own bot. He scowls. "This thing showed up a few minutes ago, and it won't stop following me."

The three bots circle each other and park themselves along the wall. If we get any more Fittest-related people in here, we'll have an entire crew.

"You've never had a surveillance bot?" I remember my first one. I was four or five, old enough to play by myself but too young to go completely unsupervised. For the first hour, I did nothing but run in circles, zig-zagging around trees and doubling back on my tracks. It took me even longer to figure out the bot was following me and not playing tag.

"I had no reason to have a surveillance bot," Master Somjing says. "Never important enough to be in any danger."

I press his arm. The council member looks as wrinkled as I feel. "Thank you for coming. My father will be happy to see you."

"It's the least I can do." He touches the holo-cube around his neck. "Your father visited me every day the year after Viola passed. I credit him with pulling me out of depression, you know."

He looks at me, then Carr, and then the three bots lined on the wall. His neck flushes red, as if he's just realized we're not the only two people in the room.

"That's not the only reason I'm here." His voice takes on a stiff, formal tone. "I have official council business to relate."

"I'll leave," Carr says.

"No, stay. This news concerns you, too."

Carr and I exchange a glance. The surveillance bots roll forward a few feet. They have no stake in the conversation, of course. But when the volume drops, they're programmed to come closer, in order to capture every word.

Whatever this news is, it can't be good.

"The council called an emergency meeting. Mistress Barnett informed us the King has recovered from the poisoning, but this episode has taxed his already weakened system."

My hand reaches out and wraps around Carr's.

"I'm sorry to say, he can't afford to wait two months for the organs transplant. We have to move up the procedure."

"Up?" My heart pounds—loud, loud, so loudly. I'm surprised the bots don't roll backwards. "How long do we have?"

"One week. The transplant's been scheduled for a week from today."

CHAPTER THIRTY-THREE

One week. Ten days. 300 hours. 18,000 minutes. 1,080,000 seconds.

With every second that passes, I die a little more. I sleep a little less. Every minute I sleep is one less minute I can be with Carr. One less minute I can spend in the control room, helping the data analysts look for Zelo. So, I stop sleeping.

I can rest anytime. After the ten-day week. After the deadline for the transplant has come and gone. After I lose or save the only boy I've ever loved.

Yes, I love him. I always have. From the moment I saw him digging for his worms to the times his voice told me to hold on. From the kid who was serious beyond his years to the boy who stood on a stone block and told me he was unworthy of love.

I love his kindness and his goodness. I love how he inspires me to be more honorable. I love how he brings order and sense to the universe—my universe, at least.

I love Carr Silver. I know that now. I always have, and I always will.

I put the search for the King's poisoner on hold. My broken friendship with Astana fades in importance. Everything else gets shoved to the background. My first priority is finding Zelo.

If I can recover his disc and reconstruct the data, I know it will reveal a mistake. Someone tampered with CORA. Carr isn't the Fittest, after all.

His salvation is within my grasp. All I have to do is find Zelo.

In the control room, the analysts and I check school records, medical records, financial records. Zilch. Birth registry, death registry, personal identification numbers. Zip. We even send investigators to the Temple and other destinations to inquire if anyone's seen him. Zero. Like the inspiration for his name, Zelo seems to have vanished onto another plane.

My saboteur is nothing if not thorough.

The days pass. Two days. Three days. Ninety hours, one hundred and twenty. And then on the fifth day, with five more days remaining until the transplant, Carr calls me out of the control room.

I meet him in the narrow corridor, so cold and metallic next to his blood-and-flesh warmth, with my surveillance bot trailing after me. Our reflections glint off the curved metal walls, but I ignore them. Just like I ignore the bot and the eyes behind it.

"Can you take a break?" He steps closer, even though there's no one in the hallway. "There's something I'd like to show you."

"Of course. Anything you want." Guilt floods my veins. Have I been in the control room too long? Should I be spending every last second of these final days with Carr?

Maybe. But foregoing my search for Zelo is like

admitting defeat. And I will not give up. I have to believe I can still stop this.

"Before we go…" He tilts my chin up. "I want you to talk to my sister."

"I've tried, Carr. She won't even look at me, and I don't blame her. If I were in her position, I'd feel the same way."

I make my tone light, as though my best friend's anger doesn't bother me. But nothing could be farther from the truth. When I lay in bed at night, not sleeping, the grief crushes me from the inside out. There are two holes inside my chest. The bigger hole is for the imminent loss of Carr, but the smaller one is for my best friend. For my sister, if not in blood, then of the heart. If I can't stop this transplant from happening, and Carr dies, then I'll lose them both. Forever.

"Try again. Please?" he asks.

When I don't respond, he sighs and pulls my head against his chest. The bot whirrs a few feet to the side, trying to get a better view of us.

"I'm not sad, Vela. For the first time in my life, I feel like I don't have anything left to prove. My life finally matters because I'm able to save Astana."

"Your life has always mattered," I whisper. I look up and do my best to imprint his caviar-black eyes and straight, thin brows into my memory.

I'll have holograms, sure. And I've made a point to take a few of him, because I know I'll regret not having them later. But I don't want to rely on some dots of light to remember him, like I do my mother. I don't want all the people I love to be confined to a little black cube.

"I worry about her." His voice stutters and halts like a faulty combine. "She's not strong like you. I don't know if she'll be able to bear the grief when I die. I would feel so much better if I knew she had you, watching over her. So please. For me. Before I die, repair your friendship."

I close my eyes, the heat burning like an iron poker against my lids. He's wrong. I'm not stronger than Astana. I won't be any better at surviving his death.

But with this speech, he's passing his life's work to me. He's entrusting me to do what he will no longer be able to do. Take care of Astana.

"Okay," I say, my words a vow to the most honorable boy on Dion. "I'll do my best."

I try everything. I apologize. I explain why I didn't use the veto, how I couldn't destroy Carr's honor. I outline every step the control room analysts and I have taken to locate Zelo.

I even remind Astana of the time we spread pond mud on our faces to give ourselves a facial. Instead of a smooth and glowing complexion, we ended up with red, splotchy skin.

I talk until my mouth dries out, until my voice goes hoarse, and still, I can't get a flicker out of her plaster-mold lips.

Okay, then. I want to keep trying, for Carr's sake, but there's only so long I can push against a boulder that won't budge. The bots tell me that Hanoi comes to visit her every day. So, perhaps, even if she never forgives me, she'll have one friend to comfort her after her brother's death.

"I'll come back tomorrow. Maybe you'll feel like talking then."

I trudge away. My bot leaves its spot by Astana's bed and scurries after me. My best friend remains at the window, the

ever-present feeding tube running from her stomach to the
stand. She's got over a week left on her regimen of expander
pills. Which means, if the transplant goes as planned, Carr
won't see his sister become an Aegis before he dies.

Yet one more thing to mourn.

All the reasons to grieve block my throat. I might choke—
but then a thought occurs to me. Something that might pique
Astana's interest.

"The Fittest gets one last request. Anything he wants,
within reason, will be granted a few hours before he dies."

Carr's request was odd. I expected him to ask for
something for his sister. Or maybe a concession for future
Fittest candidates. Not a food item. And certainly not for
himself.

"He asked for a pie," I say. "An entire strawberry pie he
wouldn't have to share with anyone, not even you. Do you
know what that means?"

Her head jerks up. "He wanted a pie?" Something I can't
read crosses her face. And then, tears are falling onto her lap.

I rush to her side and kneel by the wheelchair. "What?
What is it?"

She presses the heels of both hands against her eyes. "I
can't believe he remembers. When we were kids, Carr and I
would fantasize about eating. We would see these great big
pies leaving the royal kitchen, and we'd dream about what
we would do if we had an entire pie to ourselves. Carr, being
Carr, said he would split it with me and Mama.

"I told him he didn't have to share. 'Of course I do,' he
said, as if it were the most natural thing in the world. And
then I said…" Her voice cracks, and she drops her hands.
The splotches cover her eyes like a pair of sunglasses. "I
said, 'Before you die, I want you to have an entire pie to
yourself—and not share a single bite.'" Her face crumples.

"I guess my wish is coming true."

She breaks down, then, and I put my arms around her. She cries and cries, as if she'll use up all the water inside our bubble. As if she'll reach out into the planet and borrow its colored streams and rivers, so that the tears raining down her cheeks will turn orange and pink and red.

Her tears splash onto the ground, creating wet patches on the tile. For once, the pattern of my despair matches someone who cares about Carr as much as, or maybe even more, than I do.

"I love him, Astana," I say, the confession long overdue.

Her sobs subside. Her brother hasn't given her enough credit. Those years she allowed him to look after her? Maybe it wasn't because she needed him, but rather, because he needed her.

She wipes away the tears. "I know. You've always loved him. Even when we were kids, I would catch you sneaking looks at him."

I lower my head, a seven-year-old girl once again. Fascinated by this boy with the deep black eyes and the fistful of worms, but too shy to talk to him. "How come you never said anything?"

"I didn't think anything could come out of it. You're an Aegis. He isn't." She doesn't finish her thought. She doesn't have to. We were always only a distinct possibility because I was slated to die sixty years before him.

Now, I'd give anything to have another year with Carr, much less the rest of my truncated life. Because I'm more certain now than I've ever been before. Even if I become the Successor, I will never let someone die to extend my own life.

"Have you told him that you love him?" she asks.

"I don't know if it would make things better or worse."

"Better. My brother needs love in his life. Even if it's only for a few days."

"You don't mind?"

She studies me, as though picturing the different roles I've played in her life. Friend. Princess. Traitor. Sister. "I want my brother's last days to be happy."

"So you forgive me?"

She hesitates and then holds up her wrist. "I missed you. Hanoi has been an absolute dear, but I missed having my best friend."

My heart bobs in my chest. Just when I thought all the happiness was stripped from my life, a trickle of joy finds its way back. I press my wrist against hers. "Oh, Astana, I missed you so much."

"I also have something to confess. This colonist has gone and fallen in love with an Aegis, too. Who would have thought?"

"Denver has thirteen years left," I say. "It's not a lot compared to seventy-three, but it's still a long time. Especially now, I'm realizing how long."

"I'm glad I got sick." She looks at the feeding tubes, at her pale forearms. Instead of threads, they now resemble pasta noodles. "All my life, I've been chasing something bigger and better, when everything I've ever wanted has been right here. Someone who loves me no matter what. I don't need to do the primping and enhancements, the laughing and storytelling. I can just be me."

I squeeze her hand. "I'm so glad."

"Just think, both of us in love." She smiles, the old Astana smile, the first one she's given me since I chose not to exercise the veto. "Nobody ever told me how happy it would make me."

Nobody ever told me how much it would hurt.

CHAPTER THIRTY-FOUR

*T*he water gushes off the cliff, its roar deafening. If we had any predatory animals on Dion, this is what they would sound like. Ferocious, proud. And willing to eat you alive.

The four of us stand in front of Bubble Falls, a name too dainty to match its power. Me, Carr, and our two surveillance bots. Just one happy family.

"Any chance we can ditch the bots?" Carr asks. The falling water sprays our faces and makes the bots whirr back a few feet.

"I thought you'd never ask."

I kneel in front of my bot and press my palm against the sensor pad in its torso. "This is Princess Vela commanding you to shut down." The bot's eyes blink off and its mechanical limbs droop. I turn to Carr's bot and repeat the procedure.

He looks at me like I've solved the problem of the Aegis' shortened life spans. "That's it? We could've been free of the bots this entire time?"

I giggle. "I have a royal override. The same way my handprint can get me into any government building in the colony. Once the override is activated, it'll lock down the bot for ten minutes before it can be powered up again.

"But this trick will only work once. When Master Somjing finds out, I'm sure he'll reprogram the bot so it no longer responds to that particular command." Which, under the circumstances, will be the easiest I get off. But I'm ready to call Master Somjing's bluff. Astana and the others have improved so much. There's no way the council will take away their daily ration of food just because I want a last date with Carr. Perhaps forever.

"I wanted to save the override for a time that really counts." I wet my lips. "I was hoping today would be it."

His eyes flash. With the waterfall at his back and the sun lamps outlining his silhouette, he looks like one of the mythological gods. Apollo, maybe, god of all things enlightened and fierce protecter of his family.

"What did you want to show me?" I ask.

"Do you trust me?"

"With my life." The words should be ironic, but they're not. I'm not doing such a great job saving his life, but I trust him implicitly to take care of mine.

"Take a deep breath." Without further warning, he scoops me in his arms and jumps into the stream.

The water engulfs me, and the surge pushes us apart. I claw my way to the surface, and Carr pops up next to me. He's laughing. The sound erupts out of him like lava from a volcano and flows everywhere. To the expanding ripples caused by our cycling legs. To the slick muddy shore of the stream bank. To me.

"You could've told me we were going to jump." I shiver, from the cold water or his nearness. Probably both. "The bots wouldn't have followed us into the stream."

"But that wouldn't be as much fun, would it?"

I've never seen him like this before, so mischievous and pleased. And I can't help it. I propel myself forward and press my wet lips to his. Our limbs wind together, tangling like seaweed, and we sink deeper into the stream. We kiss all the way down, and even when the water closes over our heads, we keep on kissing.

When we finally surface for oxygen, my heart feels like it's been working as hard as my lungs.

"Ready to keep going?" he asks.

"There's more?"

"A lot. We're going to swim straight through the waterfall, okay?"

Not okay. The way the falls sputter and spew, I'm not sure I'll make it to the other side. But with Carr holding my hand, I feel like I can do anything. I nod and take a deep breath. And we begin to swim.

The stream bubbles around us, like a pot of boiling water, and the waterfall batters our backs. My body plummets half a foot in the water, but Carr tightens his grip on my hand and yanks me through.

We emerge in a dark, cool cavern, with four or five tunnels leading deeper into the planet. Everywhere I look, stalagmites sprout from the ground and stalactites drip from the ceiling, as thick as trunks and as thin as twigs.

"How did you find this place?" My voice comes out hushed. The natural, free-form beauty of this place demands it.

"By accident. Astana dared me to swim through the Falls once. I've been coming here ever since." He takes off his thin cotton shirt and wrings it.

I swallow. Whereas before, I averted my eyes when he was in front of me, shirtless, now I can't help but stare. His chest is wide and solid, his abs hard and defined.

With fumbling fingers, I remove the outer layer of my

clothes, leaving a sufficiently modest tank top and shorts. Unlike Carr's flimsy shirt, the thick material of my eating caftan has absorbed my body's weight in water. No amount of wringing will get the wet out, so I lay the caftan on a rock to dry.

When I turn back to Carr, his eyes are fixed on my bare arms and legs. "You'd better not touch me," he says in a strained voice. "Otherwise, we might not make it any further."

I flush. Did I say the cave was cool? Every square inch of my skin is burning hot.

He leads me through the stalagmites into one of the tunnels, and despite his warning not to touch him, he offers me his hand. When my fingers close over his, energy flows between us, fusing our skin together.

A short distance later, the tunnel opens into a larger cave. The walls are smoother here, and the light more muted. A single sky-hole opens the top of the cavern. And jetting straight through the middle of the cave is a river of turquoise, yellow, and magenta.

My heart stutters. "This is like the hologram." Except so much more. The colors more brilliant, the drops of water more distinct. If I kneel and stick my hand into the stream, I'd feel real, cool wetness.

"You said you wanted to see the colored streams." He looks at me as though the only thing he's ever needed to see is…me. "This is the only place I know inside the shield where you can see unfiltered water."

"It's beautiful. If a piece of a nebula broke off and fell into the water, this is what it would look like."

Unexpectedly, tears spring to my eyes. I haven't cried this entire time. Not when Carr was selected as the Fittest, not when my father collapsed. And here I am, crying at a bit of water.

Maybe my emotions were just filling up, like the maple syrup that drips from a spigot. Or maybe it's because I never needed a gift from Carr. I treasured the trinkets he gave me all those years ago, but only because they were from him. And now he's given me a piece of my dreams, based on an offhand comment.

"Don't be sad." He wipes the tear off my cheek with his finger.

"I'm not," I say, my throat tight, my chest even tighter. "I've never been happier. Truly."

He brings the finger to his lips and tastes my tear. "Doesn't taste happy to me," he whispers. "Do you know what this custom means, when a colonist tastes someone's tears?"

I shiver, even though my skin is flushed with heat. How can I be so hot and cold at the same time? "I think Astana's mentioned it, but tell me again."

He takes my hand and leads me around a boulder, where a solar blanket and some pillows have been laid on the rocky ground. He must've come here earlier. He made an extra trip so I would be more comfortable. More tears escape from my eyes.

"You have to understand how it feels not to have food," he says. We settle on the still-warm blanket. "It's like one of our senses has been taken away. We crave taste, of any sort. And one of the most intimate things you can give to another person is the taste of your emotions. The taste of your tears."

He catches another one of my tears and holds it out, as if asking my permission, before bringing it to his mouth. "When someone tastes your tears, they are making a commitment to you. They're saying: I will love you forever. In order to accept the commitment, to pledge your love in return, you would reciprocate the action."

"But you're not crying," I say and then wince. Because he hasn't said the ceremony was about us. He hasn't said he loves me.

"That's because you haven't said 'yes.'" He shifts so he is right in front of me, the colored streams of water flowing behind him. My heart aches so much it might rise out of my body and become its own entity.

"I told you earlier my life was complete. I would be able to die, satisfied my life had served a purpose." He pauses, his breath tracing my eyebrows. "But you've given me something more than purpose. You've shown me joy.

"I've never done a thing for you, and yet you care for me anyway. I'll never forget that, Vela. Wherever I am, whatever medium my soul becomes, I will love you forever. But I would never seek to bind you to me when I'm no longer on this planet. So, my question to you is: will you be mine, for the next five days?"

Just when I thought my heart couldn't shatter anymore, he has to pick it up and run it through the shredder. I fly into his arms. "You don't have to put conditions on it. I'm yours forever, whether you like it or not."

And then I see it. A shimmering at the corner of his eyes. A gathering of moisture that becomes a single perfect tear. I lean forward and catch the tear with my mouth.

The colonists know what they're doing. The drop is the most exquisite thing I've ever tasted. Wet, salty. And fully Carr. I'd give up eating if I could taste his tears over and over again.

"I don't ever want to leave you, Carr," I whisper. "I never want to say goodbye."

I'm being selfish. This situation is hard enough. I shouldn't make it even harder.

But Carr just wraps his arms around me and pulls me

close. "Then don't." His voice is hoarse with emotion and need. "Let's stay here, the two of us, and pretend like we never have to go back. Pretend like there are no bots waiting for us. No transplant looming in a few days. Pretend like we have all the time in the world. All the love in the world. Can you do that? For one night, can you pretend with me?"

My father will worry. When they find out the bots are deactivated, the security detail may even send a search party. But none of that matters right now.

I belong to Carr, and he belongs to me. Heart, soul, and body. For one night, we can be together the way we're supposed to be, the way we're meant to be. This is the only night I'll ever have with him, and the memory of it will have to last a lifetime.

I'm not holding anything back.

"Yes," I say. "I'll pretend with you."

And on a solar blanket on the rocky ground, next to the colored streams of water, we pretend. All. Night. Long.

CHAPTER THIRTY-FIVE

Yesterday was only the second time in my eating career I've failed to meet quota. Since I missed the early and late evening meals last night, and the early morning meal today, I'm desperately behind on calories. And my stomach's letting me know it.

With every rumble and gurgle and growl, Carr grins a little wider. "It's a good thing we had your stomach to wake us up. Otherwise, we might still be sleeping."

We enter Protector's Courtyard, and my eyes skip to the flagpoles on top of the shuttle. To my relief, I don't see anything unusual. No purple distress flags, no royal guards racing around with alarmed looks on their faces. Just a few people window-shopping along the row of stores, which won't be open for another hour. Business as usual.

My stomach groans, and I press my hand to my abdomen.

Carr brings my hand to his lips. "You look cute when your face is the same pink as the unfiltered streams."

"How can you joke at a time like this? What if we're in trouble?"

"Nah. The security guys aren't idiots. It was pretty clear what was going to happen when you turned off the bots. They knew we were safe the second you reactivated them this morning."

I stop short, and our two surveillance buddies cease rolling behind us. "Was I that obvious?"

"I wasn't sure." He brushes a strand of hair off my forehead. "But I was certainly hoping."

He leans forward, about to kiss me, when Denver comes bounding across the courtyard.

"Where have you been? I've been looking for you everywhere." Before we can respond, he rushes on, "Astana's not in her recovery unit. She's been gone since yesterday evening."

The blood drains from my face. Yesterday evening. After I powered off my surveillance bot. When I disappeared into a cave with Carr. The council threatened to withhold the patient's daily rations if I turned off my loop. Could this be their punishment because I shut down my bot? Could I have read the council so incorrectly?

No. They wouldn't hurt her. They couldn't.

And yet…and yet…

"Maybe they moved her to a different room," I suggest.

"They wouldn't tell me anything." Denver shoves his hands into his hair. "I don't have clearance."

My stomach rolls, and the action has nothing to do with the food I haven't eaten. "I'm sure she's fine. But we need to find her. Right away."

*H*er bed is neatly made. Creased sheet corners, a plump, fluffed-up pillow, folded solar blanket. But no Astana.

We stare at the empty bed and then look at each other.

"Where is she?" Carr croaks.

"I don't know." My voice is faint and reedy. "This is her room."

"So where is she?" He looks behind the wheelchair and the metal stand, as if she's small enough to hide behind either. "I'll check the cleansing room," he says when there's nothing left to inspect.

He leaves the unit, and my stomach lets out a large roar. I shove my fist into my mid-section. Not now! I need to think!

"Here." Denver pulls some pills from his eating caftan and hands them to me. "I just came from the Transfer Room."

"Thanks." I take them gratefully and fling them into my mouth. That's when I see Astana's surveillance bot against the wall, powered off the way mine was.

I sink to my knees in front of the bot. It is still and silent and strangely devoid of personality. It may have witnessed exactly what happened to Astana. But without a camera, and the human eyes behind it, this bot is as useless as the C-trunk in the corner. If I reactivate it, will it tell me who shut it down?

"That was me," Denver says, as if reading my thoughts. "We, uh, wanted privacy last night. I talked one of the security guys into giving me an override, and I guess I forgot to turn the bot back on."

I stand, pushing down my disappointment. The royal override is normally reserved for the King and his daughters, but I suppose he is part of the family. Besides, I can't begrudge him for wanting privacy when I did the same thing.

"Why don't you ask? They'll tell you. You're the Princess." He gestures to the call button on the bedrail.

"Good idea." I press the button that will connect me to the facility operator. When she answers, I explain as calmly as possible that Astana's not where she's supposed to be.

There's a pause, and I hear fingers tapping on the holo-desk. "She's been moved, Princess," the operator says. "Her condition worsened, and she was transferred to the TCU last night."

My heart stops. The Terminal Care Unit. But Astana's condition's not terminal! Last time I saw her, she was talking about spending the next thirteen years with Denver. She can't be in the TCU. She can't.

Carr rushes back into the room, thrusting a handheld at me. "I found this in the cleansing room. You have to read it."

The handheld appears to be Blanca's, and the document open is a report to the council. One I don't have security clearance to read. Ordinarily, I would never look at the report without her permission. But this situation's anything but ordinary.

I hold up the handheld and skim the report. My eyes snag on a few key words: "unrest," "precedent," and "collapse."

My heart sinking, I start at the beginning and read more carefully:

It is my recommendation that we do not allow Astana Silver to become a permanent Aegis, no matter what privileges her brother has earned. This course of action may have been feasible had none of the other patients been given food. But now that they are all used to eating, CORA predicts unrest among the patients when their food is taken away. If Astana is shown preferential treatment, the unrest may slide into rebellion.

Unfortunately, we do not have the resources to make all the patients Aegis. The food shortage in our colony is very real, and we cannot set a dangerous precedent. More and more colonists will steal food, in the hopes that they will enter the patient pool and be elevated to Aegis status. We would be risking the collapse of our entire colony.

I respect we must honor the privileges of the Fittest, but we cannot jeopardize our colony's future. I suggest we find a work-around. We may even have to consider termination of the patient, as distasteful as this option may be.

At the bottom of the report is Blanca's fingerprint, certifying she is the author.

Carr reads the final paragraph out loud, his voice wobbling like a tuning fork. "Termination of the patient? What does that mean?"

My words come out garbled, as if every third syllable gets stuck in my throat and has to be left behind. I take a deep breath and try again. "It means we have to hurry."

*W*e run. I don't think I've ever run so fast, not even when I was competing in the Aegis Trials. Not even when I was trying to break my father's fall from the stage.

The scream greets us as soon as we round the corner to the TCU, long and loud and shrill. I've only heard that sound one other time: when Denver tackled Astana at the Bee Park, preventing her from unlatching a cage full of bees.

I run even faster.

We reached the glassed-in room of the TCU, and I see Astana through the window. My knees buckle, and I sway once, twice. On the third swing, Carr catches me and props me next to him on the window ledge. We stare.

Tubes come out of every surface of Astana's body. Her scalp, neck, temples, arms. She looks like a mutant octopus, one who doesn't know when to stop regenerating legs. Her features are open and dilated. Bulging eyes, flaring nostrils, gaping mouth.

Medical personnel wearing scrubs move around her. Blanca's also there, conjuring diagrams and images at the holo-desk. Hanoi's not present, but that's to be expected. Blanca wouldn't want her assistant to witness such a sick patient, especially one with the same disease as herself.

As I watch, my sister's lips move, barking orders at the team. But I can't hear her words, not above Astana's screams. Not through the glass wall keeping us out of the room.

"Hey." I rap my fist against the window. "HEY!"

One of the medics looks up. It's Mistress Barnett's apprentice. He says something to my sister. Blanca turns. For a moment, I read fear in her eyes, and then she shuts down the emotion, locking it behind the cold neutrality of her regular expression.

She barks an order, and a medic grabs Astana's pale stick of an arm. He finds a vein on the inside of Astana's elbow and produces a syringe the size of a ruler. I reach my hand out, only to hit glass. My hand falls back. The needle goes in.

The screaming stops.

Except it doesn't.

Astana's contorted body gyrates back and forth, her

mouth stretches wide open. She's still screaming, but no sound comes out.

"What did you do to her?" I clench my hands into fists and drum the beat into the glass. "What. Did. You. Do?"

Rage boils inside me. How dare they silence her? How dare they hide her pain, as if it won't exist if they can't hear it?

Carr joins his fists with mine. Together, we produce a drumming so loud it must vibrate across the entire bubble. My fists are not enough, so I add my voice to the noise. Carr follows suit. The sound is ugly and discordant, but it should be. Astana can't scream so we're doing it for her.

Finally, Blanca comes out of the TCU. She grabs me by the collar, Carr by the arm, and we both stumble. "Stop it, both of you," she says. "Just stop."

That's when I notice for the first time that Denver's no longer with us. I glance around the corridor, and he's nowhere to be seen.

I look at Blanca, into the face so similar to my own. She's been my sister for seventeen years. We've shared everything, from rag dolls to my father's love to memories of an incinerator. Is it possible I never knew her at all?

"Blanca, how could you?" I whisper. "How could you do this to Astana?"

Her head snaps back. "What are you talking about? I didn't do anything to her."

"The report, Blanca. We read your report to the council."

As I say the words, a wisp of hope rises in me. Maybe Blanca didn't write the report. Maybe Astana got sick on her own, and the medics are trying to fix her. Maybe this has all been a horrible, terrible mistake.

"You didn't really write those words, did you, Blankie?" My tone is pleading now. I'm a little kid again, begging for a turn on the swings. "You couldn't have. Something faked your fingerprint. Someone forged the report. Isn't that right, Blankie?"

She flinches. Her eyes travel to Carr, and she looks away quickly, as if she can't bear to face what she's done. "Sorry, kid." Her voice is heavy with an emotion I can't identify. Regret? Guilt? Or something else? "That report was all mine."

Her words are like a sledgehammer to my knees. I stumble forward, trying to regain my balance.

And then, Denver charges down the corridor with royal guards in tow. A split second later, Carr shouts, "Look!"

His palms are spread against the window, his face plastered to the glass. Astana sits straight up in bed, and she looks directly at him. Her lips curve in a gentle smile, and she mouths the words, "I love you, Carr."

No sooner are the words out of her mouth than she seizes up. Her body contorts in odd, grotesque angles, and she's gasping, gasping, gasping for breath. The machines emit loud, insistent beeps for help, and medics rush to her bedside. One trips over a wire in his haste. His feet fly out from under him and he slams onto the ground.

The entire time, Astana's eyes never leave her brother's face.

I know the moment the life leaves her body. I know it before the machines flatline. I know it before her body goes limp. I know it because her mouth moves again. And she says the word I dread most.

Goodbye.

CHAPTER THIRTY-SIX

*P*andemonium erupts. People run everywhere, yelling at each other, pulling tubes out of Astana's chest and plunging syringes into her arm. A medic presses defibrillator paddles over her heart. Her body bucks. One time, two times, three.

But she doesn't come back to life.

"Arrest her!" Denver half bellows, half moans, pointing a finger at Blanca's cowering figure. His face is twisted into something unrecognizable. "You saw the report. She did this! She killed Astana!"

The royal guards advance on my sister, and Denver falls to his knees, sobbing uncontrollably.

So that's where he was, I think dully. Summoning the guards. He's one step ahead of me. He predicted this would happen, and he held himself together long enough to direct justice in the right direction.

"I didn't do it." Blanca's shrill voice pierces the air. "Tell them, Vela. Tell them it wasn't me. You know I would never do that. You know it!"

The guards hesitate, looking to me for the final verdict. The machines have stopped beeping. The medics have pulled a white sheet over Astana's face. All eyes are watching me. Waiting.

"I…"

I can sway them. With a word, I can postpone her arrest. I can prevent my sister from being red-celled.

But all I can see is Astana's mouth, saying the word "goodbye." All I can hear is my sister's heavy voice and those cold, cold words. *That report was all mine. All mine. All mine.*

I couldn't save Astana. So I'm not about to save her murderer. I don't care whose sister she is.

"Take her away," I say thickly. "Get her out of here."

"Vela, please." Blanca claws the air, trying to reach me, but the guards grab her, wrenching her arms behind her back. "You have to help me. Please. You're my sister. I'm begging you—"

But I'm not listening anymore, and the cries get fainter and fainter as the guards drag her away. I crawl toward a heap collapsed on the ground, one that hasn't moved since the machines went wild.

Carr.

I should say something. Touch his shoulder. But my entire body is numb. My hands, my feet. My face is frozen in the last expression it held. I'd have to look in a mirror to see what that contortion is. I'm afraid if I touch him, if I speak to him, the numbness will flow from me to him, freezing us both.

He jerks up. Meets my eyes for an infinitesimal moment, a fraction of a second I will never forget as long as I live. And then he tears himself away. Stumbles to his feet and races, races down the corridor.

Taking all my numbness with him.

*F*or the next two days, I focus all of my efforts on eating. I swallow roasted cicadas and sweet potatoes; I digest cranberry sauce and dragonfly mash. I give myself entirely to my duty. To my colony. If I can't save Astana, I have to do some good for somebody, somewhere.

In the entire history of the Aegis, I don't think there's ever been an appetite like mine. I don't just surpass the daily records. I smash them.

Carefully, thoroughly, I work through the royal cook's entire repertoire.

I eat lemongrass crickets and papaya salad, sticky rice and mango.

Vermicelli noodles and fresh spring rolls, caramelized fish in clay-mud pots.

Steamed beetle buns. Congee with ginger and fried dough. An entire grilled eel.

I have kimchi stew and barbecued spider. Stone pot rice with sizzling fish eggs.

Sushi. So much sushi. Raw shrimp, raw salmon, raw tuna, raw yellowtail. With vinegar rice, wrapped with seaweed. Red pepper flakes, sprinkled with sesame oil.

This is where I stumble. I hold up a hand roll filled with deep fried salmon skin, trying to convince myself to put it into my mouth. Refusing to think of the way Astana used to admire the bright colors. The moss green of the wasabi next to the bright orange of the fish roe, layered with pale pink tuna and deep black seaweed. I cannot remember the clay model she built in her art class, the hours she spent studying the holograms to get the details exactly right.

The tears build behind my eyes. "Eat," I whisper to

myself. "Do your duty."

Quickly, before the tears can spill out, I put some ikura in my mouth. The orange fish eggs explode on my tongue, bursting with salt. It makes me feel like I am swallowing tears. I spoon more and more ikura in my mouth, because so long as I eat these tears, my own will not, cannot, fall.

I move on to hummus and falafel and anchovy salad with olives and onions.

Squid ink paella and cod fish omelet. Fresh honeycomb with fig preserves.

I eat bee larvae and sauerkraut, cabbage-wrapped dumplings. Empanadas and corn tamales. Ceviche and fried plantains. Grasshopper au poivre, salt-encrusted grasshopper, grasshopper sautéed in a wine-shallot reduction.

This is what Astana wanted, more than anything in the world. She wanted to experience every sensation, every adventure, and the thought that her sense of taste was never to be used killed her, literally killed her.

I gave her the first bite. None of this would've happened if I had refrained from that childhood temptation. When you come right down to it, this is my fault.

I killed Astana.

And so I continue to perform my duty. Because in a world where Astana is gone, a world that must be lit by something other than her voltage-shock personality, there's nothing left.

On the third day After Astana, as I've come to think about that day, I leave the Banquet Hall in search of Carr. I find him, of all places, in the Bee Park, sitting on the grass before a free-standing cage of bees. Not just any cage, either, but *the* cage. The one for whose latch Astana reached. The place where she would've taken her own life, a week ago.

I power off my surveillance bot. Surprisingly, the manual override still works. I guess security hasn't had time to disable the command. Or maybe the council thought Astana's death was punishment enough.

I sink onto the grass next to Carr. Without a word, he places his head in my lap. I tangle my fingers in his black hair and wish life could be as simple as this. The two of us, lounging under a sun lamp, a swarm of bees buzzing over our heads.

"She forgave me before she died," I say. "That afternoon, before we went to the caves. She called me her best friend again. I'm glad for that, at least. And…" The words get stuck behind my tongue. It seems a betrayal to Astana, to find anything even remotely positive in her death. But I have to voice my thought, because it's the only thing that's pulled me from one moment to the next. The one thing that's allowed me to pick up the next morsel and put it in my mouth. "Now you no longer have to be the Fittest."

He goes perfectly still. Even his hair seems to stiffen under my fingers. I pull my hands away. I've said something wrong. I know what. But I'm not sure why.

Slowly, as if he's a bot set on lag-motion, Carr retreats from my lap. "I made a commitment," he says, so quietly I have to lean forward to hear him above the drone of bees. "Your father crowned me in front of the entire colony. I would expect the council to keep their word, whether or not the transplant is successful. Why would you think I would back down because my end of the deal didn't turn out the way I wanted?"

My heart sinks to the level of my feet. From the time

I chose not to exercise the veto, I knew Carr and Astana were a package deal. If I failed to save him, she would be dead to me, as well.

But I didn't know the reverse was also true. I didn't know Astana's death would mean I would also lose them both.

"This isn't about your honor, Carr. This is your life."

"You know that's not true. Out of all people, I would expect you to understand. For the very same reasons you didn't use your veto, I can't step down now."

I open my mouth, but nothing comes out. Because he's right. I do understand. And deep down, I probably knew all along how he would react.

My insides turn. I want to grab one of the bees and shove it into my mouth. If it stings me on the way down, so much the better.

Why, oh why, can't he be a little less worthy? Why did I have to go and fall in love with someone so good?

"Let's not talk about this anymore." His voice is as miserable as my heart.

"Okay."

He puts his head back in my lap, and we stay there, not talking, until my stomach begins to growl. I activate my bot and excuse myself to go back to the Banquet Hall.

I take my usual spot at the dining table. Ramekins of cricket pot pie are stacked before me. Carrots and celery swim with crunchy insect legs in a thick gravy, baked inside a golden crust, and the smells of onion and rosemary waft in the air.

But I don't want to eat. Because if I take a single bite, I might get pulled under for another two days, and when I resurface, it will be the day of Carr's transplant.

I can't lose these final days.

For the first time since Astana's heart stopped beating,

something other than hunger stirs in the pit of my stomach. Something hard and resolved and determined. I've already lost one Silver sibling. I'm not going to lose another.

I jump from my seat. The food preppers look curiously at my untouched ramekins, but I don't care. I've eaten enough over the past two days to fulfill my quota for a week. The time for mourning is over. I've got a boy to save.

I think Astana would approve.

CHAPTER THIRTY-SEVEN

"**Y**ou think Astana was poisoned?" My foot falls with a thud. Mistress Barnett continues gliding down the corridor of the medical facility. After a few steps, I scurry to catch up. "Why?"

"Before her body went into shock, she exhibited the same symptoms as your father," Mistress Barnett says. She wears the medic's stone-gray jacket, and since it is early afternoon, her lips are still a uniform hue. No doubt she will have chewed off the color by the evening meal. "Vomiting, dizziness, muscular weakness. The cases occurred a week apart. We can't discount the similarities."

"But that would imply the two cases are related."

"Correct." She stops in front of a patient's unit, flipping her silver hair behind her. A computer is embedded in the wall. After scanning the head medic's retinas, the computer pulls up the patient's treatment plan. She taps on the screen a few times and then turns to me. "Any reason your sister might want to poison your father?"

Again, my foot jerks in the air. Again, I stumble over

nothing. I know Blanca's sitting in the red cells. I'm the one who sent her there. But I didn't expect her guilt to be presumed.

"You think she's responsible." The words are a statement, not a question.

"I saw her report to the council, Vela." Her voice is gentle, as though she's breaking difficult news to me. *My best friend's dead*, I want to shout. *Not much is difficult compared to that.* "We think Blanca got it into her head that she needed to make a grand gesture to impress us. Something unexpected, something that would guarantee her spot as the Successor."

I don't say anything. If Blanca was receiving the same type of talks that I was, if she felt the same pressure from the council, I get it. I would've been searching for something bigger, too.

"We told her 'no,' of course. I want you to know, Vela, we struck down her suggestion as soon as she made it. Not for a moment did we consider terminating Astana." With a shake of her head, Mistress Barnett absolves herself of any blame. "But your sister just couldn't let go of the idea."

The head medic isn't walking fast. In fact, she keeps stopping to check her patients' screens. But I drop farther and farther behind, as though my brain is spinning so fast my legs fail to work.

I don't buy it. The explanation that Blanca was looking for a grand gesture, sure. The fact that she wrote the report, she admitted herself. But this conclusion that she was somehow involved in my father's poisoning?

No. Way.

"You didn't see her," I say. "After my dad toppled off the stage, she completely fell apart. Her reaction was like when my mom passed away, but worse. Because he's the only parent we have left."

"You're right. I didn't see her. But I have a hard time imagining Blanca falling apart at anything."

"She didn't poison the King. I can guarantee it." There are few things I know to the core of my being. This is one of them. Blanca loves our father. She could never hurt him.

"You may be right," Mistress Barnett says. "But for now, she's our only suspect."

We arrive at the TCU. The site of Astana's death. I've been keeping the grief at bay, but now, gushing, hot despair knocks me over.

I reach for something—anything—to keep steady and end up hugging a medical cart. The scene replays in my mind like a hologram. Astana mouthing, "I love you," to her brother. Denver's unspeakable rage. And then my sister, pleading with me. *Please, Vela*, she said. *You know I would never do that. You know it.*

I refused to listen. But I'm listening now, Blanca. I'm listening as hard as I can.

Mistress Barnett goes into the glassed room to speak to the man lying inside. He's probably my father's age, with skin more creased than forgotten laundry. Even his wrinkles have wrinkles. This is the kind of patient the TCU usually receives—people near the end of their ninety years. Not girls like Astana, whose lives have just begun.

"Vela?" a clear, bell-like voice says as a soft hand lands on my shoulder.

I look up and see riotously curly hair gathered into a ponytail. Hanoi. In all this chaos, I forgot to think about my sister's assistant. Forgot to consider how she might feel now that her boss has been imprisoned for killing a patient with the exact same condition as her.

I lunge forward, gathering her in my arms. "You don't have to worry," I say fiercely. "She's in the red cells now. She can't hurt you. If it's the last thing I do, I'll find a way out of this mess. I'll find a way for you and the others to live."

"Are you talking about Blanca?" Hanoi asks, puzzled. "I'm not afraid of your sister. In fact, she made me the exact same promise. We've been meeting with the Fittest families every day, a few at a time. She's mounted a campaign to introduce them to all her patients, so they could understand whose lives they were saving. Starting with me."

I pull back. "She had a plan to save her patients?"

"Yes!" Hanoi squeezes my hands. "That's why I'm here. There's been a terrible mistake. Blanca didn't kill Astana. She couldn't have. She may not show it much, or at all, but there's goodness at her core. I believe that with every bite of food I've eaten, with every pill that Blanca's given me."

All of a sudden, I'm certain she's right. Blanca might be cold. She might've even been willing to let me be tortured. But she's not a murderer. I know that she didn't poison our father, so it stands to reason that she didn't kill Astana, either. She may be the only suspect so far, but she's not the right one.

Now I just have to prove it.

CHAPTER THIRTY-EIGHT

I dig my fingernails into my palms as I walk into the red cells. The last time I saw my sister, she begged for my help. And I turned her down. Hard. I left her to the mercy of the royal guards. How will she react when she sees me now?

Palmetto tells me to go to the last cell in the row. I'm alone, for once. After a heated discussion with Master Somjing, he agreed to retire my surveillance bot. I was planning on turning it off any chance I got, anyhow.

What's more, I'm beginning to wonder if the murderer has access to the security feeds. Maybe that was how they knew to strike as soon as Astana's bot was shut down. If so, there's no point in broadcasting my every move.

I walk down the corridor. Scratchy Girl and Defecating Guy are still here. As soon as they see me, they shuffle to the edge of the red beams. I nod and wave, but I don't say anything. We didn't have that kind of relationship—the talking kind.

To my shock, they spread their palms against their chests and tap three times. What? No. *No.* I don't know what they've heard, but I haven't been named Successor. The King is still very much alive. The royal greeting should be reserved for him.

I tuck my chin to my chest. A ruler wouldn't act this way, but I'm not a ruler. Yet.

The word slips out. Now when did that happen? When did the Successor position go from elusive dream to reachable goal?

I arrive at Blanca's cell, and the red beams blink off long enough for me to go inside.

"Nice of you to stop by. No one's been here other than Hanoi." My sister sits on the concrete floor, her face clammy with sweat. Her hair looks like it hasn't been brushed in days, much less washed. "To what do I owe this visit, Princess? Or maybe I should call you *Successor*?"

"Nothing's been determined," I say.

She snorts. "Right. I'm an inmate, if you didn't notice. No longer in the running for any race, much less the Successor."

"I was red-celled," I point out. "And I wasn't disqualified."

Hope lights up her face, and then, like a flickering candle, it dies. She sighs and pulls on the threads at her pant cuffs. Already, one pant leg is a couple inches shorter than the other. "Even if I'm found innocent, there's the matter of the council report. I wrote it. That's enough to knock me out of the race. So congratulations, little sister. The position is as good as yours."

Her voice cracks on the last word. She's lost so much these last few days. Her freedom. Her credibility. Most importantly, her dreams. Everything she's been working toward her entire life. Without these goals, I'm not sure who my sister is anymore. I don't think she knows, either.

"I didn't do it, you know," she says, the words directed at her pant leg. "No matter what I said in the report, I would never kill Astana. I would never advocate for a policy that would hurt Hanoi."

I sit on the floor and pick up a strand of her hair. "Yes. I'm beginning to believe you."

"You do?" She blinks half a dozen times and then bursts into tears.

I drop her hair. I've never seen my sister cry. Ever. Not when she fell and skinned her knees. Not when our mother burned in the incinerator. Not even when we waited in the lounge to hear news of our father.

"The analysis…is…sound…" She gulps at the air between words. "Even CORA agrees with me." The facts seem to calm her, and after a few more gasps, she's able to talk with only a bit of hitching. "Under every scenario where Astana was made an Aegis, CORA predicted everything from unrest to systemic collapse. The council needed to be aware of the findings."

She takes a shuddering breath. "I guess I was too forceful in my word choice. I didn't mean we should actually terminate Astana. I just wanted to impress upon the council how serious the situation was."

I stare at her. "You mean, your arrest was a semantic mistake?"

"Bad luck for me, she ended up dying. So, my poor word choice became a fingerprinted confession."

I look over my shoulder. The inmate in the next cell is listening to us. After being followed day and night by a surveillance bot, the extra audience shouldn't faze me. But the murderer could be anyone. They could have ears and eyes anywhere.

I shift closer to Blanca and push a button on the electronic fob in my pocket. Immediately, a wall of silence surrounds us. Along with calling off the surveillance bot,

Master Somjing loaned me his muffler. Now that I'm tracking down my best friend's killer, he thought the device might come in handy.

"You didn't suffer bad luck." I'm taking a chance, telling my sister. If I'm wrong, I could be giving information to the enemy. But I'm not wrong. I'm staking Carr's life on it. "Astana was poisoned. If you didn't do it, somebody else did. And we have to find out who."

"How?"

I peek at our neighbor. He has his head cocked, as if puzzled why he can no longer hear us. Good. The wall seems to be working.

"It's got to be the same person who poisoned Dad. The same one who wiped the files and deleted Zelo's identity. For some reason, they don't want me to find Zelo. So I'm thinking that's a good place to start."

"Have you tried tracing Zelo through his kid?" she asks.

I shake my head. "He doesn't have a kid. That's part of the problem. He has no family whatsoever."

"Zelo Hale?" Both her voice and her eyebrows jump. "Of course he has a kid. I saw him in the patient pool a bunch of times, visiting his daughter. Just ask Hanoi."

I go still. Because I remember seeing Zelo, too. In the wait lounge, after Carr's seizure. I thought he was there to check on Carr, but could he have been visiting someone else?

"You mean that little girl is his? The one with the pigtails?"

"Yeah. Brooklyn." The confirmation makes my stomach sink. That's the one. The one who leaped off a stretcher into my arms. The one who couldn't keep in her feeding tube. Catch you, she said to me. Hold you. Save you.

"She called him 'Daddy,'" Blanca continues.

"Zelo lied to me." My voice is dull, my heart duller. He

said he had nobody in this world, no family, no friends. Certainly not an adorable little girl with flaxen pigtails. The guy whom I thought was so worthy, so deserving to be remembered in our history, lied.

What does this mean? Is he somehow connected to Astana's murderer? Could he *be* the murderer?

"The task was disbanded once I got arrested," Blanca says. "The council sent all the patients home with a month's supply of formula and told them we'd be in touch once they figure out what to do with me."

"So Brooklyn's gone?"

"Yes, but you can find her." As usual, my sister has the solution. "If Zelo never admitted to having a family in his Fittest profile, then the killer wouldn't know about Brooklyn. They wouldn't know to erase Brooklyn's file. The address is probably right where it's supposed to be. Find the girl, and you find Zelo."

Unless, of course, Zelo's behind this entire thing. In which case, he would know exactly what to delete. Still, I've got a lead I didn't have before.

"Blanca, you're brilliant."

"So they say. Unfortunately, that doesn't help me right now." Her mouth twists. "Before you run off, there's something else I want to say."

She takes a breath. And then another. As if she needs all the oxygen in this entire cell to give her the courage. "All my life, I've been so fixated on being the best, the smartest, the most logical. I'm not lovable like you. So I had to earn my position as Princess somehow. I had the rest of my future completely outlined, and I didn't think there was room for anything else. Not for friendship, not for kindness. Not even for my sister.

"That's a problem, V. It's a problem when my own sister

doesn't believe I'm innocent. That means I've been living my life very, very wrong."

"Blanca, I'm sorry—"

"No, don't apologize. You had no reason to believe me. Hanoi's the first friend I've ever had, and that's only because she wouldn't let me put up my walls. Every stone I laid, she punched out with equal force. I know I need to change. Now I just have to figure out how."

She turns her hand over, offering her wrist. That one hesitant movement means more to me than a hundred hugs from acquaintances, a thousand casual handshakes. Whatever else she's feeling, my sister's not acting now. This girl is the real Blanca, the one I used to know. The one I've always loved.

I cover her wrist with my own. "No, Blanca. You don't need to change. You just need to remember who you used to be."

CHAPTER THIRTY-NINE

I race down the corridor toward my father's recovery unit. I want to skip and jump and shout. In fact, I do, a kind of spin-hop that gets me a few inches off the ground and draws stares from the passersby and bots. The bots, because they're programmed to detect sudden movements. The medics, because they're wondering if they should be worried.

I don't care. Because I did it. I got Brooklyn Dorset's address. Colonists' Slag E3, Unit #422. The information was right there in the file, like Blanca said. In fact, CORA took less than a second to pull up the data once I keyed in the request.

I'm still not sure why Brooklyn's file was intact. Did Zelo get careless and forget to erase it? Or is he not connected to the murderer, after all?

Either way, I'm on the verge of an answer. I can feel it.

A bot whirrs up beside me. "Where are you going? Who are you seeing? Can I come?"

Since it's not *my* Nosy Bot, I put on a little speed and ditch it. And I don't even feel bad.

My breakthrough is exactly the news my father needs. He was devastated by Blanca's arrest. Oh, sure, he tried to hide his distress, but there, in the set of his lips, in the stillness of his gaze, I could see the questions. *Is this my fault? If I had been a better parent, more accessible, would this crime have happened? What could I have done better?*

I round the doorway, and my thoughts and feet stop short. My father has company.

He lies against a standard-issue pillow, eyes closed, a single wire extending from his chest to a bulky machine. His hand is on the shoulder of a young man. I can't see the guy's face—his head is lowered over clasped hands—but I'd recognize that sliver of forehead anywhere. Carr.

I sway on the threshold. Should I go in? Neither of them are speaking, and yet, I get the feeling they're having a very definite moment. One I can't bear to interrupt.

I back from the door, before either of them sees me. I no longer feel like jumping. My father and the boy I love. The two most important men in my life.

Most girls would be overjoyed to witness their connection. Not me. Because if this address doesn't pan out?

I may not get to keep them both.

*T*he fluorescent bulb in the hallway is out, so the only light comes through a broken window no one's bothered to fix. The entire floor could use a good sweeping, but as with the bulb and window, there's nobody to clean. Nobody to care.

I find the right door and slap my hand against the panel. Immediately, the door lights up and begins to flash. The Dorsets live in a similar unit to the Silvers, but I never had to light up Astana's door. I always walked right in.

Not anymore. I'll never barge in on my friend, with or without lighting her door, ever again.

My chest tightens, and I work to keep my breathing regular. In and out, in and out. Not now. This is not the time to miss my best friend.

But when? Is there ever a good time to have a hole punched through your heart?

I blink back the tears, and the door creaks open. A young woman peers out. I remember her from the medical facility. She has the same flaxen hair as Brooklyn, but instead of pigtails, it's tied in a knot at the base of her neck.

"Yes?" she asks. "May I help you?"

I give her my best harmless smile. "We met at the medical facility. I'm Princess Blanca's sister, Vela—"

"I know who you are," she interrupts. "Are you here about my baby? Are we moving back to the facility?"

There's so much hope in her voice, so much desperation. I know in this instant the council was right to push Blanca. Yes, feeding tubes are an inspired intermediate solution, but they can't give the patients back their lives. If the council doesn't come up with a better answer, if the Fittest families don't relent, little Brooklyn may not see the age of three. Hanoi may not live past the year. "I'm sorry. The council's still trying to straighten things out. How's Brooklyn doing?"

"Awful." She pushes away a strand of hair that's dislodged from her knot. "I'm on her every second, and even then, she pulls out the tube ten times a day. She's driving me crazy!"

"And you're her mother? Camden Dorset?"

She nods, her shoulders rising preemptively, as if she expects me to criticize her. She's young, in colonist years, to be a mother. It's not uncommon for Aegis to bear children this early. We only have thirty years to live, after all. But most colonists, with their longer life spans, don't have babies until later in life.

"I'm looking for Brooklyn's father," I say.

"Her father?" she echoes, her voice as blank as her face.

"Yes. Zelo Hale? Does he live here?"

Her eyes narrow, her lips tighten. If this conversation disintegrates, I have no doubt who will throw the first punch. "I have no idea who you're talking about. I've never heard that name before."

"Maybe he's an uncle, then? Or a friend? My sister saw him visiting Brooklyn at the facility."

"You have the wrong place. Sorry."

She tries to shut the door, but I stick my foot out. The door slams into it, crunching my shoe between metal and doorframe.

Ow. A supernova explodes in my head, and I swear I hear bones crack.

But at least the door doesn't close.

"Who is it, Camden? Is everything okay?" a familiar voice asks.

The door opens again, and Zelo appears, wearing a form-fitting blue shirt and pants. He doesn't look like the disciples of the Temple, with their wardrobe of flowing clothes. Nor the other candidates, with their uniform sweats. He looks exactly like who he is: a regular guy…and a father.

He does a double take when he sees me, maybe because I'm hopping on one foot and cradling the other one in my hands.

"I'm sorry." His eyes ping-pong between me and Camden. "Can I get you anything? Ice? A bandage, maybe?"

Camden crosses her arms. The only thing she's sorry about is not shutting the door harder.

"I'll be fine. I could sit for a few minutes, if you don't

mind." Before he can come up with an excuse to turn me away, I limp across the threshold, clenching my jaw with each step.

We move into the main room, and Zelo pulls the couch out of the wall. A vase of bright, blooming azaleas sits on the window ledge, and small puddles litter the floor.

Brooklyn stacks building blocks in a precarious tower. Her feeding tube lies on the ground, as silent and insidious as a snake, dripping out the nutrients that should be going inside her.

"Brooklyn, no!" Camden snatches up the tube and attaches it to the port in the little girl's stomach. A small pool of liquid remains where the tube lay. "What did Mummy say? You have to keep in the tube."

"Make you!" Brooklyn smashes her tower with so much force the tube falls down along with the blocks. Camden blows the hair out of her face and reattaches it again.

"That's her new favorite phrase," Zelo says, helping me to the couch and sitting next to me. He half laughs, half sighs, as if he doesn't know whether to be frustrated or proud. "We're at our wits' ends."

"Is all that liquid from her formula?" I count the puddles. Four…five…six…

"I have to leave the puddles there until the end of the day," Camden says. Her shoulders are in their defensive position again. "That way, I'll know how many nutrients she's lost. When she cries at night, I need to know if she's hungry."

"Do you have enough formula bags?" I ask.

"The facility sent us home with a month's supply. Only two days have passed, and she's already gone through a week's worth."

"I'll make sure you get more."

Camden's lips tremble, but no sound comes out. It's as if

she can't bring herself to thank the enemy. Without another word, she scoops up her daughter, along with the portable stand, and leaves the room.

"You may not be able to tell, but she does appreciate your generosity," Zelo says. "We both do."

We. Our. This whole visit, Zelo's been talking in the first-person plural. Back at the shuttle, during the trials, it was all "I" and "me." Language that suggested he was alone in this world. When he clearly isn't.

"So, you have a baby," I say.

"Yes." His voice is resigned, as if he knows he's past the point of lying.

"And Camden? Is she your wife?"

"Girlfriend."

"I'm guessing you also didn't receive a message from God. And he didn't tell you to die for the King."

He ducks his head. "I didn't lie about my entire background. The part about growing up at the Baby Unit, the origins of my name. That was all true. I even prayed at the Temple for a short time, when I was feeling particularly lost. But I didn't tell you the whole story."

I study his flat nose, the horizontal eyebrows. This boy I thought I knew but didn't. I built up his image in my mind. How much of my deception was fueled by his lies, and how much by my own need to believe? I wanted so badly to find the perfect candidate. Not only so I could save Carr, but also so I could sacrifice a boy without feeling remorse. The old Zelo fit every criterion.

"Why did you lie? Can you tell me the real story now?"

He sighs and picks up a rag doll lying by his feet. Tiny holes—the kind a toddler's teeth might make—puncture the doll's skirt. "When Brooklyn was born, we didn't have many pills. I was working a double shift at the glasshouses, and we still didn't make enough to feed her. Baby nutrition pills cost twice as much as adult ones. Did you know that?"

I shake my head, guilt slithering through my heart. I should've known. If I'm to be the ruler of this colony, this is the kind of information I need to have. My father has kept me too sheltered. The moment I'm selected as the Successor, and even if I'm not, things are going to change.

"She cried constantly. The only time she would stop is when we gave her a pill. When the effects of the pill wore off, she cried again. You didn't have to be a genius to figure out she was hungry."

His fingers tighten around the doll, and he stares into its opaque button eyes. "I started stealing from the glasshouses. Fruit, mostly. Bananas, avocados, peaches, pears. Soft foods that were easy to mash up. A different place every day so I wouldn't get caught." He looks up. "Brooklyn was happy for the first time in her short life. We didn't count on her body developing a resistance to the pills."

"That's why you were competing to be the Fittest? So Brooklyn can eat real food?" My voice is faint and far away. Because that's the same reason Carr chose to compete. The exact. Same. Reason.

He nods. A single tear drops onto the doll's button eyes, so it looks like she's weeping, too. "You should've heard her crying, Princess. Her sobs weren't the brash screams you hear from most babies. She was so weak her cries sounded more like musical notes. The saddest song I've ever heard."

My chest squeezes. The room is silent, but I can hear the haunting melody of her cries in my mind. The helplessness pools in my gut, the kind that makes you antsy and scared and determined all at once. And I know I would've done the same thing in his position.

"I'm sorry I lied." His shoulders move with his breath.

"But I knew there was no way you would deem me worthy if you knew who I really was. A liar and a thief."

All of a sudden, I'm certain Zelo had nothing to do with Astana's death. I was wrong about him, but not *that* wrong.

"If you're a liar and a thief, then so am I. The council forgave me for stealing food. And my motivation wasn't even as good as yours."

I take the doll out of his hands and wipe the moisture from her eyes. So that's it, then. He's not a boy on a mission from God. He has a family. A *daughter*. I want to save Carr, but not like this. Even my love for him doesn't extend to ripping a father from his child. "Take care of your family, Zelo. I'll do everything in my power to make sure Brooklyn gets well."

I get to my feet and limp to the door.

"Wait, Princess," he calls. "Why did you come?"

"No reason. No reason that's important anymore."

"You found something, didn't you? When we last spoke, you said if there was a mistake, you would find it." His eyes blaze with the zeal I'm used to seeing in the old Zelo. Only now, I know the fervor isn't for God. It's for his daughter. "Tell me. I was willing to lay down my life for your father. You owe me at least this much."

He's right. I came this far. He deserves an explanation. "The files were wiped. We're trying to reconstruct the data using the candidates' silver discs, so that we can determine if CORA made a mistake. Only one disc is missing. Yours."

He jumps off the couch, his arm swinging wide and knocking the vase of azaleas to the floor. "I'll get the disc for you."

"No, Zelo. I didn't know you had a daughter. Camden and Brooklyn need you."

"They need me to save Brooklyn's life," he says fiercely.

"You will not take this chance from me, Princess. This opportunity is my right as much as any of the candidates'."

My heart throbs in a way that's all too familiar. The council made me administrator of the Trials. Not judge, jury, and executioner. It's not my place to determine whom CORA may consider. Or is it?

"I don't have a death debt to redeem." His voice lowers, and I realize he must be a lot closer to Carr than I realized if he knows this much. "But I have a daughter whom I love very much. You gave Carr the chance to save his sister. Please, I'm begging you. Give me the chance to save my baby."

What do I say? What can I do? He's right. I did give Carr the chance. How can I treat Zelo any differently?

My head pounds with all the choices, but I don't need to make any decisions. At least not yet. "Get the silver disc. Let's see what CORA says."

"Thank you, Princess." He seizes my hand and licks it. And then frowns at the spilled vase on the floor. "I need to pick up this mess before Brooklyn eats a leaf and gets sick."

"Go ahead. I'll clean it." I kneel on the floor, the pain in my foot faded to a dull throb. "Where did these flowers come from, anyway?"

"Denver sent a vase home with each patient, as a memento of Astana. All the patients in the pool loved her, you know. He said azaleas were her favorite flower."

"They were." My heart heavy, I begin to gather the leaves and stems. So sweet of Denver. So thoughtful. I've been so consumed by my own grief, I haven't thought to check on my cousin. He must be devastated.

"Will he be taking over the task, now that Blanca's been red-celled?"

I jerk, and I cut my hand on a piece of the vase. "Why would he do that?"

"He seemed to be running things, that's all. Camden had an exit interview with him before she left, and he said he would be in touch."

Running things? Exit interviews? Denver's supposed to be mourning my best friend's death. I would think he'd be locked in his glasshouse, surrounded by his flowers and his memories. Not conducting exit interviews.

"I'll get that disc for you," Zelo says and disappears into the corridor.

I barely notice him leave. I pick up a delicate bloom. A drop of my blood falls on the petal, and I watch the stain of red spreading across the pink.

What's going on? My cousin must be grieving in his own way, determined to find a solution in honor of Astana. But he pulled himself together pretty quickly. I lost two days in the Banquet Hall, doing my duty so I wouldn't think, wouldn't feel. In order for Denver to conduct exit interviews, he'd have to go straight from the TCU to the patient pool.

I look down at the azalea. The petals flutter in the air. The movement comes from the trembling of my hand. I know that. But I feel as though the flower's trying to tell me something. What?

Zelo comes back into the room, carrying a filigree silver box. "I knew there was a reason I kept the disc in a safe place." He lays the box on the table and lifts the lid.

We stare at the crushed velvet cloth. And nothing else.

"Where's the disc?" I ask.

He shakes his head, a crease between his brows. And then his head snaps up. "Oh, dear Zeus. Camden has it."

CHAPTER FORTY

We check the three rooms of the living unit. No Camden. No Brooklyn.

"I don't understand," I say. "They were just here."

Throughout our conversation, I heard feet padding down the corridor. Toddler shrieks and giggles. Or at least, I thought I did. But maybe my imagination's filling in the blanks of my memory.

Zelo strides to the front entry, where the door has been left open a couple inches. "The door clicks when it closes. She didn't want us to hear them leave."

"Where would they go?"

His face turns winter-sky white. "The river. Dear Dion, she's going to throw the disc in the river."

He's out the door before the words exit his mouth. He dashes up the corridor and scuttles down three stories of steps cut into the rock.

I do my best to keep up. Did I think my foot was better? The scream along my bones disagrees.

"Where's the river?" I get out between pants.

"Right behind the Slag."

We hit the line of trees, and Zelo charges straight ahead. I'm assaulted by both the swing of branches and the smell of eucalyptus. Any other time, I would've stopped and let the smell transport me. Now, the scent is nothing but a wall through which to crash.

My foot catches on an exposed tree root, but I don't have time to fall. Branches scrape off the first layer of my skin, but I don't have time to feel. We run and run and run. I hear the river before I see it, a sustained roar of currents crashing over boulders.

We burst onto the shore, and I glimpse the long, unending line of water. It winds through the entire north end of our bubble. Despair fills me. How will we ever find her?

But Zelo seems to know where he's going. He heads to a cluster of boulders and slides down the back. There Camden sits, her back hunched, cradling Brooklyn between her legs. The portable stand holding the bags of formula is wedged in a rock, but the way the little girl's wiggling, she'll knock it over any second.

"Where's the disc?" Zelo kneels before his girlfriend. "Oh please, baby, tell me you haven't thrown it out. Oh please."

Camden looks up. Tears scratch down her dusty cheeks. She slowly lifts her hand and uncurls her fingers. Inside glints a silver circle.

Relief presses me up against the boulders.

But it is short-lived.

Even as I watch, Camden pulls her hand back and launches the disc into the river. Zelo grabs at the air, but it's too late. The disc disappears into a gush of white foam.

"It's gone," Camden says, her voice as grim as her face. "You're no longer in the running to be the Fittest. You're not leaving us."

"Watch me," Zelo says and dives into the icy current.

I hesitate. If the disc is gone, CORA won't be able to redo the calculation. I won't have to make a hard decision. And I won't be able to save Carr, either.

Staying on the shore would be the coward's way out. Whatever else I may be, I'm not a coward.

An instant later, I jump in after Zelo.

*T*he water swallows me up, uncomfortably cold, and my feet squish in the mud. I open my eyes underwater, and they sting, as if someone's poured oil and vinegar into them. But I can see, and that's what matters.

I surface for a breath. The water rushes against my collarbone, and the current pushes me down the river. Already, Camden is a figure in the distance.

I dive back under, twisting my neck as I try to look at every rock and vegetation that rushes by. Zelo is twenty feet downriver, and I hope he's doing the same. Our only shot is if the disc gets wrapped in some weeds or stuck in a cranny between boulders.

The water pushes me too fast. I don't have time to examine every moss and algae. Plus, I have to surface for precious seconds in order to breathe. I need to orient my feet in front so I don't smash into boulders. All of this takes time and focus from my search.

What are you doing? My lungs scream. *This is hopeless. Utterly hopeless.*

But then, as I'm rushing past two boulders in a *V* formation, something gleams at me. It could be a shiny rock. The scales of an iridescent fish. Maybe the trick of the sun lamps on my wishful eyes.

I turn my body and grab at the underwater tree roots. My first grasp isn't strong enough, and I slip farther down the river. I lunge again, both hands this time. Something sharp nicks my forearm, and the water turns cloudy red.

The roots hold.

I drag my head above the water. "Zelo! I see something! I see something!"

He must hear me. His entire body jerks, and I assume he's attempting the same maneuver as me.

My arms throb. My muscles ache. I'm not sure I can feel my toes. But I grit my teeth and painstakingly drag myself, hand over hand, up the river.

Carr's salvation might lie at those rocks. I'm going to make it there if it kills me.

Come on. Just a few more feet. You can do it.

Zelo is stronger than me, and faster, and he catches up as I arrive at the *V* formation. I brace myself against the rocks, take a breath, and duck under the water.

There it is again. That flash of silver. Were my eyes tricking me? Is it seaweed? I reach out, and for a moment, my hand wavers in the water. Afraid to touch, afraid to have my dreams destroyed.

And then I grab that gleam of color.

I feel not the slimy leaf of a plant, not the hard shell of a fish, but metal.

Sweet, glorious, manmade metal.

I've found Zelo's disc.

CHAPTER FORTY-ONE

I walk through the Bee Park in search of Carr. Path after path, honeycomb after honeycomb, green shrubs and orange flowers and purple skies.

Zelo's silver disc is with the control room analysts. Within the hour, they should be able to complete the data reconstruction and rerun the algorithms. Within the hour, we'll know whether someone tampered with CORA. Within the hour, we'll know once and for all whether Carr really is the Fittest.

Of course there was sabotage. Why else would the files be wiped? Why else would somebody delete Zelo's identity? I know this truth at the core of me, and in an hour, the rest of the colony will know it, too.

And yet, I don't feel like pumping my fist in the air. I can't shake my last glimpse of Zelo's family. Camden keening as if I've cut her heart out, her long hair dragging against the rock like a paintbrush. Zelo's face looking like the stone on which he was standing. Brooklyn clutching her father's hand like she would never let go.

Even now, Zelo's waiting at his living unit. One word from me, and he'll move into the shuttle and take Carr's place.

Carr will live. That's what's important. Right?

I reach the grassy knoll where I last spoke to him. The spot where my best friend tried to kill herself with a cage of bees, the place where her brother laid his head on my lap. Someone's cut the grass since I was here, shorn it too closely to the ground, so that the lawn looks bald. Empty. Devoid of all memories, good and bad.

The lump in my throat swells up. It hasn't gone away since Astana's death—and if I don't save Carr, I'm afraid it will never go away again.

If CORA reveals Zelo is the Fittest, it wouldn't be my fault. I didn't tamper with the data. I'm only making sure that CORA chooses the right candidate, the candidate it would've picked if there was no manipulation from the saboteur.

And no manipulation from me? a voice whispers.

Yeah, I did it. I can admit that now. I did manipulate the Trials. And I'm starting to think that if I could travel back in time, the way Blanca's always dreaming about, I would do it again. Because there's no good choice here. I don't want to dishonor the Fittest, but I don't want Carr to die, either.

Is that so wrong?

I ignore the lump and keep walking. Keep searching. Carr's not in the sculpture garden, either. Or by the bushes trimmed like serpents, or at the picnic tables around Protector's Pond.

I walk the entire Bee Park, and I can't find him anywhere. Instead, I come across a row of azalea bushes, covered with pink and white blooms. The flowers aren't as big as Denver's glasshouse variety, but the overall shape is the same.

My breath quickens, and my skin prickles. A feeling descends on me, as warm and encompassing as a bubble bath. These bushes were my destination all along. But why?

A thought niggles at the back of my mind. Something Zelo said before we discovered that the silver disc was missing. Something vital concerning these flowers.

I sit in front of the bushes and rub my foot. It's aching again, probably exacerbated by my strenuous run to the river. The real sun is on its way down outside the bubble, and the sun lamps have been dimmed. Someone must have turned on the wind machine, because a slight breeze ruffles the blooms on the bushes. The only sound I hear is the music of the nighttime insects.

A flash catches my eye, and I turn to the free-standing cages behind the bushes. As I watch, the wings of a bee light up.

"Pretty, aren't they?" a voice says.

I scramble to my feet. The voice belongs to a beekeeper dressed in a yellow jumpsuit, with a mesh veil falling from a wide-brimmed hat.

"What makes the bees light up?" I ask. "I've only seen fireflies do that."

"We have both cross-pollinators and honey-producers here at the Park." He swings a smoke canister at his side. "And we don't want anyone getting sick because we mix them up. These bees have been genetically engineered to light up when they've fed on poisonous flowers."

I go still. The scene with Zelo replays in my head, from his arm sweeping the flowers to the floor to my hand being cut on a piece of the vase. "You mean honey can be poisonous if the bees feed on the wrong nectar?"

"Oh, sure. You never want to eat honey made from oleanders, rhododendrons—"

"And azaleas?" I interrupt.

"Yep. Azaleas, too. Every part of the plant is poisonous. Stems, leaves, everything."

Better pick up this mess before Brooklyn eats a leaf and gets sick, Zelo said. He knew. Somehow, he knew that every part of the azalea plant was poisonous to the human body. How? Did Denver send the flowers home with instructions?

Denver.

Dozens of images cram my mind.

Denver encouraging me to cheer on Zelo. Denver knowing too much about the switch from oranges to apples. Denver bringing us our favorite snacks—candied crickets for me and honey toast for my father. Denver telling me not to give Astana false hope. Denver finding Blanca's incriminating memo. Denver admitting he turned off the surveillance bot. Denver siccing the guards on Blanca.

Denver, Denver, Denver.

"No," I say out loud. "No. Way."

The beekeeper jostles the smoke canister. "Excuse me, Princess?"

I try to curve my lips, but they're like rubber that's overheated under the outside sun. "Just thinking out loud. Wondering if I could, um, have some of these light-up bees as pets."

"You could. Your cousin Denver's got a whole hive of them in his glasshouse."

A blast of cold slams into my core and spreads to my hands, my feet, my nose, my ears. I can't breathe. My lungs are frosted over, and drawing in air is like trying to inhale an ice cube through a straw.

I don't believe it. I refuse to believe it. Denver isn't the enemy. He's my cousin, my friend. My longtime fort buddy. He couldn't have killed Astana. He *loved* her.

Or at least, she loved him.

I shake my head, hoping to clear it. But it's like every spider in our colony has descended on my brain, weaving cobweb on top of cobweb, suffocating logic, blocking my ability to think.

What reason does he have to kill Astana? He doesn't have political aspirations. He's content to toil away in his glasshouse, breeding his next variety of azaleas.

Or is he? He took over Blanca's task the moment she was sent to the red cells. His mother wants him to reach the highest levels of achievement. If Blanca and I were to become disqualified, he would be next in line to be the Successor.

Is it possible? Could Denver have hidden his real goals behind his charm?

The thought rises like steam along my body. Any moment now, it will blow my head off, flinging the cobwebs to the outer edges of our bubbles. Dear Dion, what if the enemy all along was Denver?

He's been everywhere this entire time. He had both knowledge and opportunity. He's had his hands in everything. And I never saw it. Until now.

"Princess, are you okay?" The beekeeper peers at me, his concern apparent even through the mesh veil.

"I have to go." I dart my eyes from bees to azaleas to trees, expecting to see my cousin pop up behind a bush. Don't be ridiculous. He's not here. He can't hurt you.

He already has.

No. I won't believe he's guilty, not until I see the proof with my own eyes.

"Thanks for the information," I say to the beekeeper.

And I run off, as fast as my injured foot will carry me.

CHAPTER FORTY-TWO

*T*he last time I visited Denver's living unit was when he and his mother moved in. The cottage is still situated at the edge of the fish farms, at the southernmost point of the colony's bubble. Moss still creeps over the stone walls, and the smells of seafood and rich black soil still tangle in the air.

Time could've stood still these last two years—except for one thing. Behind the cottage, another glasshouse has been erected, smaller and squarer than the ones growing crops at the opposite side of the bubbles. This must be Denver's lab. The place where he breeds his azaleas.

Sweat beads on my forehead, and I wipe my palms on my caftan. My muscles bunch, as if I'm back at my Aegis Trials, waiting for the bell that would signal the start of the next challenge.

The difference is: for this challenge, I'm not prepared. If I had an entire ninety-year lifetime to plan, I still wouldn't be ready.

Doesn't matter. I have to confront Denver, anyway. If he's innocent, I need to cross his name off the suspect list.

And if he's not…it won't matter how fondly I remember our childhood.

I try the door. It's locked. No matter. Denver received the funds for this glasshouse from the King, and like all government facilities, the door opens immediately with the royal override.

I step across the threshold, my toes curling around the metal cylinder wedged at the front of my shoe. The muffler Master Somjing lent me. The device that's going to convict Denver or clear his name. And my exit strategy.

Shelf after shelf of flowers greet me. There are blooms in every possible shade, with petals pointed, round, and star-shaped. As I watch, the shelves slowly rotate, so that each level gets exposed to the sun lamps and sprinkler system overhead.

I lean over and sniff the flowers. Some don't smell at all, while others have a lemony, almost spicy scent. I brush my finger over the powdery petals. As soft as a baby's kiss. Who would have guessed something so exquisite could be so deadly?

I walk to the end of the aisle and pick through the supplies scattered across a long table. A pair of rubber gloves. Empty flower pots. Cubes of dirt with a few green leaves beginning to sprout.

And then, I see a jar of honey, with an azalea decorating the glass.

My heart pounds, each beat racing the next to an unseen finish line. My legs shake, as wobbly and insubstantial as a flame. Despite the warmth of the glasshouse, despite the sweat stinging my eyes, every hair on my arms stands up. I want to run. I want to hide. I want to be anywhere but here, do anything but this, see anyone but Denver.

He did it. He actually killed Astana.

Up to this moment, part of me hoped I was wrong.

Hoped this was all a terrible misunderstanding. Hoped my cousin was still the boy who fell in love with my best friend.

But with this jar of honey, all my hopes evaporate like morning dew under the sun lamps.

I hear a buzzing and force myself to move to the end of the table, where there is a box-like shape covered with a piece of cloth. Squeezing my eyes shut, I pull off the fabric.

Bees. Hundreds of bees. Instead of one or two, every other one is lighting up. It's like a New Year's laser show in there.

"You found my pets."

I whirl around and almost scream. It's him. My cousin. And Astana's murderer. He walks toward me in a beekeeper's uniform. The same thick jumpsuit. The same wide-brimmed hat with mesh veil.

"You scared me." My voice squeaks like a toy mouse, and my hands tremble as I bring them to my throat. At least I don't have to pretend to be jumpy.

His eyes dart around me. I can't tell what he's looking for at first, but then I get it. The surveillance bot. He wants to make sure no one's watching.

"What are you doing here?" He pulls the blanket over the bees. Mild-mannered, charming Denver. That's always been his disguise, hasn't it? Everybody's friend, completely content to work in his glasshouse, breeding new varieties of flowers.

Poisonous varieties.

Heat flushes through my entire body, and red smears across my vision. Every cell inside me vibrates, and my head feels like it's going to explode.

My fear shifts, changing like a werewolf. The emotion takes a new form, one that has blood-red eyes and sharp, pointy claws.

I want to rake my nails across Denver's face. I want to sink them deep into his chest. I want to dig out his still-beating heart and slash it into thin, ragged strips. I want to feed the strips to the buzzing bees, or better yet, leave his heart at the bottom of the cage to rot and fester and decompose. And those actions still wouldn't be enough.

But I can't let my anger take over. Not yet. He poisoned my father and killed my best friend, and he's not going to get away with his crimes.

I give my cousin a sweet smile. Make that honey sweet. Poisoned-azalea sweet. "We haven't talked since Astana died. I wanted to see how you were feeling. Make sure you're okay."

"That's so nice." He walks to me and places his hands on my shoulders. His fingers curl toward my collar, feeling for the loop that's not there.

After a few swipes, he slides his arms around me. It's all I can do not to pull them out of their sockets.

"It's been hard," he says. "But I'm trying to keep busy."

"By taking over Blanca's task?"

The arms fall, and I take a few steps back, pointing the muffler in my shoe toward him.

Except it's not a muffler. The cylinder has been switched to the inverse. Instead of a wall of silence, the device amplifies the sound within a ten-foot radius. Loud enough that the security teams positioned outside the glasshouse can hear our conversation.

"I ran into one of the patients from Blanca's task," I say. "Her father said you seemed to be stepping into Blanca's role. Giving them instructions. Sending them home with your azaleas."

"I petitioned the council to put me in charge of the task." He takes the veil off his head and lays it on the table.

His tone is so mild. So smooth. "Those poor patients. They can't be set adrift because Blanca went rogue. The pressure must've gotten too much for her."

"Is that the story you're telling?" My heart bounces around my chest, about to slide right out my mouth, but I have to keep my act together. I have to stay calm until he confesses.

I pick up a pair of tweezers from the work table and test the point with my finger. "Tell me, Denver. If you assume Blanca's role, will you also inherit her candidacy for the position of Successor?"

"If that's what the council wishes."

"The council? Don't you mean it's what you wish?"

His eyes glitter. Sharp, dangerous, and nearly wild. How could I have missed that desperate need inside them? The ambition that will do anything to win. Even kill.

The acid spurts up my throat. He was my friend, that's why. My old fort buddy. I trusted him implicitly because of our childhood bond. When did the monster take the place of the boy? Was it before or after his father died? Before or after he moved from the shuttle?

Or maybe, as Blanca says, he didn't change at all. Maybe he's been this way all along, and I've simply just discovered it.

"Did you ever love her?" I whisper, sick to my stomach. Sick in my lungs, in my kidneys. Sick to my eyelashes and fingernails. Sick in every pore and chromosome of my body. "Or was she just a pawn in your vile game?"

"What are you saying, cousin?" He crosses the floor in a blink and wrenches my arms behind my back. The tweezers clatter to the ground, and I yank my hands up and out. He must've underestimated my strength, because I actually break his hold. I edge away a safe ten feet. I didn't expect him to get violent so soon, but the basic plan hasn't changed.

Keep him talking. Get him to confess.

"You're so clever." Betrayal makes my voice raspy. "Bringing us our favorite snacks before the crowning ceremony. You knew the king's favorite food was honey toast, didn't you? Lucky for you, you happened to have poisonous honey on hand, made from bees that fed on your azalea flowers. Is that how you killed Astana, too? By giving her poisoned honey?"

He advances again, and I dodge left. But this time he's ready for me. He lunges in the same direction and bands his arms around me, and no matter how I struggle, I'm no match for his superior strength.

"Get your hands off me!" I scream at the top of my lungs. I don't have any hope that he'll actually listen, but I need to let Master Somjing and the rest of the team outside know that I'm in trouble. That they should barge in as soon as he confesses.

He drags me to a foundation beam and ties my hands around it with a piece of rope. The pulse thunders at my throat, and my mouth is as dry as planetary dust. But I have to stay calm. I have to draw him into conversation.

"Why'd you poison the King?" I pant. "Astana, I can understand." *No, I can't*, my heart rages. *There's no reason, on Earth or Dion, that justifies you taking my best friend's life.* But I need to talk to him on his level. Speak in the rationale of a demon. "You found Blanca's report to the council, and you couldn't resist. She set herself up perfectly. You could disqualify Blanca in a single move, so you took it."

He grins at me, teeth flashing under the lights, as if he's pleased, finally, to be sharing his brilliance with someone.

"But the King? I don't get it. He was like a father to you."

He snorts. "You have no idea what he was to me." His eyes blaze, as hot as any incinerator. "The King wasn't my father. I didn't grow up a prince. I was the half-colonist bastard who couldn't even live in the shuttle with the rest of you."

"That was your mother's choice." I lean forward, but the rope holds me back. There's just a bit of slack in the knot, and I wiggle my wrists back and forth, trying to loosen it. "Remember? The King gave her special permission to live in the cottage, but it was a favor, not a punishment."

He shoves me back against the beam. "Nobody asked me if I wanted to give up two-thirds of my life. You got to choose, but I didn't. My father made the decision for me. He threatened to throw me out of the bubbles if I didn't get the genetic modification. And then, as soon as I became an Aegis, he had to go and die, breaking my mother's heart. I'm all she has, and I'm not leaving her, too."

I pull my hands against the binding, and the rope rubs against my skin. He didn't answer my question. I need to steer him back to the topic. I need to get him talking about the King. "Is that why you want to be Successor? So you can extend your life?"

"Among other reasons. I'd also make a pretty good king, if I say so myself." He leans over and touches my cheek. "You were a good friend to me. But the only things I ever got in this life were by taking them for myself. So that's what I'm doing."

He strides back to the cage and pulls off the blanket. The bees buzz angrily, as if they can't wait to be let out.

"Wait!" I jerk my hands, and blood trickles down my wrist. *Try harder, Vela. Try. Harder.* "I found Zelo and his silver disc. Whatever your end game is, it's not going to work. We're going to uncover the true Fittest, and it's not going to be Carr."

Denver sighs. "Oh, cuz. I didn't want my plans to come

to this. All you had to do was take some unethical action to yank Carr out of the race. The council was already wary of you. Everybody knows you always put your heart above your principles. You just had to prove one last time that you will always bend the rules when it comes to those you love, and the council would've disqualified you for good." He runs his fingers against the mesh cage, caressing his pets. "Everything I did was to help you along. Fixing CORA so that Carr was named the Fittest. Poisoning the King in order to speed up the transplant."

I release my pent-up breath. Finally. He confessed. The security teams will bound in here any second, to save me and arrest Denver.

Except they don't.

"I have to say, I'm impressed." He picks the veil off the table and slips it on his head. "I never thought you had this kind of backbone. But if you won't take yourself out of the running, I'll have to do it for you. Lucky for me, I specifically cultivated these bees to be aggressive."

He smiles at me through the mesh, his lips distorted and cruel. My entire body turns to ice.

He opens the hatch to the cage. The one with the hundreds and hundreds of bees. They pour out of the opening.

And head straight in my direction.

CHAPTER FORTY-THREE

*T*ime slows to a creep. I can see each flap of the bees' iridescent wings. Hear each distinct buzz. Feel the flutter of air against my face, as the bees fly closer and closer to me.

My father was right. My mind whirls hysterically to my mother's limp body, swollen with hundreds of bites. I do look more like her every day. I'm not allergic to bees, like she is, but with enough stings, I'll be just as bloated. Just as dead.

The bees approach. They've covered half the distance between the cage and me now. The same mantra cycles in my head: Astana's dead. Denver killed her. I'm next. Astana's dead. Denver killed her. I'm next.

The bees fly closer still. One detaches from the pack, buzzing in my face as if it's not sure what to make of me. Are you a foundation beam or a hunk of flesh?

A beam! Nothing to sting here!

But the sweat gives me away. It pours off my body, soaking my caftan, wetting my hair.

More bees surround me. Through the swarm of their thick, fuzzy bodies, I see Denver standing by the cage. I can no longer decipher his expression behind the veil, but his hands are clasped, waiting. He wants to make sure the bees do their job.

Where is security? Did the amplifier work? Is anyone coming?

No. It's been too long. I'm on my own here.

And I'm not ready to die.

I yank against the bindings with all my strength. With every rage that's simmered in my belly. With every passion that's stirred in my heart. I pour every emotion that I've ever felt into my arms, into my hands, into my wrists.

Try. Harder.

I pull with my shoulders, I tug with my core arching against the beam, I heave with my feet bracing against the dirt.

Try. Harder.

This is the man who killed Astana. And he will not kill me, too. Not like this.

Try. Harder.

The rope gives, just as a bee stings me on the neck. The shriek that rips through my body propels me forward. Before Denver can blink, I launch myself toward his torso, knocking him over. We fall to the ground, and I pull the veil away from his head.

The bees begin their attack.

Denver bellows, batting at the insects against his face. But it's too late. Even as I watch, bees swarm his face, so that I can barely make out a patch of skin. Satisfaction rushes through me for one glorious moment — and then my body goes up in flames. I feel like I'm bathing in a pool of lava. Everything screams, long and loud and never-ending. My neck. Forehead. Cheeks. Every square inch of skin not covered by my caftan.

I, too, flail my arms, trying to get the bees away. I press my exposed face into the dirt, squashing the insects that linger there. I roll my body, over and over again, trying to dislodge their companions. But it's no use. My few uncoordinated movements will not detract the bees from their purpose: stinging me to death.

This is the end. I try to think of the people I love. Carr. My father. Even Blanca. But I can't. The pain blots out everything else, and my entire body turns into one giant howl.

My last clear thought is: if I must leave this life, at least I'm taking Denver with me.

CHAPTER FORTY-FOUR

After a while, the screaming stops. My skin continues to throb, a live, pulsing thing, but I'm not getting any new stings.

I open my eyes. The bees hang in the air, stupefied. They fly drunkenly in small circles before crash-landing to the floor. The glasshouse is filled with the black uniforms of the security team, spraying the bees with gas canisters and securing cuffs around Denver. At least, I think it's my cousin—his features are so swollen that he is unrecognizable.

Finally.

Master Somjing creaks down in front of me, blinking. "Princess Vela, are you okay?"

"What took you so long?" I try to say, but my mouth isn't working right. Neither is my mind. They both feel slow, sleepy, lazy. Either I'm experiencing the after-effects of the stings, or I inhaled some of the gas meant for the bees.

"You used your handprint to open the door. The royal override locked up the system for ten minutes." Master

Somjing signals to someone behind me. The two of them pull me into a standing position. "There was nothing we could do to reach you before the ten minutes was up, short of blasting through the glass walls. We were afraid the flying shards of glass would kill you." He pauses. "We had to physically restrain Carr when we saw Denver tie you against the beam and release the bees. It's a good thing you got free. The only reason you're still alive is because you managed to kill half the bees attacking you."

The words float in my head. I can make sense of one out of every three or four. I fall forward, into a pair of familiar arms. Carr. He was the one Master Somjing signaled. The one they had to physically restrain. Somehow, some way, he found out about my mission and came along for the rescue.

"How did you—?" I start to ask.

"Shhh. It doesn't matter right now." He gathers me gently against his chest. "All that matters is that you're safe."

He stands and carries me out of the glasshouse. I want to protest. I can walk—I think. I've just got bleeding wrists and a dozen stings. And this ridiculous sleepy head.

But his even gait lulls me, and his body is warm and snug around me. Finally, I relax. *Yes. I'm safe now. It's over. It's over. It's over.*

I wake to the faint, rhythmic beeping of a machine. A clamp is fastened over my pointer finger, and my skin feels sticky, as if it's been smeared with fruit preserves.

I dreamed again of the serpent. It attacked me over and over, sinking its fangs into the flesh of my neck and face.

Does that explain the aches? The pieces of white gauze decorating my skin?

And then, I remember. Denver, not the serpent. Bees stings, not fangs. I'm in the medical facility, recovering, and my cousin is in the red cells.

Last time I saw Denver, he was being cuffed. The entire security team heard his confession. I trust that Master Somjing will make sure he's put away for a long time.

Good. I expect a burst of triumph to shoot through me, but instead, the backs of my eyes prick again. Justice, no matter how satisfying, will never bring Astana back.

I lean against the pillow, my heart pinning me to the mattress. I drown in memories of my best friend. Her mouth a perfect *O* when she first tasted a strawberry. Her mischievous laugh that turned every head in the courtyard. Her soft smile when she forgave me for the very last time.

I can never bring Astana back, but at least I exposed her killer. I invalidated the Fittest results. I saved Carr.

The events of the last few days are anchors on either side of my lips. I didn't think I would ever smile again, but the thought makes me try.

I saved Carr.

Not a moment too soon. I grope on the nightstand for my handheld and check the date. The transplant is happening today.

Today, my father will get the organs he needs to get well again. Today, Carr will be free from being the Fittest, forever. Today, we can start rebuilding the rest of our lives without Astana.

My lips pull again at the anchors, and this time, I succeed. This time, I do smile. I pull the clamp off my finger and rip the gauze from my wounds. Whatever miraculous jelly the medics used, the stings have shrunk and hardly hurt anymore.

How they look is probably a different story. But I don't pause to glance in the mirror. I don't care.

Today I get to revel in the knowledge that everyone I love—at least everyone's who's left—is safe.

*W*hen I walk into the control room, the air hiccups. The analysts don't stop what they're doing, but their hands jerk on the holo-desks, and they widen their eyes at one another. A couple stare openly at my face. Maybe I should've checked out my reflection, after all.

"Who's the new Fittest?" I ask the room at large, since they're all focused on me. "Zelo or Jupiter?"

Captain Perth clears his throat. "Princess Vela. We're all pleased you're looking so well."

"Thanks. Me, too," I say, even though I know he's lying. The way he averts his eyes is more telling than a mirror. I look a fright. "Has the Fittest been informed? What provisions do we need to make for his family?"

He takes my arm and walks me to the wall, next to the blinking control panel. But the room is so small that the extra steps don't give us any more privacy. "The disc is irrevocably water damaged. We can't retrieve any data from it."

My mouth opens. No. That can't be right. It *can't* be. "The disc wasn't in the water very long."

"One moment is all it takes."

My breath comes out in funny gasps and pants. I stumble back until I hit the switchboard. Just like my mom's body. She had 327 stings, when it would've only taken one. One sting. One moment. That's all it takes to destroy a life.

Carr's life. And mine.

"You have to keep trying." My voice is jerky, like a buzzing bee deciding where to land.

"We've been trying for the last twenty hours."

"Try. Harder." That's what I've done this entire task. I listened to Master Somjing. I gave the challenges everything I had. I broke free from my rope bindings and killed the bees that tried to end me. The result can't turn out like this, with a water-damaged disc. I refuse. "I'll talk to Mistress Barnett. Maybe we can delay the transplant a day or two, to give you more time to recover the data—"

"She was just in here. Your father's taken a turn for the worse. The transplant can't be delayed anymore if we want to save the King."

His face blurs, and the lights on the control panel blend together. Weights settle on my shoulders, my chest, my back. The pressure pushes in on me from every direction, squeezing me tighter than a trash compactor.

I want to give up, but a germ inside me won't let me. The germ grows. Try harder. I'm not back where I started. Denver admitted to fixing CORA. Carr heard him, along with the rest of the security team. I don't need the silver disc to prove the results are invalid. I have Denver's confession. Will that be enough to convince Carr to step down?

"I'm sorry." Captain Perth's voice is softer than I've ever heard it. "It's never easy to say goodbye. I know the boy is important to you."

My lips harden. The confession has to be enough. There's no other option. "I'm not saying goodbye today. Not if I can help it."

I find Carr in a room off the Banquet Hall, a small, windowless unit with just enough space for a table and two stools. He's sitting in front of a luscious fruit pie. His final request. Two hours from now, the transplant is scheduled to begin.

I push down on the despair rising in my throat like the tides of Earth. It leaves behind an acerbic aftertaste. Is this how the oceans of our origin planet tasted? A little salt, a little bitter, with a dash of longing and a whole lot of tears?

"Did you know all the Aegis passed their first meals in here?" I ask.

"I didn't know that." The light in his eyes is just a glimmer of the joy he displayed at Bubble Falls, but I take a mental snapshot anyway. This subtle humor is one more side of Carr, and I treasure every last facet. Especially now.

"Oh yeah. The young Aegis tend to be overzealous," I say. "The private room gives them the chance to grab their stomachs and moan in peace."

He grins. The scent of strawberries wraps around me and tugs me the rest of the way into the room. Not that I need any urging.

I wet my lips. "Mind if I join you?"

"Please." He pulls out the stool next to his. "I stopped by your recovery unit earlier. You were sleeping, and I didn't want to disturb your rest."

The transplant's in two hours, I want to shout. *Disturb my rest. You should've kept me awake all night, the way you did in the cave. We have to make the most of every last second.*

"You haven't taken a bite?" I ask instead, a surge of hope rising. If he doesn't want his final request, maybe he's not planning to go through with the transplant. Maybe he'll let one of the others take his place. "Are you worried how your body will react?"

"Nah. I'll be long gone before my body can feel the effects."

Maybe not. The lump in my throat grows so big I nearly choke.

"All our lives, Astana and I wanted an entire pie to ourselves. It was her daydream more than mine, so I'm going to eat the whole thing for her." He takes my hand and traces each of my fingertips with his thumb. "But you know what? I'm not thinking about the flavor that's about to explode on my tongue. Or the juices that will run down my throat, quenching my thirst in a way it's never before been quenched. All I can think, when I see the strawberries, is how they remind me of the red in your cheeks."

I cover my face with my other hand. "Especially now, with all these bee stings."

He pulls my fingers down, so both my hands are nestled in his. "You are always beautiful to me, whether you're covered with mud or bee stings."

His lips meet mine, and my tears fall into our kiss. The brushing of our lips is at once the most exquisite and painful thing I've ever experienced. He tastes like colored streams of water. Plump worms wriggling in the mud. A shiny red apple with a bite taken out of it. But most of all, he tastes like goodbye.

I wrench away, and the absence of his lips is so stark it hurts. "I'm not giving up on you. Denver confessed he manipulated the Fittest results, so we know you're not truly CORA's choice. You don't have to go through with the transplant."

He studies me as though I'm trying to trick him. "What did they find on Zelo's silver disc?"

"How do you know about Zelo's disc?"

"He told me. When he didn't hear from you last night,

he came to the shuttle. They told him you were injured and unavailable, so he came to me."

"So you know about Brooklyn...?"

"Yes. I know he wants to be the Fittest for the same reason as I do. To save someone he loves."

I lick my lips. He's right. I am trying to trick him. Or at least persuade him. I'll put on a whole magic show if it means I get to keep him. "If you respect his reasons, then you should step down, so he can take your place."

He shakes his head. "His daughter needs him. So does Camden."

The words are an echo of what I said to Zelo. But now, coming from Carr's lips, minutes before he dies, I can't accept them.

"I need you," I whisper. "Did you ever think of that?"

"No, Vela." He cups my chin in his hands. "You've never needed anybody. That's why I fell in love with you. Why you're going to be such a good ruler. Because you've never listened to anything but your own heart."

"Right now, my heart's begging you to step down."

"I've got a better idea." He releases my chin. "I'll go through with the transplant and ask that Brooklyn be the beneficiary of my sacrifice instead of Astana. That way, she can have her life and her daddy, too. The council would agree, wouldn't they? Now that Astana's gone, it seems like a reasonable request. Maybe I can even convince them to throw in Hanoi while they're at it. She was so nice to Astana."

My throat closes. His idea is more than reasonable. In fact, it's the kindest, most noble thing I've ever heard. Just like the boy in front of me.

"That's besides the point." I need my voice to be strong and sure, but it comes out shaky and weak. "Zelo wants to be the Fittest—"

Carr laughs, and the sound shatters my already fragile bones. "You think he wants to die? You think he wants to leave Brooklyn and Camden to fend for themselves? Don't fool yourself, Vela. Nobody actually wants to be the Fittest. Maybe it's the best choice we have. That doesn't make it right."

My veins fill with concrete. Because in all the times we've discussed his candidacy, he's never once spoken out against the Trials. He's never once criticized the system my father and the other council members implemented in order to extend the King's life. I've never questioned it, either.

Until now.

"What did the silver disc show?" Carr asks again.

"It was inconclusive," I croak. "The disc was too water damaged to retrieve any data."

"So according to CORA, I'm still the official Fittest?"

I don't want to say yes. I know this single word will seal Carr's decision. But my silence is answer enough.

He picks up his fork and takes a bite of pie. His expression changes when the food hits his taste buds, but he doesn't look joyous. With this action, he's telling me, as resolutely as any words, that he intends to go through with the transplant.

"Vela," he says, his voice lower, rougher than normal. "I would move mountains to have a natural lifetime with you. I'd skip nutritioning for a week if I could have another night like the one we had in the caves. But I can't let Zelo take my place.

"You know it, too. That's why you're asking me to step down, instead of making the decision yourself. You could invalidate CORA's decision, but you won't. You know in your heart Zelo doesn't deserve to die. No more than I do. Difference is, he has a daughter. And I don't."

I squeeze my eyes shut. He's right. I couldn't make the decision, so I wanted him to do it for me. When the truth is, there's no good decision. Not a single one.

"If the system's wrong," I burst out, "why do you have to be the one to fix it?"

"Who else, Vela?"

He looks straight into my eyes, and his pain breaks me. Roots out and destroys every bit of strength I have left.

I have no response.

CHAPTER FORTY-FIVE

For the next two hours, I wander around the shuttle in a daze. One foot falls in front of the other. My hand brings the fork to my mouth, but I'm not sure where I go. I don't know what I eat. I have no idea who I see.

I walk and I walk, and when my handheld vibrates in my pocket, alerting me to the time, my feet automatically take me to a glass-walled room, the one designated for step one of the transplant process.

A group of people stands around the one-way window—council members, the medical personnel, the Fittest families. Only Blanca is missing. Even with Denver's confession, I guess they haven't had time to release her from the red cells.

Everyone stares as I approach, and the crowd parts, clearing a path for me to the door. A serpent is etched in the metal, baring his fangs at me.

Of course he is. I can never escape the serpent, no matter where I go. It seems fitting that he accompany me here, too.

I grasp the door handle, my palm slick with sweat, and go inside the room. My father and Carr are already strapped into their respective transfer machines. Blankets are draped over their bodies, and all I can see are their heads. My father wears a crown of thorns, while Carr's head is bare.

My pulse throbs, in places I didn't even know had a pulse, and breathing hurts. Every mouthful of air has spikes that rip up my lungs, but I have to breathe. I have to stand here. I have to make this decision.

A technician turns from the control panel, where he was keying in the parameters of the transfer, and gestures to a red button. "Whenever you're ready, Princess. This button will start the process."

I nod, and he exits the room, leaving me with the two men I love best. The deep knowledge squirms inside me. I don't get to keep them both.

I go to Carr first. The last of my stupor clears like fog in the sun. I sense everything in sharp hyperfocus. The way a muscle twitches at his jaw, the perspiration that dots his brow. The *tsch-tsch-tsch* of the machine warming up. The crisp, clean scent of sanitizer warring with Carr's unique scent of soil and apples and goodness and life.

I want to press my face against his neck and breathe him in. I want to watch his forehead crinkle as he puzzles out a solution. I want him to laugh, joyously, with his mouth and eyes and stomach. I want one more night by the colored water, one more taste of his tears, one more kiss, anywhere and everywhere.

I want, I want, I want. I could turn myself inside out from the wanting.

Instead, I touch his warm, bristly cheek. An emotion flickers in his eyes, one I've never seen on his face before. Fear.

"Don't be afraid." My voice comes out too thin and missing consonants, as if it too were a victim to the spiky air.

"This is just the first step. The machine will transfer nutrition from one body to the other. If we get through this okay, we'll move to the surgical room, where the actual transplant will be performed. Nothing will happen yet."

"I'm not scared to die." He sounds like his regular self— confident, strong. Instead of reassuring me, the words knock down the scant barrier I built, so that my heart breaks, and then breaks again, until it is little more than dust motes floating in the air. "But I don't want to leave you. What I'm doing here has nothing to do with how I feel about you. You understand that, right? You know how much I love you."

The tears gather in my chest like condensation before the rain. "I understand. I understand perfectly."

He reaches out his hand, and I grasp it. In his grip, there is only resignation and love. No more flickers of fear, not a trace of our last conversation in front of a strawberry pie.

But I haven't forgotten the conversation. And now, as his hand settles into mine, as his fingers interlock with my fingers like two halves of a zipper, his words pound in my head again.

Who else, Vela? Who else can fix the broken system? Who else? Who else? Who else?

The tears begin to boil and creep up my throat. I drop his hand like it scalds me. And back away from this boy I love. For perhaps the final time.

I cross to the man who has been by my side my entire life. I took my first wobbly steps into his arms. When I cried out in sleep that the bad guys were chasing me, he gathered me close and raced up and down the corridor. He picked me up when I fell off my bike, taught me sums by turning the pill bank into a pretend store. He even pulled up a hologram to explain the menstrual cycle after my mom passed.

The King of a colony, but first and foremost, my father.

I reach his side, and my knees go weak. For the first time, he looks his age. Frail and thin, like his bones might poke through his skin any second. His eyes are set in wrinkles the way a jewel sits on crushed velvet, and like diamonds overdue for cleaning, they are clouded and tired. He smiles, and that, too, is weary, as though he's lived too many days, made too many decisions, known too many heartaches.

I feel the truth of Captain Perth's words. If my father is to live, he needs the transplant today.

He brings his free hand to my face, and I cover it with my own. As always, his presence steadies me. As always, his touch gives me courage. He believes in me—has always believed in me—and that belief makes me stronger than I've ever dreamed.

"You taught me to value life." Once again, I am a student, and he is my teacher. I repeat to him the lessons I've learned, to make sure I understood. To make sure he approves. "From the time I was a little girl, you showed me all life was valuable. From the dragonflies that flit by our ponds to the leaders of our colony, you taught me we must treasure and respect them equally."

I take a breath, but it's more of a gasp. The tears surge up again, burning a path from my eyes to my throat, and I don't know if I can keep them inside. I don't know if I can do what needs to be done.

Water rolls inside me, and it's a strange mix of salty tears, colored streams, and savage storms, battering at my throat, clawing at my strength. If I let down my guard, for one fraction of a second, I'll wash away on a sea of misery and grief.

I can't let go. Not now. Not when I'm the only one who can do this.

"You taught me the leader of a colony must make tough

decisions. Sometimes, for the greater good of a colony, a few people must sacrifice. We have to accept that." My voice cracks, and the water seeps out. The tears, the colored streams, the storms. The pain, the confusion, the age-old loneliness. Whether or not he approves, this is my decision. I'll shoulder the blame, I'll suffer the consequences. I'll have to live with my action for the rest of my life.

"Other times, there's a moral imperative that trumps even the most clear-cut quantitative analysis. The task of a ruler is to balance the two, to choose when the moral imperative outweighs the greater good."

"You've learned your lessons well, my eye-apple." My father smiles again, but this time, there is more than weariness. This time, there is pride.

I lick my lips, but I can't wet them. I try to swallow, but there's no moisture. In spite of the waves crashing inside me, my mouth dries like our arid moons.

And for a moment, I waver. What is right? What is wrong? My mind sees the truth, as clearly as the water cascading down Bubble Falls, but my heart, my heart, my heart. My heart is a comet shooting through the deepest, darkest space, burning so hot it will scorch itself out of existence.

I can't do this—I can't—but my father's hand is against my cheek. And I think of Astana and Zelo and Cairo Mead and Miss Sydney's son, and I know that I must.

"Do I have your permission to trust my instincts?" I whisper.

"You've never needed my permission, my eye-apple. But I'll give you my blessing."

Something crosses his face, and in that instant, I know he understands exactly what I'm asking. He knows exactly what I have to do. My father has always known me better than anyone else. In this case, I think he knew even before

I did what decision I would reach.

I take a shaky breath and then another. The tears pound at my throat, but I'm not letting them out. Not when there's still work to be done.

"I love you, Dad." I choke on the words. "More than colored streams, more than the moons. More than Dion itself. I love you. I will always love you."

The corners of his eyes crease, as soft as petals, as crinkly as leaves. With the crown on his head, he looks every inch the King. The man an entire colony reveres. "I have never been prouder of you than I am at this moment. I'm ready, my daughter. It's time."

I swipe at my eyes, and quickly, before I can change my mind, I walk to the control board. I flip a switch to reverse the transfer, and then I push the red button. The machines hum to life, and both my father and Carr lift off the recliners.

Instead of the other way around, every last nutrient is sucked out of the King and pours into Carr.

Within a minute, the machines quiet. The suction stops. Both bodies lower to the reclining chairs.

It is over. The end of an era. The King of Dion, the best, most heroic man I've ever known, my father, Adam Kunchai, is dead.

CHAPTER FORTY-SIX

*T*he instant my father's heart stops, an alarm sounds. Loud, insistent beeps that must echo through the entire shuttle. Now, they'll know. If the people watching at the window weren't sure what I was doing, now they'll know I killed my father.

Any second now, the royal guards will rush into the room. Arrest me for being a traitor of the very worst kind. Throw me in the red cells, this time for good. The council will have to find another Successor.

Doesn't matter. None of that factored into my decision. Because this was the right thing to do.

I fall to the floor. My knees smack the concrete, but I don't feel the pain. I don't feel my legs at all. Nor my arms, nor my face, nor my tongue. My entire body is as numb as the cryogenically frozen embryos in our storage rooms.

My eyes dart around the room. To the blinking lights on the control panel. To the plastic shield retracting over Carr. To my father. No, not my father. His body. His corpse.

His eyes are closed, his mouth relaxed and peaceful. For

one wild moment, I think he's only asleep. I didn't actually kill him. This is just an awful nightmare.

But then, Carr sits up. His skin is full, his face alive. He looks as healthy as I've ever seen him. And I know the truth in my bones. He received my father's nutrients. In a healthy person, a transfer of this magnitude would've only weakened the body. In my father's already compromised state, the transfer killed him.

I did it. My father is dead, and I am responsible.

Inside my head, I rage. I rip the control panel apart circuit by circuit. I take a sledgehammer and I slam it against the transfer machine, again and again, until it breaks into useless component parts, and then I take these parts and I hurl them against the generator towers, until I knock them over, until I destroy our energy shields, until our entire colony comes crumbling down around me.

Oh Dion, I can't breathe. My chest seizes up, and I miss him so much, it's like the universe has sucked all the oxygen out of my lungs.

I miss the way he would nod off during his midnight snack when he was really tired. I miss how he would never go easy on me during our chess matches, so that I never beat him in a game until I was fifteen. I miss his stern yet affectionate lectures, the ones teaching me the proper way to act, but laced with so much warmth I never doubted his affection for me. Not once in my life did I ever question whether he loved me or if he loved me enough.

He was proud of me. This is what he wanted. All along, this was the decision he wanted me to make.

The knowledge relaxes my chest enough that oxygen begins to flow again. It banks the rage inside me, turning the grief into glowing embers instead of turbulent flames.

He gave me his blessing. I'll gladly be red-celled for the

rest of my life, I'll live with the sin of killing my father, so long as I know he approved.

I lift my eyes and find Carr's. We look at each other for one searing second, and then the door bangs open.

Within a minute, the room is packed. With every council member, every royal guard, every medical personnel—with the exception of Blanca.

They form a circle around me, gawking. If this is the Circle of Shunning, we're a little beyond that.

I stand and stick my hands into the air, my wrists held close together to make it easier for the cuffs. "Go ahead. Arrest me."

Nobody moves. I feel the weight of their eyes, pushing me down, heavier than a month's worth of food.

"I won't make excuses. I'm of sound mind and body." If I'm going down for this crime, they need to know exactly why, so it won't happen again with a future ruler. Ten years from now, when the next sovereign nears the end of her reign, I hope they will reevaluate the decision to prolong her life and come out on the other side. My side.

"I did what I thought was right." My voice is quiet now, and I try to pretend I'm talking to my father. Strolling with him in the woods behind the shuttle, having one of our many discussions about right and wrong. "The King has long surpassed his natural lifespan. As pivotal a figure as he is in this colony, we cannot sacrifice an innocent life in order to extend his. We cannot trade one life for another. This is what the King wanted. This is what he wished."

Still, the guards do not come forward. Still, they do not snap handcuffs over my wrists and lead me to the red cells, where I'll spend the rest of my days.

"I loved him." I shake and shake and shake. "I loved him as much as any of you. More, probably, because I was not only his subject but also his daughter. This wasn't about me. It wasn't about saving the boy I love. I could've replaced him with another candidate, but I didn't." I lace my fingers together, the irony of it all tap-dancing on my quivering shoulders. "I did what the council asked. I looked beyond my own feelings to see the bigger picture. I just happened to reach a result none of you expected."

"That's not quite true." Master Somjing shuffles forward. He bows as low as he can before the King's body. And then, he straightens and gently removes the crown from my father's head. "Which is why I'm giving you this."

He places the crown of thorns on my head.

The world tilts one way and then the other. My head thuds with too many thoughts, too many images, too many dreams. And not a single one makes sense. "Wha-at?"

"On behalf of the council, and as a stand-in for the King, I hereby bequeath you this crown."

Every square inch of my skin tingles. If Master Somjing touched me right now, I'd probably electrocute him.

I hear his words, but I don't. Dream. Yes, that's what this is. Or maybe I've gone into shock, and I'm hallucinating. Yes. That must be the explanation.

But then, I reach for my temples and grab the thorns instead. They prick my skin, and a drop of blood wells on my fingertip. I stare at the blood. My finger hurts. This isn't a dream. "I don't understand."

"Your father was dying, Vela. He never intended to go through with the transplant." Master Somjing speaks to me, but his eyes keep drifting to the King's body, as if he can't believe his old friend is truly and irrevocably gone.

A lance of sorrow pierces through my confusion. I can't believe it, either.

"The Fittest tradition began when our colony was young,

chaotic, and unstable." His words are slow and measured, as if he's practiced this speech a hundred times. "Back then, we needed a consistent leader, especially someone who was as loved and revered as your father.

"But things have changed. Our colony is older now, more established and settled. And the King began to feel we made a mistake all those years ago. He was ready to pass the throne, but he wanted to make sure it went to someone who not only had the same moral convictions as he did, but who also had the strength to follow them through."

He gestures toward the crown on my head. The additional weight is awkward, unfamiliar. Any moment now, the crown's going to topple to the floor—and take me with it.

"This was the true test, Vela, and you passed."

"Test? What are you talking about?" Just when the room was beginning to right itself, the walls spin away again, and my mind can't keep up. I tug the crown off my head. The thorns catch on my hair and pull. "What about Carr? If I'd made a different decision, he'd be dead."

"We wouldn't have let you get that far. In fact, this was your last chance. If you didn't make the right decision now, in the transfer stage, we would've called off the entire task. The King would've wanted to spend his last few days with you. And we needed time to find a new Successor outside the genetic pool, in spite of CORA's advice to the contrary."

Carefully, stiffly, he arranges his mechanical braces so he can kneel on the ground. He looks up at me, tears shining in his eyes. "The King was certain you would pass the test. As much as you loved him, he knew what you were made of at the very core of your being. The stuff it takes to rule a colony. And can I say, my Queen"—he spreads his palm and taps three times against his chest—"how very glad I am that he was right."

I stare at him, the crown dangling from my fingertips, my hair tangled in the thorns. Not sure what to think. Not sure how to feel.

"Ladies and gentlemen," he announces. "May I present to you the new ruler of our colony. Queen Vela!"

Everyone drops to their knees, the council members and the royal guards. The medical personnel and the Fittest families. They all spread their hands on their chest and tap three times.

I open my mouth, but nothing comes out. My hand loosens, and the crown drops. This is too much. Too much. Too much.

I wait for the crown of thorns to fall to the floor. I wait for it to shatter against the concrete, breaking into a thousand pieces and destroying the illusion.

But it doesn't. Carr catches the crown, and he places it back on my head. "Your Highness," he murmurs, the blanket wrapped around his waist and love in his eyes. "I believe the Fittest families have something to say to you."

Miss Sydney emerges from behind his back. She kneels before me, her head bowed, the blue sash dragging along the floor. "Queen Vela, you have given your father to save our future sons and daughters. Your sister had nearly convinced us, but your action solidifies our decision. It would be our honor to give you our meals to save your loyal subjects."

Still, I can't speak. Still, I don't move. Hanoi will live. As will Brooklyn. As will the rest of the patients in Blanca's pool. The enormity of the situation has cut out my tongue. The shock of the last few minutes has severed the connection between my mind and my limbs.

I don't know how long I stand there. Long enough for each person to take his or her turn kneeling at my feet. Long enough for Master Somjing to clear the room. Long enough for Carr to take my hand and lead me to my father's body.

I come back to myself. My father no longer breathes, but there, at the corner of his lips, is the tiniest curve. And then I know. Wherever he is, to whatever realm he went in this short time, I know he is happy. Because he's with my mother again.

I drop a kiss onto my father's cool, waxy forehead. My breath flutters over his face, and his eyelashes move. For an infinitesimal moment, I can almost believe he is alive again.

"You believed in me when nobody else did. You believed in me even when I didn't. I won't disappoint you." My words are my vow. The first promise I make as the ruler of Dion. And as the late King taught me, the sovereign always keeps her promises.

"I couldn't imagine a better queen." Carr touches his lips to mine, and every emotion I've ever felt coalesces in that sweet, exquisite point of contact.

I'm more convinced than ever that Carr is the Fittest. Not to die for the King or anyone else. But to stand by my side and help me rule.

I look at my father one last time and imprint his image into my memory. I don't need a holo-cube to capture his image. Because for now, and the rest of my days, he will live in my heart. The man who led our colony. And taught me how to be a queen.

Carr and I glide through the door, hand in hand. The serpent scowls at us from the carving, its plump body wrapped around an ever-present red apple. But I smile as I walk away from the serpent, and I don't turn around to peek at its glistening fangs.

Not even once.

ACKNOWLEDGMENTS

This book is very special to me. Every description, every character was born from a fire burning deep inside. I wrote this story many years ago — before I was published, when I wasn't sure if I would ever be published — and it encapsulates my pure joy of writing.

Thank you to my publisher and editor, Liz Pelletier. Although it is just now releasing, *Star-Crossed* is the book that started our relationship. You saw something in me, in my stories, and I will always be grateful to you for believing in me. Big thanks to the amazing team at Entangled for turning this manuscript into a novel — Hannah Lindsey, Shayla Fereshetian, Stacy Abrams, Curtis Svehlak, and Heather Riccio. As always, my cover is an object of beauty, and the credit here goes to Erin Dameron-Hill.

My gratitude to Beth Miller, my agent. So very happy I have you on my side. Thanks for all the things, both big and small.

So many people helped to shape this story! Thank you to the following people for their support and insights: Meg Kassel, Darcy Woods, Brenda Drake, Vanessa Barneveld, Denny Bryce, Jen Malone, Stephanie Buchanan, Romily

Bernard, Natalie Richards, Danielle Meitiv, Kimberly MacCarron, and Kaitlin Khorashadi. I am indebted to the Firebirds Brainstormers, in particular Jean Willett and Jonathan Willett, for their world-building suggestions. Finally, I am very grateful to Amanda Pennington, Aimee Lim, and Amber Medland for their thoughtful reads.

I would not be the person I am today without my family and friends. You know who you are, and you know how much I love you! But this time, I'd like to give a special shout-out to my dad, Naronk Hompluem. *Star-Crossed* is dedicated to him, and this dedication has been a long time coming. I wanted to save this book for him, and if you've read *Star-Crossed*, then you know why. As Vela says about her father, "Not once in my life did I ever question whether he loved me or if he loved me enough." Thank you, Dad, for loving me unconditionally. I would say that you have given me a gift that is indescribable — but well, I wrote an entire book about it. So, I'll just say that it took that many words to sum up what you mean to me.

To my four A's — Antoine, Aksara, Atikan, and Adisai. You are the center of my world and my heart. Thank you for making me smile and laugh every day of the year.

And finally, to my readers. I appreciate every message and kind word. Thank you for reading my stories! I hope you'll love Vela and Carr's star-crossed tale!

Have you read all the books in the Forget Tomorrow series?

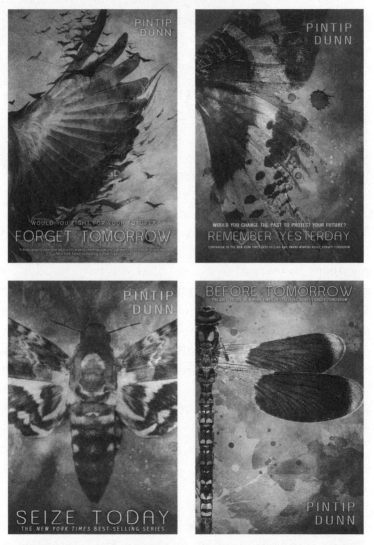

1

"The next leaf that falls will be red," my six-year-old sister Jessa announces. An instant later, a crimson leaf flutters through the air like the tail feather of a cardinal.

Jessa grabs it and tucks it into the pocket of her school uniform, a silver mesh jumpsuit that is a smaller version of mine. Crunchy leaves blanket the square, the only burst of color in Eden City's landscape. Behind our patch of a park, bullet trains shoot by in electromagnetic vacuum tubes, and metal and glass buildings vie for every inch of pavement. Their gleaming spirals do more than scrape the sky—they punch right through it.

"Now orange," Jessa says. A leaf the color of overripe squash tumbles from the tree. "Brown." Sure enough, brown as mud and just as dead.

"You going for some kind of record?" I ask.

She turns to me and grins, and I forget all about tomorrow and what is about to happen. My senses fill with my sister. The voice that lilts like music. The way her hair curves around her chin. Her eyes as warm and irresistible as roasted chestnuts.

I can almost feel the patches of dry skin on her elbows, where she refuses to apply lotion. And then, the moment passes. Knowledge seeps through me, the way a person gains consciousness after a dream. Tomorrow, I turn seventeen. I will become, by the ComA's decree, an official adult. I will receive my memory from the future.

Sometimes, I feel as if I've been waiting all my life to turn seventeen. I measure my days not by my experiences but by the time remaining until I receive my memory, *the* memory, the one that's supposed to give meaning to my life.

They tell me I won't feel so alone then. I'll know, without a shred of doubt, that somewhere in another spacetime exists a future version of me, one who turns out all right. I'll know who I'm supposed to be. And I'll never feel lost again.

Too bad I had to live through seventeen years of filler first.

"Yellow." Jessa returns to her game, and a yellow leaf detaches from a branch. "Orange."

Ten times, fifteen times, twenty, she correctly predicts the color of the next leaf to fall. I clap and cheer, even though I've seen this show, or something like it, dozens of times before.

And then I notice him. A guy wearing my school's uniform, sitting on a curved metal bench thirty feet away. Watching us.

The back of my neck prickles. He can't possibly hear us. He's too far away. But he's looking. Why is he looking? Maybe he has super-sensitive hearing. Maybe the wind has picked up our words and carried them to him.

How could I be so stupid? I never let Jessa stop in the park. I always march her straight home after school, just like my mother orders. But today, I wanted—I needed—the sun, if only for a few minutes.

I place a hand on my sister's arm, and she stills. "We need to leave. Now." My tone implies the rest of the sentence: before the guy reports your psychic abilities to the authorities.

Jessa doesn't even nod. She knows the drill. She drops into step beside me, and we head for the train station on the other side of the square. Out of the corner of my eye, I see him stand up and follow us. I bite my lip so hard I taste blood. What now? Make a run for it? Talk to him and attempt damage control?

His face comes into view. He has closely cropped blond hair and a ridiculously charming grin, but that's not why my knees go weak.

It's my classmate, Logan Russell, swim team captain and owner of what my best friend Marisa calls the best pecs in this spacetime. Harmless. Sure, he has the nerve to smile at me after ignoring me for five years, but he's no threat to Jessa's well-being.

When we were kids, his brother Mikey made a racquetball hover above the court. Without touching it. ComA whisked him away, and he hasn't been seen since. Logan's not about to report my sister to anyone.

"Calla, wait up," he says, as if it's been days instead of years since we sat next to each other in the T-minus five classroom.

I stop walking, and Jessa clutches my hand. I give her three squeezes to let her know we're safe. "My friends call me 'Callie,'" I tell Logan. "But if you don't already know that, maybe you should use my birthday."

"All right, then." Coming to a stop in front of us, he jams his hands in his pockets. "You must be nervous, October Twenty-eight. About tomorrow, I mean."

I lift my eyebrow. "How would you have the first clue

what my feelings are?"

"We used to be friends."

"Right," I say. "I still remember the time you peed your pants on our way to the Outdoor Core."

He meets my gaze head on. "Ditto for the part where you splashed us both with water from the fountain so no one else would know."

He remembers? I look away, but it's too late. I can smell the protein pellets we made a pact never to eat, feel the touch on my shoulder when Amy Willows compared my hair to straw.

"Forget her," the twelve-year-old Logan had whispered, as the credits rolled on the documentary on farming methods before the Technology Boom. "Scarecrows are the coolest ever."

I had gone home and daydreamed I'd received the memory from my future self, and in it Logan Russell was my husband. Of course, that was before I learned the older girls waited until a boy received his future memory before deciding if he was a good match. Who cares if Logan has dimples, if his future doesn't show sufficient credits to provide for his family? He may have a swimmer's physique today, but it might very well melt into fat twenty years from now.

By the time I figured out my crush was premature, it didn't matter. The boy of my dreams had already stopped talking to me.

I cross my arms. "What do you want, October Twenty-six?"

Instead of responding, he moves behind Jessa. She's taken the leaves from her jumpsuit and is twisting them around each other to make them look like the petals of a flower. Logan sinks down beside her, helping her tie off the "bud" with a sturdy stem.

Jessa beams as if he's given her a rainbow on a plate. So he makes my sister smile. It's going to take more than a measly stem to compensate for five years of silence.

They fool around with the leaves—making more "roses," combining them into a bouquet—for what seems like forever. And then Logan holds one of the roses up to me. "I got my memory yesterday."

My arms and mouth drop at the same time. Of course he did. I'd just used his school name. How could I forget?

Logan's birthday is two days before mine. It's why we sat next to each other all those years. That's how the school orders us—not by last name or height or grades, but by time remaining until we receive our future memory.

I notice the hourglass insignia, half an inch wide, tattooed on the inside of his wrist. Everyone who's received a future memory has one. Underneath the tattoo, a computer chip containing your future memory is implanted, where it can be scanned by prospective employers, loan officers, even would-be parents-in-law.

In Eden City, your future memory is your biggest recommendation. More than your grades, more than your credit history. Because your memory is more than a predictor. It's a guarantee.

"Congratulations," I say. "To whom am I speaking? A future ComA official? Professional swimmer? Maybe I should get your autograph now, while I still have the chance."

Logan gets to his feet and brushes the dirt from his pants. "I did see myself as a gold-star swimmer. But there was something else, too. Something…unexpected."

"What do you mean?"

He takes a step closer. I'd forgotten his eyes are green. They're the green of grass before summer, a sheen caught somewhere between vibrant and dull, as if the color can't decide whether to thrive in the sun or wither in its heat.

"It wasn't like how we were taught, Callie. My memory didn't answer my questions. I don't feel at peace or aligned with the world. I just feel confused."

I lick my lips. "Maybe you didn't follow the rules. Maybe your future self messed up and sent the wrong memory."

I can't believe I said that. We spend our entire childhood learning how to choose the proper memory, one that will get us through the difficult times. And here I am, telling another person he screwed up the only test that matters. I didn't think I had it in me.

"Maybe," he says, but we both know it's not true. Logan is smart, too smart to be beat by me in the T-minus seven spelling bee, and too smart to mess this up.

And then I get it. "You're kidding. In the future, you're the best swimmer the country has ever seen. Right?"

Something I can't identify passes over his face. And then he says, "Right. I have so many medals, I need to build an addition to my house in order to display them."

He wasn't kidding, something inside me yells. *He's trying to tell you something.*

But if Logan's one of the anomalies I've heard rumors about—the ones who receive a bad memory, or worse, no memory at all—I don't want to know about it. We haven't been friends for half a decade. I'm not going to worry about him just because he's deemed me worthy of his attention again.

Suddenly, I can't wait for the conversation to end. I reach for Jessa's hand and connect with her elbow. "Sorry," I say to Logan, "but we need to get going."

Jessa hands him the bouquet of leaves, and I tug her away. We are almost out of earshot when he calls, "Callie? Happy Memory's Eve. May the joy of the future sustain you through the trials of the present."

It's the standard salutation, spoken the day before everyone's seventeenth birthday. In the past, Logan's address would have filled my cheeks with warmth, but this time his words only send a chill creeping up my spine.

We walk into the house to the smell of chocolate cake. My mother's in the eating area, her dark brown hair twisted into a bun, still wearing her uniform with the ComA insignia stitched across the pocket. She's a bot supervisor at one of the agencies, but she gets paid by the Committee of Agencies, or ComA, the governmental entity that runs our nation.

We drop our school bags and run. I hug my mother from behind as Jessa attacks her legs. "Mom! You're home!"

My mother turns. Powdered sugar clings to her cheek, and chocolate frosting darkens one eyebrow. The red light that normally blinks on our Meal Assembler is off. Actual ingredients—packets of flour, a small carton of milk, *real* eggs—lay strewn across the eating table.

I raise my eyebrows. "Mom, are you cooking? Manually?"

"It's not every day my daughter turns seventeen. I thought I'd try making a cake, in honor of my future Manual Chef."

"But how did you…" My voice trails off as I spot the small rectangular machine on the floor. It has a glass door with knobs along one side, two metal racks, and a coil that turns red when it's hot.

An oven. My mother bought me a functioning oven.

My hand shoots to my mouth. "Mom, this must have cost a hundred credits! What if…what if my memory doesn't show me as a successful chef?"

"It wasn't easy to find, I'll give you that." She takes off the rag around her waist and shakes it. A cloud of flour puffs into the air. "But I have complete faith in you. Happy Memory's Eve, dear heart."

She hoists Jessa onto her hip and pulls me into a hug so that we are in a circle of her arms, the way it's always been. Just the three of us.

I have few memories of my father. He is not so much a gaping hole in my life as he is a shadow who lurks around the corner, just out of reach. I used to pester my mom for details, but tonight, on the eve of my seventeenth birthday, the heavy knowledge of him is enough.

My mother begins to clear the ingredients off the table, the bare, gleaming skin of her wrist catching the light that emanates from the walls. She doesn't have a tattoo. Future memories didn't arrive systematically until a few years ago, and my mother wasn't lucky enough to receive one.

Maybe if she had, she wouldn't have lost her job. My mother used to be a medical aide, but as more and more applicants came with memory chips showing futures as competent diagnosticians, it had only been a matter of time before she got downgraded to bot supervisor. "You can hardly blame them," she had said with a shrug. "Why take a risk when you can bet on a sure thing?"

We sit down to a dinner usually reserved for the New Year. Everything has the slightly plastic taste of food prepared in the Meal Assembler, but the spread itself is unrivaled by the best manual cooking establishments. A whole roast chicken, its skin golden brown and crispy. Mashed potatoes fluffy with butter. Sugar snap peas sautéed with cloves of garlic.

We don't talk through most of dinner—can't talk, our mouths are so full. Jessa savors the snap peas like they are candy, nibbling at the ends and rolling them around her mouth before sucking the entire pods down.

"We should have invited that boy to dinner," she says, a snap pea dangling from her mouth. "We've got so much food."

Mom's hand stills on the serving spoon. "What boy?" she pries.

"Just one of my classmates." I feel my cheeks growing red and then remind myself that I have no reason to be embarrassed. I don't like Logan anymore. I help myself to more dark meat. "We ran into him at the park. It was no big deal."

"Why were you even there in the first place?"

The chicken suddenly feels dry in my mouth. I messed up. I know that. But I couldn't bear to be stuck inside today. I needed to feel the sun's warmth on my face, to look at the leaves and imagine my future.

"We only talked to him for a minute, Mom. Jessa was calling out the color of the leaves before they fell, and I wanted to make sure he didn't hear—"

"Wait a minute. She was doing what?"

Uh oh. Wrong answer. "It's no big deal—"

"How many times?"

"About twenty," I admit.

My mother pulls the necklace from under her shirt, where it normally resides, and rubs the cross between her fingers. We're not supposed to wear religious symbols in public. It's not that religion is illegal. Just…unnecessary. The traditions of the pre-Boom era gave their believers comfort, hope, and reassurance—in short, everything that future memory provides us now. The only difference is we actually have proof that the future exists. When we do pray, it's not to any god, but to Fate herself and the predetermined course she's set.

But my mom can be excused for clinging to one of the old faiths. She never got her glimpse of the future, after all.

"Calla Ann Stone." She grips the cross. "I depend on you to keep your sister safe. That means you do not allow her to speak to strangers. You do not stop in a park on your way home from school. And you do not display her abilities for anyone to see."

I look at my hands. "I'm sorry, Mom. It was just this once. Jessa is safe, I promise. Logan's own brother was taken by ComA. He would never tell on her."

At least, I don't think he would. Why *did* he talk to me today? For all I know, he was spying on Jessa. Maybe he's working for ComA now. Maybe his report will be the one that sends my sister away.

Or maybe it has nothing to do with Jessa. Maybe the falling leaves reminded him of another time, when we used to be friends. My mind drifts to an old book of poems Mom gave me for my twelfth birthday. Pressed in between the pages, next to a poem by Emily Brontë, is a crumbling red leaf. The first leaf Logan ever gave me. A small piece of my heart, one I didn't even know still existed, knocks against my chest.

"You were lucky." My mother strides to the counter and snaps up the cake stand. "Next time might not work out so well."

She plunks the stand on the eating table and lifts the dome. The chocolate cake is higher on one side than the other, the frosting glopped on and messy. Each mark of the handmade-ness reproaches me. See how hard your mother worked? This is how you repay her?

"There's not going to be a next time," I say. "I'm sorry."

"Don't apologize to me. Think how you would feel if you never saw your sister again."

The chocolate cake swims before my eyes. This is so unfair. I would never let them take Jessa away from us. My mother knows this. I just wanted to see the sun. The world is not over.

"That's not going to happen," I say.

"You don't know that."

"I will! You'll see. I'll get my memory tomorrow, and in it we'll be happy and safe and together forever. Then you won't be able to yell at me anymore!" I leap to my feet, and my arm knocks the stand. It tips onto the floor, breaking the cake into a hundred different pieces.

Jessa cries out and runs from the room. I'd forgotten she was still here.

My mom sighs and moves around the table to put her hand on my shoulder. The tension melts away, leaving behind our shared guilt for arguing in front of Jessa.

"Which do you want? Clean up this mess, or talk to your sister?"

"I'll talk to Jessa." I usually leave the hard stuff to Mom, but I can't bear to sift through the chocolate cake, hunting for the few parts I can salvage.

Mom squeezes my shoulder. "Okay."

I turn to leave and see the eating table with its empty plates and balled-up napkins, crumbs layering the floor like an overturned flowerbox. "I'm sorry about the cake, Mom."

"I love you, dear heart," my mother says, which isn't a reply but answers everything that matters.

Jessa is curled on the bed, her purple stuffed dog, Princess, tucked under her chin. Her walls have been dimmed, so the only illumination comes from the moonlight slithering through the blinds.

"Knock, knock," I say at the door.

She mumbles something, and I walk into the room. Sitting on the bed, I rub her back between the shoulder blades. Where do I start? Mom's so much better at this than me, but since she took an extra shift at work, I've had to pinch hit for her more and more.

I used to worry I wouldn't say the right thing. When I told Mom, she blew the bangs off her forehead. "You think I know what I'm doing? I make it up as I go along."

So I gave my sister a bowl of ice cream when Alice Bitterman told her they were no longer friends. And when Jessa said she was afraid of the monsters under her bed? I gave her a toy Taser and told her to shoot them.

Maybe it's not the best parenting in the world, but I'm not a parent.

Jessa turns her head, and in the glow of the walls, I see tears in her eyes. My heart twists. I would give up every bite of my dinner to take the sadness away. But it's too late. The food lodges in my stomach, heavy and dense.

"I don't want to leave," she says. "I want to stay here, with you and Mom."

I gather her in my arms. Her knees poke into my ribs, and her head doesn't quite fit under my chin. Princess tumbles to the floor. "You're not going anywhere. I promise."

"But Mom said—"

"She's scared. People say all kinds of things when they're scared."

She sticks a knuckle into her mouth and gnaws. We weaned her from the thumb-sucking years ago, but old habits die hard. "You don't get scared."

If she only knew. I'm scared of everything. Heights. Small, enclosed places. I'm scared no one will ever love me the way my father loved my mother. I'm scared tomorrow won't give me the answers I've been waiting for.

"That's not true," I say out loud. "I'm scared of one thing."

"What?"

"The tickle monster!" I attack. She shrieks and squirms away, her head flinging out. I wince as her face almost smacks the metal headboard. But this is what I want. A laugh that jerks her entire body. Screams that come from the pit of her belly.

After a full twenty seconds, I stop. Jessa flops across her pillow, her arms dangling over the edge. If only I could wipe out the topic so easily.

"What do they want me for?" she says, when her breathing slows. "I'm only six."

I sigh. Should've tickled her longer. "I'm not sure. The scientists think psychic abilities are the cutting edge of technology. They want to study them so they can learn."

She sits up and swings her legs over the bed. "Learn what?"

"Learn more, I guess."

I look at her scrawny legs, the knees scabbed over from falling off her hovercraft. She's right. This is ridiculous. Jessa's talent is a parlor trick, nothing more. She can see a couple of minutes into the future, but she's never been able to tell me anything really important—how I'll do on a big test, say, or when I'll get my first kiss.

Jessa's frown relaxes as she snuggles into her pillow. "Well, tell them, okay? Tell them I don't know anything, and then they'll leave us alone."

"Sure thing, Jessa."

She closes her eyes, and a few minutes later I hear her slow, even breathing. Standing up, I'm about to slip out when she calls, "Callie?"

I turn around. "Yes?"

"Can you stay with me? Not until I fall asleep. Can you stay with me all night long?"

It's the eve of my seventeenth birthday. I need to call Marisa, speculate with her one last time what my memory will be—if I'll see myself as a Manual Chef or have a different profession altogether.

It's been known to happen. Look at Rita Richards, in the class ahead of me. Never touched a keyboard in her life, but her memory showed her as an accomplished concert pianist. Now, she's off studying at the conservatory, all expenses paid.

And earlier this year, Tiana Rae showed up to school with bloodshot eyes when her memory revealed a future career as a teacher instead of a professional singer. Still, we all agreed it was better to find out now that it wasn't meant to be, rather than spend an entire life trying and failing.

Whatever the possibilities, one thing is clear: I need to be in my own bed tonight, alone with my thoughts. But Jessa won't notice if I leave ten minutes after she falls asleep. And tomorrow, she won't remember she asked me to stay.

"Okay." I cross back to her bed.

"Promise me you won't leave. Promise you'll stay forever."

"I promise." It's a lie, but a small one, so white it's practically translucent. I can't be concerned. This is it. The moment I've been waiting for all my life.

Tomorrow, everything changes.

Grab the Entangled Teen releases readers are talking about!

Frequency
by Christopher Krovatin

Fiona's not a kid anymore. She can handle the darkness she sees in the Pit Viper, a DJ whose wicked tattoos and hypnotic music seem to speak to every teen in town…except her. She can handle watching as each of her friends seems to be nearly possessed by the music. She can even handle her suspicion that the DJ is hell-bent on revenge. But she's not sure she can handle falling in love with him.

Bring Me Their Hearts
by Sara Wolf

Zera is a Heartless—the immortal, unaging soldier of the witch Nightsinger. With her heart in a jar under Nightsinger's control, she serves the witch unquestioningly. Until Nightsinger asks Zera for a prince's heart in exchange for her own.

No one can challenge Crown Prince Lucien d'Malvane… until the arrival of Lady Zera. She's inelegant, smart-mouthed, carefree, and out for his blood. The prince's honor has him quickly aiming for her throat.

So begins a game of cat and mouse between a girl with nothing to lose and a boy who has it all.

Winner takes the loser's heart.

Literally.

KISS OF THE ROYAL
BY LINDSEY DUGA

Ivy's magic is more powerful than any other Royal's, but she needs a battle partner to help her harness it. Prince Zach's unparalleled skill with a sword should make them an unstoppable pair—if they could agree on...well, anything.

Zach believes Ivy's magic is dangerous. Ivy believes they'll never win the war without it. Two warriors, one goal, and the fate of their world on the line. But only one of them can be right...

SEVENTH BORN
BY MONICA SANZ

A Witchling Academy Novel

Sera dreams of becoming a detective and finding her family. When the brooding yet handsome Professor Barrington offers to assist her if she becomes his assistant, Sera is thrust into a world where someone is raising the dead and burning seventhborns alive. As Sera and Barrington work together to find the killer, she'll discover that some secrets are best left buried...and fire isn't the only thing that makes a witch burn.

entangled teen

an imprint of Entangled Publishing LLC